CHAD'TU

A WESTERN NOVEL

IN THE STYLE OF LOUIS L'AMOUR

KELSIE R. GATES

To order additional copies of this book, contact:
Bookwhip
1-855-339-3589
www.bookwhip.com

THIS NOVEL IS
DEDICATED TO LINDA

Thanks to the following people for their encouragement and support without whom I would still be struggling.
Tami Frias
Jack Morris
Don Coach
Warren Fenton

PROLOGUE

HIS NAME WAS Chad'tu, a name with a reputation. He was a white man, even though he had an Indian name. Chad'tu had a reputation that followed him, and sometimes even preceded him. A reputation that made men's blood run cold with fear. A man feared for the fastness of his guns and the deadly precision with which he used them.

He was a ruggedly handsome man, tall with dark skin and piercing black eyes of a devil. A mane of black hair touched his broad muscular shoulders, and sensuous lips that could on a moment twist from friendly, into a sardonic grin. He wore two Colt forty-four guns strapped around his narrow waist and tie to each leg. A man called Chad'tu by some, and to others he was just Chad, a fun loving man.

However, to one he was a loving husband.

CHAPTER 1

I RODE DOWN from the ridge of the Black Mountain range. Bone weary, I urged the horse down the rocky hillside. Covered with dust, I was dirty, thirsty and hungry. My horse, an off-white appaloosa with scattered spots of rusty brown across her rump, was also tired. Faith was an amazing horse, tall and with the strength and spirit of five. I had raised her from the time she was a year old.

Head down, she slowly picked her way, slipping and sliding, down the steep rocky mountainside, headed toward home. It took all my strength to remain in the saddle as we descended the steep slope to the valley. I thought of the beautiful red-haired woman with the mischievous deep green eyes that the door throw her arms around me, and smother me in kisses.

—∘∘◦━❮◉❯━◦∘∘—

I'd gone to the Black Mountains looking for a place to settle and raise cattle and maybe a son or daughter or both with God's blessing. Not finding a suitable place after passing over a lot of country, I had finally settled on a grassy mesa edged high up against the granite side of Black Mountain. At first sight, I knew this was the place to build and start my ranch and raise a family. Far from the towns that held the corruption of gamblers and drunken cowboys. Yes, this was the place to raise my family.

From high atop the mountain, a roaring waterfall tumbled several hundred feet down the shear granite rocks into a pond and then ran off into a creek and trickled on down the mountainside, slowly winding its way around aspens and sycamores. The creek finally ran off through the knee-deep grass. Signs of deer, wild pig, and turkey, along with coyote and wolf tracks were evidence of an abundant wildlife.

It took some time to build the cabin on this high plateau, which overlooked the vast surrounding country. For the convenience of the water, I had built close to a spring in the mountainside that flowed from the ground and meandered like a snake slowly back and forth across the downward slope until it joined into the waterfall. The view from the ranch was more than a man could ask for. It was about twelve miles from a new town.

The small town was so new it still had no name. A rock strewn dirt street ran through the town. Across from the hotel was the Overland Stage stop. Next door was a stable with an adjacent corral. Next to the stable was the blacksmith shop, owned by John Hurley. A huge man that probable weighed close to two fifty, with arms as large as his head and a belly that matched. Everyone called him "Big John." He was a man you would not want to mess with.

Everyone who lived in town called it, 'No Name.' What the town did have was a general mercantile store, owned and run by John and Sara Bartlett, both hard working and friendly people. A saloon with a newly painted white sign that read in rather large gaudy red letters 'Pair-a-Dice' owned by a large handsome woman by the name of Maybelle. Those that were acquainted with her called her Belle. The saloon had a long bar down one side and games of chance on the other. A stairway in the back led to rooms above, some to let and others … girls for an evening of entertainment.

The sheriff's office sat on a slight curve the street took at the edge of town, where usually you would find the sheriff, kicked back in his chair, his scuffed boots resting against the railing of the porch, puffing on a cigar with an overview of the street. Sheriff Jay Reardon was a gentle man but if he got riled, you'd better watch your step. The people in town were mostly friendly with the exception of the few rowdies that occasionally would pass through on their way headed west.

—∘∘❖∘∘—

During the summer in this part of the country, the climate was good and the weather was mild, with only a few hot days. The several thundershowers that usually occurred kept the grass growing so there was plenty of grass to graze cattle. Winters were mild, with slight snowfalls that seldom covered more than two feet, three where the wind had blown snowdrifts up against a sharp out jutting of stone or over a gully.

Today, there was a gentle summer breeze blowing through the canyon. I was up before dawn and out rounding up strays. With an open range, they sometimes wander up canyons for no apparent reason that I could tell.

After two years of hard work, with one bull and fifty or so head of cattle, I figured I was doing okay. My cattle, some with newborn calves were increasing nicely. Trying to increase the herd I could not afford to let them wander far from the ranch, a mountain lion might get hungry. I'd tried my best to keep the few cattle I had in one spot. With no fences, it was a full time job. It was worth the effort because of the beautiful woman, who supported my efforts, my wife who loved and adored me.

Rounding up loose cattle and leaving them with the herd, I'd headed for the cabin. Thoughts of my woman with long flaming red hair, which cascaded like a beautiful waterfall down past her shoulders, drifted into my head. A woman with a touch of the Irish spirit, as wild as she was beautiful.

With one hand, I pushed my hat back and wiped the sweat from my forehead and neck with a red bandanna. It was hot and muggy. I rode along thinking of Jaydeen. The shadows were growing long as the sun slowly slipped behind Black Mountain. The temperature started to cool somewhat. I couldn't wait to get to the ranch and wrap her in my arms.

With that thought and a cooling breeze, I urged Faith on. Faith knew we were close to home and eagerly picked up the pace, ears forward and alert in anticipation of the wolf that usually bound out to greet us.

Approaching the ranch, I looked for the wolf called Track, which I and Jaydeen had nursed back to health. He had grown into a magnificent beast, which had bonded to both me and Jaydeen, like a brother. With pleasant thoughts, I remembered the day I had found Track.

━◦◦❀◦◦━

I'd been out rounding up strays, when I heard the most pitiful cries of an animal. It sounded more like a whimper. Searching for the source, I found a small wolf cub in a small indentation in the side of a short bluff.

It looked like the bluff had collapsed from a recent thunderstorm, bringing down brush and dirt, partially covering the small hole that concealed a pitiful starving wolf pup. It appeared to have been abandoned by its mother. For what reason I didn't know, maybe she couldn't get to it, and left it to die. Nevertheless, I took a sharp look around making sure the mother was not nearby.

A snarling vicious skinny ball of fur had greeted me as I pulled brush from the opening. Seeing a man, the pup tried to hide, but was too weak. Even though it was small, it snarled, trying to bite with its small razor sharp teeth. Taking no chances, I wrapped the snarling, biting, and kicking, wolf cub into my bedroll, gathered it up and taken it home.

'Track,' I had named the wolf … usual ran out to greet me.

As I approached the cabin, I noticed there was no smoke coming from the chimney. Strange I thought it was unlike Jaydeen not to having a fire going this time of day. The sun was almost beyond the horizon. It was starting to chill a little.

I rode up to the house wondering why Track had not greeted me. Dismounting I tied my horse to the hitching rail. I looked around wondering, and then stepped up onto the porch, walked to the door that stood slightly ajar and pushed it open and stepped inside.

Quickly I looked around and called her name. "Jaydeen … Honey where are you?" She didn't answer. Then I noticed the broken dish on the floor and the overturned chair lying next to a red smear of blood on the stone floor. Worried, I called her name again. She did not answer.

I noticed a blood smear on the side of the doorway that I'd missed before. Was it her blood? Maybe someone or something had attacked her. I hoped it was not her blood. Something terrible must have happened. Concerned, I hurried to the barn she might be there. The stable was empty. Her horse was gone. She would never leave the ranch without telling me. A dark grey shape in the corner caught my eye. As I approached, the sound of a whimper cut the quiet.

Bending, I found my wolf beaten but still alive. Stroking and speaking softly, I soothed Track, running my hands over him feeling for broken bones or flesh wounds. There was none, only a patch of sticky fur. After some effort and with my help I got Track to stand. "What happened boy?" I said, stroking him gently. Standing with some effort, Track leaned against me, licked my hand, and feebly wagged his tail. I'd noticed Track had dried blood around his mouth. He must have gotten a good bite of someone. I said, "You'll be okay, seems like you got kicked, and …" my voice trailing off I thought of Jaydeen and stepped out of the stall.

I checked the ground in front of the stable. Along with Jaydeen's there were three sets of boot prints in the soft earth. I bent and memorized them; I noticed one print was slightly drug through the dirt. It looked like Track did get a piece of someone. Mixed in among the boot prints were the fresh hoof prints made by three horses, hoof prints I did not recognize. I studied them so as not to forget them.

Becoming very worried, I went back to the house, with Track limping after. I tried to visualize what the hell had happened.

She must have struggled and put up one hell of a good fight from the looks of the kitchen. Still, someone had taken her. She would never leave the ranch voluntarily. Why had they taken her? Was it her blood on the floor or that of her attackers? For what reason had they taken her? I didn't know. There were many questions, for which I didn't have answers.

I only knew what would happen when I caught up with them, and I would catch up with them. I vowed. As surely as the sun rises and sets, I would catch them. They had no idea who they were dealing with. When I caught up to them … what would I do … Kill Them?

Getting a bucket of oats, I fed Faith. Going into the house, I hurriedly stuffed supplies into my saddlebag. I checked my Colt guns that I wore tied down. When I caught the men that had taken Jaydeen, I would kill them one and all. Grabbing the Winchester from the gun rack along with more ammunition for the rifle and guns, I went outside.

Faith had finished eating and I led her over to the water tank to drink her fill. With her nose to the water drinking, she seemed to sense my unease.

I suddenly remembered the supplies went back into the house picked up the saddlebag that held food for a week or two, which ought to be enough. Faith had drunk her fill when I returned and was pawing the ground as if to say lets go.

Shoving the Winchester into the boot, I turned and quickly filled up two canteens I'd snagged hanging from a hook beside the door. I lashed down the saddlebag and bedroll and looping the straps of the canteens across the saddle horn, grabbed the saddle horn and jumping up, slid my boot into the stirrup and with one smooth motion, flipped the other leg over and stuck my boot into the stirrup.

The sun set low and was dropping rapidly to merge with the horizon. I gathered up the reins, took a long last look around before starting to track the four sets of hoof prints. If I were to catch them before dark, I'd not have much time. I looked back over my shoulder one last time as I urged Faith forward out of the yard at a fast trot.

The wolf limping slightly had started after me not wanting to be left behind. I quickly pulled up the horse and in a commanding voice said, "Stay. Track Stay … Stay," I said to the wolf as I turned Faith and again headed out of the yard.

Track lay down and watched his master ride away. As soon as Chad and Faith were out of sight, he arose to follow. Track had a mind of his own and followed after them, limping slightly with his head down smelling the scent.

The anger and vengeance that burned hot and heavy in my heart spurred me on. My anger grew more with every breath. I had renewed energy, with but a single purpose, find and punish those responsible.

Faith sensing my mood started down the sloping hillside at a fast pace without urging, her head up and ears forward and alert. The sun dipped lower into the horizon, the sky turned grey and the shadows grew longer by the minute. Don't think just hurry and catch up, was the only thought on my mind. I started to lose hope as the shadows turned from grey to black and the sun quickly set beyond Black Mountain. I could not follow their trail in the dark.

Stopping Faith, I stood as tall as possible in the stirrups looking and smelling for a sign of smoke or the light from a campfire. Surely, they could not be more than four or five hours ahead. If so, I might see their campfire. All I saw was the black of night.

Riding over to a grove of Sycamore trees that grew close by, I dismounted and tied my horse to a low branch. Somewhere off in the dark a night owl hooted. I hastily started to climb the tree with the thought if I could get high enough I could see farther and spot their fire. Fifty feet up the tree, I stopped and catching my breath, looked hopefully out into the darkness. Nothing, no glow in the night sky, just the black of night sprinkled with a few stars. Then a wolf howled close by.

Smiling to myself, I slowly and carefully made my way down the tree. Waiting at the bottom was Track. If wolves could smile then he was smiling and happy to be with me.

Well one thing was for darn sure; I couldn't follow their trail in the dark. Searching about I gather some small dried out mesquite and dead branches from the sycamore and built a small sheltered fire in a gully that couldn't be seen if anyone looked this way. I put on my worn buckskin coat as the chill of the night started to creep in.

I filled the coffee pot with water and makings for coffee, setting it on rocks next to the fire to heat. While the coffee was making, I took the saddle off of Faith, setting it well back in the shadows of the trees away from the fire where I would sleep and not be a target. No one would surprise me. I grabbed a couple handfuls of dried grass and gave Faith a good rub down.

Track lay close to the fire, rested the dancing flames he watched every his head on his paws, his eyes reflecting move I made.

Pouring a cup of coffee, I sat on the ground next to my loyal wolf. "You and me, we'll get her back." At the sound of my voice, Tracks ears perked up and he thumped his tail. I gave him a pat and a piece of jerky I'd taken from the saddlebags. I chewed on my piece and Track on his.

Being tired, I rolled out my bedroll by the saddle, placed the Winchester's barrel on the saddle close at hand if needed and banked the fire. I lay down back in the shadows, a man could not be too careful in this country. If a man was not right careful, he could wake up dead. Shot or with an arrow sticking from his chest. I looked up at the stars through the branches, what would tomorrow bring? Track moved over and lay next to me. Throwing an arm over him, I soon fell into a fitful sleep.

I was up before the first light of dawn. Track had disappeared into the trees sometime during the dark morning hours. The wolf's leg had seemed much better. I stoked up the fire and cooked breakfast, bacon and red eye gravy along with coffee. While eating, I watched for Track.

I poured a second cup of coffee. Track appeared as silent as a ghost from the edge of the trees, carrying in his mouth the bloody remains of a half-eaten rabbit. He approached the fire, dropped the rabbit at my feet, then lay down and finished the rest, fur, bones, and all. When he finished he licked his lips and looked up at me as if to say, my breakfast was better than yours.

In the cold morning hours before the first light peaked over the horizon. I kicked dirt on the dying embers of what remained of the fire, making sure it was out, turned up the collar of my coat and buttoned it, and packed up the gear.

I was ready to mount Faith when I had a sudden impulse. Flipping the leather thong from the hammer of my Colt that held it secure in its holster, I pulled the gun in one smooth fast motion pointing it toward the horizon and fanned close to the hammer, with my left hand, while crouching making a noise like a kid when they shoot make believe guns.

Satisfied with my draw … I double checked the cartridges, replaced the Colt into the holster fastening the thong over the hammer to keep it in the holster if I had to ride hard. Satisfied, I stepped into the leather and was on my way.

Track would lope along ahead and sometimes he would range out to the side with his head down smelling and sniffing. He ran as if his leg no longer bothered him. It appeared that he was almost fully recovered. Occasionally he would lift his head above the scrubby brush to make sure I was still in sight. He was a magnificent animal I loved dearly, but not as much as I loved Jaydeen.

I rode slowly till the sun peeked over the horizon, throwing enough light to see by. Finally, I picked up their hoof prints left in the dirt. Picking up their trail was easy and from the spacing of the hoof prints. It seemed they were taking their time wherever they were headed. Not knowing they were being pursued was all to my advantage.

I urged Faith into a slow gallop following the tracks in the direction the four horses and their riders had taken. With the dawning sun, sagebrush and yucca appeared from the plains. I urged Faith to a faster pace.

Trailing after them, the sun rose ever higher into a cloudless blue grey sky. I could tell it was going to be another hot day. Moving fast hour after hour, I tried to catch them. I couldn't tell if they were headed for the town called 'No Name.' Their trail looked to be angling off and heading past the town. I wondered where they might be headed.

A couple of times I lost the trail and started making wide swings and loops till I picked it up again. Why had they taken Jaydeen I kept wondering? There was no reason I could think of. I thought maybe it had to do with something that had happened in my past. I could have made a few enemies in the line of work I'd done in my younger days.

It got me thinking as I tracked the four riders relentlessly, hour after hour in the blistering heat. I kept after the riders, who were somewhere still ahead. ... With the heat beating down my thoughts drifted back to the past ... back to every year of my past life that I could remember. I searched through my memories for an answer. What had I done in the past to deserve this?

CHAPTER 2

THINKING ABOUT MY past life, I didn't remember much of my life before I was ten. I remembered that I'd been in a wagon train. One of the wagons belonged to my father and mother. Crossing the high mountains and the great prairies, we werelifheaded west to start a new life.

Sometimes I rode in the wagon, setting on a hard board seat my mother had covered with a blanket. To me it seemed a great adventure. Other times, I remembered walking alongside the wagon in the dirt and the dust stirred up by the wheels, and the times playing and throwing rocks with boys from the other wagons, until someone would yell for us to stop the foolishness and help our folks.

The wagon train had stopped after a nasty river crossing, almost losing a wagon in the swift waist-high current as they crossed. It had taken several men with ropes and their horses, shouting and yelling to each other to keep it steady, not letting it tip over.

I had no idea what trouble it would cause if the wagon turned over. To me it was just another river crossing. A river I didn't even know the name of, but to me with all the yelling and everyone hustling to save the wagon, it was exciting.

When all the wagons were safely across the wagon master called a halt so the teams of horses and the few cattle could catch their breath. People rested and chatted with one another as they ate their noon day lunch sitting in the shade of the wagons.

Bored I had wondered off back toward the river. As I walked, I kicked a few stones until I was back to the riverbanks. It sure was hot. I looked down at the deceptively slow-moving muddy water. A nice swim in the river would really feel good. I knew I would get in trouble if I were caught.

I looked around making sure no one was watching. Removing my clothes, I hid them in a pile under a bush. Naked, I slipped down the dirt bank and waded into the water. Boy, it sure was cold. I took a deep breath and shivering waded deeper into the river, till the water reached my shoulders. It was still cold but not as much. It felt good after the hot sun. My body slowly got use to the cold muddy water.

Doing a frog stroke I reached the middle of the river and slowly turned over floating on my back, I looked up at the tree branches that hung over the river as they slowly moved past. The current started moving faster as the river narrowed, the banks becoming somewhat higher. I floated blissfully along unaware the river was moving me swiftly farther downstream.

I started to get goose bumps. Time to get out and dressed before anyone found out about my swim. I surely didn't want to get into trouble. It seemed I was always getting into trouble with my mom. My dad would say to her, "he's only a boy doing what boys do, leave him be."

Swimming to the bank, I found it steeper than I'd remembered. It was much harder to climb up than it had been to come down. Finally reaching the top, I looked around for my clothes. I had left them here by this tree … no it had been a much smaller tree I thought. After several minutes of looking, I couldn't find them. Where had my clothes gone?

It came to me. I must have drifted down river, but how long and how far had I drifted?

Starting to get scared, I went up the riverbank to the edge of the prairie looking for the wagon train. No wagons were in sight as far as my eye could see. My mind numb, I sat on a dead branch that had fallen from a cotton-wood tree and thought. They will come for me, and they will search till they find me.

⸺••◦⊙◦••⸺

Chad's Ma and Pa had reported Chad missing to the wagon master. He in turn wasting no time rounded up twenty volunteers from the wagons, most of them had kids of their own. The group spread out and started to search for the boy. They started back toward the river calling out his name. They continued searching up and down the riverbank yelling out Chad's name.

Sometime later, someone yelled, "Over here, I think I found something." The nearby searchers gathered around, as 'Big Bill' pointed down at the muddy bank. A bank that held small foot prints, leading down and disappearing into the water.

'Big Bill' looked down river with an expression of not much hope, shook his head and shrugged his shoulders. He didn't know how good a swimmer Chad was, and voiced his opinion that the current was too fast and Chad had probably drowned. The river had claimed him.

They searched for a couple of more hours down stream and some went up stream calling out Chad's name. They found no other sign of the boy. The day was wearing on as the sun moved across the sky. Heardon, the wagon master, was getting anxious and a little worried as the day wore on. The wagons needed to get a move on.

Finally the wagon master, felt having done his duty, called a halt to the searching and declared.

Chad must have drowned, and the current washed his body downstream. "We've wasted enough time." he said gruffly, "We must get these wagons moving."

Returning to the wagons, Chad's mother was in tears as she stumbled along. Chad's father steadied her as she stumbled, with his arm around his wife, he tried to comfort her. Grant, a smaller boy, Chad's age, ran to greet them. "Where's Chad?" he asked in a scared little voice, "Didn't you find him?" Chad's mother started crying even harder, as the question was asked. Chad's father replied in a choked voice, "Chad" ... he choked, "Chad won't be coming back ... the river got him."

—•○○—▪◻▪—○○•—

Being naked, I was embarrassed. If I could find my clothes, no one would know. With this thought in my head, I started walking back up the river. I didn't know how far I had drifted, but I hoped I had not drifted far. As the day progressed, I started to lose hope and just trudged on, thinking I was really in a lot of trouble.

I started to get hungry but walked on becoming more and more tired.

The sun was low on the horizon, I had to find my clothes before night fell, or I would be mighty cold. If I didn't find them, what would I do?

The river started getting wider and the banks were lower and further apart. I thought this must have been the place the wagon train had crossed, I hoped.

Searching for the tree where I had hidden my clothes, I remembered I had shoved them under a low bush to hide them. Running from tree to tree, I looked for one with a bush close by. Slowing down I stopped, took a deep breath and went over my actions I'd taken when I hid my clothes. Suddenly I remembered there was also a large rock the bush was growing by.

With new hope, I turned slowly in a full circle and taking my time, looked around for a bush with a large rock. My eyes fell upon such a bush about fifty yards from where I stood.

Running forward I tripped in my haste. Struggling up I brushed myself off, and with my heart beating fast ran to the bush. Getting down on my hands and knees, with my fingers crossed for good luck I looked under the bush. There were my clothes in a bundle just as I had left them. Pulling out my clothes, I quickly dressed and thanked God.

No longer embarrassed I continued walking farther along the bank. I came across the tracks made by the wagon wheels where they had crossed the river. I followed the tracks with my eyes as far as I could see ... no wagons were in sight. I wondered what to do? I decided to follow the wagon tracks and catch up to the wagon train.

CHAPTER 3

A S I THOUGHT of what lay ahead my mouth became suddenly dry. I realized I was very thirsty. I turned back to the river, slid down to the water and, laying down on my belly; put my hands into the river to divert the dead leaves, branches or anything else that might come floating along. I drank as much of the muddy water as I could, my hunger forgotten for the moment.

I followed along the ruts made by the wagon wheels, walking fast as I could. I'd just have to catch up. The sun moved down past a slight rise of the trail that lay ahead. The sky becoming grey as it set farther into the earth. It appeared that a storm might be in the making.

The sun dropped past the horizon and soon it became cooler. My relief was short lived. It became darker and colder. I was alone on the desert plains, without a coat, food or water, or a means to start a fire. The night closed over me. Exhausted, I laid down on top of a flat boulder that protruded slightly from the ground; the heat it retained kept me warm for part of the night as I slept.

The next day I awoke to the sun shining on my face. Rubbing my eyes and sitting up, I didn't remember for a second where I was. Then it all came flooding back: the swim, then trying to catch up to the wagon train. Sore from lying on the hard boulder, I stood rubbing my arms and legs. Biting my lip, I hurried on after the wagons.

The sun grew hotter and hotter as the day wore on. The heat was getting to me. My throat was dry and my lips didn't feel right as I licked them with a dry tongue. All day I'd followed the tracks leading straight across the dry parched plains. Stopping now and then to rest, I looked through the heat waves across the desert toward the horizon for the wagons. Nothing as far as my eye could see. There was no dust, no noise, just a couple of birds coasting on the heat that arose from the desert. Probably vultures waiting for me to die, I thought.

Night came swiftly and soon it was dark. Still I struggled on, not giving up hope. Thirsty and hungry, I licked my parched lips wishing I had something to eat and drink. Still I stumbled on falling down time after time ... I started crying, but getting up I staggered on thinking I was going to die. No longer able to continue on I collapsed into a wagon rut. Wrapping my arms around my chest, I drew my knees up to my belly trying to keep warm. Shivering from the cold it was hard to fall asleep.

I awoke sometime in the night to the yapping of a Coyote. Too weak to move, I just lay there waiting. If the coyote came for me, what could I do? My hand found a good size rock in the dirt. Clutching it in my hand like a weapon, I dozed off again.

Something woke me in the grey dawn. Suddenly I opened my eyes, looking up at an Indian who stood over me holding a very sharp knife. Too afraid and weak to scream, I just looked at the Indian. The Indian came closer and closer, crouched toward me with the knife. I thought so this was how my life would end. I closed my eyes in fear. No, No! ... I thought. Eyes closed are the cowards' way. I opened my eyes and frowning hard stared at the Indian in defiance.

The Indian paused, took in the defiant look and the rock clutched in my hand. The Indian with his eyes squinting and half-closed grunted something. Then opening his eyes wide, he smiled and pulled the knife back as if to stab it into my gut. Instead, the Indian stuck the knife into its sheath. As his hand came forward, the knife was gone and in its stead was a small leather pouch.

The Indian moved closer, grabbed me by the hair, and roughly pulled my head up from the rut. He pressed the leather bag gently against my blistered, cracked lips, and poured water down my throat. After I got over choking, sputtering, and coughing, I took a few swallows.

The Indian was smiling and talking. I had no ideal what he was saying. For some reason, he seemed very excited. I just lay there, too exhausted to move, and watched as the Indian did a little dance with his arms raised toward the sky and chanting. He seemed to be giving thanks to his gods above. After a few moments, the Indian stopped dancing and turned toward me.

He walked slowly over, looked down at me for a long moment with a disbelieving look. His face, old, weather-beaten, and sunburned showed the stress of many years. Suddenly he let out a blood-curdling scream as he reached down and picked me up. Holding me in both arms, he walked fifty paces and around a large boulder to a horse tethered to a mesquite bush.

The Indian dressed in deerskin was very strong for being old. He tossed me onto the horse's back face down and sprang up immediately behind. He gathered up the reins, whispered something to the horse. The horse shook his head up and down snorting as if it understood and slowly started off.

Lying across the horse on my stomach was not the most comfortable position. I couldn't see where I was being taken. Then I lost consciousness. I had no idea how long I was out or how far we'd traveled or in what direction. Even if I could escape, I probably couldn't find the wagon train now. Still, I would wait for the chance to escape. Then I passed out again.

The sound of hooves grating on shale and rock brought me back to awareness. The horse was struggling as it climbed up a rocky slope. I tried to raise his head to look, but the Indian pushed me down hard and uttered something. I didn't understand what the Indian had said, but I sure got his meaning.

After a time we reached sort of a shelf or plateau on the mountainside. Stopping the horse the Indian slid off to the ground. He led the horse along a narrow trail concealed by brush to a small crevice in the granite hillside. We passed through the narrow space with my head and feet scraping the sides. It was barely wide enough for a horse, let along a boy draped across its back.

We emerged from the crevice onto a small grassy piece of ground. The temperature was noticeably cooler this high up above the desert plains. A slight breeze sent ripples across the grassy meadow, like waves on the ocean. It was deathly quiet. There was no other sound, only the sound of rustling leaves moved by the wind.

The meadow lay concealed by craggy mountains reaching high into the pale blue sky. Still we went on, through the deep grass toward an outcrop of the mountain. As we approached the outcrop, a cave came into view. We stopped near a seep in the ground that held crystal-clear water in its rocky basin. The horse started drinking as the Indian came around reached up and jerked me from the horse. I fell hitting the ground. The Indian grunted something reached down grabbed me by the arms and dragged me into the partially concealed cave. Looking around I could see that someone lived here, made obvious by the bedding of animal skins, and things with which to cook.

Letting go of me the Indian picked up a bowl and went out, only to return shortly. The bowl filled with water, which he offered to me with a nod of his head. I hesitated, the Indian thrust the bowl forward with another nod. I took the bowl at his urging. My eyes never left the Indians face while I drank greedily of the ice-cold mountain water. The water tasted good, but it was so cold it hurt my teeth. I could feel the water as it went down into my stomach. My stomach growled with pain, I quickly realized hunger was making the pains.

The Indian squatted there watching me drink. Then turned and went to a far corner of the cave, reached up to a shelf in the rock. Reaching he put his arm into a hole on top of the shelf. Feeling around he pulled from the opening a leather bag. He dropped it to the ground opened it and reached in and pulled out a small pouch. Grunting in the language, which I could not under stand, he stood and walked over to me and offered the pouch.

So I took it, the Indian nodded his head in approval. Opening the bag I saw it contained something that looked like a cross between wood chips and shredded cow manure. I looked at the Indian, who nodded and made a gesture to his mouth with a chewing motion. He wanted me to eat. I smelled what was in the pouch. It did not smell like cow manure. I looked back at my captor who smiled and shook his head up and down. With trepidation, I reached in and grasped with two fingers a small piece. Trembling I smelled it. Not much smell, so I slowly put it to my mouth. I stuck my tongue to it, and then carefully put it into my mouth. I did not know what it was, but it was food and it tasted wonderful. I reached into the pouch, got a handful, and stuffed my mouth. The Indian sat down in front of me crossed his knees and smiled.

With my belly full and my thirst quenched, I laid back on the fur robes and fell asleep.

A full day later, I awoke with a start. I was still in the cave and there was no sign of the Indian. I thought this was my chance to escape. Leaping to my feet, I rushed toward the cave opening but was jerked bask off my feet. What happened? Something was around my neck. Tied around my neck was a raw-hide cord, and like a dog, I was staked to the ground.

I tried to untie the rawhide. After several attempts, I gave up and sat on the skins waiting for my captor to return. There was a bowl of water close by and some more of whatever I had eaten earlier. I drank and ate my fill and waiting fell back asleep.

I awoke to the smell of cooking meat. I yelled, "Untie me." I waited awhile ... and yelled again at the top of my lungs. The Indian silently appeared in the opening of the cave. He covered his mouth with one hand and shook his head side to side. I got his meaning; he wanted me to be quiet. He walked over, then bent to the stake driven deep into the ground and with some effort untied my leash and dropped it. He turned his back to me and walked out of the cave.

I stood for a second, thinking about running. Then quickly discarded the idea, the Indian was bigger and faster. Slowly I went to the mouth of the cave and looked out. The Indian was squatted by a small fire over which the meat cooked. The smoky smell of cooking meat made my mouth water. The Indian took no notice of me. With the leash trailing in the dirt and the smell of cooking meat upon my nose, I approached the Indian who hardly glanced up and with a hand made a gesture to sit.

Taking the meat from the fire, the Indian placed it onto a small flat boulder that was close to the fire. In the high mountain air, the meat cooled quickly. He drew his knife and with an effortlessly move sliced off a piece. Holding the meat to his mouth he blew on it then carefully took a bite.

The Indian looked toward me and then tossed the remaining piece into the air in my direction. I jumped catching the meat in midair like a dog; I sat down and started eating. The Indian watched smiling. I guessed I really was the Indian's dog. After all, I did have the leash around my neck.

I started following the Indian around, as a good dog would follow its master. The Indian was not lazy, he was always doing something. Wood we had gathered was piled just inside the cave's entrance, keeping it dry for future fires.

One morning after a few days passed, the Indian could see I was no longer trying to escape. Taking out his knife, he cut the rawhide thong from around my neck.

CHAPTER 4

THE INDIAN'S NAME was Shatika. Shatika would carve a hook from bone with his knife, and using a piece of rawhide, make a fishing line, that he would bait with a kicking grasshopper or some other insect he'd caught.

The Indian and I went through the crevice to the lower plateau, where there was a flowing stream which held fish. I used my leash as a line for the hook I'd made, with Shatika's help.

Shatika taught me how to fish, where to drop the hook and not to let my shadow fall on the water. Together we caught several fish. Some we ate, and some we smoked and stored for future use.

One day Shatika looked at my ragged overalls, shaking his head and frowning. Taking deerskins from a pile, he discarded some and selected others. There was an old tree stump he'd dragged into the cave. Sitting on it, he unsheathed his knife, took a flat stone and started sharpening the blade, now and then stopping to carefully run a thumb across it. Satisfied he took a deer-skin and laying it on the hard dirt floor started cutting with his knife. I just looked on not knowing what the Indian had in mind.

The Indian again looked at me and cut more pieces. Taking a small, very sharp, pointed stick, he punched holes along the edge of each piece. Grunting he held up the pieces. Smiling at his handy work, he picked up a thin strip of rawhide, and started lacing it through the holes in the skin, while he sang.

I didn't understand what he was making. When Shatika was through, he tossed it to me, with a grin on his face. He made a sign for me to take off my torn and ragged overalls and put on the deerskin he'd tossed to me. I did as Shatika wanted. The next day Shatika made a pair of moccasins, and the day after he made a shirt. After he had finished making the garments and given the last one to me. Shatika stood tall and proud turning me around, admired his handy work. I looked down at my legs, sheathed in deerskin leggings. They felt soft against my skin and much better than my threadbare overalls.

With my new garments, a thought occurred to me. Except for the color of my skin, I now appeared to be an Indian.

Taking me by the shoulders, and with a grunt he turned me to face him. Speaking and pointed at himself said, "Shatika." I did not understand. The Indian repeated the word Shatika several more times pointing at himself. I guessed it must be his name. Then he pointed at me.

I tried saying Shatika. It did not sound the same as when the Indian said it, but Shatika seemed to approve.

Then he pointed at me and grunted. I guessed he wanted my name. I pointed to myself and said, "Chad."

Shatika got it right away. He tried saying my name several times, but he had as much trouble saying Chad, as I did saying Shatika. He frowned, seeming not to like the sound of my name when spoken. He shook his head not satisfied with the name Chad.

So, he changed my name to his liking. He called me Chadtu. He walked back and forth, saying "Chad—tu, Chadtu." All the while, with a frown on his face. He walked around and around the cave. Then he said the name twice again, "Chad'tu, Chad'tu. Yes!" Satisfied with the name he had given me, he left the cave. Now I had an Indian name and wore the clothes of an Indian.

It dawned on me one day that I was no longer afraid of this Indian and actually was having fun. Although the fun was, sometimes more like work.

Shatika started teaching me his language through trial and effort. He would point to different objects and speak their names. Then he would point to me, it would be my turn to say the words he had spoken. He made me repeat the words over and over till he was satisfied.

Sometimes when we were out he would suddenly point at something and ask what this is? If I answered with the right word, I would be praised. When I said a word that was not right, Shatika would get mad, throw his arms in the air and utter a long string of words. Then we would have another lesson on how a captive pale face boy should speak the Indian language.

The language lessons went on and on for days, that dragged on into weeks, which dragged on into months. After several months, I felt I was speaking the Comanche language as well as any Comanche Indian. I hoped.

Winter was coming, and soon the snows.

One morning we awoke to a chill in the air and frost at the mouth of the cave. Stepping out into the cold my breath turned to steam as I exhaled. This was the first winter I would spend without Pa and Ma. I felt sad. I thought of the Indian Shatika, who had taken care of me after finding me dying in a wagon rut on the plains; Shatika who had nursed me back to health and taught me so much this last year.

He was now like a father to me.

Soon after I had become somewhat fluent in speaking and understanding the Comanche language, Shatika told me, with some hesitation in his voice, of his wife and his son who had died in a horrible massacre. He spoke of wounds he had received doing battle trying to defend them. After the battle, everyone in the village had been left for dead. Later in the day he had revived only, to find his wife and son were dead. He told me this with tears in his eyes.

He said he'd been surprised to find me that day with the wagon train long gone. At first, he thought I was dead and he was going to take my scalp. When I had opened my eyes, it stunned him. Then he looked into my defiant black eyes, my black hair and saw only his son. Overcome with emotion he could not kill this boy, who reminded him so much of his dead son. He thought the gods had sent me to replace the son he had lost. That explained the dance and singing that he did.

Now after all this time, I did feel like I was his son, and he my father.

The winter snow was deep in some places and not so deep in others. Shatika taught me how to make snowshoes, using young saplings that bent readily and rawhide lacing. We did not often venture forth into the cold winter air. It was with snowshoes when we did, and then only to check on the snares and traps. Which were set to catch rabbits and squirrels and sometimes something larger?

There was not much to do during the long winter months. Shatika would sometimes take his knife from its sheath, flip it into the air, catch it by the point, and throw it at the tree stump, where it always hit point first and stuck with a vibrating twang. He never missed. "How can you do that?" I asked.

"With much practice." he said.

"Can I try? Can you teach me?" He handed me the knife and stepped behind me. I do not think he trusted me completely yet. Holding the knife by its tip, I pulled my arm upward and threw the knife at the stump, missing it completely. It clattered harmlessly to the floor. I ran to retrieve it, but Shatika was there before me, laughing as he picked up the knife.

He taught me to be very careful of the sharp blade. He showed me how to hold the blade for throwing, and the different ways to hold it, for attacking or defending when fighting an enemy. He showed me how to skin all the animals he killed and someday that I would kill.

Sometimes Shatika would give me a stick as long as his knife and we would have mock knife fights. Shatika always won. And each time we fought, I would try harder. Toward the end of winter, I won once, or maybe Shatika let me win.

Shatika had given me a knife one day and said it was mine to keep. He must have had it hidden away somewhere. I wondered what else he had hidden away.

All winter I would practice all that I had learned. After much time, I was good with that knife. By spring, I was skilled in the way of knives. Then he started me on the lance, defending and attacking with it. When I had that pretty down pat, he started me on using the hatchet and throwing at a tree, as if the tree were an enemy. What else am I going to have to learn I thought? It was fun most of the time, but sometimes it was too much like work, with all the practice.

When we were not practicing, Shatika told stories of his people, and the adventures he'd had growing up. His stories always fascinated me. I told him of my life, living in different towns, my pa trying to make a living for my ma and me. Then one-day pa hitched up with the wagon train to head west to some far off place called California. How I became separated from the wagons by my foolish swim. Shatika laughed at me so long and hard that I started laughing with him at my own stupidity.

Gradually, winter dwindled into spring. Grass started to grow; the trees grew a new set of leaves, the ice on the seep melted, and the weather turned noticeably warmer. Now and then, we'd have a couple of cold days, followed by warm ones. Sometimes we got thundershowers that nourished the earth and washed away the remaining snow.

With the coming of spring, I felt renewed and invigorated. Once able to get out into the open, with the warmer weather, I made a notch with my new knife in the trunk of the tree that grew by the seep, one notch for each year.

CHAPTER 5

THE OUTDOOR LIFE and the way of the Indian showed in my rapid growth. Since I had been with Shatika, I had grown a lot taller and filled out some. He never gave up on my training. The taller I grew the more training he pushed onto me.

He would make me run with him. We ran like the wind till my lungs burned, and my legs would ache. Winded I would have to stop. For being old, he never seemed to tire. I guessed he could run all day without resting. Not an ounce of fat was on him, just hard sinewy, muscle covered his bones. With all the training, my body soon became a smaller version of his. I could run almost as fast and far and for as long as he could. Almost.

I did not know how old he was and he could not tell me. I admired him. I wanted to be just like him. Shatika felt that in me. It made him proud. Still he never let up on me always pushing me harder and harder. Some of the time, he called me his son and would put his arm around my shoulder and hug me to him, telling me I was learning fast. Soon, he said, I would be a warrior.

With the warmer weather, we traveled farther from the cave into the lower meadow and even farther, sometimes onto the desert plains. Usually we went on foot for two reasons: first, to keep our bodies tough, second, his horse was getting old and did not have the energy or stamina to go any distance.

At times, he would stop and point out different tracks made by different animals. He taught me to track them all. He taught me how to make and set snares and traps without leaving the scent of man. When hunting, always approach the animal being hunted from downwind, he told me. They can smell man scent for a long ways.

I became so adept at tracking that I could follow the trail running fast, leaping over the smaller boulders and trees that had fallen, without losing the trail, except for the deer that sometimes traveled in great bounds. Then I would have to slow up, but not much.

He showed me how to make a bow from the branch of a certain tree and string it with a piece of seasoned rawhide, along with arrows fetched with bird feathers. Next, I learned to make a lance and adorn it with feathers tied to the shaft with rawhide. Little did I realize at the time the value of everything that I'd learned, would stand me in good stead, later on in life.

Since I had no horse and his horse was getting old, we usually would hunt on foot carrying our bows. We were out one day when suddenly, Shatika held up a hand. Stopping and squatting down beside a stream we listened, all was quiet except for the gurgling mountain stream. He pointed out fresh hoof prints made by several deer that had stopped to drink from the stream. The tracks crossed the bubbling stream and then wandered aimlessly into the nearby woods.

We crossed the stream as it rushed rapidly over rocks that lay on the creek bottom. The stream, not quiet to the knee was icy cold. Carefully, not making a sound we moved silently up the bank into the trees and notched arrows to our bows. The only sound heard was the rustling of leaves as the wind stirred them.

Shatika motioned me downstream, he went up stream. When we were about twenty paces from each other, he made the low sound of the dove. I looked up and he motioned towards the woods. Slipping into the woods, we disappeared among the trees. Silent as ghosts we moved through the shadows, in search of the deer.

Some time and several steps later, I approached the edge of a small clearing. In its center were three deer with their heads down chomping at the grass. A large buck would raise his head occasionally, sniff the air, look around then go back to eating. The two does that were with him just kept eating.

I felt the air as it blew across my face, it was a good sign. I was down wind and they could not smell me. I was excited. My palms became damp with sweat. I suddenly became nervous and uneasy. I had practiced many hours with the bow and I hit what I wanted, but I had never killed a live animal with an arrow.

I must have made a noise. Something had alerted them for all three heads shot into the air together. They stood like statues frozen for an instant. Then as if shot from a canon they turned and bounded off.

Without thinking, in one fluid motion I pulled the notched arrow to my cheek and released it with a resounding twang of the string. The arrow struck the doe in mid leap. The doe fell to the ground, kicked and then lay still. The arrow had flown straight and true striking her through the chest. I didn't know if I was happy or sad.

My Indian father came from the woods went to the deer and cut its throat. He turned to me, took me in his arms and hugged me. He said now I truly was a warrior. He turned back, knelt and started gutting the deer, taking out the parts that would taint the meat. We rejoiced. We talked happily, as we gutted my first kill. Now we would have meat for some time along with a nice hide.

We only had to get it back up the mountainside and to the cave. With rawhide strips that Shatika wore wrapped around his waist like a belt, we tied the doe's front legs together, then the rear legs in a like manner. Sliding a pole cut from a small tree through the tied legs we lifted, Shatika at one end and me at the other. We started up the hillside. It was not easy but we managed with a few rest stops along the way.

That was my first kill. After that I had too many to count.

—∞◦❘❭◦∞—

Too soon, the warm weather turned to autumn. There were now four notches on the tree that stood between the mountain and the seep.

I was now as tall as my Indian father, Shatika. I was skilled in all things that he had taught me. There was only one thing in my mind about all my skills. No matter how hard I tried, Shatika could always best me. I promised myself, as well as Shatika, that one day I would best him at all things. He laughed at me as a proud father would laugh at his son, telling him that some day when I was bigger, I would be the best.

Shatika really did love me as a son. I could tell by his actions. For all he had taught me and the affection he had shown, I loved him as a father. Sometimes he would get a far away look in his eyes and I could tell he was thinking about his murdered wife and son. Then he would come back from where ever his thoughts had been, look over at me, and smile a happy smile that somehow held a hint of sadness in it.

High up in the mountains as we were, no one could find our hidden little valley, unless by accident. With No one to bother us, we had good times.

CHAPTER 6

WE WERE MOSTLY alone until one day we were hunting out on the meadow of the lower plateau. It was getting late, we were about to return empty handed to the upper meadow and the cave, when we both smelled smoke.

We hit the ground quickly. Lying close to one another and hidden by the knee-high grass, we raised our heads, looked around and saw no one. We didn't speak but made sign language. We crawled forward through the grass toward the smell of burning wood. Topping a slight rise and parting the grass, we looked down toward a group of trees. We saw a whisper of smoke rising above the trees.

Where the grass met the trees, there was a camp of sort. Two horses were tethered to a small cottonwood. A white man was bent down, cooking something over the fire. We watched for a while and then slowly retreated the way we had come. The man was alone and did not seem to be worried about an attack. I wondered about that.

Out of sight of the white man, we rose up and were making our way out of the tall grass, Shatika bent over suddenly, grabbed at his stomach, and fell into the dirt.

He lay there moaning and groaning in pain.

I went quickly to him and knelt down, I touched him and asked, "What is the matter father?"

He only moaned and said, "Take me to the cave." I helped him up and put an arm around his waist. He put one arm over my shoulder, and we started toward the cave. It was slow going up hill with most of Shatika's weight on me.

He stopped moaning after a while and seemed to be better. I could tell he still had some pain. He was moving better and we eventually made it through the crevice to the safety of the cave. I laid him gently upon the hide on which he slept. I took a gourd and brought him fresh water from the seep. He drank and curled up with his knees against his chest groaning softly. Not knowing what else to do, I covered him

I prayed to the Indian gods and then to the white man's god. I didn't know what else I could do. Shatika finally fell asleep. Yet, he moaned as he slept.

The next day Shatika was better but still weak. I made soup with a little meat and some wild onions that grew close by. I fed it to him. It seemed to give him strength. That evening he was almost his old self. More soup and back to bed he went.

I worried most of the night, hoping he would get well. My other thought, what would I do if he died? I would be here all alone.

What was I now, fourteen, or fifteen or maybe even sixteen? I did not know. Whatever the age, I was tall and broad of shoulder with no fat. If he died, I could take care of myself. I am a man now ... and a warrior, I told myself. I will manage somehow. He had taught and trained me well. I thought like an Indian and I could survive off the land. I dozed off only to awaken several times during the night. Worried. with its bright light awoke

Morning came. The sun shinning into the cave me. I jumped up and ran to Shatika to see how he was. "Shatika, Shatika!" I spoke his name, "Are you okay?" I bent and took his arm, "Shatika, Shatika, wake up." He did not move. He did not put his arms around me with the usual bear hug. Shatika was dead.

I sat there my mind numb to all feeling. How long I sat holding my father's hand, I don't know. Then the tears trickled down my cheeks. Slowly at first the tears fell, then the reality of it all hit, and the tears turned to a stream. Men don't cry I told myself, but as much as I tried, I could not make them stop. I just sat there holding his cold lifeless hand, sobbing and cried like a child. I did not care about anything. My reason for living was gone from me. I sat there and cried, and cried till the tears stopped flowing.

Putting his arms across his chest, I let go of his hand. I covered him up to his chin with a soft deerskin. I stood up and walked outside the cave. Feeling dizzy, I steadied myself with a hand against the mouth of the cave. My stomach felt like I was going to vomit. I wiped my eyes and took several deep breaths of the fresh, crisp mountain air. The urge to vomit passed. Feeling slightly better, I looked up toward the sun that was now high in the sky. I must have cried for several hours. I walked aimlessly around till my senses finally returned. I sat on a dead tree trunk and thought—then thought some more.

I was on my own now, all alone, with no one to turn to in time of trouble, no one to take care of me. I would have to take care of myself now. I could not just take off; I would have to bury Shatika.

Walking back into the cave, I went to Shatika and looked down at him. He looked peaceful lying there. He looked as if he were sleeping. In a sense, he was sleeping—the long sleep.

I went from the cave looking for a suitable place to bury my Indian father. Someplace he would like, someplace he would be happy. Forever. I found a place next to the Sycamore tree he had like to sit under when the weather was hot. I thought he would like it there under his favorite tree. I dug a long hole using my hatchet and knife, deep enough to keep any animals from digging up my father.

Returning to my father, I picked him up gently in my arms, along with his blanket and carried him to his burial place. I laid him gently into the trough of the cold earth. I placed all of his weapons alongside his body, except for his knife. I'd admired that knife and he had told me upon his death, I could have it. With sadness in my heart, I pulled the deerskin over his body and with a final last look, over his face.

Kneeling beside the grave, I raised my face to the sky and prayed to the Indian gods, then to the white man's god. "Please take my father to your happy hunting ground in heaven and let him be happy there."

With my eyes glassy, I hurriedly grabbed my hatchet and started dragging dirt into the hole, till I no longer could see the man who had given me so much and now was gone. The dirt now made a slight mound. Searching the area, I gathered stones and place them on the fresh earth till the mound was completely covered. Now I had lost two fathers. The first was my fault. The second was not.

I sat close beside the grave my mind vacant until I suddenly got chilled. I became aware that it was becoming dark. Still I sat there, not moving, listening to the sounds of the night.

With the cold of night, I finally went into the cave, made a small fire, and warmed myself. I stared into the flickering flames as they jumped and danced, my mind slowly returned. I contemplated the choices that were open to me.

There were not many.

CHAPTER 7

THE FIRST THING that came to mind, I needed a horse, a good horse. The white man we had seen a few days ago had two horses that appeared to be in good condition. What does a man need with two horses? He can only ride one at a time. It should not be hard for a warrior like me to take one while he slept, if he still had a camp there.

I would see in the morning, but at this moment, I was just tired. Emotionally my mind was devastated. What I needed was sleep, so I slept. I slept like the dead, no thoughts, no dreams, nothing.

I awoke the next morning before sunrise my mind clear and finally focused. Gathered up things I would need looked around at my home one last time, and then left without a backward glance. Pausing at the crevice, I turned looking back at the sycamore with mixed emotions, of sadness. Wondering how my life would be without Shatika. Would I ever find happiness?

Once through the crevice, I traveled rapidly. Running swiftly on foot I left the cleft in the granite behind. Going down to the lower meadow and on to the rise where we first saw the white man's camp. Would he still be there?

Close to the ridge, I hit the ground and rapidly crawled forward my heart beating fast, parted the grass and looked. The white man's camp was still there. I did not see the white man, only the two horses and my chance for freedom. Should I go down now or wait for nighttime? My chances would be better if I waited for the darkness of night, I waited.

I lay in the grass under the heat from the hot blazing sun the Comanche way. I sweated and itched. Bugs were pestering me. Ants crawled over my skin. The worst were the flies. Ignoring them all, I lay there on my stomach watching the camp, waiting for dark of night.

The dark blackness of the night was an answer for which I had been praying. There was no moon. A heavy mist somehow covered the stars. I could not see my hand in front of my face. Everything was perfect.

Silently, I arose and made my way toward the white man's camp. Pausing, I stopped to listen. I heard nothing. Then suddenly an owl flapped its wings, on the hunt, as was I. The man must surely be asleep by now. Like a snake in the grass, I slowly crawled forward pausing now and then to listen. No sounds came from his camp only the soft glow from his banked fire. The only sound I heard was the restless movement of the horses when they blew and snorted.

Crawling forward, to within ten feet of the horses. I thought this is too easy the white man is a fool. I could take both horses and he would be stranded. Then I thought that is not the way. Take only what you need, or can use, my Indian father would say.

Moving closer the horses caught my scent and started to move around making a slight noise. Moving slowly step by step, I approached them. In a soft whisper, I tried to calm them. As I reached to undo the tether of the first horse, I heard movement behind me. A gun in his hand the white man stood there facing me. I moved toward him, pulling my knife. He did not fire he just waited. When I was close, I lunged and thrust my knife at him. He quickly twisted and stepped back, I missed. The momentum of my lunge carried me past him, my head exploded in a brilliant burst of pain as he brought the butt of his pistol down.

When I regained consciousness, my head was throbbing with a pain I had never felt before. Opening my eyes, everything was black. Thoroughly disoriented, I must be blind I thought. Gradually my eyes adapted to the darkness and I could see vague outlines in the dim light. I remembered the white man had outsmarted me somehow. He must not be as foolish and stupid as I had thought.

I listened not hearing anything. I started to get up and could not move. I realized I'd been tied hand and foot, and so tightly, the only thing I could do was breathe. I struggled against the ropes but they were too tight. If I could get my hands on my knife, I could cut myself loose. I wiggled my hand around to my side where my knife was sheathed. The sheath was empty. I carried two knives, one at my waist, the other in a sheath concealed in my tall moccasins. Both were empty.

I looked around to the extent that my bindings would allow. I could not see the man who had captured me or his horses, only the glow from the fire where he had dragged me close. Struggling I tried to loosen the ropes enough to escape but it was no use, they were too tight. I quit trying and lay still, waiting …

My eyes darted fearfully about. Was the white man going to kill me? Some warrior I turned out to be. After spending the hot day lying in the sun and my failed theft of the horse, I was tired. My Indian father would not be proud. I closed my eyes and must have fallen asleep my head still throbbing.

I awoke to the sound of chirping birds the next morning. The escapade of the night came flooding back to me, along with the throbbing pain in my head. My arms and legs had become numb they were tied so tightly. The light hurt my eyes, so I closed them. I would be killed for trying to steal a horse. My eyes tight shut with dread and fear at the thought. My thoughts running wild I waited, expecting the worst.

Soon I smelled a smell that pulled at my memory. What was that smell? I knew what it was, but I could not quiet place it. Then I remembered with an onrush of thoughts that flooded my mind. It was coffee. With the recognition of the word coffee, my mind became a confusing rush of thoughts, swirling around inside my throbbing head. Soon my thoughts settled down. I remembered the wagon train, the swim in the river, the Indian who had saved me. I remembered it all as clear as if it had been yesterday.

A kick to my feet suddenly interrupted my thoughts. My eyes flew open with a flash of hate in them. Who was this white man that could treat me thus, with a kick from his booted foot? It did not hurt but he should not kick me. I looked up at the tall man as he studied me.

While he was studying me, I was studying him. He was twenty-five or thirty, and tall, around six feet or more, broad of shoulder and slender in the hips. His blond hair hung down touching the collar of a faded denim shirt. He wore a flat wide brim black hat that tilted down over his pale blue eyes. The black leather pants were worn, shiny with long use and ended covering a pair of black scuffed boots. Two crisscrossed cartridge belts buckled around his waist, slung low, holding two pistols in holsters and tied around his legs.

I had never seen anyone dressed as he was. Maybe he was a sheriff or a famous gun fighter, or an outlaw. My mind started going in circles with many thoughts. I lay there wide-eyed, my imagination running wild.

The white man stood over me, staring down into my face, as he drank from a cup. He quickly backed off, at the angry look on my face. "What am I to do with you," he said, pushing his hat up from his forehead. With a shrug of his shoulders, he turned and walked back toward the fire and added more wood. Soon I smelled the aroma of frying bacon, along with other smells, as he busied himself in the chore of cooking. I realized I had not eaten since I had buried my Indian father a day ago. At the smell of cooking food, I stopped struggling with the rope.

While the food was cooking, he returned with a cup of coffee and setting it on a nearby rock, turned and walked cautiously to me, grabbed me and put me into a sitting position. He picked up the cup and held it toward me. When I did not move he came closer and held the cup to my lips while making a smacking sound. He wanted me to drink and I went along. Taking sips very carefully of the hot coffee. It burned a little going down but it tasted good. It had been a long time since I had had coffee.

Twice I had been on my own and what had come of it? I had been captured both times. What would be next? I didn't know what to expect from this tall white man. Stranger yet, one moment he was hitting me in the head, the next he was offering me coffee. I didn't know what to make of it.

CHAPTER 8

I WAS JOLTED back to the present, by the quick movement of Faith as she jumped sideways from her forward motion. I stopped thinking of the past and quickly looked to see what had spooked her. I spotted the coiled rattler almost instantly and stopped Faith, calming her down; I took a quick look around for Track. He was sitting on the trail fifty yards ahead. Waiting with his head cocked to one side watching to see if everything was okay.

I stepped down from the saddle. By then the snake had slithered off into the sagebrush. Stretching my legs, I knelt down checking the tracks of the four horses I was trailing. The hoof prints still showed they were in no hurry. From the imprint of the hooves and the amount of sand that had blown into them, I guessed they were still about four hours ahead.

Remounting Faith, I rode on m ore slowly. Why were the abductors not in a hurry? Maybe they wanted me to catch up to them. They sure weren't trying to hide their trail. May be it was me they wanted. Maybe an ambush lay ahead. I would have to be very careful when I got closer. I rode on trying not to let my mind wander so much. Still … I had to puzzle out the mystery of why this was all happening. I trailed on as my mind slipped back … to the tall white man.

He must have tired of holding the cup to my lips for he set it back onto the rock. He looked me square in the face and said for me not to try anything, or he would shoot me. With that said, he started untying my hands, leaving my feet still tied. My understanding of English was coming back somewhat after all this time. He handed me the cup. My hands were so numb and trembling from the ropes I almost dropped it.

He watched me sharply as he went to the fire, not trusting me, and not turning his back. He filled two tin plates. Returning he handed one to me.

The feeling was finally returning to my hands. I reached out and took the plate of bacon and beans. I started to use my fingers to eat, when he handed me a spoon. I did not talk. I just ate ravenously, as if I were starving.

I finished before this man, who sat there watching me, while he ate. I licked the tin plate clean with my tongue. He shook his head sadly. He finished shortly thereafter, stood and took my plate. I was still hungry as he walked away. I wanted to ask for more. I searched for the right words that were somewhere in my memory, and spoke. The sound that came out was not what I wanted. But it got his attention.

I had started speaking Comanche and had said, "Aegeh." I stopped quickly. I knew in my mind I had said the wrong word as soon as the words left my lips. I would have to think in the other language, English. Starting over I said, "Ah, Ah … moor," and pointed at my open mouth.

Pushing his hat up on his forehead said, "Well I'll be dang, if that don't beat all!" He stood there dumbfounded, an unbelieving look upon his face.

"What did you say? Do you understand English?" he asked.

"Ah 'ee … ah … soam … soom …some," I finally got out.

"You want more to eat?" he asked pointing at his mouth.

"Yis … Yes, more," I said, shaking my head up and down.

"I understand you, but you don't speak good English. Still, some is better than nothing, I suppose." he muttered to himself. W hile getting me more beans he started talking more and more to me. The more he talked the more familiar the sounds became.

My memories and understanding of English were slowly coming back. He kept talking while I finished off the beans. When I finished eating, I said, "Good, that good."

"How did you learn to speak English?" he said with a thoughtful look. Speaking with Comanche and bro ken English, I told my story as best I could. Stopping often, I struggled trying to get the words to come out right. He kept interrupting with questions.

With his interruptions and my searc hing for the right words, it took some time telling about our move f rom the east and moving west with the wagon train. My getting lost out on the plains and almost dying, but saved by an Indian. The Indian had become a father to me, his dying and me burying him, ending in my present predicament trying to steal a horse

Not speaking he sat there thinking. "So you are not an Indian." It was more a statement than a question. "You are a white boy, whose skin has turned dark from sun and dirt." Pausing … he then continued. "You also smell bad. What you need is a good scrubbing to get the dirt and smell off."

He said, "I'm going to untie you if you promise not to run."

"If I not promise, what happen then?"

"Then I will just shoot you and put you out of your misery."

With that, he bent picked up a rock and flung it high into the air over his shoulder. The rock arched high into the air and started falling back to the ground. Without paying attention to the rock, he looked like he had all the time in the world. He whirled empty handed and suddenly a pistol appeared in his hand as if by magic. Finding the stone as it fell, he fired one shot that struck the rock shattering it.

I looked from where the stone had been back to the man who stood there empty handed with a smile on his face. I could not believe what I had seen, or maybe I should say what I hadn't seen. I could not believe anyone could move that fast and be so accurate.

I believed maybe he would shoot me.

CHAPTER 9

HE SEEMED TO be a fair man, from his words and actions, so I promised. "By the way if you had gotten one of my horses, what were you goin' to do with it?" He asked.

"I was gonna ride away and go somewhere," I said.

"And just where is this somewhere you were goin' to ride to?" he asked. "I don't know, I didn't think, I was just gonna ride."

"What were you goin' to eat on the way to somewhere?"

"I would kill something to eat. I am a warrior and a man." I said standing a and puffing out my chest as the last of the rope was cut from my ankles.

He laughed. "Do you know what would happen to you out there? The first time a rancher or a gunman saw you they'd shoot first and ask questions while you lay dying." he said, looking me straight in the eyes. "How old are you anyway? You're fairly tall but with all that dirt, it's hard to tell.

Shrugging my shoulders I replied, "I think I'm fourteen or fifteen or maybe sixteen. I don't really know for sure how old I am."

"You really don't know much do you. You think you're all grown-up and smart, but you know very little. What's your name?"

"Ah … ah, what you mean? 1 not understand."

"You know … what do they call … what did your Indian father call you? What word does he say, when he wants your attention?"

"Oh! … I think … I understand. What my father Shatika call me when he want me to come. He call me Chadtu. No is not right, he call me Chad'tu. Yes … Chad'tu is Indian name my father gives me."

"Well Chad'tu, that's a strange name that you answer to. You can call me Brett. The whole name is Brett Tishman. Most everyone calls me Brett. A few refer to me as Mister Tishman, and some call me the 'The Devils

Gunsmith.' You probable never heard of me, being a kid and tucked away in these here mountains, away from civilization and all."

"No, I never hear that name before." I said watching the man intently, as he strode back and forth. With my reply, he took charge and said that was enough. He told me it was time for me to clean myself of the sweat and dirt. He led me through the trees to a trickling creek. It must have somehow found its way down the mountain from the seep by the cave.

I thought of escaping but where would I go. He was right. Where would I go? I didn't know what was over the next hill, let alone as far as the eye could see, toward where the sun slept. I guess I was not as grown up and smart as I thought.

Shedding my clothes, I stepped into the cold water of the creek. Brett handed me an old bar of soap that had turned grey with age and a small towel. "Use these and keep scrubbing till I can see what color you might be under all that dirt." After a moment or two of splashing cold water all over my body and hitting a spot here and there with soap, I was ready to get out. I started for the bank.

Brett yelled, "Hey! That's not enough, get your ornery hide back and do some real scrubbing, or I'll come in and scrub it for you." With his large hand, he gave me a push sending me sprawling into the middle of the creek. He burst out laughing as I lay there splashing and sputtering.

Brett sat on a large granite boulder and watched as I scrubbed and scrubbed with the rough cloth and the hard bar of soap. After several minutes that seemed like an hour, he said, "That's enough you can get out. I rinsed off the soap and was back on the bank in less than a minute.

"You sure were fast getting out. You ain't afraid of a little water are you?" He asked, chuckling.

I stepped from the freezing creek dripping water and shivering. Brett tossed me a blanket to dry with. I turned my back embarrassed. After drying, I put on the clothes I had shed earlier. When I was dressed, I turn to Brett and said, "You happy now?"

"Yeah, you look like a white boy ... er man, I mean." He moved toward the fire with me close behind. I stepped close to the fire to warm myself. He poured himself a cup of coffee, and then handed the cup to me. "Here this will warm you."

This man was trusting and kind I thought. He poured a second cup for himself. Settling back and sipping his coffee, he said, "Chad'tu … I been thinking … you don't know what life is all about out there. As soon as you step out there you are gonna get yourself killed. Somehow, for some reason, I like you. You don't lie. I can see now you're white. You tell the truth. I like that in a man … And by damn, if I don't think you are a man, what kind I don't know yet. But I will find out."

I sat sipping my coffee listening as Brett spoke. For a while, there was silence as we both looked into the flickering fire mesmerized by the flames. I was starting to get warm and sleepy when the silence was broken by Brett's deep voice.

"Chad'tu, I have a proposition for you. Since you will only get yourself in trouble out there, here's my proposition. I'm a gunsmith by trade, and the best. You can be my helper, apprentice or whatever, you call it. I'll teach you the gunsmith trade. I will teach you how to handle and shoot the guns you repair or modify for their owners. I will show you how to use them, for good or bad that choice will be up to you. I will help you to speak proper English. So, what do you say? … Before you answer," he added, "Think carefully of what I offer."

"I have had several that wanted to work under me. Until now, I was not interested in teaching anyone. You … you're different. There's something about you I can't quiet place. Maybe it's you remind me of myself when I was about your age."

"As I said, whether fixing or modifying guns, or in a gun fight, I am the best." Going on he said, "I'm one of the fairest gunman … still alive." He stopped speaking. He sat there thinking, maybe of his past, while waiting for my answer.

"What are my choices? I go with you … or I go on my way … maybe get killed. Not much choice."

"Chad'tu, if you decide to stay, it would make my heart happy, as you would say. If you decide to go, I will return to you all your weapons. You must make these choices for yourself. Stay or go it's up to you. I will understand whatever you decide."

I thought for only a moment then said, "I will go with you … for now, but I have a question. There is one thing I can't figure out."

Brett stood up and walked over, "And what might that be?" he asked, with a frown on his face.

"I have but one question to ask. You have been camped on this little plateau for some time now. My father and I saw you here several weeks ago and you are still here. … Why?"

"Ah, that's a long story my young friend, it's getting late. Let us turn in and get some shut-eye. I'll tell you why I'm still here in the morning. Okay?"

CHAPTER 10

WE WERE BOTH up before the night sky lightened to grey. Brett stoked up the embers of last night's fire and added some of the wood that I had gathered. We didn't speak but communicated with looks. He collected more wood and I helped.

A pregrey dawn preceded that first burst of sunlight still to come from over the distant mountaintops. It was a cold brisk morning. I hadn't slept much, wondering about Brett, why he was still lingering here. Soon the fire was burning well and dispelling the chilled air. Brett came from the creek carrying the coffee pot filled with water to make coffee. The strong smell of coffee soon filled the air.

Brett got out the makings for breakfast. I looked for wild onions that grew plentiful in this area. While searching I came across the nest of a bird which held three eggs. Walking from the woods with eggs in one hand and wild onions in the other, I yelled, "Brett, look what I found."

"Well, it looks like were going to have ourselves a good breakfast," he said, taking the eggs. We sat eating our bacon and eggs, sipping on hot black coffee. Chewing a piece of salty bacon and a little nervous, I ask Brett, "You were going to tell me why your still here?"

"Yeah, it plumb slipped my mind. Let's see, you wanted to know why I've been here so long. Wasn't that it?" he said, Taking a sip of coffee.

"Come on Brett you know that's it. So quit stalling and tell me."

—◦◦]◦[◦◦—

I rode along fondly remembering Brett and his past life, as if it were yesterday. It seemed close and at the same time so far away.

I looked up from the hoof tracks I followed and whistled at Track to stay close. My eyes snapped back to the trail of the men who had taken my wife.

My thoughts drifted back to the telling of Brett's past escapade.

⚬⚬❦⚬⚬

Brett started in. "Alright then, you wanted to know how come I was here so long. This here is the story as it happened. And don't you interrupt."

Brett began, "I had a disagreement with a man I didn't know. It happened in the town of Bisbee, just across the Mexican border from a shack town call Naco. The sun was getting low on the horizon and I'd been riding all day. I was tired and thirsty. You might say I was more than a little thirsty. I rode slowly, down the winding street of Bisbee, paying little attention to the people that glanced my way."

"Leading my pack horse, I rode along the narrow, wagon rutted street, which wound its way haphazardly down the side of the hill through this western town. The horses kicked up dust, which the warm evening breeze quickly blew down the dusty street. I looked for a saloon where I could get a drink, and wash the dust out of my throat. I drifted past several old wooden buildings built of similar construction searching for a drinking place."

"Rounding a bend and sidestepping my horse around a large pothole in the middle of the dirt street. I heard the faint tinkling sound of a piano coming from a building some fifty yards further on. When I got closer, a sign in large gold letters on its front read, 'The Brass Spittoon Saloon.' In smaller letters it stated, 'Gambling and Rooms to let. Sliding from the saddle, I tied my horse and packhorse to the hitching rail. Stepping up on the wood porch, I glanced up and down the street and walked through the short swinging doors into the smoke filled saloon.

Stepping quickly to the side as was my habit, I stopped and taking a quick glance made a survey of the large open room. A long bar ran down the right side with several fellers drinking and talking. Some looked in my direction. Everything seemed normal. Playing poker at several of the green card tables were a variety of types, a mixture of cowboys, ranchers, some locals, a few shifty looking hombres and of course, a card sharp. Some were smoking, betting, drinking, and in general all seemed to be normal. Toward the rear, a staircase led up along the sidewall to the second floor rooms.

Stepping into an open space at the bar, I made a motion to get the bartenders attention. The men at the bar paid me no more attention and went back to their drinking. With all the yelling and telling stories, everyone was having a good time. Some rested their elbows on the well-used, shiny wood topped bar. Some had a boot on the brass rail that ran below the bar, punctuated by several brass spittoons; hence the name.

Wiping a glass as he came down, the big, burly, mustached bartender smiled and asked, "Whadda ya have friend? Name yur poison."

"Give me a shot of rye and branch water," I said. Placing a few silver coins on the bar and looked up into the smoke-covered mirror that hung behind the bar. From where I stood I could see the entire room or any sign of trouble that might crop up.

The bartender returned and set a glass of branch water along with an empty glass on the bar, uncorked the rye, and poured me a decent drink. Taking some of my money and leaving some, asked, "New in town?"

"Yeah, I just rode in from up Tombstone way. It looks a little stormy out, maybe we'll get some weather." I said, making small talk to get the feel of the place. Downing the first drink, I poured myself another and said, "Let me know when my money runs out."

"Sure thing," He replied, "When I need more, I'll let ya know. By the way, my name is Ramber, Jeffe Ramber. Everyone calls me Ram. I own this place." He extended his hand toward me and asked, "What's your'n?"

I tossed down the second drink. Taking hold of Ram's extended hand and watching the expression on his pudgy face said, "Mine is Brett Tishman, pleased to make your acquaintance."

On hearing my name, he let go of my hand as if he had been bitten by a rattler and hurriedly stepped back. A frown quickly replaced his smile, "We don't want no trouble in here Mr. Tishman; I heard of you, I heard you're mighty fast with a gun too."

"I'm not looking for trouble." I replied, "Just thirsty. I won't start any trouble, but if someone starts something, I'll try to walk away, if at all possible. If not ... the trouble will be with the others. All I want is a few drinks, and I might just try my hand at one of your tables, and maybe a room for a night, fair enough?"

"If you don't cause no trouble, I might have a room. We'll see," Ram said, not looking at all happy. "I sure hope there's no trouble. I don't want my bar broken up," he muttered walking off down the bar. While getting drinks for three cowboys, he kept looking back toward me.

Soon I started feeling better. Some of the stiffness had started leaving my aching body—Helped along some by the whisky I'm sure.

I looked up into the mirror behind the bar at the poker tables behind me.

I suddenly felt lucky.

Picking up my change and drink and tossed a coin on the bar. I turned and walked over to a table that had an empty chair, where a mixed group was playing poker. The table stood at the end of the stairs and an empty chair sat next to the wall. From which vantage point, I would have a view of everything including the stairs. I could keep an eye on the whole place.

"Mind if I set in for a few hands?" I asked the players. Watching their eyes for any reaction to the question, I took a sip of my whisky. Hardly looking up, they continued with their play.

Two players across from the empty chair looked up and said, "Shore stranger, your money's as good as the next fellow's, I s'pose. Ain't that right, Mort?" he winked at his friend, and then looked at the card slick setting across from him. Maybe I shouldn't have sat at this table and in this particular chair. I had a premonition that told me not to play at this table. Ignoring the thought, I pulled the chair out and sat anyway.

I lost a few hands and won a few. Not betting too heavy I played trying to get a feel for the table, players, and how they bet. After a few more drinks and sometime later, I hit my stride, and started winning more than I was losing.

Drinking and playing cards for hours into the night, I had won a handsome amount. I play cards pretty good, but this night I was just plain lucky. With the large stack of money, setting on the table in front of me and the amount still left in front of the better players. I could see I still had a ways to go. There was no beating me.

Suddenly I caught a whiff of sweet-smelling perfume. It reminded me of roses. With the pleasant scent came the woman wearing it. Long blond hair down past her shoulders wearing a slinky red dress cut low. It looked like I might get even luckier.

She walked right up to me and placed a long white-gloved hand on my shoulder, "My name is Lou, what's yours big boy?" I just sat there for a moment ... dumbfounded. I gulped down the drink and stood, knocking over my chair.

"Ma'am," I started and choked on the swallow of whisky. Everyone at the table started laughing at my befuddlement. Taking off my hat and holding it in front of me like it would protect me from this lovely creature, I started over. "Ma'am ... my name is Brett." Then I bent and sat the chair upright my face flushed a beet red.

She toyed with her necklace as she ran the other hand through my hair. A shiver of pleasure ran through my body. "Mind if I set beside you? You look like my kind of man," she said, and kissed me on the cheek.

I smiled my most women-getting smile. "All right, but don't be distracting me while I'm playing, okay?" It was Blackey's, the card sharp's deal. I watched closely as he dealt the cards making sure he wasn't dealing from the bottom of the deck. If' he was, he was slicker than anyone I had seen, and I had seen a few. I had a pair of queens and some low number cards. The first man opened, and the next called, the next folded. My turn, I called and raised the pot. The next two just called.

Slick asked each player still in how many cards they wanted. The man that had opened asked for two cards. He looked at his cards, and then bet.

This raised the pot to a goodly amount. The two in front of me folded after receiving their draw cards.

I called. The two after me tossed in their cards. When it was Blackey's turn, he called and raised. The opening bid looked at his cards, and tossed them as he folded. This left me heads on to mister sharp.

He beat me with three deuces.

I started losing more hands than I was winning, which was not good. I started thinking ... I was winning before Lou had sat down at my side, with her sweet smelling perfume, rubbing my back, running her hand through my hair, and slightly touching my thigh with hers.

I had not won to many hands since Lou had arrived. I started paying more attention to Lou as I played out my hands. I noticed she fiddled with her necklace a lot. Then I noticed light reflected on the wall from the necklace as she fingered her throat.

Without drawing attention, I looked closer at her necklace. It was made of little round mirror's that reflected the light and any thing else they might reflect, such as the cards that I held in my hand. I watched Blackey and Lou closely and could tell they were in cahoots with each other.

I finally had had enough. Standing I said to mister slick, card sharp, that he was cheating. The rest at the table looked stunned. "Are you callin' me a cheat?" Slick said. He stood and kicked back his chair. An ugly look spread across his face. With a curled lip, he snarled at me, "No one calls me a cheat and gets away with it!"

I said, "I don't want no trouble, but it's plain as day you and this here lady are in cahoots." As the word 'day' fell from my lips, he drew his Colt. I stood there watching ... as he slowly drew the Colt from its holster. Time slowed for me. Suddenly a large hole appeared in Slick's gun hand, followed by the roar of the gun that had appeared suddenly in my hand.

The shock of the bullet as it passed through his hand made the grip on the gun loosen. He dropped his Colt in surprise. Looking down at the bloody hole in his hand where the bullet had ripped through it. He turned pale at the sight of his gun hand dripping blood onto the floor. He stood with a shocked expression on his face as his gun fell to the floor. His snarl had been replaced with a sign of fear.

Hardly had I realized that I had drawn and fired my gun beefore he had cleared leather. A subconscious reaction on my part, learned through long hours and much practice.

The saloon was suddenly quiet as they all looked for the disturbance of the shot. I grabbed my money from the table. Keeping an eye on everyone with my colt still smoking, I backed slowly through the swinging butterfly doors. Once through the doors I holstered my gun turned and ran swiftly to my horses. I jerked the tethers loose, swiftly mounted and was away before anyone had time to come through the swinging doors.

I didn't know where I was going. I only knew I had to get out of town fast. The horses had revived somewhat and I didn't see any sign of immediate pursuit, so after the first few minutes I didn't push them.

Riding most of the night, I went to the high ground, came across this creek with the woods and all, seemed like a good place to rest up, and maybe let all those folks cool down a bit. That's why I've been here so long. "Does that answer your question?"

"Yeah, but Brett how can you shoot so fast an still hit what your aiming at? The gun just seems to suddenly appear in your hand, it's like magic. How can you do that?"

"Practice, practice and more practice, till you're sick and tired and want to quit. Then you practice some more, a lot more. And then one day ... without thinking ... it just comes natural and automatic ... It's like breathing, you are hardly aware you're doing it."

CHAPTER 11

W ITH THE ABILITY to end someone's life, shooting is not something to be takin' lightly. It carries with it a lot of responsibility."

"Brett, could you teach me to shoot like you?"

"Yeah, I suppose I could."

"When can we start? I'm ready now."

"There are certain things you need to learn first. You need to learn how to repair all the different makes and types of pistols, short guns, and rifles, and shot guns, and how to modify them to their owner's wishes."

"If you are willing to do all of that, I will teach you . If not, you can leave here and I won't stop you. But you'll leave as you came, afoot. So what will it be? Will you be my apprentice and helper? If you say yes, you must promise to never give up on any task, I set you. What do you say?"

"I make this promise to you, Brett. I will do what ever you want! Just teach me to shoot like you. Okay?"

"Alright, we agree. Now the first thing I want you to do …"

"What?" I said with excitement edging my voice. "What do you want me to do first, Brett?" I asked wide-eyed, eager and impatient to learn. "First thing I want you to do," Brett paused, and then said, "Get me some more coffee."

"Aw... Brett, that's not fair. I don't want to be your slave. I want to learn."

"First you have to learn to follow orders and not to speak back. Understood?"

"Oh! Alright, I'll get you more coffee." I took Brett's cup, walked over to the fire and carefully took the hot coffee pot from the fire and filled his cup. I brought Brett the steaming hot coffee. "Are you happy now?" I asked, with a wave of my arm.

"Chad'tu, the most important thing you have to learn is, never ever ... ever question me on anything I say or do, or tell you to do! Understood?" I sat down, crossed my legs the Indian way, picked up a pebble, looked at it, and then tossed it at a nearby ground squirrel that had poked its head up. It quickly ducked down its hole.

I sat thinking. First, I'm a dog on a leash with Shatika. That had turned out okay ... better than okay. Now if I go along with Brett it seemed I would be his slave. I really liked this man and he could teach me a lot. He had been places, done things, and seen things that I could not imagine. He could teach me how to get along out there among people.

"Okay, Brett! I won't question you ever again. Now can we be friends?"

Brett reached out took my hand in his and we shook. "Fine," he said, "then friends it is." Then he gave me a brotherly hug. "As a matter of fact a couple more days on this here plateau and I think it will be safe to leave."

"Where will we go?" I asked bright-eyed, eager and curious. "Tombstone is not far and it would be a good place to start on your training. You need getting reacquainted with some of the more civilized people. I'm known and respected there and the people are friendly. It's a new town with not many folks there yet, but that will change due to the discovery of silver. It's an ideal place for you to learn your trade and me to teach you."

Two sunrises later, we left the plateau in the early hours of a chilly predawn morning. We rode out after breakfast, just as the sun was peeking over the horizon tinting the clouds a pale rose color. Brett on his beautiful steel grey stallion and me on the buckskin pack horse, along with the saddlebags and packs. I was excited.

Finally, I was going to a real town. I was g oing to see real people and things that I couldn't remember seeing before.

We rode all day stopping now and then to let the horses rest. Having never ridden a horse, I was uncomforta ble with the motion. I mostly just hung on and let the horse do its own thing. Walking the horses along slowly was not too ba d, but when we went faster, I bounced up as the horse went down, and then I came down and met the horse coming up. After a few hours, it ceased being fun and became painful.

Getting close to Tombstone, Brett stopped his horse. He slid off of the stallion dropping to the ground, saying it was time we stretch our legs and limber up a bit. I jumped down took a couple of steps feeling a sore pain in my rear. I could hardly walk it hurt so much. I complained to Brett.

He just laughed at me and said, "You'll get use to it."

It seemed a long time ago that my rear had hurt so much. Brett had been right; I did get use to it. It had taken some time. Now I rode in pursuit, on the trail of the people that had taken my wife.

The motion of Faith was an easy rolling gait and my rear didn't hurt at all. My thoughts were not on my rear but on Jaydeen. As I trailed them, my thoughts drifted again to Brett and the past, trying to figure this thing out.

After a brief break and letting the horses rest some, we mounted up and continued on toward Tombstone. Scattered about the landscape were boulders and rock -strewn gravel, punctuated with a few cactus and scraggly sagebrush. An occasional lizard or snake was all that greeted my eye. This is awful country.

CHAPTER 12

THE SUN WAS setting as we rode into town. The heat of the day was starting to cool somewhat. Brett rode down the wide dirt street of Tomb-stone, I followed not knowing what to expect, ready for anything.

A few people were walking on the boards in front of the stores. Storekeepers were moving the goods that had been displayed on their porches inside for the night. The sun was slowly sinking beyond a cloudless horizon. Brett turned his horse to a building, slid off and tied it to the rail. He motioned and indicated for me to do the same.

"This here is a boardinghouse. See the sign? It reads, 'Rooms and Eats, by the day, week, or month.' If we can get a room, this is where we'll stay."

There was light shining across the wooden porch from a kerosene lantern that hung just inside the open wood door. Upon entering, there was the strong smell of kerosene. A short, bald, portly man stood behind the high counter. He looked up as we approached. "What can I do for you folks?" he asked, wiping the sweat from his shining head and adjusted his glasses. It was hot and stuffy in the small-enclosed entryway.

"We just arrived in town. We're looking for a place where we might get a room for a night or two, or maybe longer. It depends." Brett said.

"Depends on what?" he wanted to know. Then without taking a breath, "My name is Ben Barlow and I own this here place."

"Well, as I said, we just now got into town. I'm a gunsmith by trade-of some renown, I might add. People hereabouts know of my work, and this young buck is my apprentice."

Barlow gave Chad'tu a hard look but didn't say anything.

"We'll be staying … if you have room … for several days or until I find a suitable place to open a gun shop. Can you accommodate us, sir? Oh!

And one other thing, we would like a room in the front overlooking the street if possible."

"Well this sure is your lucky day. Just this morning I was full up till a young feller got his-self kilt right out front. I think it was over a dancing girl over at the Rio Cantina and her jealous boyfriend."

"So gentlemen, I do have a room that is available. I haven't had time to straighten it up and it's only got one bed, but I could throw in a cot at no extra charge. Take it or leave it. Don't matter much to me, seeing as how rooms are scarce in town and it sure won't stay vacant long. And it is a street front room with a window door that opens onto the balcony."

"What might the charges be, for such a spectacular room with a view?" Brett asked facetiously, poking fun at him.

He missed Brett's play on humor and thought a moment. Then he replied, "Normally I charge six bits a day per person, but seeing how I ain't cleaned it. The two of you can have it for four-bit's a day, if you want to eat make it a dollar that'll include the meals."

Brett paid for five days, laying out five silver dollars on the wooden counter.

Mr. Barlow picked up the coins and inspected each one. Making sure, they weren't shaved on their edges. Satisfied, he stuck them in his pocket. Saying, "You can't be too careful nowadays; matter-of-fact some people scrape the edges for the silver shavings you know."

Ben wrote out a receipt for five dollars, then taking a key from a drawer handed both to Brett. "Shore is hot and muggy for this time of year," he said, wiping his brow and neck again.

Brett just stood there waiting. Barlow looked at us wonderingly. "Oh yeah, I plumb forgot, the room is up those stairs." he said pointing. "It's the first door on the right down the hallway."

"Thank ya kindly, we'll just get our belongings and be out of your hair." Brett said touching the brim of his hat. As we turned to go Brett stopped, "By the way, what time are meals served?"

"Well, supper starts at sunset and breakfast is at sunrise." He thought a moment, "And iffen you get real hungry and lucky, you might get the cook to make you something around noon time. For your horses, there's a stable on down the street. Tell Jeb I sent you, he'll treat you fair."

We got our belongings and carried them up the steep, rickety stairs. Turning right at the top into a dimly lit, narrow hallway, Brett found the door locked. Fumbling in the dim light he unlocked the door. Opening the door wide, he said, "Well this is our new home Chad'tu, come on in." In the dim light, it didn't look too bad.

"Ah, Brett, I got to tell you something. Since all the talkin', we been doing, I starting to remember things. I think my name is Chad. And did you see the look that Barlow gave me?"

Brett lit a lantern, put the glass chimney on, and adjusted the wick. He took a long look at me and my Indian clothing. "Yeah Chad'tu, I did. He probable thinks you're an Indian the way you're dressed. Maybe we should get you some different clothes and I'll start calling you Chad, might make things easier."

There was still a bucket of water setting on a table, beside a washbasin. We could smell the cooking of supper as it rose up through the wood floor. We washed the dirt and dried sweat from our faces and hands. Feeling some-what freshened and presentable, we hurried down the unsteady wood stairs into the dining room.

After eating our fill of biscuits, redeye gravy and fried chicken, we strolled out on the porch. "That was a dang good meal." I said, rubbing my stomach.

"Yep, that was a right good supper," Brett nodded. We should probably take the horses down to the stables before it gets too dark. After we get them settled in, let's take a walk around town and see what's going on. That sound okay, Chad?"

"Sure, I ain't ever been in a real western frontier town before." I said excitedly, as I jumped off the porch and went to the horses.

Leading the horses down the dark street, we passed by a noisy saloon and several darkened store fronts, before we found the stable. A small building without a light, sat slightly in front and to one side. Sitting on the porch in the dark was a man. Getting closer Brett said, "Howdy. Do you know where I might find the man that runs this stable?"

"That would be me." he replied, spitting over the porch edge. "What can I do fer you folks?"

"I'd like to board two horses for awhile if you got room."

"We got plenty of space in the corral and there is room in the barn for two more Cayuses." He spit his chaw-in-tobacco again and said. "I figure two bits a day aught to about cover it. Course, feed is included in that figure. How long you all figure on leaving them?"

Brett shrugged his shoulders, "Well I don't rightly know. We just rode into town and I'm looking for a place to open my business. You wouldn't per chance have an idea of a small store that might be vacant and for rent would you?"

"We got in too late to look around and now it's dark. Tomorrow were going to start looking for a place. If you got any ideas, it would be of a great help to us." Brett handed the man four bits, "This ought to cover my horses for two days worth."

The man stood and taking Brett's money said, "The name's Brannon, and there are a few empty buildings in town you can probably rent cheap. Might warn you also, there's a lot of shootin' going on in this here town. Day and night it never ceases."

"Don't worry," Brett said, "If it comes to trouble my Colts will protect me."

"By the way there young feller, I didn't catch your name. And being a mite curious, just what kind of business y'all figure to open anyway?" He asked, as he spit off the porch again.

"Mister Brannon. The name is Brett and this young lad's name is Chad. With all the shooting that's going on in this town, it would seem a likely place to open a gunsmith shop. Wouldn't you say? And that's what I intend to do." Brett started to walk away and stopping he turned and said, "By the way old man, for your information my full name is Brett ... Brett Tishman." With that said, Brett turned and started to walk away.

"Wait ... Wait, Mister Tishman." called out Brannon. Brett paused, turning back once again. "Yes, what is it?"

With a quiver in his voice, Brannon asked. "You're not that Tishman are you?"

"What Tishman are you referring to Mr. Brannon?"

"You know the one from down El Paso way. The one ... the one no one can ..." He faltered. Then said, "Beat to the draw ... The one who's shot and kilt" ... Brannon swallowed hard ... "six men?" He quickly added, "I heard they 'twas all fair fights."

"I guess you might say that I am that Tishman— except for one thing, Mister Brannon. You know what that one thing is. Actually it isn't one thing, its four things." Before Brannon could answer Brett said, "This Tishman you say killed six men could not be me. For I have ended ten lives. That's four more than you said. So you see, how could I, be that Tishman."

"Mister Tishman, sir, I didn't mean nothing, I apologize."

"Forget about it. I was not offended by your remarks, Brannon." Brett turned and walked off down the dark street. He motioned for me to follow, "Come on Chad let's see what's going on around town."

CHAPTER 13

EXCEPT FOR THE noise coming from the saloons, the town was quiet, until they heard distant shots fired. Brett said not to worry, probably only a drunk cowboy letting off steam. Brett stopped in front of one such saloon and said, "See that sign beside the doorway?"

"Yeah I see it." I answered. "What about it?"

"Read it for me."

"Aw, Brett, you know I can't read." I said, kicking the steps leading up the porch. "I forgot how."

"Well that's something we can fix. It says Longhorn Saloon. Along with teaching you to repair guns and rifles, I guess I'll have to teach you how to read. It shouldn't be too hard, seeing as how you told me at one time you could read pretty well." Brett stepped up to the doors leading into the saloon. "You never been in a saloon, would you like to go in?"

"I guess so," I said. Stepping up on the wooden porch, we pushed through the well-worn swinging doors. The saloon was somewhat less noisy than the others we had passed, smoke hanging in the air slowly drifted out through the open doors and windows.

I didn't know what to think. I looked at the drunken cowboys, carrying on with the women serving them drinks. Some of those women were drinking right along with those cowboys. Laughing, kissing, and hugging, they looked to be having a real good time.

The smoke filled room was hot and stuffy. A long bar ran down the side. As I stood gawking, Brett grabbed me by the shoulder and pushed me toward the bar. Behind the bar was a skinny man, wrapped in a white apron and wearing a blue, long sleeved shirt, with garters on his arms asked with an accent, "What can I get you gents?"

Brett looked at me and laughed, shaking his head, he ordered two beers. The bartender took two large glasses and filled them. Slopping over with white foam, he sat them on the counter in front of us. The beer still foaming over ran down the side of the glasses and onto the bar. Not knowing what I should do, I watched Brett. He picked up his beer and holding it toward me said, "Pick up your beer my young friend."

I picked up my glass. Brett said, "Here's to you and me and a long life for us both." With that said, he took a swallow, and set his glass down and wiped the white mustache from his upper lip. He motion for me to drink.

I put the glass to my mouth, took a swallow as I had seen Brett do. Choking, I spewed a small amount of beer onto the bar. Embarrassed I looked around. No one took noticed what I had done, except Brett. He looked around to see if anyone was paying attention to us.

He Looked at me and laughed, "You should a seen the look on your face when you took that swallow. It was the funniest thing I've seen in a long time. How do you like the taste of beer?" he asked, as he lifted his glass. Taking another long swallow, he let out a loud belch.

"It tastes sorta bitter." I said, picking up my glass. I bent my head down and sniffed at the yellow brew. It had a strong smell which I had never smell the likes of. Satisfied I took a small sip, not a swallow. This time I got a good taste of this thing called beer. "It tastes not too bad." I said, as I took a couple of large swallows.

Brett finished his beer and ordered two more. I still had half a glass of beer left. "Drink up," he urged. "You don't want to fall behind. It's too hard to catch up." With that encouragement, I tilted the glass and downed the rest of the liquid.

"That's more like it." he said, while sliding one of the two beers over to me. The second beer went down much more easily and much faster. Brett ordered two more beers and it wasn't long after the second beer there was a third and ...

CHAPTER 14

I WAS AWAKENED the next morning by the shaking of my bed. Disoriented and confused for the moment, I jumped from the bed ready to fight. I looked quickly around my eyes coming to rest on Brett's face. Brett held up his hands and backed away taking no chances, then stood there with a smile on his face.

"Okay, Sunshine! Its time to be up and about, and you'd better hurry or you're going to miss breakfast. The cook just rang the bell. So get a move on seeing we got a lot to do today."

"What … what happened? My head hurts something fierce." I felt a pounding throbbing feeling, behind my eyes, like a bunch of little men trying to get out of my head. I didn't understand the feeling. It was something I hadn't ever felt before and didn't ever want to feel again.

"Brett, what happened last night? I don't remember anything after that third beer. And how did I get here undressed and in bed?" I asked, rubbing my pounding head

"Well you weren't feeling no pain after five beers. You kept saying you wanted more. I thought you'd had enough so I called it a night, and helped you back to the room and to bed." Handing my clothes to me he said, "Get dressed and wash up, make it quick."

—∞◦❂◦∞—

Bringing my thoughts back to the present, I smiled to myself of that past memory. Pulling Faith up, I stepped down from the saddle, knelt and carefully looked at the hoof tracks. They were spaced further apart; the group seemed to be traveling faster. Standing and stretching my legs a moment, I looked down the trail hoping for any sign of a dust cloud. There was none.

I swung up into the saddle reached forward and rubbed Faith's neck. "Good girl." I praised her. Her cars twitched back at the sound of my voice and tossing her head she snorted as if saying, let's get moving. I gave out a long loud whistle, and looked about for Track. The independent thinking wolf was far ahead. I yelled, "Track, stay close."

Picking up the pace, I rode, looking down at the trail then up at the surrounding countryside. After a couple of hours, I still had not caught sight of any riders. Once I thought I saw a dust cloud far off, but I couldn't be sure. I rode with my head down moving swiftly along. Suddenly, there was a difference in the pattern of prints. Stopping Faith, I pulled to one side and gave the prints a slow thoughtful perusal. Studying the tracks it appeared that they had stopped and had some sort of discussion, or maybe even a disagreement. Hard to tell if good or bad, I didn't know.

The tracks moved back and forth overlaying one another. Then they split apart, two sets went northward and two sets looked like they were headed to the town, which was maybe five miles over the hill that lay between me and it.

It was a hard decision I faced. Which of the trails should I follow? The one headed north or the one headed for town? It appeared they had not harmed Jaydeen, so far. I didn't know where the trail north led, or how far their destination. I was pretty sure the other would lead into the town. For what reason was not clear to me. I had a choice to make. Since the town was closer, I decided to head that way and check it out. If I chose right, maybe just maybe, Jaydeen would be there unharmed.

Anxiously, I decided to follow the two sets of tracks headed for town. If one set were Jaydeen's, there would be only one man to confront. It would be a cinch to get her back. Unless they had others waiting to meet up with them. The thought crossed my mind, but I'd deal with it when the time came, if that was the case. It wouldn't take long to settle my account with the two riders if Jaydeen were not there. I could still catch up to the northbound ones, with little time lost.

I headed toward the town … and my thoughts again drifted back to my past.

CHAPTER 15

TAKING MY CLOTHES, I dressed quickly. My head was still hurting. Taking the wash pan with Brett's dirty water, I emptied it through the open window. I poured fresh water from the bucket and washed the dirt from my face and then my arms. Satisfied, I hurried after Brett who had not waited.

I caught up just as he was seating himself at a small table, covered with a bright red and white checkered tablecloth. Brett sat looking out the window beside the table. He watched the early risers as they moved up and down the street. He was always looking for any sign of trouble.

Dressed as I was in Indian buckskin and leggings, with long black hair tied back and hanging past my shoulders, several people glanced apprehensively at me, some with a worried look as I entered the dining room. I had grown to be almost six feet tall and was big for my age, whatever that might be. Pulling out a chair, I sat across from Brett. A few diners whispered to one another casting a nervous glance in our direction.

"Why are those people staring at me?" I asked Brett.

Brett had noticed the stir I had caused. Brett looked at me and said. "If an Indian stepped into the room, while you were having breakfast, and if you were town folk, you might be just a little frightened at the sight."

"But, I'm white, as anyone with eyes can see its plain as day."

"Yeah, I know but your clothes and hair says you're an Indian. I heard somewhere that clothes make the man, but in your case the Indian. I suppose a new set of clothes wouldn't hurt none either."

Four large plates of food were set in front of us by a big-boned blond woman. We stopped talking as our breakfast of bacon and eggs and pancakes was served along with hot strong black coffee.

"What are we going to do today?" I asked between mouthfuls.

"Well, first we get the horses and ride about town and see if we can find something suitable for our gun shop. While were doing that we can find out what kind of people we'll be dealing with. Oh! And I guess we could get you some different duds."

Finishing our food, we stood. Brett left a couple of coins on the table and we walked out amid the stares of several of the diners.

I walked along the boardwalk, excited to see all the stores in the daytime. I kept stopping and looking in windows, at the things stacked on shelves, and some on the floor, and all were for sale. Brett was ahead of me several steps and yelled for me to hurry up.

I turned from the window quickly and bumped into a young cowboy coming from the store. He swore at me. Calling me a damn, dumb Indian, that didn't know anything. The blood rushed to my head, and in a fit of rage, I grabbed him and threw him from the stores porch into the dirt street. Still cussing, he rolled up on one knee facing me and drew his gun. That was his second mistake. I jumped from the porch and taking two quick steps kicked the gun out of his hand.

The commotion had brought Brett back. He stood on the porch and watched, as I jumped off after the one, I had tossed into the street. The smart-aleck cowboy was about my age. Seein' his gun wasn't going to help, he stood up angry and mad, ready to fight man to man.

I doubled up my right fist and with all my might; I swung, punching him in the gut. With my left, I swung for his jaw missing as he ducked, but I was ready with my right. As he ducked the left, I punched up with my right catching his chin as he tried ducking down. He staggered back wiping blood from his lips

About that time, an older cowboy came from the store to see what all the yelling was about. He took one look at the two fighters. Stopping, his hand reached for his Colt. Brett moved into the cowboys' line of sight getting his attention. Brett tapped the butt of his own pistol and shook his head no. "I wouldn't do that if I was you. Just let em fight," he told the cowboy. The cow-boy looked Brett up and down, saw his tied down guns and wisely decided against drawing down on the fighting young buck.

He wiped the blood from his bruised lips, rushed forward grabbing for my throat. I had practiced fighting with my Indian father many times and learned much about the art of fighting hand to hand from him. Grasping his shirt as the cowboy connected with me, I rolled onto my back and pulling him with me, I pushed his body up with my legs into the air. He landed flat on his back with a loud groan.

No sooner had he landed than I was sitting astride his chest as I would sit a horse. I drew back my fist ready to strike, then stopped and asked, "You had enough, or you want more."

He was at a disadvantage and knew it. "Okay, you win. I quit." he said, as I got off letting him up.

Brett chuckled, "That was a right good fight if I say so. Yes sir a mighty good fight." He turned to the cowboy standing next to him, "Don't you agree mister?"

The cowboy answered grudgingly. "Yeah, I guess so." He turned and started down the street. With a gruff, disapproving tone in his voice, he said to the young cowboy, "Sid! I want to talk to you later."

Brett then turned to the boys standing in the middle of the street, brushing the dirt from their clothes, while trying to catch their breath. "Now boys," he said, "I want you to shake hands and say no hard feelings, Okay?"

The young cowboy extended his hand and I grasped it in mine and we shook, saying we were sorry. He picked up his hat that had fallen off and holstered his gun.

He said. "Boy, I never did see any one who could fight that good. My name is Sid ... Sid Brucker. We have a ranch a little ways out from town. Maybe you could visit sometime. What's your name?"

My name ... I have had so many what should I say? "Ah, ah ... my name is Chad."

Sid stood waiting. "Well what's your last name; you know ... your surname?"

I thought for a moment. Surely, I must have a last name but I could not remember my last name. I could make one up. Everyone has a last name; otherwise, you wouldn't know one Bill from another Bill.

Sid said, "Everyone has a last name tell me yours. What is your fathers' last name?"

My fathers name. ... Suddenly I blurted out, "Chadtu ... Chad'tu," the words felt strange as they left my lips.

"Okay Chad. Please, do come see me." Then he added, "Not many boys my age around to do things with. Well, I guess I'd better go see what my father has to say. That was him standing up on the porch with your father. I dread it ... sometimes he can get purty mad. Well come on out, were only about, maybe six, seven miles northwest of town. Hope to see you again. Bye for now." he said, and walked off down the street.

CHAPTER 16

SID WAS SORT of like me, he was okay after all. We both seemed to have short fuses, and were fast to anger. Something about Sid made me like him. He was my first friend I thought, as I watched him walk off down the street. I'd forgotten about Brett. I saw him setting on the edge of the porch, smoking a cigarette and looking up and down the street. He was always watching everything that went on. He got up and said, "You got all that itch and anger out of your system now?"

"I'm sorry Brett, but he called me names and I got so mad I couldn't see straight. And I had to fight him."

"Let me point out what you said. You said you were so mad you couldn't see straight. Is that right?"

"Yeah, and that's the dang truth!"

"Don't cuss." Brett said sternly, taking a drag off his smoke. "Now let's stop and think about this for a minute, and don't interrupt me. Let's say you could shoot as good as me and we are going to have a showdown between you and me. Drawing our guns and shooting to kill or wound the other." He took a long pause ... "Who do you think would win that shootout?"

He waited as I thought about it. "If we were both equally good and had no advantage over the other, it would be a tie, right? We both would be shot dead, through the heart at the same instant, right?" I replied smugly.

"Wrong! Wrong! Wrong! Think how you were today, so mad ... so mad, over nothing. Some few words spoken by another made you see red. In a fit of red hot anger, do you think you could draw and shoot faster than a person who was cold, calm, and calculating?"

Brett went on, "The first rule is never, and I repeat this, never ever lose your temper, or you will be a dead man. Do you understand?"

"Yeah," I said sheepishly, "Got it."

"That is your first lesson, and the most important one you'll ever learn. Never forget it. The golden rule is 'Never Lose Your Temper.' Let's get the horses; you've had enough fun for the day." That was the first lesson of many, and I never forgot it. It has saved my life many times.

We saddled up the horses. Brannon had groomed and fed them. He had taken great care of the animals after finding out who Brett was. Sometimes it pays to have a reputation that people respect or fear.

We rode up and down the streets that comprised the town of Tombstone. Streets that ran haphazardly, without much thought or planning, in several directions.

The few stores that were vacant were located on the main street that wandered through the town. After we checked out the town, we enquired about the availability and cost of renting some of the stores. Two of the empty stores were next to or close to saloons. Brett didn't want to be that close he said, to all the noise of the drunks and the shooting that sometimes happened when they did get drunk.

After riding the streets for two or three hours, Brett was exasperated not being able to find exactly what he wanted. The perfect place seemed to elude us. Frustrated, Brett turned in his saddle and said, "The next saloon we come to, I'm going to stop, get down off this here horse, tie it to the hitching post... and I'm walking in that there saloon, and I'm gonna have me a beer!" Taking off his hat, he wiped his forehead with his sleeve. "What do you say Chad? Want to join me?"

After last night, I was not sure if I ever wanted another beer. My head still throbbed slightly. I told Brett I was not sure I could drink another beer after last night.

He laughed at my hesitation. Then withh aa good-natured laugh said, "What you need is a bit of the tail of the dog that bit you! That will fix you up right quick."

"I don't want no dog tail and I'm not to sure about the beer either." I said frowning and making a face.

It wasn't long before we came to a saloon called The Last Chance Saloon, at the edge of town. Tying up the horses along side several others, we stepped inside through the swinging doors and into the coolness of the bar. I noticed the bar was not crowded; being it was early in the day. Heck it wasn't even time for lunch yet.

Brett stepped up to the bar, easing in alongside a shabby dressed old man, ordered two beers. Taking a swallow of beer Brett turned to the old man and said. "Howdy, how you all doin' today? My name is Brett and this here lad is called Chad. What's your'n?"

"The name is Johnston." He said, looking at Brett and taking in the tied down guns strapped to his hips, but you can call me Bill. Everyone else does. So you might just as well too."

"Are you from around here Bill?"

"Well that depends on how you look at it. You see over yonder to the west, those grey mountains, I got me a little mine. It ain't much of a mine, but I get by. I come in to town maybe once a month or so, depending if I need supplies, or a drink, or something else." He paused and looked at Brett with a knowing smile. "How come that Indian has Chad for a name?"

"He's really not an Indian. I guess though you might call him a white Indian. He's a white boy that got lost sometime back. It's a long story. Right now, I'm looking for a place to set up a business. So far, I haven't found a place I like. You probable wouldn't know of any thing, seeing that your not here all that often."

Bill scratched the back of his head, squinted up one eye, and said. "As a matter of fact I just might know of a place you might like. I pass by it every time I come into town." Bill took a sip of his whisky and said, "But it's not in town. It's a small shack that sits about a mile or so out from town, it's situated right alongside the road that leads into town. It's vacant and I ain't seen no one living in it for a long time now."

Brett was drinking his beer as he talked with the miner. I looked at my beer for a long time as if it were a poisonous snake that might bite me at any moment. The longer I looked at it the thirstier I became. I bent and smelled it. It smelled like beer and it didn't bite. I looked at Brett; he was still a talking and drinking.

I picked up the beer and smelled it, then slowly took a sip. It tasted like the beer I had drank the night before, and it did have a slight bitter bite to it. I hoped it was not a fatal bite, cause I was not ready to die just yet. It didn't taste too bad. I had drunk water that tasted worse. After a few bitter sips, it started tasting better so I finished it off.

Brett was still talking, so I ordered another. Brett held up a hand to the bartender and said, "No more we have things to do."

Walking out of the saloon, we were momentarily blinded by the bright day light. As our eyes were adjusting to the bright sunshine, we untied our horses and stepped into the saddle.

"Where we going, Brett?" I asked.

"What about we take a ride out of town and take a look at that place the old miner spoke of, okay with you?"

"Its okay with me, you're the boss." I said with a shrug of my shoulders. "Whatever you say is okay by me."

As we rode along, I pointed out the plants that I knew, calling them by their Indian names, trying to impress Brett. I told Brett what uses each plant had. He was impressed.

In the far distance, you could see the hazy, grey mountains the old miner had spoke of. Up there somewhere in those mountains, the miner had his mine.

There was not a cloud in the sky. Two birds were coasting along on the rising thermals of heat, effortlessly tilting one way, then the other. I watched them for a second. Not much to look at around here I thought. I soon became bored as the horses moved along.

CHAPTER 17

I T SEEMED LIKE a long time but it took only a few minutes before we sighted the building the old man had spoke of. It didn't look like much from the distance.

Brett picked up the pace and in a short time, we stopped the horses in front of the dilapidated old building. Brett sat on his horse for a few minutes, taking in the shack, the outlying buildings, and the surrounding countryside. A huge, old cottonwood tree spread its branches wide over the site. Its green leaves rustling in the sunlight by a slight breeze.

After a moment, Brett stepped down from his horse, saying, "Let's take a look around."

I slid off my horse and following Brett stepped carefully onto the porch and tread past several large open holes in the broken wood floor. The front door was sagging, held on by one rusted hinge. It fell in a cloud of dust as Brett tried to open it. Coughing and waving the dust away, we entered the structure.

It appeared on the verge of collapsing at any second. Cobwebs and the scurrying sound of tiny feet in the walls and ceiling told of rats. It had three smaller rooms and the larger room we had made our way through.

"Not to bad," Brett said to no one. "Not to bad at all. The place has possibilities! Let's see what's out back."

In back, was a lean-to shed used for whatever? It was in disrepair too. There was a well between the house and the lean-to. The giant cottonwood grew between the lean-to and the house. Out further and down the slope a ways was a really small building with a moon like crescent cut high in the door.

About three hundred yards further out were a line of cottonwoods that snaked around as they followed the low-lying contour of the land.

Cotton-woods were tough, but they still needed water, there must be a stream or a creek running through here.

"Okay, let's head back to town, we seen enough." Brett said, "I think this place would do right nicely for the two of us. It's nice and quiet out here, no whooping and hollering, or shooting going on. Yes ... I do believe this is the right place. Close enough to town to do business and far enough away for peace and quiet. Yes sir, this will do mighty fine. When we get back to town, maybe we can find out who owns it." Brett added with a thoughtful expression on his face.

I looked at the old shack, the run down buildings and the piles of discarded garbage stacked here and there among the different rooms. Along with some broken windows and what might have been doors at one time. It was hard to tell what they had been from their condition.

I was afraid to ask. Finally getting up the courage as we walked out to where we had the horses tied. I asked. "Brett, You aren't serious about this place are you?"

Mounting the horses, Brett sat for a moment looking at the place. Contemplating and picturing it, as he had visualized what it could be, with some effort and a little work.

"Chad, use your imagination! Can't you see what this place could become with a little work?" As he said this, I could see he was thinking. "Chad think, use your brain. That big front room could be our show room for the guns we will sell."

He started speaking rapidly and with such enthusiasm and excitement in his voice. I looked and tried to see what he saw as he spoke. "One of the smaller rooms could be a safe room for the ammunition and storage of supplies for gun parts. Another room could be sleeping quarters and the fourth room could be where we do the work and modifications on the guns. Don't you see that? Surely you must?" He waited for no answer but continued on...

"We can build a corral next to the shed for the horses. Maybe expand the shed to hold hay and feed. There's water and land aplenty here. We would be self-efficient and beholden to no one. Don't you see the advantages we could have?"

He paused almost out of breath and pointed out past the outbuildings. "And the best part I saved for last. You see that large boulder sticking up out of the ground in that slight depression about a hundred yards past everything else?"

"Yeah, I see it. What about it? It's just an old boulder."

He had a smile on his face as he said, "That's where I will teach you to shoot. We can set up some sort of target, out towards those cottonwoods. It's away from the house so you won't shoot anyone accidentally and another good thing, no one in town will be able to hear the gunshots. Now do you see the possibilities that I speak of?"

"Gosh darn it Brett! ... Why didn't you say that in the first place? Yeah I'm all for it. When do we start?" I said excitedly.

⁓••◦◦❂◦◦••⁓

Back in town and riding down the main street, I noticed people staring. I leaned over toward Brett and whispered just loud enough for him to hear. "Brett people are staring at me."

"Dad gum it, I plumb forgot all about getting you new duds. Well let's fix that right now." He looked around, "You're in luck the emporium store is right over there. They sell everything." he said, reining his horse up in front of the store.

Stepping down from the saddle, he tied his horse to the hitching rail, looked up at me and said, "You coming, or are you just going to set there like a bump on a log?" He motioned for me to come on, as he went into the emporium. Quickly I jumped down, tied up and hurried into the store.

I ain't seen much in my days, but I ain't ever seen a store like this one. Stuff on shelves that ran along the walls, was stacked from the floor to the ceiling and not one empty space did I see. In the middle were shelves and racks with more stuff. There were shovels, hammers, nails, saddles, horse things, hats, spurs, boots and clothes for both men and woman. I never did see the likes of such a place. My mouth hung open and I stood there staring dumb-founded in awe.

Brett came over. "You just gonna stand there with your mouth open, gawking! Come on we ain't got all day." He said giving me a jerk.

An older man, the owner maybe, asked Brett, "What can I help you folks with today?" he glanced nervously at me.

"My young friend needs a new ... a new set of ... As you can see; he needs some different clothes so he will fit in better with the surroundings. Can you handle that?"

"Yes, Yes. Indeed, we have the best variety of garments in all of Tombstone and in fact the whole territory." he added smugly, hooking his thumbs under his suspenders and rocking back on his heels.

Brett did the picking of the clothes. A pair of blue grey denim pants, a wide shinny black cowhide belt, two shirts, one blue the other was green and red plaid. Then it was over to the other side of the store, for socks and rawhide black boots. They didn't shine but they sure were black. Brett kept stacking everything on my outstretched arms. I could hardly hold everything; my arms were so heavily loaded.

The clerk or owner whichever he might be was tallying up the bill as the pile in my arms grew larger.

"Oh, I almost forgot, we need an appropriate hat. And toss in a couple of bandannas." Brett said, pointing to a stack of colorful bandannas as we walked by on the way to the hat section.

Brett said, "Okay Chad, pick out a hat you like.

I laid the armful of clothes on a counter and looked at the hats. There were several different types. I tried on a couple, looked in the full-length mirror that stood nearby and made faces in disgust. I didn't like any of them. Then I spotted one setting high up on the top shelf, it was black. I asked if I could try that black one setting way up there.

The clerk frowning in an off hand manner said, "I suppose." He fetched a short ladder and climbed up to get the hat. Stepping down he handed the hat to me. It had a wide brim and a flat crown. I put it on. It fit better than the others. I looked in the mirror.

"I like this one," I said to Brett.

"I like that one too. It makes you look like a ... a real gun slick. ... I mean a real gunsmith." He said a little embarrassed.

The clerk finished adding up everything. As Brett paid the bill, he asked, "Can we leave our purchased goods in your hands while we take care of some business."

"Certainly sir, I can oblige you."

"Oh! One other thing, might you have a place where my young friend might change into his new clothes?"

"Yes of course, follow me." he led me to a corner enclosed with a heavy curtain strung on a heavy wire.

"You can change in here." he indicated the small corner.

Closing the curtain, I took off all my clothes and dressed in the new ones.

I gathered up my old clothes, pulled the curtain aside and stepped out.

Brett was standing there waiting. "Damn!" He said, "If you don't look good." Brett gathered up my old and the remaining new clothes. Handing them to the clerk, he said, "Keep these till we return, we have to see someone about some property that I would like to buy."

"What property might that be?" he asked. "I've been in town some years now. I might be able to help. I know most everything that's for sale here-abouts."

Brett responded, "Well its not exactly in town you see, it's about two miles north on the road out of town. Do you know the place I'm talking about?"

"Sure do. You must be talking about the old Smith place. Ain't worth much, appears it's about ready to fall down if you ask me. Ain't no one lived there, let me see," he said thinking out loud, "I reckon maybe six, seven years now."

"Who should I see about buying it?" Brett asked.

"Probably you should see the mayor or maybe the judge." the clerk replied nonchalantly.

"And just where might the mayor or the judge be found?" Brett asked questioningly.

"Well it just so happens they have offices in the same building." Before Brett could ask its location, the clerk continued, "Go down the street to the corner and then make a right turn, it's in the second building on the left."

"And if they are not there where would they be?"

The clerk pulled a pocket watch by its gold chain from his vest pocket, and flipping open the cover, looked at the time. It was ten minutes past noon. "Well if they aren't there they would most likely be having lunch at the Lucky Lady saloon." The clerk closed the watch and carefully tucked it back in its pocket with a pat. He paused. Held up a hand, and said, "I know, I know. The Lucky Lady Saloon is not hard to find beings it's directly across the street from their office."

We left the clerk holding the remaining purchased clothes, for safekeeping. On the way out and not being able to stand the temptation, I stopped to look at myself in the full-length oval shaped mirror, which stood by the door held up by its swivel supports. I turned this way and that admiring my new clothes.

"Okay, Peacock! Come on we ain't got all day." Brett said with a jerk of his head toward the door. I glanced in the mirror one last time and hurried after Brett.

Walking awkwardly in the new boots I tried to keep up. "Brett, I like these new clothes. I look like you in these clothes, don't you think? The only difference between you and me is my boots are nice and black and yours are all scuffed up." I said laughing out loud.

"Yeah, well don't you be laughing so loud or so quickly, my boots are broken in and very comfortable. While you still have to break yours in. Wait and see, then we will decide who has the last laugh."

We mounted up turned our horses down the street, headed in the direction we had been given.

I didn't know at the time, what Brett was talking about, but I figured I would find out sooner or later. It didn't take long—maybe half an hour. My feet were used to my soft moccasins not stiff cowhide boots that didn't bend much.

We rode down the street, turned right at the first corner and look for the second building on the left. Most of the buildings were built right up tight to the building next to it. It was hard to distinguish where one building ended and another started.

A sign hanging out front read, Offices of the Mayor, and the Judge of Tombstone. After tying the horses to the hitching rail, we stepped up to the door. A sign attached to the door read, having lunch, back sometime today.

Turning we left the horses where they were and crossed the dusty street on foot. I crossed wobbling in my new boots, and dodging out of the path of a hurrying cowboy on horseback.

Pushing through the swinging doors, we entered the cool interior of the Lucky Lady. We looked for someone that was dressed like a judge or a mayor, there were two over weight and stuffily dressed older men sitting at a table in back near a stairway.

"That has to be the judge and the mayor." Brett said to no one particular as he made his way toward the table.

"Please excuse the intrusion, but could one of you be the Mayor?" Brett said with a most engaging smile.

The younger, but much fatter man spoke first. "Yes, I am the Mayor, what may I do for you sir." he said, sitting back in his chair with a questioning look on his face.

"I'm interested in some property in Tombstone, that I possible might be interested in purchasing. I was told to see either the mayor or the judge." Brett said, acting as if he was not that interested and if he was turned down, it was no big deal.

"My name is Devlin, Bill Devlin, and I am the mayor of Tombstone and this is Judge Bradshaw of Tombstone." He paused as he looked us over and then said. "I didn't catch your name sir, how may I address you?"

"My name is Brett. Can either or both of you help me?"

The mayor looked at the judge and winked. "Yes I think the judge and I might be able to assist you in your needs. What do you think, Jim? Can we help this young fellow?"

The judge sat up straighter and grabbed his lapel with his free hand, thinking for a moment, of the extra money they could make off this stranger. Putting down his fork and wiping his mouth on his sleeve, said, "Young man if it can be arranged you have certainly come to the right people. What property did you have in mind?"

Brett hesitated, and then said, "Well it's not exactly in the town. It appears to be an old abandon farm about two miles out north of town with a rundown shack on it. Do you know about it?"

The judge and the mayor looked at one another and smiled knowingly. They both said, "Yes we know of it."

There was a long pause, the three of them looking at one another. I stood off to the side watching. Everyone must be thinking about dollars.

Brett finally broke the silence, saying, "I spoke with a few people. They all said no one has lived there in six, seven years. It's in such poor shape I'd say it's not worth a whole lot. If you can handle it, I would surely be obliged to you. If you can't handle it, please be kind enough to direct me to who may be of help."

"Oh! By the way, if we make a deal. I will need a written bill of sale, along with a bona fide signed deed, so gentlemen, what do you say? Can we deal or not?"

The mayor said, "Please can you excuse us for a moment, the judge and I need to talk." They bent an ear to each other and spoke in low tones to one another. After some debate, they came to an agreement.

The judge said, "Mister Brett, the mayor and I have come to an agreement. We will draw up the deed and bill of sale for ... shall we say in the amount of two hundred dollars. To do this and make it legal, we will need your full name for the paper work. Is it a deal?"

"No it's not a deal! That place, in the condition it's in, is not worth more than thirty dollars. However, tell you what ... I feel generous today. I'll give you fifty dollars for that shack, if you throw in lets say, an extra hundred acres. My offer is good only till sundown. I will need the deed and bill of sale signed by you both and in my hand before the sun sets over boot hill, if that is agreeable with you. You may make out the deed, and bill of sale in the name of Brett Tishman."

The judge and mayor gave each other a nervous look. Perspiration appeared suddenly on their foreheads as the name Tishman registered. The sweat slowly started to trickle down.

The mayor looked at Brett and then looked at the judge, who looked like he was having an apoplexy attack, then back to Brett. The mayor took a handkerchief from a pocket wiped his forehead, and said, "That's more than fair Mister Tishman, you will have your deed and bill of sell before the sun gets much lower."

The mayor said, "Jim, I seem to have lost my appetite, I think I'll head on back to the office and get started on that deed. You staying or going?" he looked at the judge waiting for an answer.

Jim stood abruptly. "That a good idea Bill, I think I'll join you." He then turned to Brett and said, "Mister Tishman you will have all the paperwork within the hour."

Brett watched the judge and mayor as they hurried across the street back to their office. He yelled after them. "I thank you both for doing your civil duties and if I can ever be of help with anything please let me know. I'll be over shortly, for those papers."

He turned to me and said, "That went quiet well don't you think?" Without waiting for an answer, he said, "Let's go pick up those clothes of yours we left at the emporium, and take them back to the hotel. Maybe we can talk the cook out of a couple sandwiches."

And we did get those sandwiches. We sat in the hotel dining room eating cold roast beef sandwiches, along with a glass of milk for me and coffee for Brett.

We finished eating and Brett called the cook from the kitchen. Her name we found out was Charlene. She must have weighed two hundred pounds, but on her, it looked good. She had a pleasant face and looked to be about forty-five.

Brett took out a bill and taking Charlene's hand pressed the bill into her palm and leaning over kissed her lightly on the cheek and said, "Charlene this is for you sweetheart, for taking such good care of my friend and me."

Blushing a bright red she giggled and stepping back, she shyly said, "Mister Brett, why thank you but you needn't do that," as she quickly stuck the money in her pocket.

Brett sure was a charmer when he chose to be, especially with the woman. Maybe it was his boyish good looks. He could charm women into doing anything he wanted, and sometimes the men as well. In addition, the men he couldn't charm, he sometimes handled another way, much to their regret.

Everyone liked Brett, including those that were afraid of him. The latter didn't really like him so much as they respected him. They respected him for the things he could do and the reputation that preceded him. Mostly … for the reputation that seem to always follow him. He seemed to lead a charmed life. I wanted to be just like him.

It was afternoon when we left Charlene standing dazed, in the dining room, all aglow with the echo of Brett's sweet words in her ear.

As we left the dining room, I ask Brett a question. "Why do you always butter every one up so much, especially the woman? You're always leaving a lot of money for small services."

He didn't answer as he thought of what he would say.

Going out on the hotel porch Brett rolled a smoke and then he said, "Let's sit a spell and rest, while those politicians have a chance to finish our paper work."

We sat on a wooden bench that butted up against the hotel wall. I was glad to sit; my feet were hurting something awful, from the new boots. Relaxing Brett smoked, watching the people coming and going. Some were riding, some walking and some just talking.

"Brett you didn't answer my question. Why do you butter every one up?"

"You never know when or where a favor might come in handy. Always treat everyone that you come into contact with ..." he paused, "and I want you to remember this! Treat them better than anyone else and they will always remember you. The reason being, someday you might need a favor or help to get out of a situation. If it comes down to them choosing. Would they help the person that treated them badly, or the person that treated them better than anyone else had? You understand what I'm telling you?"

"Yeah, I guess so. Try to make friends of everyone, because friends will help you?"

Brett blew a puff of smoke into the air, and said, "Yeah, that's sort of the idea, and I don't want you to forget it! That's your second lesson!"

CHAPTER 18

STOPPING FAITH, I paused in tracking those that had taken Jaydeen. I sat thinking about my past … way back in my past and what Brett had said. 'Make friends of everyone,' and mostly I had. Somewhere along the way, I must have also made a few enemies. Someone wanted to hurt me by taking the one thing I held closest and dearest to me.

I renewed the chase with determination. My thoughts soon wandered and strayed back to the past, trying to determine who I had wronged.

—∘∘⊱◈⊰∘∘—

So far Brett and I had purty much accomplished, all we had set out to do today, and it wasn't even three o'clock yet.

Brett stood, dropped his cigarette and stepped on it. He said, "Shall we mosey on over and pick up those papers to our property? They should be ready by now, don't you think."

I could tell Brett was feeling good by his cocky attitude.

"Brett, after we get those papers, what're we going to do then?" I asked. "Well Chad, we're going to swing by the Emporium, and I'm going to order some gun supplies for the gun shop, along with a few other things we'll be needin'."

We walked into the mayor and judge's office. I think they called it Tomb-stone Town Hall or some such name. Things were becoming civilized in this part of the country it seemed.

As we shut the door, both men jumped up and spoke, each trying to talk over the other. The mayor finally won. "Mister Tishman we … the judge and me have the deed and bill of sale all made out and ready for your inspection," he said, handing Brett a brown envelope.

Taking the papers from the envelope Brett read them. Tipped his hat and said, "Mayor, Judge, I thank you kindly. It's been a pleasure doing business with you." He put the papers into the envelope and handed it to me. Reaching into his pocket, he pulled forth some bills and counted out fifty dollars. Handing the money to the judge, said, "This will seal our deal. Thank you gentleman," he turned and walked out with me close on his heels.

A few minutes later at the Emporium, Brett spoke to the same clerk that had help us in the selection of clothes. He must be the owner I guessed, because he acted more like an owner than a lowly clerk.

This time, Brett started the conversation with a short introduction of himself and me. We found out that he was the owner, and his name was Samuel Elliot. After we all shook hands Brett said he had just purchased the old ranch house that was north of town, and that we intended to repair and make it a suitable place to open a gunsmith business.

"Sam … you don't mind if I call you Sam do you?"

"Why should I mind, that's what every one calls me."

"Well Sam, you and me, we're gonna to do a lot of business together." Sam looked pleased. "That's just fine by me Brett, what is it that you need?"

Brett smiled, "The better question to ask would be what I don't need. I'll make out a list of things I'll need, and those you can't supply, you'll have to order from back east." Brett thought about all the things and made out his list as I slowly wandered around the store looking at everything.

Sam said, "That's a mighty long list." His eyes followed his finger down the list. He smiled to himself thinking of the profit he would make. He looked up saying, "I got most of the things on your list and what I don't have I can order for you. You're sure lucky. On your list is lumber, which is hard to come by. However, you're in luck—a shipment of milled lumber arrived ten days ago. The nails, hammers, hinges, hardware, wire, food supplies, all those things I stock and have."

Brett said, "I was wondering about lumber and if any would be available. It's mighty good to hear you have a good supply of it. I don't know how much I will need, but you can be sure it will be a lot." He frowned, scratched his head and said. "I have one slight problem Sam, concerning that lumber. How am I to get it out to the property? You know anybody with a wagon I can borrow or rent?"

Sam smiled even bigger than before if that was possible and said, "Mister Brett, you're in luck. It so happens I have a wagon and a team, and with all of the supplies that you purchased, I see no reason why I can't haul them out there for you. It's not all that far out to the old Smith place."

"With an order this large, it'll take a good part of the day to load, and a couple hours to haul out," Sam said, removing his glasses and cleaning them. He cleared his throat and continued, "It's too late in the day to load now." Putting his glasses on, he looked at the large round clock that hung on the wall. "It's getting close on to supper time. Tomorrow bright and early I can load up, and I think I can have everything out there— lets say by two o'clock or thereabouts. How's that sound?"

Brett said that was fine and perhaps we could all ride out together. They shook hands over the transaction. In parting, Brett said, "Good afternoon and we'll see you sometime tomorrow, Sam"

——◦◦◦◦◦◦——

After a good nights sleep, we were up as daylight broke across the sage-brush sandy plains and peeked in through the window. We dressed, washed up and went down the rickety stairs to an early breakfast.

Charlene the waitress and cook, hurried over as soon as she laid eyes on Brett. "Oh! Mister Brett, what can I get you for breakfast?" She cooed in a soft, butter-sweet voice.

Brett leaned toward Charlene and said in his smoothest soft voice, "Charlene you're looking very pretty this fine morning. But what of the people who were here before us?" Brett nodded his head toward them saying, "Don't you want to wait on them first?"

Charlene was blushing from Brett's greeting. "Oh, them, they can just wait, they're nobody anyway. So what can I get for you all this morning?" She said looking at Brett with a dimpled smile, which held an invitation.

"I'll have steak and eggs with some fried potatoes and black coffee. What about you, Chad?" he asked.

"Brett, that surely sounds good." A little shyly, I said to Charlene, "Could I maybe have some of that there white gravy too? Please."

"Shor thing, honey, you can have whatever you want." She said, patting me on the back. She licked her lips and winked at Brett. I thought Brett was somewhat taken aback.

After Charlene had left, Brett leaned across the table and in a low voice said, "See what I mean about being nice to people? It gets you places that you sometimes couldn't get to any other way. Even if sometimes you have to do a little 'buttering up' as you put it."

After breakfast, we went to the stables and saddled up. Brett paid the bill and said we were going out of town for a while. We said our goodbyes and rode back toward the hotel. At the hotel, we packed our belongings into the saddlebags and went down those rickety stairs for the last time, I hoped.

On the way out Brett paid the hotel bill at the desk. We said our good-byes. Then Ben the hotel owner said in an offhand way, "Charlene is going to miss you. She's taken a real fancy to you."

"Well were not leaving for good, we'll be back. Tell Charlene good by for me." Brett said as he turned from the counter. We crossed the porch and mounted our horses which stood impatiently swishing tails at the biting flies.

We wheeled the horses about and headed for the Emporium, riding at a fast trot, through the uncrowded early morning streets. At the Emporium, we reined up and tied the horses. Sam was still loading the wagon, positioned close to the loading platform.

Sam saw us as we approach and yelled out, "Brett, were almost done loading, should be ready to go shortly after noon. We got an early start; every thing is going smoothly and ahead of schedule."

"That's great you can drive out and get unloaded before it gets dark." Brett was enthusiastic.

Sam and a helper threw a heavy canvas cover over the wagon and tied it down over the load that was heaped high. Sam had taken care in the loading of the wagon, keeping it balanced out, so it would ride evenly.

The slow ride out was boring. I only saw a mangy coyote, skulking off through the mesquite and a couple of rattlers, side winding across the dusty ruts of the road. Upon arriving at the old house, Sam stopped the team of horses. "Brett where do you want these supplies unloaded?"

Brett thought a moment, "How about under the roof of the lean-to? I know it don't look like much, but it will give some protection from the sun. And the tree will shade it some also, what do you think Sam?"

"That'd be my choice if it were left up to me. But it's your call, Brett."

"Okay let's unload there. You can drive your team right up close to it." We got everything unloaded in a couple of hours and still had some daylight left before dark. We covered everything with a tarp we'd bought for that purpose. Sam and Brett talked awhile. Then Sam said he had to get on back to town. He drove off whistling through his teeth at the horses and yelling, "Haw! Haw!" He slapped at the horses with the reins running through the harness. A cloud of dust left behind slowly settled to the ground as the wagon rolled out.

Soon it was quiet, except for the sound as the wind whispered through the tall grass and on across the prairie.

Brett said we better get busy and set up camp before dark. We used the end of the lean-to, closest to the house. He hung a kerosene lantern from a beam that partially held up the roof. We tethered and fed the horses, from one of the several bales of hay that had been bought. We scattered more hay on the dirt of the lean-to, up close to the wall and laid out our bedrolls on it. It was almost as good as a mattress.

Daylight was fading fast. Brett made a fire for coffee before it got completely dark. Too tired to cook we ate jerked beef, washed down with hot coffee.

Afterwards, in the dark, we talked about tomorrow and the start of something new in our life. Brett said we should stop talking and get some shuteye. I lay there looking up at all the stars, too excited to sleep. Restless with anticipation, I turned toward Brett. "Brett what are we going to do first ... tomorrow?"

He answered with sleep in his voice, "Shut up and go to sleep." There was a long pause. "Sorry Chad tomorrow will come soon enough so get some rest. We work hard from here on out."

Brett was up before sunrise. He was making so much noise, banging pots and pans, it was impossible to sleep. Rubbing my eyes and yawning, I yelled at him, "Brett it's the middle of the night. Why the heck are you making all that noise?"

He replied by making more noise and said, "Hey! Don't yell at me. It will be light soon. And by the time it is, we should be finished with breakfast." Grumbling, I dressed, pulling on my still stiff boots last. They were not broken in yet. Brett was right as usual, it took time to break in boots. We finished breakfast just as the sun rose over the distant horizon.

We started clearing the house of the clutter of broken and decayed pieces of wood that lay about in every room. We carried it out away from the side of the house and tossed it on the ground. We soon had a sizeable pile. The house had two doors. One in front that opened onto the porch, and one on the side almost to the back of the house. It faced out toward the lean-to and the little house with the crescent cut in its door.

After we cleared the debris from the house, we got to work fixing the room with the door that opened to our supply of lumber stacked in the lean-to. I carried the lumber and Brett sawed boards to fit into the empty spaces. There were a lot of spaces to fill in. We started on the floor so we wouldn't trip or fall through. We both nailed boards into the spaces. Then it was on to patching the walls. He sawed and I carried. Brett finished knocking the glass out of a broken window and said, "We'll fix the windows last after we get the rest of the house fixed."

It took us almost three hours to patch up that one room and that was only the floor and walls. We still had the ceiling, and the roof, and the outside walls to do. I thought at this slow pace it would probably take ... Let's see this was one of the smaller rooms ... the other rooms were larger ... I gave up trying to figure out how long it would take us to finish. I guessed it would take maybe two or three weeks, maybe longer.

Once, or twice a day someone would ride by. Some rode slowly past and looked curiously at what was going on. Sometimes three or four would ride by in one hell of a hurry. I guessed they couldn't wait to get to Tombstone for a drink. They stirred up a lot of dust on the dirt road, which ran across the front edge of the property.

Once, two cowpokes stopped and asked what we were doing. Brett stopped work as they rode over. He took off his hat, his long blond hair blowing in the slight breeze. Mopping the sweat from his forehead he replaced his hat and said, "We ... my partner and me" ... he jerked a thumb in my direction. "We're gonna open a gun repair shop. Gonna fix any kind of gun you might have and make them shoot better than brand new."

One of the cowpokes crossed his arms as he leaned on the saddle horn and said, "My name is Hess, and this here hombre's name is Jesse. What's yorn?" Spitting a wad of tobacco juice, he hit a wandering ant dead on. The one doing the talking and the asking looked mean and tough.

Brett answered. "They call me Brett, and my side kick, you can call Chad," he said smiling up at the man.

Hess started to pull his six-gun from the holster.

Brett had pulled his gun before Hess had barely touched his and holding it up said to a startled Hess. "I want you to look at this fine example of the kind of work I do." Hess had stopped chewing; his hand was frozen in mid-motion. Slowly very slowly, he eased the Navy Colt back into it holster. Beads of sweat appeared on Hess's forehead. Jesse sat his horse not saying or making any sudden movement, just watching as the scene played out.

Brett, holding up his gun nonchalantly cocked it. Both Hess and Jesse were getting very, nervous and a little uneasy. Still smiling Brett took a step back and began to remove the cartridges from the gun. He dropped the cartridges into his shirt pocket. Then he un-cocked and, putting the hammer back down, took the gun by the barrel, and still with that deadly smile on his face, extended the pistol to Hess butt first and said, "Just take a look at the fine workmanship on this Colt. I customized it to my needs, it has a hair trigger, and it only needs a very slight pull to fire it. What do you think, nice huh?"

Hess reached out and very carefully took the offered pistol. Holding it in both hands, Hess looked at Jesse and then he took a deep breath, which he'd been unaware of holding for so long and let out a long sigh of relief.

Brett said, "Hess, you look a little pale, are you okay? Maybe you need to get down and rest a spell?"

"Mister, I thought you were going to shoot me." Hess replied, with a slight stutter in his voice. "I ain't ever seen a gun appear that fast in a hand." Brett with a shrug of his shoulders said, "You think that was fast? That was my slow draw when I want to show somebody how good I am ... I mean when I want to show them my gun and the workmanship and detail that I put into it."

Now that Hess had calmed down, he looked the Colt over, turning it this way and that way. "Shor does feel good," he said, cocking and feeling the smooth action of the well-oiled mechanism. "That's a mighty fine gun." he exclaimed as he handed it to Brett.

Brett said, "Thank you." He reloaded the cartridges into the Colt and holstered it.

Hess asked, "When you all going to be open to do business? I got some guns that don't work too well. And some that don't work at all." He spit at a lizard and missed. I guess he was still nervous. "I was going to show you my Navy Colt ... then you had your'n out and cocked so I put mine back. I sure don't want to get shot for doing something dumb. You all know what I mean." he said, still a bit nervous.

Brett, still smiling that grim smile said, "Okay show me the Navy." he paused looking Hess straight in the eyes, "Just be sure to hold it by the barrel when you hand it to me." he added.

"What do you want me to see? Is something wrong with it?"

Hess carefully holding his pistol by the barrel handed it to Brett, saying, "The hammer catches some when I cock it. And then when I fire it, it hesitates somewhat."

Brett taking the gun by the grip looked it over and cocked and uncocked it several times. He nodded his head and said "H'm," as if he knew what the problem was. Brett bent and picking up a rock, tossed it high in the air.

I knew what he was going to do, but Hess and Jesse had no idea. The rock reached its peak and started back to earth. Brett quickly cocked the gun and fired. The rock hit the dirt in one piece and rolled to a stop. Hess said, "You ain't a very good shot mister, you missed it." He went on "See what I mean? It hesitates some, don't she?"

"Yeah, she does more than hesitate ... she plumb goes to sleep." Then Brett added, "You're gonna to get yourself killed with this here gun, or worse some innocent bystander. Hess what you need is a new Colt, and soon."

Hess answered, "Yeah I know, but I didn't think it was that bad. Can you fix it? I can pay."

"Well, I can fix it, but you can see were not really ready for business. He paused then said Chad get the black bag from the lean-to? It has my gun tools in it."

I ran over to the lean-to and got the bag. Returning, "Here, is this the one you wanted?" I asked, handing it to Brett.

"Yep, that's the one." He said, as he took a brown canvas roll out of the bag and laying it on the porch unrolled it. He kept one eye on the cowpokes as he laid out his tools. He removed the cartridges from the cylinders and quickly had the Navy Colt dismantled into several parts. Picking up a file, he filed some on the cocking mechanism and then some on the trigger. He blew metal filings from the parts, as he worked. Finally satisfied, he wiped the parts with an oily rag, and reassembled the Colt.

Aiming at a small boulder, he cocked and dry fired the gun several times. Reloading the gun with cartridges, he bent and picked up a stone, and again tossed it high up. On its way back to the ground, it was shattered by the smoking colt that Brett held. He handed the Navy Colt back to Hess barrel first. "Hess that should make your old gun last a bit longer. But you still need to replace it as soon as you can."

Hess carefully took the gun and slid it into his holster. He looked at Brett and asked, "Mind if I try it?"

"Sure go ahead," Brett said, pointing at a rusty old can, out away from us and the house. "Shoot that old can out there." Hess turned his horse to get a more comfortable shooting angle. He drew the Colt, cocked it, took aim and fired. The can didn't move but the dirt beside it erupted in a cloud of dust.

Hess turned back to Brett. "I can't believe this is the same gun" he said with a smile and looked at the Colt in amazement. "Iffen I didn't see you do whatever you did to my gun, I would not think it the same gun. It's amazing. It shoots like new." he kept going on and on about his gun.

Soon he stopped his rattling on and looking at Brett said, "What do I owe you for making my gun shoot like new?"

Brett thought for a moment then looked at the old house, then back to Hess. "Nothing," he said laughing, "Nothing at all, it's on the house you owe me nothing. Seeing we ain't really open for business yet, but soon we will be." Brett still laughing said, "Be sure and tell all your friends about us, and the fine work we do." Saying goodbye, Hess and Jesse rode off toward town. They both said they would certainly spread the word.

After they had gone, I said to Brett, "Why didn't you charge them? Don't you need the money?"

Brett's reply was, "It took me less than half an hour to fix that gun. How much is that worth Chad? There are always two ways to look at everything. One way is what I can get now or what can I get further down the road. Use your head Chad that's what its there for. So let's say, I get two or maybe three dollars now for that little amount of work. On the other hand, let's say I do it for no fee. Only for the goodwill, it will bring me. So tell me what you'd rather have, two or three dollars or the word of mouth from two cowpokes that will tell everyone they meet about us and this place we are opening?"

"You choose. Two happy cowpokes or the many people they will tell. Those people they tell will seek us out and many people will come. You choose?" he paused. "Look at it this way, fix one gun and get two dollars. Fix fifty people's guns get fifty dollars or maybe more. Throw in a new gun or rifle we sell now and then. We'll be making hundreds. Again you choose."

"Okay. I get your point. You are always right, so far. But can I ask you something?"

Brett rolled his eyes. "What is it now? Ask away if you must."

"When you handed your gun to Hess, Jesse could have shot you. If I knew how to shoot, I could have backed you up. Brett, when are you gonna teach me to shoot?"

"Chad, I will start training you as soon as the house is finished. About the other remark you made, you think Jesse could've shot me. You think I was distracted by talking with Hess and wasn't watching Jesse is that it. Don't answer. You notice I wear two guns. You have seen me draw and fire them both at the same time and at different targets. True? Did I ever miss? No! What do you say to that?"

"What do I say? I say lets get back to work on the old house. We have done wasted enough time fixing up old broken down guns." I said, smart-aleck like, as I rolled up Brett's gun tools and stuck them in the black bag and took them out to the lean-to.

By the time, I got back to the house Brett was sawing and hammering away like crazy. I must have made him mad, I guessed. We worked the rest of the day without any more interruptions.

We ate supper as the sun dropped from the cloudless sky, and set beyond the hazy blue grey mountains rising up out of the plains in the far distance.

CHAPTER 19

THERE WERE THREE of them and they had ridden in slowly. Hearing hooves and the snorting of horses, Jaydeen stepped out on the porch, and raised a hand to her forehead, shielding the bright morning sun from her eyes.

The rough looking men sat their horses uneasy. They kept looking nervous toward the barn as if expecting someone to come from it at any moment. The horsemen appeared more gunslingers than cowboys Jaydeen thought. She suddenly became somewhat apprehensive and worried. Chad was off taking care of the cattle, and wouldn't be back till sundown.

She called for Track with a whistle of her soft lips. Instantly a large grey wolf came through the open door and sat by her side. Track watched the riders. His mouth hung open, his tongue lolling across large white teeth. His large head reached higher than the women's waist. A fearsome sight for sure. The large yellow eyes never once moved from them. A low growl rumbled from his throat upon sensing Jaydeen's nervousness.

Startled upon seeing the wolf, the three riders pulled up their horses and stopped. The biggest of the three removed his hat said, "Ma'am, we didn't mean to startle you. We saw smoke rising from your chimney and thought maybe we could water our horses and maybe get a drink for ourselves?"

"I suppose its okay." She answered looking at the men uneasily. Something about the way these men acted disturbed her. "I'll get you some drinking water from the house." she said, stepping hack into the house. The wolf followed.

Out of sight of the men, Jaydeen reached for the Winchester that sat in a rack beside the door.

Ackerman following grabbed her from behind pulling her away from the rifle. Track let out a deep, loud growl and leaped for Ackerman.

Shorty was right on Ackerman's heels as Track lunged for the man who held a screaming Jaydeen. Shorty hit Track in the head with his rifle butt. Dazed, Track hit the floor and rolled. As he tried to get up and attack again, Shorty ran over and kicked him in the ribs.

Jaydeen broke lose and tried to get Shorty off of Track, but Ackerman was there. She grabbed a plate from the table and threw it hitting Ackerman in the head and slowing him for the moment.

She jumped on Shorty's back, pulling him backwards. Then Ackerman grabbed her again. His grip like iron, there would be no getting away this time.

Shorty tried to get up from where he had fallen. Track got back on his feet and leaped for the man who had kicked him. With a blood-chilling growl, Track sank his teeth deep into Shorty's leg and jerked it, trying to pull it off. Shorty let out an even louder yell as Track tore at his leg.

Slade sat his horse waiting outside and keeping watch heard the yelling coming out of the house. He jumped from his horse and rushed through the open doorway as the wolf sank his teeth deep into Shorty.

Shorty screamed! "Get this damn wolf off me, for god's sake!" Slade took his rifle and hit Track in the head. This time Track lay there, not moving. Slade helped Shorty get to his feet. Shorty hobbled over and tried to kick the wolf that he assumed was dead. He almost fell as the badly bitten leg would not support him.

"To hell with it," Shorty said, and pulled his gun to shoot the wolf. Ackerman yelled at Shorty, "No shooting, remember what the boss said." Shorty hobbled over to a chair and tied his bandanna around his leg to stop the blood flowing from the wound.

Ackerman, dragging the fighting, kicking, biting, clawing, hellcat of a woman, yelled, "Slade help Shorty to his horse, and get hers Saddled up. Then help me with this wildcat, so we can get the hell out of here, before her husband comes back. Get a move on."

Slade staggered helping Shorty out the door. The bloody leg brushed against the doorframe leaving a smear of blood. Shorty groaned. Slade pushed Shorty up onto his horse.

Slade hurried to the barn and saddled Jaydeen's horse. Trying to still Jaydeen, Ackerman said gruffly, "Be still lady we ain't gonna hurt ya if you behave." Slade took a strip of leather and while Ackerman held Jaydeen, he tied her hands. Together they lifted her onto her horse then tied the leather strip holding her hands to the saddle horn.

Ackerman led Jaydeen's horse out of the barn, he and Slade then mounted up, and the four riders turned and headed down the mountain. They rode swiftly not speaking, with an occasional glance back to see if any one followed.

A while after the four riders had gone, the beaten and almost dead wolf, dragged himself through the open door. He lay on the porch, whimpering and moaning. After a short rest, he crawled towards the barn. Resting several times, he made it into the barn. He looked for Jaydeen but didn't find her. Finally, he crawled into a far corner and collapsed. His eyes watched the door, the thought of Jaydeen keeping him alive.

⸺∘∘🟐∘∘⸺

It took Brett and me three or four weeks to finish the repairs to the house. It was a mild summer. The weather was warm with an occasion thunderstorm, but no rain. We were lucky, but when wasn't Brett lucky? By the time we finished with the house we thought we were expert house builders.

The house done, we started on the lean-to. After the house, the lean-to was easy. We put in new post, repaired the back wall, and extended the roof further out, adding several new posts to support it. Brett said, "We still have lumber left over, should we build some sides for the lean-to?"

I don't know why he asked. He always did what he wanted, with or without my permission. "Yeah Brett, sounds like a good idea, lets do it."

We had to move some of the lumber out of the way. In doing so, I came across two old wagon wheels. One had a broken spoke; the other seemed to be okay. "Brett, I found a couple of old wagon wheels, what do you want to do with them? I could roll them down the hill toward the creek and see how far they'd go. That'd be fun, don't you think?"

Brett came over and looked at the wheels. Rubbing his chin, he thought for a moment and then his face brightened. "Lets save them, I got a good idea how we can use them."

I was happy with all the work we had done. I thought now we can open the business and make money and Brett can teach me to repair and

90

shoot all the different types of guns we would be selling, but no, Brett wasn't happy yet!

He said to me, "You see our horses?"

"Yeah, I see them. What about them?"

"Do they look happy to you?"

"I don't know. How do you tell a happy horse from a sad horse?"

"Well do you see them running around and kicking up their heels and rolling in the dirt?"

"They can't do that because they're tied up."

"Chad, that's a keen observation, so we can just let them loose. Then they can play and run and roll around in the dirt?"

"No we can't do that! They would run away wouldn't they?"

"Well if we untie them so they can play and be happy, how are we going to keep them from running away?"

I finally got the drift of Brett's questions. "Okay, Okay, I get it; we have to build them a corral."

Brett stood there smiling. "Chad that's a great idea, I don't know why I didn't think of that." then he laughed.

It took another four days to build the corral.

———∞∘◦❉◦∘∞———

I thought back to the days when I was young without problems, to that time we had redone the old Smith house, turning it into a gunsmith store. So far, my life had been one unbelievable experience after another.

We'd fixed up the old house. Redid the lean-to and built a new corral from branches that had broken and fallen from the cottonwood trees that ran along the edge of the creek, along with some we had cut. The horses were happy. Brett was happy. And I ... I was almost happy; soon I'd be learning how to shoot.

Brett taught me to take apart the different guns and rifles, how to clean them and then how to put all the parts together again. I only made a few mistakes. Sometimes I had extra parts left over and I didn't know where they went. Brett was patient; he would make me take the gun apart again, and showed me where the parts went and why those pieces were important. I learned fast.

We soon had a thriving small gunsmith business going. Brett was right, word of mouth was spreading. I was doing a lot of the repairing and Brett was doing most of the customizing. We almost had more work than we could handle from the cowpokes, town folk and a few farmers.

Then there were the gunslingers. Brett always handled them. He said he didn't want me to get into any trouble, before I was ready and able to handle it.

⁂

Jaydeen kept asking, "Why are you doing this to me?" She never got an answer to her question. The men for the most part ignored her, except for Slade.

After a couple of hours of hard riding, the four slowed the horses to a fast walk. They didn't want to tire them in case they needed to make a run for it.

"We ain't gonna hurt you lady, you're just bait … for the big fish," Slade said. Riding up close, and patting her backside, he smiled.

"Slade shut your mouth. Ya hear!" Ackerman said. "You know what the boss said. And keep your damn hands to yur'self." he added with disgust.

"Okay, okay, don't get all het up, I was only fooling some," Slade said as he rode away from the woman.

Ackerman turned to Shorty, "How's that leg, you goin' to make it?"

"I don't know how fer I can go on, it pains me something awful. If I can't make it back to the ranch … maybe I can stop at that there town we passed on our way here," Shorty said, groaning through clenched teeth. "They must have a doc don't ya think?"

CHAPTER 20

ONE MORNING AFTER breakfast Brett said, "Chad, I think its time for your next lesson. Are you ready?"

"What lesson might that be? I done learned ever thing haven't I."

"What's the one thing you haven't learned yet and so desperately want?"

"Well it sure would be nice if I could learn to shoot. I want to shoot so bad I can taste it. I want to shoot as good as you Brett, you know that or did you forget?"

"No, I didn't forget. I was waiting for the right time. I think that time has arrived. I have taught you most everything I know, except for one thing."

"Chad, how old would you say are now, sixteen, seventeen or maybe even eighteen?"

I didn't have an answer to that question so I said, "Yeah one of those must be right."

Brett went on, "We don't rightly know for sure do we. You're big enough, six feet I'd say. You're strong enough; you almost beat me at arm wrestling, and you're smart enough, though not as smart as me. And you're learning some patience, but it still needs work."

"Chad, I have a present for you. Just stay seated at the table while I go fetch it." Brett said, going into the next room. He returned carrying a large wood box that looked to measure maybe twenty-four inches long and eighteen inches wide and about ten inches high. He handed the wood box to me saying, "I don't know if it's your birthday or not ... but happy birthday."

—∘∘❮❙❘❙❯∘∘—

The first night after taking Jaydeen, Ackerman and the others made camp in a low ravine. They staked out a picket line and tied the four horses to it. Removing the saddles, they placed them on the ground to sit upon.

They had no way of knowing that only nine short miles separated their camp from their pursuer Chad's camp.

Making a small sheltered fire that could not easily be seen, they made coffee and cooked a meal. Too soon, it became dark, but that's the way it was on the desert plains. The men rolled out bedrolls, placing them by their saddles to use as a backrest. Ackerman took an extra blanket he'd brought along for the woman and rolled it out by her saddle. Her hands had been untied so she could eat and then retied.

Ackerman asked Shorty how he was holding up. Shorty moaned. "It ain't good." Shorty hadn't eaten, his pain was too great, and he'd only had coffee. The men smoked their cigarettes and talked some, then turned in to get some sleep.

—∞∘◦❋◦∘∞—

The box was fairly heavy. I took it from Brett's hands and set it on the table, and asked excitedly, "What is it Brett? I ain't ever had a present before."

He handed me a hammer, "Open it and find out."

I opened the box. My jaw dropped. Stunned, I sat down and stared at the contents that lay neatly packed inside the box.

"Well say something," Brett said. "Do you like them?"

I couldn't speak. For inside the box rested two new shiny .44 caliber Colt Peacemakers, along with a box of cartridges. And wrapped in paper were two black cartridge belts with holsters. Tears fogged my eyes. I jumped up and hugged Brett before he could step back. "Brett this is the happiest day of my life." Excitedly I went on, "How in the world did you get these without me knowing? And when?"

"You remember, last month when I ordered those gun parts? Well, I ordered these at the same time. Do you like 'em or should I sell them to somebody else?" He said jokingly.

"Over my dead body," I joked back. "I love them." I said picking up one of the Colts and turning it over in my hand.

Jaydeen lay wrapped in the blanket Ackerman had laid out for her. She looked up at the stars unable to sleep and wondered what Chad was doing. She thought about Track her faithful wolf, which had tried to protect her. She hoped he was alive.

Was Chad even now tracking them? Surely he must be. She wondered what would happen when he caught up. So many unanswered questions filled her mind that sleeping was difficult. There was no question in her mind; he would catch them. She hoped it would be soon. She missed him dreadfully. She wanted desperately to be held safe in his big strong arms.

The next morning after a quick breakfast, the fire was extinguished, the horses saddled. Ackerman with Slade, helped a moaning Shorty, onto his horse, his bloody leg looked worse. The group again headed northwestward, planning on bypassing the small town they had avoided on their way to Black Mountain and Chad's ranch.

Brett helped me put on the rig and adjusted it for my arm length, so my hand would fall easily to the grips. Brett got his guns and strapping them on, we went out to where the big boulder stuck out of the ground. It was a wonderful day. I was happy as I loaded the Colts, slipping the cartridges into the cylinder one by one. Brett carried a plank of wood that he leaned against the boulder. Then he stepped off fifty paces and marked a line with his boot in the dirt and weeds.

Brett stood behind and slightly to one side. He said, "Okay, you ready? You see that knot in the plank. I want you to shoot it out."

"You want me to shoot from way back here? That's a mighty long way, and that board ain't all that wide either." I complained.

"Just shoot will you." Brett said. "Hell I can hit that board with my eyes shut."

The Colts hanging from my waist felt heavy. I was not use to the weight. It felt uncomfortable. I pulled the right hand Colt out. Cocking the hammer back, I took aim at the knot that was smackdab in the middle of the board and pulling the trigger, fired.

The gun jumped in my hand and I almost dropped it. After the smoke cleared I looked at the slab of wood to see where the shot had gone. The wood didn't look any different than before. The knot was still there.

Brett said, "For your first shot that was a good one. You missed the board but you did hit the granite boulder. Try again."

I tried again … and again. I shot for half an hour. I think I hit the board once. The hit was nowhere near the knot. I was discouraged.

"Don't feel bad, the first time I shot, was at the side of a barn, and I missed it." He laughed, "You're doing fine."

"Watch this. I am going to do this real slow, so you can see what is happening." He pulled his gun, cocked and fired in one fluid motion; follow by another cock and fired, followed by four more shots, all done so smoothly it was like … Like a dance.

I looked at the board. There were six holes dead center and spaced about an inch apart running down the center of the board. My knot was still there.

"That's how it's done." Walking toward the house he said, "Keep shooting till you run out of ammo." He walked to the house and closed the door.

A little over four hours later, I came across the riders' camp. Getting down from Faith I knelt by the cold remains of the fire. Stirring its remains, I looked for any sparks or heat. There was none. Assessing the fire, I figured I must be four or five hours behind. I thought of Jaydeen my loving wife, with her dark green eyes and her long red hair. I prayed she was okay.

I figured I might catch them before dark. I stepped into the saddle and gave a loud whistle for Track, and rode fast in the direction the four riders had taken.

An hour later, I saw a cloud of dust in the far distance. Maybe kicked up by their horses or maybe a dust devil. It was still a long way off.

After shooting for another half hour I had used up all the ammo. Walking over to the board I looked to see where … if I was lucky, I had hit it. Counting Brett's six holes and the first hole I made, there were now eleven holes in the board. That meant I had hit the board only five times.

Not too good, but the boulder had a lot of scars on it. Which meant if I were shooting at a man on a horse, I probable would hit the horse. Not good I thought.

Disgusted I went into the house, slamming the door after me. Brett looked up from a gun he was working on and said, jokingly, "Well did you kill that board?"

"Yeah, with all the shots I fired, I only hit that dang board five times; I ain't worth a hoot. I unbuckled the gun belts laying them aside, said, "Don't you think fifty paces is too far for me to start from?"

"So you think it's too far. Where do you think you should start from?" Brett asked.

"I don't know, just a little closer, maybe from half the distance." I looked questioningly at Brett.

Brett sat thinking, and then said, "I have an idea. You start ten paces from the target and for every bullet, you put through that piece of wood, you back away one pace. How does that sound … fair enough?"

"Gosh, Brett, you sure it's okay? I don't want you to be mad."

"I ain't mad Chad. Maybe you would be better off starting closer. Lets try it that way." and he continued, "I'll betcha before two weeks, you're at the fifty pace line. What do you say?"

"Okay by me. What shall we bet? Cause we have to bet something to make it a real bet, don't we?"

"Alright, how about this, if you're shooting from the fifty pace mark by the end of week two, I'll clean the stable for a week. If you're not shooting from fifty paces in two weeks, you clean the stables for a week. Fair?"

We made our agreement and shook hands on it.

Sitting on the corral fence two weeks later, I watched Brett while he worked at cleaning the stable. Having lost the bet, he was happy to do it and I was happy too.

Standing on the fifty pace mark I was now hitting the board. No longer were there weeds at that spot, they had been worn away by my boots.

Starting closer to the target had helped. I hit the target more often, which gave me more confidence. Brett showed me a lot of things, how to draw and cock the Colt with my thumb as I raised it to fire. To look with both eyes open, toward where I wanted the bullet to hit, and staying focused on that spot.

I felt good about my shooting and Brett was proud of my progress. My draw was getting faster and my accuracy was improving by leaps and bounds. I had shot the knot out some time back and had replaced it with a stone which since then had been replaced several times. I could shatter that stone from the fifty pace line time after time. It took more time to replace the stone than it did to shoot it out.

On day, I was out shooting. Brett watched, giving me pointers and encouragement. "Hold on there Chad. You remember those wagon wheels we saved. Well now's the time to put my idea to work. Give me a hand."

We dragged out one of the wheels and part of a broken axle and some lumber. We hauled it down to the boulder and Brett started building some sort of contraption. It ended up with the spokes of the wheel facing the shooting line. He gave the wheel a spin, it rotated on the broken axle, and then slowly came to a stop. What he had built looked quiet stable.

He looked at me with a grin, "How do you like it?"

"I don't know… what the hell is it?"

"It's your new target."

"What part am I supposed to shoot at?"

Going back to the house, he returned with a pack of cards. "Brett? I'm supposed to be shooting and you want to play cards?"

"Wait." He held up a hand stopping me. "Look." He nailed six cards spaced out evenly around the circular part of the wheel. "Well what do you think?"

"It looks pretty, but what is it?"

"I want you to go back to the shooting line and I want you to shoot each one of these cards dead center.

———∘∘●∘∘———

Ackerman's trail angled off away from the town. He wanted no one from town seeing them or getting close enough to start asking questions.

Ackerman was leading the way when he stopped and waited for the rest to draw up even. He looked at Shorty's face which had a pale greenish cast to it and said, "Shorty you don't look so good. You're in no shape to go on. You ought to go to that town yonder, maybe they got a doctor." The horses milled around pawing at the ground, stirring dust, while the men discussed Shorty's predicament.

Slade was a hired fast gun, the boss back at the ranch had hired, in case he might be needed. Ackerman said, "Slade you go with him and help him stay in the saddle till you find someone that can help him … and Slade, try to stay out of trouble. Slade you got that?"

"Yeah, Ackerman, I got it." he said, grumbling. "I sure won't go looking for no trouble, but I ain't a running from it either." He said, rubbing the handle of his Colts in anticipation.

Ackerman said, "I thought I saw a small cloud of dust on our back trail. Any of you boys checked our back trail this morning. It could just be the wind blowing a dust devil, or it could be someone riding hard and fast to catch us. Could be the man the boss is looking for."

"It's probably for the best we split up anyway. If it is the man, he will have to make a choice, follow the two riders going north, or the two headed for that town. I'd say that town is only three or four miles from here, so I think he'll head for town. That will give me and the woman a better chance of reaching Mr. Bernard's, Rocking BB ranch."

"Slade, if it is the man, try and protect Shorty, and don't go stirring up any trouble. You understand me. Now let's get a move on." They couldn't stop Jaydeen from hearing their conversation. It thrilled her to know it could be Chad. Her heart pounded with a surge of hope

—◦◦◦❑◦◦◦—

Brett stood to one side of the wheel. I walked off fifty paces then turned to face the wheel my gun in hand. Brett yelled, "Now be real careful that you don't shoot me. Okay? Are you ready? Now don't shoot till I tell you. Get ready?" He gave the wheel a spin and quickly stepped away. "Shoot he yelled." I was caught completely off balance I wasn't expecting him to spin the wheel. The unexpected move surprised me. Regaining my thoughts, I raised the Colt and shot six times. The wheel slowly stopped spinning coming to a stop.

I ran back to the wheel to see how I did. Brett was there before me, shaking his head. He didn't say a word. I looked at the cards. All except one had a hole in it and that one had a nick in the spoke beside it. I looked at Brett. He was grinning like crazy. "That wasn't bad shooting for being surprised, but look. You missed the three of spades completely. And only one card hit dead center."

"I'm sorry Brett, you took me by surprise. It took me a little time to refocus."

Slade and Shorty started down the trail toward town, moving at a slow pace, since Shorty could hardly stay in the saddle. Slade stopped his horse and taking a look at their back trail. He saw a cloud of dust a few miles back that appeared to be moving fast in their direction.

"Chad there'll be many times when you'll be completely surprised. You won't have time to think or refocus. You will be dead." He looked at me, and said, "I'm proud, you did well." He put six new cards on the wheel. "Now go back and try it again. I'll try not to surprise you again."

I had reloaded while we talked. Brett had taught me to always reload after firing as soon as possible. It didn't matter if it was one shot or six, always reload. It would not be good being caught with an empty gun.

I walked back to the firing line wondering if he was going to pull something else on me. I didn't trust Brett. He was always pulling some sort of shenanigan. I reached the shooting line and yelled. "Okay Brett, give that wheel a spin."

He did ... in the opposite direction of the first spin. Damn!

I was not caught as completely unaware as the first time. I was sort of expecting him to try something. It threw me off some. Still, my reaction time was pretty fast. I quickly fired six shots, feeling I'd done better this time. I walked down and stood beside Brett looking at the cards.

All six of the cards had neat little holes dead center. Smiling, he said, "Not bad for a greenhorn gunslinger." He put his arm around my shoulder. "Not bad, not bad at all. I think you're about there." Walking uphill toward the house Brett said, "I been pushing you on this shooting purty hard.

Sometimes it helps to step back and relax awhile. It will then seem more natural when you come back to it. It'll seem like you knew it all your life."

Reaching the house and stomping the dust from our boots Brett said, "Hey! I've got an idea. Why don't you go visit that young feller you had the fight with? You two seemed to hit it off after it was all said and done. He did invite you out to their ranch as I recollect. It would do you some good to get away for a while. I can manage without you for a week. Sid did say their ranch was not far."

There was no use to argue with Brett. He had decided, and that was it.

The next morning I packed my saddlebags, saddled my horse, said goodbye to Brett and headed in the direction of Sid's ranch.

Slade said, "Shorty that cloud of dust is moving fast, someone is riding hard. Appears we could be getting company real quick. You think you can ride a little faster. We sure don't want to be caught out here in the open, we'd be sittin' ducks. If we can make it to town before that rider gets here we'll be okay."

Shorty moaning with pain tried to ride faster. A mile further down the trail Slade could tell the cloud of dust was catching up. It was almost upon them when it disappeared.

Slade sat his horse watching the cloud of dust dissipate in the wind. What the hell? He thought. The rider must have come to the place where they had parted from Ackerman and the girl.

CHAPTER 21

TOPPING THE CREST of the hill, a wide beautiful expanse of green grass covered the small valley, caught between two ridges of mountains. Sid had said the ranch wasn't far out from town. He was right, if this was the right ranch. I stopped the horse and gazed in amazement at all the green before me. Only a small hill separated it from the sagebrush-covered desert. A stream of water meandered as it ran through the lush meadows dotted here and there with grazing cattle.

Off in the distance sitting on a knoll that rose above the valley, I saw smoke rising from the chimney of a low laying ranch house. After a fashion, I found the road that led to the house. I rode slowly toward the house not wanting to alarm anyone that might be about. A man could get shot if they weren't expecting you. Two horses were tied to the rail in front. As I approached the house, I gave a holler, "Anybody home?" No one answered. I gave a louder yell, "Anyone here?" I sat my horse impatiently and waited.

Shortly after, a man appeared in the door holding a rifle. I assumed it was loaded and cocked. The man looked me over and said, "Stranger if you got no business here you'd better get before this here rifle goes off accidentally." I held up my hands, palms forward showing no animosity. "Friend, I come to see Sid ... Sid Brucker. Is this the Brucker ranch?" I asked. The man wore a gun, chaps, denim shirt, and top off by a creased, greasy cowboy hat.

A gun slick for sure, dressed as a cowpoke.

"And just who is asking?" He said in a gruff voice, as he swung the barrel in my direction.

"I'm a friend of Sid's. We met in town about three, maybe four months ago. My name is Chad." I was feeling a little cocky. "Or if you like you can call me Chad'tu," I said. My Indian temper starting to heat up some. I carefully lowered my hands. I looked at the man. He had a slight advantage over me. He stood holding a rifle on me as he thought over what I'd said. I could take him I thought.

Then I thought of Brett, he always said don't get angry, be cool. Edging my horse around, I asked, "Just who are you to be asking my name, and what might your name be? Is this the Brucker Ranch or not?" I said starting to heat up even more.

He took a step toward me and started to speak. Sid stepped through the doorway and putting up a hand shaded his eyes from the bright midday sun and asked. "Who is it Trace?"

"Its some gunslinger with tied down guns, been asking about you. I ain't taking no chances till I find out for sure. Sid, you know him?" Trace asked, not taking his eyes off me.

"Hi Sid, how you been? It's me, Chad, from down Tombstone way. Remember?"

Sid stepped to the edge of the wood porch and taking a closer look at me said, "Yeah, I do remember you. You're the one that whipped the pants off me." He turned to Trace and said, "Its okay Trace, I know this fellow."

"Okay, if you're for sure you know him I can relax then." Trace said, leaning the rifle against the wall.

"Get down off that cayuse and let's talk some." Sid said, with a wave of an arm he invited me in. "What the hell you doing up this way? You lost or something?"

Stepping down from the saddle, I tied my horse and reached to shake hands. Sid reached out his hand, grasped mine tightly and jerked me forward. Caught by surprise my body met his and his arms wrapping around crushed me in a big hug. Stepping back he said, "It's really good to see you again my friend. I often wondered what had become of you." He smiled a good-natured grin and poked me in the arm.

He turned to Trace saying, "I want you to meet the only man that beat me fair and square in a fist fight. Trace this here is Chad. Chad this is our foreman Trace, he runs things for us around here."

We shook hands, his grip was strong.

Sid went on, "What brings you up this way? Let's go in the house out of this hot sun. We need to do some talkin'. I need to get caught up what's been happening with you." With his arm around my shoulder, we went up the steps and into the house.

Slade and Shorty, the two gun-slinging cowboys hired by Bernard Black-burn, sat their horses watching their back trail. One wanting only a doctor and the other wanting only blood.

Sid and I walked into the large main room, Trace followed. "Sure is a nice place you got here, curtains and everything. It looks more like a woman lives here than a man. Whose idea was that, yours or Trace's?" I said in a friendly off hand way.

"Oh that, that's my sister's idea. She thinks it looks homier to hang up curtains." Sid said with a shrug.

"Sid, I didn't know you had a sister. I thought you were an only child the way you acted on our first meeting. Spoiled and all, you know." I laughed at the look he gave me. "Is she older or younger than you? Is she as ugly as you?" I teased, punching him in the shoulder.

"Actually, she's much better looking than me, and you can see how really good looking I am." He smiled, punching me back. "Jay's my younger sister. She's a year younger than me and she's a real handful, I might add. Feisty, and as ornery a tomboy you ever did see."

"She's not here right now or I'd let you meet her. She's out riding her horse somewhere, who knows. It's a good thing you didn't bump into her in town, the way you bumped into me, because she would have kicked the heck out of you."

"She's that tough is she?" I visualized his sister must look like a big, tough bull rider. "I can hardly wait to meet this tomboy sister of yours. Sid if you got room, could you put up with me for a week long visit?"

"Chad I can't think of anything better than you staying for a week. Heck, you can stay as long as you want, Dad won't care. As a matter of fact, he took off a week ago to visit his sister, my Aunt Tillie. He shouldn't be back for quiet a spell. There is one thing though, I should tell you. We're having cattle problems. You might not want to get involved."

"What kind of trouble are you having? Maybe I can help?"

"The count on our cattle don't tally up, it keeps dropping. What we ... Dad, Trace and me, think maybe we have got some rustlers working the herd. We haven't found any dead cattle, but sometimes we find horse tracks."

"We're going out tomorrow to round up stray cattle, and search the northwest range more closely for hoof prints. Why don't you ride out with us? You're more than welcome to come along if you'd like." The more he talked about lost cattle and cattle rustlers the angrier he became. He looked at me, then down at my guns, "You any good with those? They look mighty fancy. As a matter of fact you didn't have a gun the last time we met."

"No I didn't have a gun then, and yes, I am good with them. Very, very good you might say."

Sid smiled, "Chad, think you can shoot better'n me?"

"Is that a challenge, Sid?" I asked with a lopsided grin. "There's only one way you'll find out."

He grinned. "Let's do it." he said with excitement in his voice. "There's a place out back of the barn, where I shoot sometimes. Let's go, ought to be fun." So engrossed with each other, like a couple of kids, we had forgotten all about Trace.

Until he said, "You boys don't mine if I tag along and watch? We ain't had any fun around here for sometime now. This should be interestin' to see which of you boys can shoot the best. Do you mind?"

We both spoke at the same time. "Trace you're more than welcome to watch if you want."

CHAPTER 22

"**S**HORTY HOLD ON, were going to get you fixed up real soon." Slade hoped the rider that was coming fast would take the trail after Ackerman. He could then get Shorty to the doc. He thought about that drink he wanted so badly. They rode on, casting nervous glances over their shoulder, wondering would the cloud of dust angle off to the west after Ackerman or would the rider head their direction?

Too soon, Slade saw Ackerman had been right; the dust cloud was still headed their way, but not as fast as before. Slade new they couldn't make town before the unknown rider caught up with them. If only Shorty could ride faster, they might make it. No chance of that … if only there was a place, he could conceal himself and Shorty; he might have a chance to bushwhack whoever was on their trail.

Out behind the barn Sid stopped, and looked for something to shoot at. In a gulley some rusty tin cans were scattered about, probably the cook had tossed them there. "Chad you want to shoot at a tin can?" He said looking at the pile of cans. "We've got plenty of them."

"Sure, anything you want to shoot at is okay with me."

Sid picked up a can, walked ten paces out and set the can on top of a small boulder. Coming back he marked off a line with his boot, saying, "We'll shoot from here, okay?" It was about thirty feet away

"Sure, wherever you want to shoot from is okay with me. It's your challenge." Thirty feet would be a snap. "You picked the spot, and the target, and now we'll see if I can kick your ass again." I laughed. "Would you like to wager anything?" I asked, not expecting an answer.

Sid thought for a moment, "Hey, that's a good idea. Let's make a bet. I have a beautiful appaloosa foal, about six months old that I would put up. What would you put up Chad?"

I thought me and my big mouth. My mouth was always getting me into trouble. What did I have that I could bet … nothing? "Well … if you out-shoot me, I will help you in your quest to find your lost cattle. Is it a bet or not?" and I added, "Before you answer, just remember one thing. I'm an expert tracker. I can follow most any trail others would lose."

Sid didn't hesitate. "We might be able to use a good tracker." I could tell he was cocky. He didn't think he could lose, it showed. He said, "That sounds like a fair bet. You're on. Trace can be the judge of who wins, since he's only going to watch. Okay? … Is that okay Trace?"

Trace answered first, "Since you both trust me, I guess I could judge."

"That's fine by me," I said, "You go first Sid, it's your challenge."

Slade looked around the countryside looking for an advantage. The day was starting to warm. It must be around ten o'clock. He glanced up at the pale blue sky. Two buzzards drifting and tilting, circled slowly high up, on the heated wind. Where buzzards circled there was usual something dead. It was not a good omen.

He looked at the ground below where the Buzzards circled above. Then he saw it, the advantage he was looking for.

Sid pulled his Colt peacemaker and making sure, he didn't step over the line, took aim and fired. He hit the can and it went tumbling end over end.

Before it came to a stop, I crouched, drew and fired hitting the can while it was still in motion, sending it into the air. Before it could hit the ground, still with the trigger held down, I fanned the hammer with my left hand and each time the gun fired the can danced to the tune of the bullets that struck it. As the last shot hit the can, I flipped my gun and slid it into its holster in one quick fluid motion.

I turned to Sid, who stood there open-mouthed, looking at me in amazement. "How was that?" I asked. Trace took off his hat and shaking his head looked perplexed.

Trace spoke first, "I'll be damn! If I didn't see it, I wouldn't have believed it. That was mighty pretty shootin' young fellow. I ain't seen no shootin' like that in a long time, a mighty long time. The last time I saw anything like it, was at a gunfight down El Paso way. How the hell did you learn to shoot like that boy?" Sticking his hat back on, rubbing his chin he asked dubiously. "Was that luck or skill?" He eyed me not sure which.

"You might say I had a teacher that was very good with guns. He made me practice a lot." I said, while I reloaded my Colt and putting it back into the holster.

"You want to shoot some more Sid? I'm ready if you want more."

"No … No, I think I had enough. It's clear you won the bet." he said in awe, looking at me with a newfound respect, reflected in his voice. "Maybe Trace would like to try you. What do you say Trace, you're better with a gun than I am?" he said grinning. "Want to try him?"

—⋅∘∘🞷∘∘⋅—

A short distance away, on a slight rise were a number of huge boulders, rising out of the dry, dusty, desert plains. Slade hurried Shorty along, thinking it'd be a good spot for an ambush.

They made the rocks in good time and riding around to the backside of the grey boulders. Slade pulled the Sharps rifle from its scabbard and jumped down running for a place up in the rocks where he could see the trail and the approaching rider.

—⋅∘∘🞷∘∘⋅—

Trace looked at me questioningly; he wanted to but was not sure. I shrugged my shoulders implying it was out of my hands, it rested with Trace.

"Sure why not." he said, with a long sigh of resignation. "We both have double rig gun setups. Lets see how fast on the draw you are."

He picked up two tin cans and walked about thirty paces, placing the cans in an upright position about six feet apart he walked back.

"Okay, here are the rules." He picked up a rock and handing it to Sid, said, "When I say toss, I want you to toss that rock into the air. I don't care how high you toss it but make it fairly high." He turned to me and said, "When that rock hit's the dirt we draw and shoot. You shoot the can that's to the right and I shoot the can that's to the left, okay, any questions?"

"Okay Sid, get ready … Toss." Sid flung the rock high into the air it hung for an instant then headed down. The rock hit the dirt and we both drew and fired. Both cans flew into the air.

Trace and I looked at each other and then at Sid. "Okay, Sid who was the fastest?" Trace asked.

Sid held up his hands and shrugging his shoulders said, "I couldn't tell, let's call it a tie."

From the look on Trace's face, I could tell he wasn't happy with the call of a tie. I said, "Okay, it's my turn." Walking to the pile of rusted cans I called, "Give me a hand here Sid, please." Giving six cans to Sid and taking six cans myself, I walked off forty paces with Sid following. We sat the cans upright, six to a side and spaced two feet apart.

Trace stood watching, he smiled. He knew what was coming.

Slade called to Shorty to quiet down and stop all his moaning. "It'll be over shortly," he said, "Then we can go on to town and get you a doc."

Picking a spot among the rocks, he chambered a round into the Sharps. Lying in the crevice where two boulders met, he had chosen the perfect spot.

"Trace, same rules as before, only this time you can draw either gun or both, your choice. And shoot all of the six cans." I said, a little anxiously.

The only one I had competed with was Brett. Brett was faster and always shot better than me, but I had improved a lot. I was almost as good as Brett but not quiet. I still thought I could out shoot Trace, but I wasn't sure. Trace and I got set and waited as Sid picked up another rock. "Ready?" he said, and tossed the rock up.

Brett had told me when he was in a shooting situation. Time seemed to slow for him. Sometimes I had a similar feeling. I had that feeling now as the rock seem to slow its descent toward the ground. I couldn't explain the feeling. It felt like I had all the time in the world. Finally, the rock hit the dirt.

I felt like I was moving very slowly as I drew and fired and holding the trigger down I fanned the hammer sending six shots at the six cans. I holstered my gun and watched the cans, all of the six in a row as they fell. I looked over at Trace who was shooting his last shot.

Sid stood there looking at me, a vague expression on his face, verging on fear and with his mouth agape again.

He finally recovered and said, "How the hell did you do that?" he looked at Trace who had the same sort of look on his face.

Trace said, "Damn boy! You're surely fast. I don't know if I every seen a young'un," he pause thinking … "or for that part a grown up as fast and as accurate. You drew and shot those six cans before I hardly cleared leather." He looked toward the scattered cans. "And damn if I didn't leave one still standing. Chad that makes you the winner." then Trace asked, "Chad, you ever shoot a man?"

"No Trace, I never shot a man or even at one. I have only shot at targets and different things."

"Well Chad, I have shot and killed a man, I'm sorry to say. He was stealing some cattle that didn't belong to him. And I might add it's a might harder to shoot a man than a can."

—∞⊰◉⊱∞—

Slade had plenty of time; he could relax, and enjoy this killing. Leaning back against the warm boulder, he laid his rifle aside and rolling a cigarette lit it and sucked in the smoke.

Between puffs, he looked back up the trail. It wouldn't be long now. The cloud of dust was closer. He finished the smoke and flipped it away.

—∞⊰◉⊱∞—

Walking back to the ranch house, Trace asked, "Chad if you don't mind my askin'. Who the hell taught you to shoot like that? The style reminds me of someone. But I just can't put my finger on whom."

Chad said, "I don't mind. He's a fine man, and more than fair in his dealings and I ain't near as good as he is with a gun. He can take any gun and out shoot anyone."

Traced stopped walking. "Well are you going to tell me his name or are you just going to rattle on?"

"Oh Sorry, he goes by the name of Brett … Brett Tishman."

The name seemed to register on Trace's face. Thinking hard he said, "I saw a gun fight down in El Paso once. One shooter was so fast; the gun just suddenly seemed to appear in his hand. I remember he shot the other fellows gun clean out of his hand. And then he turned and walked off and didn't look back."

"I heard someone say a name. Tishman I think it was. I wonder … could it be the same Tishman. I only saw him that one time. There's something in your manner that reminds me of him."

"I don't know where Brett's from. He's been in almost ever town he says. Sometimes he acts like he's my father. Other times, he's like a big brother to me."

Slade started to sweat. He knew it wasn't the sun. He always got the sweats when he was about to kill someone. The thrill of killing turned the sweats into a rush of adrenaline. He always got a little nervous when it came to gunfights. However, this was not a gunfight, only a killin'. A killin' old 'BB', that's what everyone on the ranch called him, but not to his face, might approve of, hell, he might even get a bonus he thought. Slade's body was sweating, his hands clammy, as he lay in the baking sun and waited. He waited for the dead man that was coming fast.

As the three talked and walked out from behind the barn. Sid saw Jaydeen's horse tied to the hitching rail. He said, "Jay's back. Come on Chad I want you to meet her. She will be excited. We hardly ever get any company living way out here."

I glanced up and saw the sorrel still damp from sweat, tied up beside the other horses. We stepped onto the porch and went on into the large front room. Sid yelled, "Hey sis! We got us some company, come see."

She entered into the room and upon seeing me, stopped abruptly. Standing in front of a window silhouetted by the sun light that angled through, stood the most beautiful young woman I had ever seen. I caught my breath, breath which the sight of her had taken from me. I could not take my eyes from her. The light streaming through the window lit her red hair, like a flaming torch, as it tumbled past her shoulders. Our eyes locked and held for a moment, and then she looked away self-consciously. I was somewhat embarrassed myself, that I had stared so blatantly.

The silence was finally broken by Sid. "Sis, I want you to meet my friend." She sashayed toward us with a walk that fell somewhere between that of a tomboy's and a woman's. "Jay, this is my friend Chad. Chad this is my sister Jay." She reached out her hand and taking mine, shook it like a man.

I was so nervous I could hardly talk. In a choked voice, I finally got out a "Pleased to meetcha ma'am."

I took notice of her large emerald green eyes. She smiled, and looking me in the eye said, "Chad, you can let go of my hand now."

I was so smitten. I hadn't realized I still held her hand. I quickly let her hand go and apologized. "Sorry, I didn't realize ..." I stammered letting the rest of the sentence trail off not knowing what to say.

She laughed with amusement at my discomfort. "Are you okay? You act kind of funny."

I knew I was in love from the moment I first saw her. She didn't know it yet, but somehow I was going to marry this woman and make her my wife. I wanted this woman more than anything I'd ever wanted in my life.

CHAPTER 23

THE RIDER WAS fast approaching. Slade reached for the Sharps rifle that leaned against the boulder. Laying flat on his stomach, he looked down at the trail from the niche between the two boulders. It was the perfect spot for an ambush. He made sure of the cartridge he'd chambered earlier into the receiver and braced his elbows firmly into the ground. This was going to be too easy.

Suddenly, the rider pulled up sharply and glanced toward the boulders. The sudden stop threw Slade aim off the rider's intended path, but only for an instant. He adjusted his aim slightly aiming for the rider's chest and squeezed off the shot.

Just as he fired, the rider's horse kicked up. The rider knocked from his saddle, by the force of the bullet, tumbled and fell from the horse into the dirt. He lay not moving. His horse had stepped from the trail and stood looking at its rider lying in the dirt. A rider that was no longer moving. The man never had a chance.

I saw the glint of the sun off the rifle barrel and pulled up Faith. I had been expecting an ambush and was on the look out for one. I started to ride on when Faith gave a little kick, a kick that saved my life.

I felt the bullet hit me. Falling from the saddle, the sound from the Sharps echoed off the rocks. I hit the dirt and lay still. I'd drawn my Colt and cocked it before I hit the ground, the momentum of the fall rolled me onto my stomach.

Only my eyes moved searching for the shooter. The shot came from somewhere up in the rocks. I watched to see if anyone would come to make sure I was dead. If they did, I had a surprise for them. They would meet hot lead from my Colt.

Slade got to his knees and watched the fallen man for a few moments, making sure he was dead. The man never moved. He lay there dead.

Slade looked up at the two buzzards still circling high up in the sky. He laughed crazily and said, "Buzzards, your dinner is waiting. Come on down and get it." He laughed again looking toward the man. Satisfied he was dead; he stood, walked to his horse, shoved his rifle in the scabbard, and stepped into the leather.

He thought about catching the man's horse, to sell or maybe to keep for himself. It was a pretty appaloosa, a breed not seen much in this part of the country. He could get top dollar for it. He thought for a moment, it'd be hard to explain how he'd come by the horse. A horse like that, people were sure to ask questions. Someone was bound to recognize it.

Slade didn't know how close he'd come to dying … If he'd gone for the horse.

Shorty was hardly able to stay in the saddle as they rode toward the town. "Hang on Shorty, were almost there. Won't be long now till we can find a doc and get you fixed up." Slade said, as he thought about the drink of whisky he was going to have.

—∘∘⊱❖⊰∘∘—

While my eyes searched the rocks, I lay there remembering. I'd been an Indian, with the name Chad'tu. The hot sun beat down on me unmercifully; the biting flies crawled over every piece of exposed skin. I lay there waiting, thinking of both pleasant and unpleasant memories.

My senses tuned to any sounds of movement. An ant crawled up the side of my face. I did not move. I felt the blood oozing as it slowly trickled down my arm soaking my sleeve with a dark stain. I needed to stop the blood flow I knew. Still I waited, showing not a sign or movement of life. I lay there only a few minutes when I thought I heard horses riding off. Still I played dead, in case they had left anyone behind. I lay there for another hour at least.

I thought of my wolf, Track. Where the hell was he? If Track had been here, I could have given the commanded to attack. The wolf would have found the shooter or shooters and then who knew what would happen. Track was probably off chasing a rabbit or some other varmint. Maybe he'd found a female and was in love. Who knew?

Track was lying under a mesquite bush chewing on a rabbit he had out-run. While he ate … his thoughts wondered. Chad was somewhere ahead. I should be with him he might need me. He continued to eat on the rabbit. He ate the last bit of meat, bone and all, along with bits of fur, and then belched.

I had trained Faith to stay close, for just such a situation as this and she was doing just that. She stood maybe five steps away and watched me. I gave a low whistle and Faith slowly walked over and gave me a playful nudge with her nose. I rolled onto my knees and slowly stood in a low crouch, my gun at the ready. Moving quickly and keeping Faith between the rocks and me, I stood using Faith as a shield. The only sound I heard was the breathing of the horse.

I took a deep breath and removed my shirt to check the wound. Luckily, the bullet had only past through the fleshy part of my arm without hitting the bone.

I tied my bandanna around my arm just below the armpit, and pulled it tight using my teeth and right hand, till the blood oozing from the wound slowed and stopped. Satisfied, I put the bloody shirt back on. If anyone looked at me, it would be hard to tell I'd been shot. I didn't want to draw attention from the folks in town. I mounted Faith and rode slowly toward town, keeping an eye on the lookout for those who had shot me.

Track, after devouring the rabbit, got to his feet and loped off in search of Chad. He ran in the general direction they had been traveling. With his nose close to the ground, he crisscrossed the prairie with a slow lope. He smelled for the scent of Faith.

It was not long until he picked up Faith's scent, and not in any big hurry, he loped along, sniffing at the ground and moving at a good pace. He came to a place where Faith had stopped. He sniffed around in circles for a moment, and then slowly wandered farther down the trail. He caught the smell of blood with his nose and lifting his head he looked around. Nothing moved. His eyes took in the surrounding countryside. He sensed that danger lay ahead. He followed the smell of blood to where Chad had fallen from his horse, rolled across the ground and soaked it with blood.

Track had come to late to the party. He circled and smelled of the blood for several minutes. He didn't know it was Chad's blood. He circled around a moment and picked up Chad's scent, mingled along with Faith's horse scent. The trail led toward town and he followed it cautiously, aware if he was seen he'd be shot.

Slade and Shorty rode slowly over a low rise and there, a short distant off, sat a small town.

The first building was a stable with a corral. A man was tossing hay from a wagon to the corralled horses. Slade called out to the man, "Hey mister is this here town got a doctor? My friend is in a bad way and a lot of pain."

"Yeah, we got a damn fine doc. What seems to ail your friend anyway?" Slade thought fast and made up a story. "Well we were out hunting when we ran across this crazy, lobo wolf that attacked my friend and damn near chewed off his leg."

The man came down off the wagon, walked over, and looked at Shorty's leg. "That's a purty ugly wound. You'd best get him to the doc fast before he bleeds to death." He went on … you see that house down t'other end of the street. The white one, that's Doc's house. He works out of his house he does. I wouldn't waste any time if 'n I was you."

Without a word of thanks, Slade led Shorty's horse toward where the man had pointed them. On their way, they rode past a saloon. My next stop, Slade thought. While Shorty is getting fixed, I'll be having myself a little libation in that there saloon.

CHAPTER 24

I WAS UPSET at myself for not paying more attention to my gut feelin'. I was angry and mad as hell at whoever had tried to kill me. Whoever it was, I was sure I would find them in town. Probably in a saloon getting drunk and celebrating my death.

Maybe it'd be better if I let the man think I was dead. I could move around town more freely if they thought I was dead. I had only one problem with that idea, Faith. Whoever shot me would recognize the horse.

Well I couldn't stand here all day thinking about it. I slipped a foot into the stirrup grabbed the saddle horn, and careful of my arm, swung the other leg over and started for town thinking about my problem.

Slade reached up and helped Shorty out of his saddle onto the ground. Shorty could hardly stand, let along walk. Slade got one of Shorty's arms over his shoulder and putting an arm around Shorty's waist, lugged him up and onto the porch, then dropped him into an old wooden chair that sat by the door.

He knocked on the wood door and stood waiting impatiently for someone to answer his knock. On the verge of passing out, Shorty slumped in the chair, moaning in pain. Slade being short on patience knocked again, this time a lot harder. He could hear movement inside. Someone was coming to the door.

The wait felt like an eternity to Slade. The door opened and an older man with grey hair looked at Slade. "Yes, yes ... you don't have to knock the door down. What can I do for you?"

Then the grey haired man hearing a moan looked down and noticed Shorty. He said quickly, "I'm the town doctor, names Brester, Jim Brester. We'd better get him inside so I can see what's ailing your friend."

"I'll tell you what's ailing my friend, Slade said angrily; he's been bit and mauled by a wolf." he said this with little feeling and an attitude. "He was bit yesterday and he's lost a lot of blood. Can you help him any Doc? If you can't help him none, maybe we should just shoot him and put him out of his misery. We'd be doing him a favor."

The doc gave Slade a sharp look of disgust, and started to say something when he noticed Slade's strapped down guns. The doc thought better of the sharp rebuke that was on the tip of his tongue.

Instead, the doc said, "Help me get him up on my operating table," he motioned toward a tall narrow wooden table." Together they lifted Shorty onto the table. Shorty was mostly out of it now; his jabbering was so incoherent he could not be understood.

Doc looked at the shredded pant leg and taking a large pair of scissors from a drawer, he cut the pant leg off above the knee. He studied the leg below the knee. It was a bloody mess. The doc took Shorty's boot off and shook his head. "This sure is a nasty wound. He might lose his leg." Using a clean cloth and water, the doctor cleaned off most of the dried blood from the wound.

"The leg looks like it might be infected." he stated looking at Slade. "I hope I can save it. If infection has already set in, that's not good. You say he was bit by a crazed wolf?" The doc asked skeptically, as he started to cleanse the gashed wound with an antiseptic solution.

"Yeah, that damn wolf came out of nowhere an attacked Shorty, my friend here. For no reason a 'tall."

"So the wolf was acting crazy, you say? Did you notice if it was slobbering and foaming at the mouth?" The doc asked, with concern in his voice. "That wolf could have had rabies. If that's the case, there won't be much we can do for your friend."

The doctor looked up at Slade, "Mister, this is going to take me some time to clean and bandage and put on some medication to stop the infection. Some of these wounds are clean to the bone. I'll need to sew those up." The doc stopped and looked up, "I don't believe I caught your name mister?"

"The name's Slade," he said, without further comment. He didn't give a hoot about Shorty. He was just another hired hand. Slade thought only about the drink that was waiting at the saloon for him.

"Well Slade, if you got business or something to tend to, I suggest you go do it. I should be through in maybe three hours or thereabouts."

"I passed a saloon on the way here." Slade said, "That's where I'll be if 'n you need me."

Slade started for the door. The doctor spoke, "You better make that four hours. I surely should be finished by then, Mister Slade."

Slade opened the door and said over his shoulder, "Sure thing Doc, four hours it is," as the door slammed shut behind him.

Slade jumped in the saddle, jerked his horse about and headed for the saloon. Finally!

CHAPTER 25

I T'D BE BETTER if I didn't use the main street, I thought. I could circle around and come into town from the other side. If they were watching for me, they wouldn't expect me to come from that direction.

A few small houses were built out back of the stores, occupied by the stores owners. I decided I would ride in that way using the houses as cover. A dog barked somewhere. Someone yelled for it to shut up.

This was the town of 'No Name' that I'd visited often for supplies and maybe a beer or two. I didn't know all its citizens by name and only a few knew who I was, which worked to my advantage.

My best bet was to get my horse out of sight somewhere, but where? The stable might he the best bet. Hide h er in with the other horses and she might blend in and go unnoticed. Now what was the stable owner's name? We had only spoken once. Was it Branson or Hanson? It was something like that, I couldn't remember for sure. I reined Faith up behind the stable. Still thinking about the owner's name, I stepped down from the saddle. As my foot touched the ground, it came to me. The man's name was Jenson. Yeah! That was it, Jenson.

My arm was starting to pain me. I gritted my teeth; I had stood worse pain than this. I spit on the ground and looked cautiously around. By the time, I got to the stable it was becoming late afternoon. I led Faith to the back door of the stable, and tied her to a nearby post stuck in the ground, close by the door. Then I went looking for Jenson. I didn't have long to look or far to go.

Jenson was inside cleaning out some stalls. He was a slender but muscular man who handled himself well. He wore a floppy old weathered hat. From his upper lip sprouted a huge handlebar mustache. As I approached, he looked up, surprised to see someone coming through the back door.

He didn't recognize me so I spoke first. "Mister Jenson? Isn't it?"

"Yes I'm Jenson, what can I do for you, young fella?" he said, somewhat startled.

"I need a stall for my horse and some feed, can you accommodate me? She's been out in the sun all day. I've been riding her hard and she needs some rest."

Jenson looked hard at me and asked, "Do I know you?"

"You probably don't remember me, my name is Chad'tu. I think we met once, when I was in town picking up supplies. I think it was down at the Emporium. I bet you remember my wife, everyone that sees or meets her, remembers her. She has flaming red hair down past her shoulders. And, I might add, a figure to go with it." I could see Jenson was thinking. I waited a bit and asked, "You remember now?"

"Yeah, now that you mention it ... I do remember her. You're a lucky man to have such a woman. You say she's your wife. How is she?"

I didn't know what to say. I couldn't say someone had taken her. "Oh, she's fine. So, mister Jenson, can you take care of my horse? She's just out back."

"Chad'tu you startled me coming in the back way like you did, and me not knowing who you were and all." He agreed to care for Faith.

While talking, he took notice of the blood dripping from my fingertips. The kerchief had loosened and I hadn't noticed I was bleeding again, till Jenson said, "Good god Chad'tu, what's happened to your arm? You're bleeding?"

"Oh, it's nothing just a little scratch I got a couple hours ago. Someone tried to bushwhack me on the trail into town."

"It appears to me the way that blood is dripping off your fingers, you should get yourself to the doc right fast," Jenson said with concern in his voice, "Before you bleed to death."

"That's where I was headed, but I wanted to take care of my horse first." I walked between the two large faded weather beaten, red barn doors and out toward the street. I turned and asked Jenson, "You, seen any strangers about in the last hour or two?"

"Not that I took notice of," he replied.

I left Jenson and started on foot to see the doc. I walked cautiously my senses alert along the boardwalk in front of the stores, being extra careful when passing the walk-through between buildings. The hold-down thongs on my holstered guns were unfastened. My Colts were ready for use if the need should arise. I passed a walk through and stepping up on the porch of a building; I heard the tinny sounds of a piano coming out its open doors. Inside those open doors was a saloon.

Standing in the shadows, I took a peek through the window trying to see if anyone looked like a shooter. Suddenly down the street came a rider, riding hell-bent for leather, he swerved in toward the hitching rail, pulling his horse up sharply; it slid with its haunches crouched down to a stop.

The rider jumped down, quickly tied his horse and stepping in a big hurry onto the porch started inside.

Stepping back from the window into the shadows, I stood watching the man. With a hand on the swinging doors, he started to go in. Suddenly he noticed me standing there. He stopped and took a step back taking another quick look in my direction. He seemed to be thinking, maybe trying to place me. Then he shook his head and entered the saloon.

The man's behavior was odd to say the least. I wondered if he might be the man that had shot me, or just a man in a hurry to get a drink. I didn't know. Stepping back to the window I took a second look. Nothing seemed unusual. The man who had almost bumped into me was downing a drink.

I arrived at the doc's house and knocking on the door, I waited. After some time, I was ready to knock again when the door suddenly opened. I lowered my closed fist and asked, "Are you the doctor?"

The grey-haired man that stood there in a white, blood-splattered apron said, "Yes, I'm the doctor and I am very busy. What do you want?"

"Well if you're not too busy, I'd like for you to take a look at my arm and maybe sew it up. I been shot, and it doesn't seem as if it wants to stop bleeding."

He held the door wide and motioned me in. He told me to take off my shirt so he could see what I was talking about. He handed me a clean towel so I wouldn't drip blood on the floor.

"Who shot you son? Are you on the run from the law, makes no difference to me one way or t'other?"

I took my shirt off, and the doc inspected my arm front and back. "Passed clean through, it did." He commented with a nod of his head. He retied my kerchief tighter. "Have a seat over there." He pointed at an old wooden chair. "Your wound can wait a bit its not life threatening. However, the other fellow I'm working on needs my attention now. He was mauled by a crazed wolf."

Seems I'd interrupted his sewing on another patient.

At the mention of a wolf, I tensed. Taking a deep breath, I asked "How did it happen?" I knew wolf bites were rare. Wolves usually steered clear of humans and would not attack unless cornered or protecting their offspring or maybe someone they loved that was being threatened.

"Doc, you mind if I watch while you finish up?"

"Well, you might be of some help at that. Especially if he comes out of that dose of chloroform, I gave him. You're big enough to hold him down should he awaken and starts to thrash around."

I took one look at the man's leg and thought I was going to vomit. It was laid open to the bare bone in several places. It surely was a bloody mess even with all the stitching the doc had already done. This surely must be the work Track had done, trying to protect Jaydeen.

"Did he say when he was bitten by a wolf?"

"This one didn't say anything that was understandable. The fellow that brought him didn't have much to say either. Said his name was Slade. It seemed to me he didn't care one way or the other, whether this fellow lived or died. Only thing he was interested in was getting to the saloon and having him a drink."

"What did this other fellow look like? He could be the one that tried to kill me."

While the doc sewed, he described the man. His description fit the man who had almost bumped into me in his hurry to get into the saloon.

CHAPTER 26

RACK FOLLOWED FAITH'S scent along the edge of houses behind the stores, and ending at the back of the barn. Warily, Track approached the barns closed doors, cautiously sniffing around the ground. He smelled Faith's scent but not that of Chad's. Track made several circles tryingingto pick up Chad's scent, to no avail.

Dusk arrived as the sun disappeared behind the wood sided buildings. Not giving up, Track move to the edge of the barn and peered down the darkening walkthrough. Not seeing anyone, he slinked forward keeping close to the edge of the building.

Night fell, the shadows became darker. Track, becoming more aggressive, moved along the dark street. He picked up Chad's scent where he'd crossed and stepped onto the boardwalk. Track, slipping in and out of darkness, cast from the buildings followed the scent. With his grey-colored fur, he had not been seen or he would have been shot.

The only light on the street came through the open doors and windows of the saloon, casting shadows across the dirt street. With the dark of night, the saloon became busier. The boots of many, coming and going had wiped out Chad's scent. Track skirted around the saloon looking for him, he might be inside.

The light streamed from an open door along with voices, in back of the saloon. Track heard a voice he'd heard before. Stopping, he gave a low growl, his hackles bristled. It was the voice of one of the men that had been at the ranch. A porch and four steps led up to the open door. Still searching for Chad's scent, he cautious approached the steps. Keeping tight against the building and hidden by its shadow, he crawled under the steps, squeezing through an opening that was barely large enough. Out of sight, he waited for the man to come out.

—◦◦▰◦◦—

The doc finished up with his stitching of Shorty's leg.

Washing and drying his hands, he reached for a bottle of antiseptic liquid, which he poured over his hands. He turned and said, "You want some of that chloroform to put you to sleep while I sew you up?"

"No Doc, I want to keep my senses about me. After you sew me up there's something I've got to do and I need to be alert to do it. Just give me a swig of laudanum."

Shorty was stirring and starting to wake as the doc finished with me. Doc took the last stitch, to my great relief, finally closing my wound completely.

After tucking in my shirt, I paid the doc, and thanked him for his service. I had but one thought on my mind. Belting my guns around my waist, I grabbed my hat and headed out the door, on my way to the saloon and the man that had been in such a god-awful hurry.

The Doc told me to take it easy and not do any heavy lifting for a while, as I closed the door behind me. I stopped long enough to check my guns making sure they were loaded. Hurrying along it was not long before I heard the tinny piano music coming from the saloon.

Stepping up onto the porch, I carefully moved to a window and had a look inside. Damn, just my luck, it was crowded with a lot of drinking going on. Looking at each of the man carefully one by one, I looked down the bar. I didn't see the man from where I stood. Being a careful man, I studied the situation, not wanting to step into the lit bar till I was sure where my man stood.

It was then I noticed an open door towards the back of the room. Slowly I eased away from the window and made my way down the dark space between the saloon and the next building. I could see light streaming through the doorway as I crept closer.

Stopping when I reached the steps, I started to look through the doorway. Suddenly I heard the scratching sound of claws on dirt. Jumping back in surprise, I looked down to see Track emerge from beneath the steps.

125

I was completely taken aback. Reaching down I gave him an affectionate pat and whispering said, "What are you doing under there?" He didn't answer but wagged his tail happy to see me.

Maybe one of the men who took Jaydeen was in there. I took a look inside. I spotted my man almost instantly. Knowing the man's name helped some. I worked out a plan in my head. I'd leave Track guarding the back door while I went in the front way. There would be no escaping. I didn't want to kill this man till I found out where they'd taken Jay.

I knelt down and taking Track's head between my hands, I told him to stay by the door and stop anyone that tried to leave. I stood and keeping an eye on Track, I moved back toward the front of the saloon. Track stood there watching me as I disappeared in the darkness. What more could a man ask of a loyal wolf.

At the swinging double doors, I reached down and checked making sure the leather thongs were off the hammers of my guns. I walked through those doors and stood while my eyes adjusted to the light.

No one had even looked up.

I was as ready, as I would ever be. Over the sounds made by the crowd, I called out the name Slade, in a loud voice. Instantly, all the noise and conversations stopped. All eyes turned in my direction.

Slade stepped back from the bar and took a really hard look at me. His expression changed when he recognized me. The man he thought he'd killed.

I said, "Take a good look at the man you shot and left for dead."

His hand started down for his gun. He could see that my guns were holstered.

"I wouldn't draw that gun unless you're ready to die." I said with cold tight lips. What happened next I could hardly believe?

Track had snuck in quietly and unnoticed by anyone, now stood not four feet from Slade. In the silence that hung in the bar, a sound caught everyone's attention, including Slade's. As Slade's hand started down for his gun, Track, with his teeth bared, let out a bone chilling deep-throated growl. Slade looked around at the sound. He turned pale at the sight of Track baring razor sharp teeth that dripped with spittle.

Every man standing at the bar diverted their eyes from me, to stare in disbelief at the huge grey wolf, which now stood in their midst growling viciously.

I spoke loudly so everyone could hear. "I don't want any of you fine citizens to move or be afraid. The crazed wild looking wolf you see before you belongs to me. He would not harm any of you, unless you meant to do me or my family harm. As for you Slade, I can't make that promise. If I was you Slade, I would be especially afraid. I had put great emphasis on the word 'family' for Slade's benefit. You make one move and I'm sure that wolf has a grudge against you and would probably rip that hand clean off your arm with one bite."

No one moved especially Slade.

I walked up to Slade. Taking his gun from its holster I said, "You're coming with me Slade." Then I said, "Anyone object to us leaving now?"

No one objected.

———•••◦●◦•••———

I awoke the next morning in a small room of the only hotel in town. After a good night's sleep, I washed up, dressed and unlocking the door to a small closet, I let my prisoner out.

Slade looked no better this morning than he had when I locked him in last night. Due I'm sure to the cramp space of the small closet. Hell, I was lucky the room had a closet I could lock. Most rooms were just that, four walls and a bed.

I hadn't decided yet what I was going to do with Slade. I could not just shoot him, now that I'd taken him without firing a shot. I could make him suffer some. First, I needed to find out if Jay had been harmed and where they had taken her.

There was an alcove off the downstairs hallway, which held an old wooden table along with some ladder-back chairs. The owner would sometimes accommodate with a cooked meal, if the need be, which he served upon it. The fare was not the greatest but it would suffice. The coffee was weak but hot. The biscuits with white gravy were filling but had no taste. Over breakfast, I found answers to some of the questions I had. To lure me into following them, Jaydeen had been taken. Slade said the last he'd seen of her, she had not been mistreated or harmed. He told me there were three of them that had been involved in the taking. They'd been following orders given them by their boss 'B-B', Bernard Blackburn. Slade was not sure why the boss had wanted me to follow them.

Blackburn was a big cattle and horse rancher that ruled his spread with an iron fist. A valley of several thousand acres situated at the base of the Whitlock Mountains, which held many head of cattle and horses. Some were his and others rustled. He said old "B-B' was not particular on how he acquired his stock.

Leading Slade's horse, we walked down to the stable. I kept an eye out for Track. He was probable around somewhere close at hand, hiding. I paid Jenson for Faith and saddling her stepped into the leather, keeping an eye on Slade as he mounted up.

Leaving town we headed north toward the Whitlock Mountains. Slade said it would take maybe four days riding to reach the ranch. Slade kept asking what I was going to do with him. I thought I should shoot him and leave his worthless hide for the buzzards to pick over.

We rode out across the windblown desert plains. I kept thinking about Slade, and what I should do with him. I got an idea when the sun was high overhead and beating down mercilessly. I stopped and said, "Slade give me your gun belt."

He unbuckled and handed me the belt. "What'd ya want that for?" Still thinking I didn't speak right away, "Slade, I've decided to let you go." A smile crept across his face. He liked that idea.

"There's one slight catch to your freedom. I'm going to let you go, and I want you to ride west. I want you to ride west and don't ever come back. Cause, if ever I see your sneaking, ornery face again, you're gonna be a dead man. You understand?"

"You gonna send me out in the desert with no gun or food. The Indians will kill me."

"Well you got your canteen of water and maybe you might run across someone that will help you out. Who knows? Now get ... before I change my mine and shoot you."

I sat my horse and watched Slade ride off in a cloud of dust, headed in a westerly direction. Then I turned my attention north to finding those Whit-lock Mountains. At least, I now knew that an old cattle rustling rancher was behind her abduction. What I still didn't have was the reason why he had taken her. It wouldn't be long before I had my answer to that question.

CHAPTER 27

WALKING BACK TO the house Trace and I talked while Sid not having said a word broke his silence saying "Chad ... Trace and me was going to head up to the northwest pasture tomorrow, check on the cattle, scout along the foothills and look for signs of rustlers. You're welcome to come along. The way you shoot, we'd sure like you to ride with us. You'd be a great help if we run across rustling going on. Isn't that right Trace?"

Trace said, "Yeah, we'd surely like you to come along. You can show us just how well you can track. That is if we run across hoof prints that don't belong to us."

"Sure, I'd like to come along, if only to keep an eye on you two. I might even learn a thing or two about cattle." I said, in an off hand way.

Sid said, "Okay, it's settled then. Tomorrow before the sun comes up we'll be riding out the front gate."

At supper that evening, Sid said. "Sis, tomorrow the three of us are heading out northwest to have a look around. We shouldn't be more than two or three days at the most, unless we run into trouble. We'd appreciate it, if you could put together a sack of grub that would last that long?"

"Sure little brother, I would be more than happy to fix up a trail bag of something." She glanced at me smiling, showing a flash of white teeth.

Before dawn the next morning we rolled out of bed, dressed, washed up and was sitting down to steak and eggs, along with fried potatoes and coffee that our beautiful cook, Jaydeen had made. With the kerosene lamp casting a dull light over the table, we finished breakfast while it was still dark outside. With full stomachs, we headed out to the barn and saddled the horses.

It was still dark but far out across the horizon the sky was getting some color, mostly streaks of reds and some blue.

By the time it was light enough to see, we'd covered two or three miles. We talked as we rode in a northward direction. I told Sid about my life and he told me about his. I thought to myself that my life had been more exciting. I had done a lot of things and he only knew about cows.

High noon came and we stopped in the shade of a string of Cottonwood trees that grew along side a small stream. We sat on the bank resting and having a chaw of jerked beef, while the horses drank.

This part of the country was beautiful. It had everything a rancher wanted, green grass up to the belly of the cattle, an abundance of tall trees, and plenty of clear fresh water running through it.

Someday after I married Jaydeen, we would get a place like this. I sat daydreaming of how to tell her she was going to be my wife. I would think of something.

That evening we made camp at the base of the foothills in a gully that had been carved by rushing water that came down off the hills. We stacked rocks in a circle, gathered up firewood and made a small fire in its center. We cooked coffee and roasted some salt pork for dinner. After we ate, we scoured the tin plates with sandy soil to clean them. Then we wiped them with a cloth Jay had put in along with the food.

Trace rolled a smoke and taking a small branch from the fire lit it. The three of us sat around the fire and talked awhile. Then wanting to get an early start, we banked the fire, rolled out our bedrolls, and crawled in.

I lay on my back with my hands behind my head looking at the stars, my thoughts making pictures in my head, of Jaydeen with her long red hair and dark green eyes. Somewhere off in the trees an owl hooted.

Up again before daybreak, we stirred up the fire, put more wood on, made and finished breakfast, and were in the saddle ready to ride before first light.

We rode awhile before coming to a deep ravine that held hoof prints of cattle heading up it. After riding for a couple hours up the ravine, we came across cattle droppings. I stopped my horse, and as I slid off, Sid asked, "What are you doing Chad?"

I knelt down and felt the cow patty with my fingertips. "I told you I could trail anything." I replied.

Sid asked, "Just what does feeling of a cow patty got to do with tracking?"

"If it's hot or warm or cold it will tell us about how long ago they passed this way." I said.

"So what is it?"

I stood saying, "It's cold to my touch but still soft. Which means it isn't a day old."

Leading my horse, I walked slowly on looking closely at the ground. "Hey! I got me some hoof prints here. Made by at least two, maybe three different horses and their hooves are shod."

Sid and Trace stepped down off their horses and walking closer squatted down and looked to where I pointed out the tracks. The three of us stood up and looked at each other. Trace was the first to speak. "Boys, it looks like we got some rustling going on here. If that's the case we'd better be mighty careful from here on."

He went on, "If they see us, for sure they will shoot to kill, and failing that they'll try to make a run for it. I've been through this all before down in Texas." He paused, "You know down Texas way the punishment for rustling is hanging. And these boys were going after, know what they'll get if their caught."

"Chad can you track 'em?" They both wanted to know.

"Sure it should be easy, all we got to do is follow the cattle trail. We'd better check our guns and rifles, make sure their loaded, and ready. Keep a sharp lookout; we don't want them to know we're around and after them. We mounted and being more careful rode in the direction the cattle had taken. The ravine curled around the hills like a snake going across a prairie. As we followed the trail, the dirt wash that lay between the hills, became rockier.

Every so often, we would come across a cow patty. I would jump down and feel of it. Soon some were still a little warm. I knew we must still be a couple hours from catching up to them.

It was getting on toward evening and we still had not heard or caught sight of the cattle or the men who were driving them. It was going to get dark fairly fast being down in the deep ravine. For sure, we didn't want to come up on them in the dark, not knowing how many they were.

The three of us decided it would be best if we settled in for the night. A rocky outcrop of rock jutting out of the hillside looked like a good place to make camp. We gathered dry dead branches from hillside brush that would burn clean with no smoke. I made a small Indian fire, the way Shatika had taught me, it emitted no smoke. My Indian ways and knowledge were becoming useful. I was in charge.

We sat discussing strategy. Eventually we arrived at the conclusion we'd just have to wait and play it out as it happened. Suddenly I snapped my fingers and said, "I know."

"What is it you know?" They wanted to know also.

"You remember, I told you my story of being raised by an Indian."

"So?" Sid said questioningly.

"Don't you see, I was raised by an Indian," they still didn't get it. "After dark I can shuck my clothes down to my long underwear and sneak up on their camp. Check on how many they are and get a feel for their layout. Then I can return and we can discuss the best way to handle them. It shouldn't take me more than a couple hours." I asked Sid and Trace what they thought.

"You can do that without them knowing you were ever there?" Sid asked, frowning.

"You think I was an Indian for years without learning about the Indian ways of getting in and out of places without being seen. Come on, you think I'd do this if I didn't think I could pull it off?" I went on, "Can't wear boots they'd make to much noise if they scraped against a rock."

Damn I thought. If I'd known, I was going to be doing Indian work I'd have brought my moccasins. "I'll wear my socks their pretty thick. They should hold up for a short scouting trip. I won't take my guns they'd only slow me up. I have to move rapidly."

What happens if they catch you? If you don't take your guns, how will you protect yourself? They both wanted to know.

I reached up and scratching the back of my head, drew and threw the knife, which hung between my shoulder blades in a special sheath. So quick the motion, it was a blur. It stuck into the ground an inch from Sid's boot.

Sid Jumped up in shock. "Damn where'd that come from?"

Trace jumped to his feet, "What the hell? Chad you're scratching your head and suddenly a knife appears by Sid's boot."

"It is my Indian father's knife and embedded in the knife is the spirit and courage of Shatika. I carry it in a sheath strapped between my shoulder blades. It's easy to reach and throw as you can see. Just before he died, he told me it has a curse … anyone who tried to harm either of us, would die by the knife. I believed him and I have not told anyone of this, not even Brett. It was my secret."

Taking off my boots for my journey to the rustler's campsite, I said, "And another thing," I pulled another knife from a sheath inside of my boot. "I have my own knife." The blade flashed in the firelight, as it spun through the air on its way toward Traces boot. It stuck close to his boot.

Trace jump back. "Damn it Chad, don't do that. You scare me more with those knives then you do with your shootin', and that scares me plenty."

"Okay. Now that you know I can handle myself, I think I'll go scouting." I said.

Stripping down to my socks and long underwear and retrieving Shatikas knife I slipped it into the sheath between my shoulder blades. I picked up the other knife and stuck it into its sheath in my boot. I said to Sid and Trace, "Take care of my things. I'll be back in a couple of hours. Want me to bring you a scalp?"

Laughing I disappeared into the night without waiting for an answer. One moment I was there and the next, I had vanished into the night like a ghost.

CHAPTER 28

I SILENTLY RAN along the bottom of the ravine, stepping lightly on stones, some large and some small. Oh, it felt good to be an Indian again. I ran like the wind without making a sound. Stopping once I listened for sounds, none reached my ears. I ran on and stopping again to catch mybreath, I smelled smoke.

Their campfire reflected off the hillside around the bend. In the dark shadows, moving cautiously forward, I went to high ground on the opposite hill. I had been taught the high ground held the advantage in warfare and this was surely warfare.

Shatika I remembered, had always said, 'The ground squirrel sees very little, but the eagle that flies high in the sky sees everything.' I wanted to be above and look down at their camp. I wanted to be the eagle.

Working my way closer I spotted an outcrop of rock jutting from the hillside. This was across and somewhat above their large flickering fire. Making my way to the outcropping and lying flat on the cold hard stone, I inched forward stopping at its edge for a closer view. I lay within a hundred yards of their fire across the gulley. I watched and listened. It was pure luck tonight that no moon was shining its bright light down. I figured it must be close to midnight.

They had left one man to watch that the herd didn't wander too far. He sat back away from the fire in the dark, his back against a tree. Hidden except for the glow of his cigarette.

With the running and the coolness of the night, dressed as I was, I started to get cold. My eyes shifted to the bedrolls that lay close to the fire. I counted the bedrolls. There were four. I could not tell if they all had a sleeping rustler in them or not. Had the man on watch not laid out a bedroll? If he had not unrolled his bed, the count would be five.

Saddles I thought. They all rode a horse. Count the saddles. There were four.

Easing back from the edge of the outcrop in a low crouch, I slowly made my way back in the direction from which I had come. When I was far enough away, I stood thinking for a moment, before heading back and reporting what I'd seen. At the bottom of the ravine, I stopped and looked back making sure I had not been seen. I stood frozen to the spot for a couple of minutes, watching for any sign of pursuit. There was none.

Turning I ran toward our camp like a wild Indian. Taking long, leaping strides through the cold night air. Knowing the location of their camp and distance, I had traveled. It took me a little over half the time to get back. I didn't have to be careful of alerting those rustling cowpokes.

Slowing from running to a walk, I cautiously approached our camp knowing both Sid and Trace were light sleepers. I didn't want to be accidently shot by my friends. I called out softly, "It's me … Chad, I'm coming in, don't shoot." They hadn't heard a sound

"Well?" They both wanted to know, what I'd found out.

"Give me a minute, let me catch my breath." I said. Picking up my canteen, I took a long swig of water. "Okay, what do you want to know?"

"Come on Chad, this is no time to be fooling around." Sid said. "You … Trace cut Sid off, saying. "You made good time up and back. They must be pretty close. You weren't gone all that long. How many are they?"

"It took me a couple of hours of running till I came to their camp. They had built a large fire. All but one was asleep, he was their lookout but he wasn't very alert. They don't seem to have a care in the world from all the snoring I heard."

Sid broke in, "Damn it, will you cut out all the jawing and get to it."

"That's what I'm trying to do if you'll let me."

"Okay, we won't say another word, now let's have it." Trace interjected with finality in his voice.

"I counted four saddles, so there's four of 'em. And they don't know they're being trailed."

Trace asked, "Have you got a plan? What do you think we ought to do?"

"I think we should go to bed and get some rest, cause I got a feeling, tomorrow is going to be a very busy day. We need to be rested and ready to hit 'em early, while they're having breakfast. They won't be expecting anything so early in the day." They agreed and soon all was quiet except for a snore now and then.

We got two hours more of sleep. Awakening I stoked the fire for coffee and a quick breakfast. After getting the cobwebs out of our thinking, we checked our guns and rifles one last time, saddled the horses and headed apprehensively up the ravine toward the rustler's camp. Not knowing what would happen when we tangled with the rustlers or for that matter, what the outcome of it would be. One thing I knew for certain they would not be taking any of Bucker's cattle any further.

Plans often go astray, as did ours. We arrived a few minutes too late to catch them as they slept. The rustlers had just finishing saddling their horses. We did surprise them though, just not the way we wanted.

They were not quiet ready to go, but they were close enough. They quickly mounted their horses and sat wondering if they should run or stand their ground. One pulled his rifle from its boot. The four riders faced us. One with his rifle butt resting on a leg the barrel pointing up, ready. The others sat their horses and kept their hands close to their guns.

The three of us slowly walked our horses forward, watching for any sudden movement on their part, as we approached. We were about fifty yards away, when one of the four called out. "That's close enough. What you boys want?" he asked. He was younger than his three cohorts' maybe sixteen or seventeen at the most, but I was no judge of age, being young myself. He spoke like he was the one in charge.

Sid his lips stretched tight replied. "We came to get our cattle. They seem to have strayed a bit far from where they're supposed to be." Sid was scared, his voice quavered. The rustlers wouldn't know he was scared, not ever having heard his voice.

"What makes you think these cattle are your'n?" the young cowpoke replied with a cocky attitude, as he slowly inched his hand closer to his gun.

I saw the movement and quickly said, "Mister I wouldn't get my hand any closer to that gun if I was you." His hand froze and stopped moving toward his gun. We had spread out as we rode closer blocking anyone that wanted to go the way we had come. Trace stopped his horse. Sid on his left stopped his, and I stopped on the far right

I spoke directing my words to the cocky one that seem to be in charge. He looked like he fancied himself to be a gun-slick. Two pearl handled

Colts jutted out from silver studded holsters, black striped pants tucked into his boot tops, a red cowboy shirt and a matching black hat on his head.

Yeah, he thinks he's something all right. A real want-to-be gunslinger. "My name is Chad and who might you be?" I asked, leaning forward in the saddle. "And are you saying these cattle are yours?"

"Yeah, that's what I'm saying. These here cattle belong to me." The young gunslinger answered," and the name is Brice …Brice Blackburn." And if you want these cattle you're gonna have to take them from us." His three companions nervously sat their horses waiting to see how this all played out. His men were getting restless. I could tell they didn't want a shootout. They only wanted to get the hell out of here, with their hide in one piece.

Being the fastest gun among the three of us, it looked like I had been elected to be the spokesman for our group, whether I wanted to be or not. I said, "Sid you take the man straight in front of you. If he moves shoot him. Trace, you take care of the man in front of you. And if Sid needs help you're his man." I finished giving my orders saying, "And I'll take on Mr. Brice Blackburn, the cocky young kid that wants to be a gunfighter, and that other fellow back there holding onto his rifle. They're mine, okay?"

I didn't wait for an answer. "Now then Brice, this is the way I see it. You have two choices. First choice, you and your men can turn your horses and leave peaceably. Second choice, we kill you and leave you to the wolves and coyotes along with a few buzzards … Or if you prefer, we can settle this by roping a cow and checking the brand on its rump. Which will it be Brice?"

Brice turned and looked at his men. He could tell they were extremely nervous. He said to Chad, "Okay, we don't want no trouble. We'll just ride out of here now." He turned his horse and said to his men, "Let's go boys."

They started to ride slowly away through the bunched up cattle they had rustled. Brice yelled, "This ain't the end of this, you'll hear from me again."

I yelled after him as he rode off, "Yeah, when you grow up, do come back and see us. We'll have a party and celebrate."

In a flash of fury, the kid drew his iron, turned his horse and starting firing at us. He was so angry the only way he would hit us at that distance would be pure luck. Not wanting to take that chance I pull my Winchester aimed and fired. Suddenly everyone was shooting and yelling. The horses were all jumping around, and it was hard to get a decent shot, over the backs of the moving cattle.

I glanced at Sid, and Trace, they were okay and firing back. Bullets were flying in every direction. We galloped towards the rustlers with all guns blazing. Two of the rustlers fell from their horses and went down. Whether dead or only wounded, I didn't know.

Bryce and another rider were making their way through the milling cattle trying to get away. I started after them. It was a wonder the cattle hadn't stampeded with all the shooting and yelling going on.

By the time I was clear of the herd, Brice and the other rider were pretty far out and riding hard. I hurriedly jumped to the ground knelt on one knee, raised my rifle and taking careful aim, held my breath and squeezed off a shot.

With the sound of the shot still ringing in my ears I saw Brice lurch forward in his saddle. He did not fall, but his body was hanging at an awkward angle over the saddle horn, still he rode on. I figured I had hit him. Quickly, I jacked another cartridge into the chamber, aimed and fired at the other rider. I watch to see if the shot had found its target. The rider kept going, I guess I had missed.

Riding back through the cattle I looked anxiously for Sid and Trace. After getting clear of the cattle, I saw that they were okay and bent over one of the rustlers. I rode over. "You all okay?" I asked getting off my horse.

Trace said. "Yeah we're okay, but these two didn't fare so well." He pointed, "That one over there is dead and this here one is wounded. He got shot in the arm. And if he don't stop whining like a baby, I might just shoot him in the other arm." He said loud enough for the whiner to hear. After that there was no more whining.

"We should bury the dead one, but we don't have anything to dig with." Trace said to no one in particular.

"Well," Sid pushed his hat back, scratched his head and said, "We could take them into town and let the sheriff decide what to do with them."

I said, "That's a damn good idea Sid. Don't you agree Trace?" I added, "At least it will keep us out of trouble with the sheriff if there are any complaints."

"The sheriff will want a sworn deposition." Trace said.

Between the three of us, we decided it would be best to take the dead one and the shot one on into Tombstone and let the sheriff deal with it. There was just one problem. From our location, it would take at least three days to reach Tombstone. By then the dead one would probably start stinking before we could get him to the sheriff. We were discussing this when Sid mentioned a short cut to town. He said we wouldn't have to go back to the ranch, we could angle off and bypass the ranch and cut off several hours.

I said, "Well, no sense us all going. You all got to get these cattle back where they belong. I'll take the wounded one and the dead one in to the sheriff in Tombstone. I'll come back another time to finish my holiday."

We rolled the dead cowpoke in his bedroll and tied it tight around his body. Trace rounded up the rustler's horses which had not wandered far. We lifted the dead cowboy onto the horse, belly down and tied him securely. We used a kerchief to bind up the wound in the other hombre's arm, and then tied his hands so he had limited use of them.

The three of us herded the cattle ahead and out of the ravine. I let Sid and Trace do most of the herding. I led two horses behind me, on one sat a man with his hands tied to the saddle horn. On the other face down and tied hands and feet beneath the horse's belly rode the dead rustler. Moving along behind the herd, we made our way out of the canyon onto the valley floor.

The cattle knew where they were headed and needed little effort to keep them moving in the right direction. Sid along with Trace pulled back from the herd, turned their horses, and waited for me to come up. Sid pointed down the valley and said, "Chad you see that notch the hills make down about a half mile where they don't quiet come together?"

I looked in the direction Sid was pointing. "You mean where that one hill sort 'a sets back behind the other and appears to make a notch?" I replied. "Yeah, I see where the hills dip down low, is that where you mean?"

"There's a trail between those two hills that leads down to the plains and across it and on into town. If you take that trail instead of going back the way you come out from town, it'll cut your time to town almost in half. It's a short cut."

"I wouldn't waste any time if I was you. That body's going to start smelling bad in a couple days with the hot sun and all." Trace threw in.

I said goodbye to Sid and Trace and started to head for that short cut. My horse had taken only a few steps when I pulled him up. Stopping I turned my head and said, "Tell Jaydeen I'm sorry I didn't get to know her better. Tell her I'll be back and see her another time. On the other hand, if she gets down to town maybe she could stop by our place, the gun-shop. I surely would like to see her again."

If what they had said was true, I should make Tombstone two or maybe three days. I hoped it would be two days. I rode hard pushing us to the limit.

I found out the name of the one that was still alive. He said his name was Ben, Ben Crackett and he had no idea what the hell was going on. He said he had been hired by the BB cattle company to herd cattle. He didn't know anything about no rustling. They had said they were only rounding up strays. How far had these so-called stray cattle strayed from the BB ranch? I asked.

"I can't tell distance too well, but maybe thirty miles, give or take." He answered.

"Don't you consider that quiet a distance for wandering cattle to stray when there is plenty of grass and water where they were?"

"Yeah, I did wonder some about that. But I don't ask questions, I just follow orders."

"Even if it gets you killed, like it did your partner here, that's belly down on his horse and dead." I said.

"Hey mister, I don't know what's going on, I was just rounding up cattle."

"Sure," I said. We pushed on toward Tombstone and rode till it was to dark to see. Stopping we made camp, shared some cold food. We rolled out our bedrolls and turned in. I rested ten, fifteen feet away from Ben. We said our good nights and there was no more conversation.

Pulling my Colt from its holster the sound of my cocking it was loud in the still night air. I said, "Ben, my gun is out and cocked and I'm a very light sleeper, get some sleep, we'll be riding before dawn."

I held the cocked Colt in my hand and crossing my arm over my chest I went to sleep. Twice Sin the night, I awoke and checked on my prisoner. He laid there on his back snoring.

CHAPTER 29

LEADING BEN AND the dead man tied to his horse, we rode into Tombstone in the late morning of the third day. Drawing the stares of several curious citizens, we rode slowly toward the sheriff' office. We soon had a small crowd of people following us and talking excitedly among themselves. Stopping in front of the sheriff's office, I slid down off my horse and tied him to the hitching post. Tying the other horses along side mine, I untied Ben's hands from the saddle horn and reached up helping him down out of his saddle.

Pushing Ben ahead of me, we went up the steps, past a man in a chair leaning with his back to the wall, whittling on a piece of wood. "Howdy" I said, He didn't answer. As we walked by, I took notice he wore no badge. Opening the front door we stepped through, Ben in front, with me close behind.

The office was empty. I went to the back of the office and opened the door that led to the jail part. It was empty, not even a drunk sleeping it off. I told Ben, "Pick out a cell you like and set yourself down in it."

While he was deciding, if he liked the one on the left or the one on the right, I found the keys hanging on the wall behind the sheriff's desk. Returning, Ben was sitting on the bunk in the first cell. He had a sour look on his face. I told Ben, "I got to find the sheriff. Don't go any where while I'm gone." As if, he could. I locked the cell door.

Closing the door to the sheriff's office, I looked down the street to my right and took notice of the man still sitting in the chair leaning against the wall. He looked up at me, his eyes crinkled with humor, and a smile spread itself across his ugly face. I said, "Howdy friend, you seen the sheriff?"

"Sure have."

I waited for an answer. He just sat there, with his silly grin and watched me. I became impatient. "Well? ... Where the hell is he?"

"He's out at Boot hill." He said nothing more and went back to his whittling. He still wore that silly grin on his face.

"Well, when will the sheriff be back you think?" This odd person has got to be the town idiot.

"Not any time soon." the idiot replied.

"What's he doing out there?" I asked, "Burying some one?"

"No, he ain't burying nobody, because we done planted the sheriff yesterday."

"What happened?" I asked.

"Just a bunch of them cowboys was getting drunk down at the Lucky Lady Saloon. You know how cowboys are when they get drunk. They got a little too rowdy. They started shooting up the place. He went down to put a stop to it. Got shot up bad, hung on for two ... three days, then he up and died."

"Is there a deputy sheriff about?"

Still grinning, he said, "They all left town. Ain't had a deputy for six months."

"Damn it all to Hell!" I said getting mad, "Who's in charge? Have they selected another sheriff?"

"Nope they ain't. Cause nobody wants to get shot at and maybe kill't." I could tell I was getting nowhere with this idiot. I was just wasting my breath and time trying to talk to him. I stood on the porch in front of the jail scratching my head thinking. The body still draped over the horse caught my eye along with a slight smell that I'd been noticing the last few hours. Well at least I could take him to the undertaker. I could then find out what to do with my prisoner that I'd locked up.

I untied the horses, eased into my saddle and led the horses down the street. Coming to 3rd street I looked to my right, three buildings down on the left, I saw the undertakers' sign. Tying the horses to the rail, I stepped through the open door into a dimly lit parlor. A tall, thin, bony man dressed in black, was bent over working on a body. Upon seeing me, he straightened up. "Yes sir, what can I do for you?"

I didn't quiet know how to begin. This was the first time I'd had to deal with a dead person. "Well ... I ... I got a customer for you." I blurted out. "He's just outside. If you give me a hand we can bring him in."

The undertaker wiping his hands on a towel, said, "Surely, lets take a look at what you got." He picked up a black, straight crown hat and stuck it on his head. It reminded me of a short piece of stovepipe with a brim.

Smithers was his name, walked up to the wrapped body hanging over the saddle, pulled out an arm, and felt the stiff wrist. "Yes, this man is certainly dead. How did it happen?"

"My friends and me caught four men rustling our cattle. We had a slight disagreement and in the ensuing fight, this one was shot dead. Two of 'em rode away fast. I think one of 'em might have caught some lead. How badly he was hurt I don't know. I have another man locked up down at the jail, but the jail don't seem to have a sheriff, at least one that's alive."

"Well, best we get this fellow down and into my parlor." Smithers said. We laid the body on a table which was in the back of the room. Smithers turned to me and asked, "Do you know who the next of kin might be?"

"Hell! I don't even know this mans name, let along who he might be related to. The only thing I heard before all the shooting started, someone said something about a Bernard Blackburn that they referred to as BB. I never heard the name before and I don't know who that might be."

Smithers rolled the name around, "BB ... Bernard ... Bernard Blackburn. H'm ... let me think." Holding his thoughts for a moment, he stroked his long droopy mustache, "Seems like I do recall the name."

He paused, thinking some more. "Some time ago. I passed through the small town of Pearce, before I came to Tombstone. I was looking for a place to start my business but Pearce was too small to support a business like mine."

"Anyway, I stayed the night in Pearce. I was having a drink at the local saloon. I believed the name Bernard Blackburn came up in a heated argument between two young fellows. I remember now, they were arguing about who's ranch was the biggest."

"The smaller of the two said his pa's ranch up at the edge of the Dragoon Mountains ran for miles and part way up into the mountains. The larger young one called the small one a liar. He then accused the smaller one and his father of building their ranch with stolen cattle."

"Suddenly this little pipsqueak jumps up in a fit of rage, draws his gun and shoots the other one dead. Damnedest thing I ever did see." Stroking his mustache, he paused again … "All over whose ranch was the largest. If that don't beat all."

"What happened then?" I asked. Curious as to what the outcome had been.

"Well that's the thing. The kid asked if anyone else wanted some of what he was offering. No one did. The kid then said to the people sitting at tables and those standing at the bar, 'You all saw this was a fair fight. Anyone here disagree?' The kid still had his gun in hand. No one disagreed."

The undertaker taking a deep breath went on. "The bartender and another man dragged the young dead man into a back room, leaving him there. Everyone acted like nothing had happened. Damnedest thing,"

"That's quiet a story. Sounds almost like the same kid that was rustling our cattle. But those mountains are a ways out there." Starting to leave I said, "I got to go see who's going to take care of my prisoner."

Smithers said, "Don't worry about the fee. The town will take care of it; they have a special fund for this sort of thing."

CHAPTER 30

I FOUND THE mayor's office and asked what he could do about the situation. His reply was slow in coming. "Not a lot I can do son. No one wants to be sheriff."

"What about the judge? Can't he make someone takethejob?" I asked with desperation in my voice.

"He surely could appoint someone. He has the power to do that. But have you ever heard the old saying, 'you can lead a horse to water, but you can't make it drink.'"

"Yeah, I heard that." I shrugged, "But that doesn't help me with my problem."

The mayor took a better look at me, and his face suddenly brightened. "Say, aren't you the young fellow that was with that Mister Tishman?"

"Yeah, that would be me. Now I'm older and wiser. The name's Chad in case you've forgotten. My friends call me Chad'tu."

"Chad, my young friend," he said with his best vote getting smile, "The last time I saw you, you weren't as tall, and if I recollect rightly, you weren't wearing guns. Now I see you're packing two, hanging low and tied down. Do you know how to use them, or are they just for show?"

"They were a gift from Brett." I said, caressing the butts of the Colts hanging from my waist.

"You any good with those guns?" the Mayor questioned.

"You could say I'm right handy with them." I drew both Colts in a blur of motion with lighting speed, twirled them around my index fingers, flipped the right Colt into the air caught it, and shoved both guns back into their holsters.

I shouldn't have showed off. Brett had told me to never show off and tip your hand to the other fellow what you got. The mayor was so condescending, talking down to me. Something deep inside snapped.

Maybe it was anger at the way he talked to me like a boy—I was a man and I felt compelled to show him.

The mayor stepped back stunned, a little pale, at my display. "Brett taught me how to handle them real good." I said, "Don't you think?"

The mayor recovered quickly. He put on his vote-getting smile and put his arm around my shoulders, "Chad my boy, how would you like to be the new sheriff?" He went on quickly before I could reply, "I can arrange it. Just think you would be the Sheriff of Tombstone and all the surrounding countryside." He looked at me.

I didn't like his arm around my shoulders. I started to back away. I wasn't looking for a job—I already had one with Brett. This isn't what I'd wanted or expected. I finally found my voice and said, "No sir. No disrespect, but I don't want to be sheriff of Tombstone."

The mayor wasn't about to give up. He said, "We'll pay you fifty dollars a month and expenses. What do you say?"

I thought about it for a second. Fifty dollars was a lot of money. Then I thought about Brett back at the house, thinking I was having a good time out at my friend's ranch. "No, Mister Mayor, I can't see how I can be sheriff and run our gun business with Brett. I wouldn't have much time to do either very well. Whatever I do, I want to do it well."

"Well Chad … Chad'tu, Oh hell! I think I'll call you Chad'tu. It's a different name, it'll make people sit up and take notice. Don't you think? Well, Chad'tu, you drive a hard bargain. Say we make it sixty dollars a month, plus expenses, and we throw in room and board."

Sixty dollars a month was a lot of money, especially for a kid like me. A wagon creaked as it rolled by down the middle of the street. I thought on it … I thought hard about those sixty dollars. I was about to speak when the mayor interrupted my thoughts. I was about to say I might consider his offer. But I needed to talk to Brett first. My loyalty stood with Brett, not the mayor, or the town of Tombstone.

The mayor saw he almost had me, "Chad'tu I can see that you're thinking. You can come and go as it pleases you, no set hours. Jurisdiction for Tombstone is the town and out for a distance of fifty miles, or thereabouts. After fifty miles anything happens, it's up to the federal marshal. The only thing we would require is your presence be seen in town two or three times a day unless you're out of town on business. You can ride or walk the streets as you see fit. And another thing, remember that gunsmith business of yours is only two miles out and its part of the town. You could make that part of your daily rounds. Now then, what do you say?"

I could do this. It sure was tempting. I could help Brett at the gunsmith store, ride into town, and make an appearance now and then. How hard could that be? I asked myself. The mayor had said a fifty-mile radius was my territory to cover, which would mean I had a lot of territory to cover. I could travel out to the Brucker ranch and see Jaydeen anytime I wanted. Yeah! Sweet Jaydeen, the woman I was going to marry, although she didn't know it yet. The woman of my dreams was on my mind day and night.

I thought this just might work out. I was excited about the prospects of the deal, but I didn't know what Brett would say. "Okay, Okay, mayor you can shut up now! I'll take the job." Then as an afterthought, I added, "For the time being."

The mayor was aghast that I would speak to him in that manner. He said "Well I never ... no one speaks to me like that ... no one!"

"Did you hear what I said Mister Mayor? I'll take the job for now. But if I don't like it you'll have to find someone else to be your sheriff."

The mayor hemmed, hawed, and finally replied, "That's fine". He was beaming, "I accept you as our new sheriff and on your terms. The judge will have to swear you in as sheriff. You'll be on probation for thirty days. You start today, as will your pay, even if the day is half-gone already. You can quit or I can fire you within thirty days with no disgrace. Agreed?"

"I agreed." I stood there in a stupor. What had I done?

On one hand, I didn't really want to be the sheriff. On the other hand, I wanted to be the sheriff. It would give me a lot of power and it might somehow even help our gunsmith business. I didn't see what it could hurt.

I started to say something to the mayor. Then I forgot what I was going to say as the mayor opened a drawer in his desk took out a new shiny badge and handed it to me. I stood there holding the shiny five-pointed silver badge with Sheriff written across it.

"Welcome Sheriff Chad or Chad'tu. Oh hell, I guess Chad'tu will do. Anyway it's good to have someone of your caliber on the right side of the law." the mayor said.

I looked at the mayor. I wanted to say something but no words were forthcoming. I guess it was because I had a large lump in my throat. My eyes glassy I finally got out a thank you to the mayor. Then I just stood there not knowing what to do next.

The mayor took the badge back, "Here son, let me help you to pin that on your shirt."

"Chad'tu," the mayor called to me as I started to leave. "I'll tell Jim Brad-shaw, he's the judge, you'll be in to see him about setting up a trial for your cattle rustler. While your there he can swear you in, just to make things legal and proper."

I felt like the cock of the walk as I strutted down the street showing off my shiny new badge.

Suddenly I stopped. Brett would not act like this. What was I thinking and doing? I wasn't thinking that was for sure. Brett always said to keep a low profile. If no one took notice of you, you were less likely to get shot or shot at.

I went back to the jail and checked on the prisoner. He was sitting on the bunk, still with his head down.

I caught the smell of cooking food. Suddenly I got a hunger pain. I'd forgotten about eating with all I'd been doing. It had been awhile since I'd eaten, I realized. I called out, "Ben you hungry? If you are, I'll get you something from the hotel."

He answered sounding down and depressed, "Yeah Chad'tu, I s 'pose I could get something down."

I walked across Main Street and down past the saddle shop, following the smell of the cooking food I went into the hotel.

An older man stood behind a counter took notice of the badge as I said, "I'm the new sheriff in town. My name is Chad'tu; I got a hungry prisoner over at the jail. Can we get something to eat from your kitchen?"

"Sheriff you can call me Barlow. I'm the owner of this hotel. To answer your question, yes, you can eat here, or we can bring something to the jail, whichever is convenient. Which would you like?"

"Well I don't have any money," I sheepishly replied. "The mayor just made me sheriff. He said the town would pay for all my expenses."

"That is correct Mister Chad'tu. We have an agreement with the town, room and board for the sheriff, and food for any prisoners; you have in your jail. All you have to do is sign your name on the bill. Then we turn it in at the end of the month to the town hall."

"Look, I'm new at this sheriff thing and any help would surely be appreciated. You can drop the 'Mister', just call me Chad'tu. Okay?"

"How about I just call you Sheriff?"

It sounded so odd for someone to be calling me sheriff, but I guessed I would get use to it. "Sure, that's fine by me."

Barlow had beef stew delivered over to the jail by a young and pretty serving girl from the hotel.

While she was dishing out two bowls of stew for me and Ben, she kept smiling at me. She had me sign the bill. As she handed me a pencil to sign with, our hands touched for a moment. She looked me in the eye and smiled, saying she would be back later to collect the dishes. Then she winked at me and was gone.

CHAPTER 31

THE NEXT DAY after having breakfast at the hotel, I rode out to see Brett. I pulled up in front of the house; there was a new sign out front. It read, "GUNSMITHS, shooting weapons, large or small, we repair them all." While tying my horse to the hitching rail, Brett stepped out onto the porch and greeted me in his usual friendly manner. "I heard you ride up, Chad. You're back early from your time off. You surprised me I didn't expect you for another couple days." He held out his hands in a questioning manner. "What's happened? You rode out going north and now you're riding in from the south?"

He took notice of the silver badge pinned above my heart, as I stepped from the hitching rail to the porch. He walked over and gave me a big hug, "I missed you Chad. It's been lonely here without you." He stepped back and said, "What is that thing you got pinned on your shirt?" As if, he didn't know. He damn well new what it was.

"It's a badge." I said.

"I can see it's a badge." He said in a perturbed, slightly disturbed voice. "What the hell have you gone and done now?"

I answered his question with one of my own. "You got coffee on?"

"Yeah, I got coffee on, fresh-made this morning. It's probable pretty strong by now. It'll probably taste like mud. I'll getcha a cup while you catch me up.

We went into the house. Brett poured two cups of coffee. Carrying the steaming mugs out onto the porch, we sat in a couple of rickety old wood chairs. I sipped my coffee and it did taste like mud, only stronger. Brett said, "I sent you out to have some time off, and you come back wearing a badge. What the hell happened?"

I took a sip of mud and started telling my story. By the time I'd finished, I had drunk two cups of what Brett called coffee, and I called mud.

Brett said, "Well, I guess I should congratulate you on your new position as sheriff. What happened to the regular sheriff?"

"He got shot and died. No one wanted the job. Too high risk I'd say. You might say I was in the wrong place at the right time. Or the right place at the wrong time." I gave a shrug, "The mayor talked me into it."

"Well, now that you're the sheriff, see that you do the position honor." He took me by the shoulders and turned me, till I was facing him. He looked me in the eye with a serious look on his face and said, "You're young. Be careful, you hear? I have taught you all I can; now it's up to you. You know, if you need help, I will always be here for you."

"Um, Brett, there's one other thing I forgot to tell you."

Brett, rolling his eyes the way he always did, when I acted like a kid, said, "Okay what is it now? What other news did you forget to tell me?"

"Um" … I didn't know what I should say. I was kind of embarrassed. I said, "I'm in love."

"Chad you're not even gone for a week. You come back and tell me you had a gunfight with rustlers, killing one, taking one prisoner, and taking him to jail. And now you're the sheriff, and you're in love." He took a deep breath. "God, Chad, don't you think that's a lot to do in less than a week." He ranted and raved, on and on. I could tell he was proud of me, and happy I was still alive.

"For god's sake Chad, the rustlers I can understand, but how can you be in love? You've hardly been gone a week." He walked around in a circle, not saying anything. Finally he said, "Who is it some girl in town? Maybe one that works in a saloon?" He raised his eyebrows expectantly and waited for an answer.

"Aw Brett, no it ain't nothin' like that. It's Sid's sister. Heck Brett, She's the most beautiful woman I ever did lay eyes on, and I intend to marry her." I could see Brett was stunned by my announcement.

"So when is the wedding?"

"I don't know. She doesn't know I'm going to marry her, yet."

"I just want to know one thing. If she doesn't know you're going to marry her, just how are you going to pull this off?"

"I haven't figured that out yet, but I will. You can bet your life on it." On the porch, beside my best friend, I sat thinking of Jaydeen. The sun shone over the horizon for an instant, splashing the sky with streaks of red and yellow and then was gone. Dusk set in. The stars started to light up in the night sky. A cool breeze had started up. It was a glorious evening. I was happy.

Brett said, "Let's go in and fix some supper. You are going to stay the night." The last was not a question; it was a statement of fact.

Brett was up and rattling around the next morning before me, as he started to cook breakfast on the wood stove bought from the emporium. It was still dark and he had lit a kerosene lantern to see by. It was summer, so we didn't need a fire. It was warm enough already.

Setting out on the porch relaxing after breakfast, we watched as the sun rose in the east. We sat there drinking our coffee not talking, Brett smoking. The morning was cool and quiet.

After I helped Brett clean up the mess from breakfast, he said. "It's getting on and I got work to do. Don't you think you should head on back to town and check on the man you got locked up? You don't know what might be happening."

"Yeah, I guess I probably should, but I hate to leave good company."

"Well from what you told me you pretty much have free rein to do as you like." Brett said, "But I wouldn't abuse it if I were you."

"Okay, Okay, I can tell when I'm not wanted." I said in jest.

I saddled up my horse, gave the cinch one more tightening tug, and stepped into the saddle and said, "Brett, see ya," and rode away.

Brett yelled. "You be careful and remember everything I taught you.

Don't go taking any chances." He spoke those last words to a cloud of dust.

CHAPTER 32

I RODE DOWN the main street like I owned it. In a sense, I guess I did own it. I was the man in charge of keeping the streets of Tombstone safe from gun fighters, drunks and anyone that wanted to cause trouble for its law-abiding citizens.

The town was peaceful. I rode slowly down the street keeping a sharp eye for trouble or anything which looked as if it might be developing in that direction.

People throughout town were greeting me with a warm smile, and a 'Good morning to you Sheriff.' I wondered how so many people could know I was the new sheriff, in only one day. Did they have a town meeting? Maybe the mayor had had a few too many and spread the word? I rode up and down, back and forth, through most of Tombstone's streets.

With the exception of few, most of the people greeted me the same way. "Hello Sheriff,"

"Have a good day Sheriff,"

"Bye for now Sheriff." There were a few that didn't say hello, those who just stared at me with meanness and hate showing on their faces.

It sounded strange to my ears everyone calling me sheriff. After a time, I got used to bring called sheriff and decided I liked being called sheriff. I started tipping my hat to the ladies and saying hello to everyone. I liked it till I had my first squabble

Everything was fine till I pulled up in front of the Lucky Lady Saloon. Tying my horse to the rail, I was set to go in when the double butterfly-wing doors to the saloon busted open wide. A man was tossed out through them headfirst. He hit the porch, slid on off into the dusty street, and rolled, stopping at my feet in a cloud of dust.

I reached down and helped the stranger to his feet. He was shorter than my six feet. He had a small potbelly, which had a gun belt tied below it that still had a gun in it.

He shook his head like you see the bulls at a bullfight shake their head, when they are really mad and angry, ready to charge. That's what this older bearded stranger reminded me of, a crazed bull. He had that crazed, glassy look in his eyes, the charging look of a bull.

He started to go back into the saloon but he couldn't. I had ahold of his collar, stopping him. He looked up at me, then took notice of the badge and calmed somewhat.

"What's the trouble here stranger?" I asked in a firm voice. The saloon doors were still swinging back and forth, when a man pushed through them with a crumpled-up hat in his hand that he threw at the old man and said, "Stay out of this here saloon and don't come back if 'n you know what's good fer you."

Pulling the old man along I took a step forward toward the man on the porch. I noticed he had a gun worn low, tied down and still in its holster. I felt like I was caught somewhere between the bull and the bullfighter.

"What's the problem?" I said to the man on the porch above me.

"Mind your business and stay out of this," was his sharp reply.

"Friend, this is my business. I'm the sheriff in Tombstone and I take care of any trouble that goes on." I let go of the old man and still keeping an eye on him, I took another step toward the man on the porch.

"Mister ... I'm gonna ask you one more time nice and polite." I said, taking another step forward, I raised my left arm to emphasize what I was saying, and also to distract. "What is going on between you two?"

While he watched my left hand, my right hand brushed close to my gun and swiftly checked that the thong holding the hammer down was undone. Good, he hadn't noticed.

"It ain't none of your business, but I'm gonna tell you anyway. This here dirty old man called me a cheat. We were playing cards and he said I was dealing from the bottom of the deck. Them is killin' words where I come from, but I felt sorry for the old coot, and didn't shoot him. I only tossed him out." I glanced to the old man and said, "What's your side of the story? You got anything you want to say?"

"This card sharp dealt himself four aces and the last one was dealt from the bottom. I know cause I accidentally seen the bottom card as he was dealing. If'n an ace was on the bottom. How did it get into his hand, making the fourth ace for sure?"

The card sharp's face turned red and his hand started down for his gun. I could see he was about to draw his gun.

I took another step forward and said, "Mister I wouldn't do that if I was you. You don't want to shoot nobody, because then we'd have to hang you. And I know you wouldn't like that one dang bit."

He stopped for a second thinking. While he paused I said, "But you know, hanging a man cost a lot of money. So to save the town money, I would just have to shoot you dead where you stand. What do you say? It's your call?" By the look on his face, he had no idea if I was bluffing. Cardsharp's face was now the color of a fresh cut beet. He sputtered and said, "What makes you so sure you can shoot me before I shoot you?"

"Well if you don't want to live any longer—and you're sure you want to see who's the fastest, go ahead and draw. Oh, one more thing, you'll be dead before your gun clears leather. Your choice friend," I said smiling that terrible smile.

With the killing glint in my eyes showing, I started going into the zone where everything slowed down. 'The killing zone,' I called it. It was like Brett had described to me. Everything moved in slow motion, except me. I was ready.

"Oh hell, the hell with it," The card sharp said, throwing up his hands turned and walked back into the Lucky Lady Saloon.

The dirty old man was a little paler than he'd been two minutes earlier. He calmed a bit. "You know who that was, you was a talkin' to?" he said in a shaky voice.

"Never laid eyes on the man before, how could I know who he is?" I said looking at the old man. "Who is he?"

"That was Travers, Bill Travers."

"I don't know of him. Who is this Bill Travers?" I asked.

"I hear'd tell he's from down New Orleans way. Somebody said he was one of them riverboat gamblers you hear about. Hear'd he shot and killed one man too many and he run off before they could hang him." the old man said, picking up his hat and slapping it against his leg, knocking the dust off.

Straightening his hat, he stuck it on his head and scratched his stubble of a beard. "A real conniving cheat and double-dealing card sharp that's handy with a gun." He went on. "Why, I hear'd tell he even has a tiny little gun stuck up his sleeve or somewhere, I don't rightly know for sure."

You sure were brave to stand up to him like you did. He won't be a' forgetin that. No sirree, he won't be a' forgetin. Sheriff, I thank 'e kindly for your help. He might have shot me. All I can say is, you be mighty careful and watch your step when he's around."

With that said, he turned and stumbled, tipsily, along down the wooden boardwalk in the direction of the next saloon. I pondered what the old man had said along with his warning. I would have to keep a close eye on this man named Bill Travers.

When I'd tied up out front, my intention was to go in the Lucky Lady and get acquainted while having a beer. And that was just what I was going to do.

I made sure my guns had the leather loops slipped from their hammers. If I needed to draw fast, I didn't want anything to slow me up. I walked through the swinging doors into the dim smoke-filled room. I stepped to one side of the door, so as not to be silhouetted from the bright sun, while my eyes adjusted.

A long typical bar ran down the wall on my left, card tables in the back on the right side and drinking tables filled the rest. Bill Travers sat at one of the table's playing cards and chewing on a cigar stuck between his teeth. He sat with his back to a corner, facing the door and the open room. Nothing would escape his attention.

The bar toward the front curved around and ended at the wall. Standing at the end of the bar where I had an overview of the room, I ordered a beer. The bartender said his name was McCrae, but I could call him John.

"John," I said, taking a sip of beer. "I'm the new sheriff, just thought I'd stop in and get acquainted. How are things going, any trouble with anybody?" I said looking in the direction of Travers.

The bartender leaned on the bar and said, "I didn't catch your name Sheriff?"

I thought about my name for a second, and then replied, "Its Chad'tu."

"That's a strange name. What is it … Indian?"

"Yeah, it's Indian."

John looked me up and down, "You don't look like an Indian." He said. I pondered that for a moment, and said, "John … You might say I'm a white Indian."

Seeing the look on my face, he didn't pursue the issue any further.

"Chad'tu we don't have much trouble in here, only a spat now and then.

You know how it is in a saloon. It goes with the territory."

"What about the man playing cards over there? The man called Travers. Does he cause trouble?"

"Funny you should ask. He's a stranger, not one of the regulars. He showed up about a week ago and started playing cards. He hasn't given me any trouble so far. Only the disagreement you saw today. The people who play cards with him don't like him particularly. They say there's something about the way he plays that ain't quiet right. No one can quite put a finger on what it is. Mostly he wins and they lose. Lately he is becoming more commanding and demanding. It's almost like he thinks he owns this place."

"Well if he causes any trouble, send for me. Okay?"

"Okay Sheriff. If I have any trouble, you'll be the first to know." He wiped a glass and looking at it, said in a low voice, "Sheriff, just so you know, I keep a double-barrel twelve-gauge shotgun loaded and right handy, here behind the bar." He looked at my empty glass and said, "You want another beer?"

"Naw, it's too early in the day. I want to check out all the saloons and brothels around town and get a feel for where trouble might start."

I started to leave. "Sheriff," John hesitated … "Chad'tu, can I ask you a question?"

"Sure. Ask away."

"You seem awfully young to be Sheriff, you sure you can handle the trouble and problems that come up?"

I thought about his question. "Yeah I can handle anything that might happen. And if I need help, it's only two miles away." I said smiling, thinking of Brett. I put my empty glass on the bar and said, "I'll see you around John." By the end of the day, I was tired. I had visited six bars and three brothels.

I was feeling a little light-headed from the beers I had drunk.

As I left the last brothel called 'Kate's Place', I was thinking Kate sure had some pretty girls working for her, but none as pretty as Jaydeen.

I stopped by the jail to see how Ben was doing. He was still unhappy. I checked the doors making sure they were locked. I told Ben I'd see him in the morning. Back at my room in the hotel, I took off my clothes, fell across the bed and went to sleep.

The next morning after breakfast, I told the young girl that usually delivered meals to the jail; I'd take Ben's breakfast over to him.

I sat watching Ben eat his breakfast. He wasn't much hungry I could see. I guess he'd lost his appetite, thinking about hanging. He asked, "Chad you think they'll hang me?" I could tell he was scared.

"I don't know what they'll do with you. That's up to the judge and the jury."

He looked so pitiful. I said, "Ben I have gotten to know you a little. I'm starting to believe you when you say you really didn't know those weren't your outfits' cows. I believe you just got hornswaggled into a shady deal. For what it's worth, I'll put in a good word for you to the judge. It couldn't hurt none and it might do some good. Cheer up. Who knows what might happen?"

CHAPTER 33

A WEEK HAD passed since I'd been made Sheriff. I made my morning rounds of the town. Not much was happening. It was too durn peaceful for Tombstone. I was uneasy; it felt like something was about to happen. It was just a feeling I got sometimes. It was like that saying I'd heard somewhere, 'The lull before the storm.'

Morning came and went. I still had that uneasy feeling. I put the feeling down to the hot sticky weather. My stomach rumbled, telling me it was time to get something to eat.

It had rained yesterday, but today the sun was shining brightly. It was one of those days that were so common after a rain. A hot muggy day with not a breeze stirring that I could feel. A few dirty, low-floating clouds were still visible. I crossed the street and headed for the hotel to fill the empty space in my belly.

It was a little after one o'clock by the big regulator clock that hung on the wall of the hotel lobby. I took my time eating, I flirted some with the waitress while I finished my meal. Then signed the bill she'd brought.

Walking out through the lobby, I glance again at the big clock. To my surprise, it now said two fifteen. Damn, I thought, how could I spend that much time having a meal? It must be that girl Faye that had waited on me. Smiling, I thought to myself, she sure does like to flirt.

It was so hot and muggy; you could see steam rising from the ground as the sun baked it. My shirt clung to me like a wet towel. There was a tension in the air like something was about to happen, I didn't know what.

I contemplated all this as I sat in a chair on the porch of the jail, my boots propped up on the porch railing, sweating and watching the citizens going about their business. All in all, it was pretty calm, except for the tension I felt. It was just too quiet; I still had that uneasy feeling.

The sun moved slowly across the sky and far in the distance was on its way to meet the earth. The shadows from the buildings were getting longer as the sun moved lower. A young Mexican boy came running up the street toward me. He stopped in front of the jail out of breath. Breathing hard and trying to catch his breath, he said, "Señor … Señor, Sheriff, you must come quick, there is mucho trouble at the Lady that is Lucky."

"You mean, The Lucky Lady?"

"Si … Si, that iss what I say, but you must hurry …you must hurry, somebody get hurt or killed maybe. Hurry señor, please hurry. Mister John, he say for you to hurry."

Not wanting to miss any of the action, the kid having delivered his message, turned and started running back to the saloon.

We were not far from the saloon, so I just ran after the Mexican kid to the Lucky Lady. He stopped out front and pointed to the saloon. I didn't hear any noise coming out of the saloon. Usually it was noisy. You could normally here people talking in loud voices and yelling in even louder voices, along with cursing.

I started up the steps and stopped. I motioned for the Mexican kid to come close to me. When he was close I said, "Do you know what kind of trouble is going on in there?"

"Si, Si … iss the man sits at back table, he play cards."

"Yeah I know him, a real mean hombre."

"Si, that be hem, he say he gon' to shoot somebody, He say … maybe that stinkin' Sheriff."

I thought better about going in the front way through those two swinging doors. Anyone waiting on the other side would have the drop on whoever came through. I backed slowly down the steps keeping my eyes on those doors for any movement. I stopped on the bottom step and flipped the leather thong off the hammer of my Colt.

Best I go around and come into the Lucky Lady by the side door. As I remembered it, it was across the room from the card table, where the card sharp usually sat. I knew he was armed, but what I didn't know was, how ready he would be to use his gun. I only had the kid's word for everything, no reason to take chances, though.

I pulled the Colt and turning the knob on the door, I stood to one side and slowly eased it open a crack. Staying low, I looked through the crack. I couldn't see much, only an edge of a table and a booted foot sticking out. Looking at the angle the boot rested on the floor, I decided whoever was in that boot was facing to the front, with an eye on those two swinging doors.

Then I noticed an arm extending out across the wooden floor. It looked like it was reaching for something. It lay out-stretched next to one of the card tables' legs, unmoving. Not seeing the body I couldn't tell whose arm it might be.

I couldn't just stand out in this alley all day. I would have to go in and control the situation. I didn't want an innocent person getting hurt, if there was shooting, and I expected there would be. I paused, thinking ... I had never faced a man up close, face to face before. Hell, come to think of it, I'd never faced a man with a gun.

Taking a deep breath, I loosened the thong from my other Colt, in case I needed both guns for the extra firepower. Taking another deep breath, I stood back and gave the door a kick. The door swung open wide making a loud noise as it hit the wall.

The door banging against the wall startled Travers, who had expected me to come in the front way.

Travers sat at the card table with eyes glued to those swinging front doors. The light from the opened door fell across the room and onto his table. He had a gun in his hand pointed in the direction he had expected me to come from. Surprise flashed across his face.

He jerked around at the sound of my voice. "Travers, if you want to live, put down your gun." I yelled loud and clear one more time. "Travers don't do it, if you want to live." My mind slipped into the slow-motion killing zone.

The surprise was gone from Travers face. He turned in slow motion, raised his gun, and fired hitting the doorjamb to my left. He was blinded by the bright sun that streamed into the darken room and fell across the table and his face.

Moving quickly to the side of the door I snapped off a quick shot. The bullet struck Travers in the chest and spun him around, he fell across the table. He fired two more shots, one in my direction and the second into the floor. He slid off the table and his body hit the floor. He tried to rise up then fell back and moved no more. Travers was dead.

I noticed movement down at the end of the bar next to the swinging doors. A man stood there holding a gun that was aimed at me. Everyone at the bar had ducked down when they heard the man say, "Chad'tu, I'm gonna kill you."

In the deathly silence that followed those words. The only sound was the tick of the regulator clock and the click of the hammer on his gun as he pulled it back.

I had a Colt in each hand and I didn't have time to turn and shoot right-handed. That thought flashed through my brain like a bolt of lightning. Without thinking, my body shielding my movement, I whipped up my left hand and holding the Colt across my chest, I turned my head toward the man and fired. I felt the heat from the barrel as the Colt bucked in my hand. I stood and watched as the man slowly dropped his gun unfired and grabbed at his throat.

I stood there shaking; Travers was the first man I had killed up close. I could hardly remember what had happened. I didn't know what the condition of the man at the end of the bar might be.

Right now, I didn't really care. All I knew was that I was still alive. It had all happened so fast, after the slow motion of the killing zone.

The citizens that had ducked stood up, and a couple of them ran over to the man lying on the floor, with the outstretched arm. Everyone else started talking excitedly. His name I heard someone say was Bill. Someone else said Bill's still breathing, best we get him to the doctor fast.

I walked unsteady to the bar and leaned against it, shaken I guess. I must have looked a little pale. John the bartender came up to me. He was holding a bar cloth to his right shoulder with his left hand. "Are you okay Chad'tu? Are you shot? You look a little pale."

"Yeah, I'm fine. What happen to your shoulder John? You get hit by a stray bullet?"

"I'll be okay Chad'tu. I was trying to get Travers to leave. He was drinking too much and harassing the other customers. They was playing cards and he just up and shot poor ole Bill for no reason a' tall. I'd started for the shotgun that was tucked under the bar. That's when the sneaky sonabitch done shot me with a Derringer he had tucked up his sleeve."

"That's when I sent Miguel for you. Things seemed to be getting out of hand. Chad'tu that was sure some good shooting, too bad, you had to kill him and that fellow at the end of the bar. I think they both were out to get ya. I think they were in cahoots together and planned the whole thing."

"You don't look so good; you want some whiskey?" He didn't wait for an answer; he poured out a half glass of whisky and sat it down on the bar in front of me. My hand shook slightly as I picked up the glass. I took a sip. The liquid burned going down then I felt a small warm feeling starting to grow. A second sip made the warm feeling expand. I started to calm down somewhat.

"Well, John," I said, "I guess you can send Miguel for the undertaker. I don't think Mr. Travers is going anywhere but down, six feet down and then further on to hell." Having said all that, I finished the last of the whisky in the glass. I almost felt like myself again.

"Sheriff," someone called from the far end of the bar. "This man over here is still alive, but I don't think he's gonna last long, with all the blood running out his neck. I think he's trying to say something. He seems to want to talk. But with all the blood in his throat it's hard to understand his gurgled words."

Setting my empty glass on the bar, I hurried to the dying man lying on the floor.

He was lying in a pool of blood, his blood, and the pool was steadily growing larger. Blood was splattered across the wall where he'd been standing.

I knelt down and asked, "What's your name?"

His eyelids fluttered open and the man looked up. His glazed unseeing eyes could not focus. He tried to speak. It was garbled from the blood. I reached under the dying mans shoulders and lifted him into an more upright position thinking it might help to keep the blood out of his throat. It did seem to help a little.

A hand clutched my arm. I looked down at the clutching hand that belonged to the bleeding man. He said something I could not make out. Bending my ear closer to his lips, I urged him to say what he could get out. The best I could understand the garbled words, sounded like he said, "We ... we were ... to kill ... you ... told to ... hired ..." the man took a gasping breath then started choking.

"Who sent you to kill me?" I said, shaking the man gently. "Who sent you? Who wants me dead?"

Coughing and sputtering blood in a rasping voice he managed, "Kill ... you ... hired ... by ... by ... B ..." were the last words he would ever speak.

He died while I held him in my arms. My arms were drenched with his blood.

All I could think was, Damn, Damn, Damn. Why couldn't he have lived just a little longer? Long enough to tell me who had hired him and Travers to kill me? I was no closer to who it might be or why. Damn.

I stood and walked down the bar to where John looked at me expectantly. "Well?" John asked.

"Well, I think I need another of whatever that was you gave me earlier." John refilled my glass with whisky. This time he poured it all the way to the top. I guess he thought I needed it. I guess I did because I didn't object to his pour. As he finished pouring, he again asked. "Well? Did he say anything about who might have put them up to this?"

"It was all a garbled bunch of words. The only thing I could make out for sure was that someone hired them to kill me."

"This whole thing was a set up to get me at a disadvantage and it almost worked, except for Miguel. Where is that little Mexican anyway?" I looked around and saw Miguel's head peeking in from under the red swinging doors. His eyes were wide with awe and admiration. "Miguel," I called. "Get over here now."

"Si, Señor, Sheriff." He got up, ran over, and looking up, said, "Señor Sheriff you shoot good."

"Miguel I thank you for your speed in telling me of the trouble here." I rubbed my hand through his black hair with affection and said, "How old are you?"

"I think maybe I be nine." he paused, shrugging his shoulders he looked up, smiled and said, "Maybe ten. I no know for sure."

I reached in my pocket and fetched out a penny. Handing it to Miguel I said, "Take this. Call it a reward for all your trouble and your help. You might want to go over to the Emporium and buy some candy."

"Miguel, any time you want, you come see me, and if you see any trouble come running fast and tell me. Okay?"

"Si Señor, I weel remember what you say. Any trouble I see, I run fast to you."

CHAPTER 34

WAS WORN out and suddenly very tired. Without eating, I went to my room in the hotel, took off my clothes, fell into bed and was fast asleep as soon as I hit the mattress.

The next morning I awoke sometime after eight o'clock. I normally awoke around six o' clock or before, but today I was late. I hurriedly washed up and went down to eat. I was in luck they were still serving breakfast. I was ravenous. I ordered steak, eggs, and coffee. As I ate, I thought about the events of the day before.

I couldn't believe what had happened. I felt lucky to still be alive. I had to tell Brett what had happened. After breakfast, I saddled up and headed out of town to see Brett.

It was before noon when I rode up to our place. Brett stepped out on the porch as I finished tying up my horse. "Howdy, Sheriff, how are you this fine morning?"

"Brett, I need to talk to you."

"Well I got coffee on, so come on in partner and tell me what's on your mind."

"Brett you won't believe what I'm going to tell you." I said excitedly." Brett held up a hand to stop my blabbering. Pouring two cups of coffee he calmly said, "I bet you're going to tell me you were in a situation, and had to kill two men that had set you up. And now you don't know whether to be proud or sad for the killing."

I was amazed that Brett knew about the shootout and the killings. "How do you know all that?" I asked questioningly.

He laughed at my consternation and said, "It's magic, I know everything that goes on."

I could tell he was joking. He was trying to get me to loosen up and let go of all my terrible thoughts, and his jesting with me did just that.

Brett said, "An early traveler passed by this morning and told me the sheriff had shot and killed two men in a saloon. He didn't know what it was about. Why don't you fill me in? Tell me what really happened and how it went down."

I poured out my guts to Brett telling the story just as it had happened.

After I got through with the telling, I felt much better. I'm not a Catholic, but it must have been like a confession.

Brett said, "You were damn lucky you didn't go in the front way through those swinging doors. If you had, you'd be dead. Shot through the head by the man who was waiting for you at the end of the bar. He would have had a clear shot and standing only ten feet away he wouldn't have missed. You're damn lucky."

Brett took a sip of coffee and sat there looking at me, a slight frown creasing his forehead. I could tell he was happy I was alive. He took another swallow of coffee and asked, "Chad, just out of curiosity, tell me why you went in the rear side door instead of walking in the front way like a normal person would?"

I took a deep breath and a swallow of coffee. "I don't rightly know Brett… I had started for those swinging doors and was almost to them when I stopped. I looked at Miguel. Miguel looked back with a frightened look on his face like something terrible was about to happen. I knew the man that waited for me would be in the back and probably watching those doors expecting me to come through them. I needed to surprise him and I would then have the advantage."

"Then I thought about what you had always said. You told me to always do the unexpected. So I did. I remembered that side door and decided to go in that way, which helped me also with the other shooter, by putting more distance between us. And that was just pure luck on my part, because I didn't know there were two shooters."

Brett smiled at my explanation of how it had all happened and gone down. He rolled a smoke and lit it. "I'm glad some of the things I tried to teach you sunk into that hard head of yours. I'm more than glad you're still alive. Thank God for that." Then teasingly added, "I don't know what I would do if I didn't have you for a partner … partner." He rolled his eyes up toward the ceiling in the way that only Brett can do.

I knew what Brett was getting at. I hadn't been much help lately at our gunsmith store. I stood up. I knew what Brett was trying to say in a round about way. "Brett as soon as I find a deputy to help with the keeping of law and order in Tombstone, I'll be able to spend more time out here."

"There are several problems in Tombstone and I got a few ideas about how I might handle them. And another thing, I haven't even had a chance to visit the love of my life, the woman who's going to be my future wife." I went on, "There's a lot of things I want to do that I don't have time for just now." It was good seeing Brett after all that had just happened. I didn't want to, but I left around noontime. I had to get back to town, there were a few things I wanted to do. I was glad to see Brett, but my circumstances bothered me. The sun sat high in the pale blue sky as I rode off, in the far distance above a butte hung a solitary white cloud.

I needed a deputy, that's all there was to it. I didn't know how I was going to get one. I was just spread too thin to take care of everything.

Back in Tombstone, I stopped at the jail. Checked on Ben then made my rounds of the town. Ben wanted to know when we were going to hang him. He said he was tired of waiting to die. "Do it and get it over with," he said.

I told him not to be in such a hurry to get his neck stretched. "Who knows what the judge will decide. You're getting free room and board so enjoy it."

Walking over to the hotel I'd made up my mind, tomorrow I would see the town printer about my idea. Thinking about the events of the last day, I had supper.

The next day after breakfast, I stopped in front of the building they called the Town Hall of Tombstone. The offices of the judge and mayor were located in this building and they were both in their separate rooms, having just arrived shortly before me.

I was ushered into the judge's office by a frumpy-looking, middle-aged woman. The Judge looked up and said, "Oh! Sheriff, what can I do for you? What brings you in so early to my office?"

"I came to see the mayor about an idea I had. Your outer door was open so I stopped here first. I have a question or two. It's about Ben, the fella I got locked up over at the jail."

The judge leaned back in his chair and adjusting his glasses, said, "Alright Sheriff, what about this Ben feller? That's the one you caught red-handed, rustling cattle?"

"That's what I wanted to talk to you about judge. I have a pretty good feel about things and this thing with Ben is wrong. And yes we did catch him with a few others that were herding cattle with the wrong brand on their hind quarters."

"Alright, I know all that, so what's the problem?"

"He keeps telling me he was hired as an extra hand to round up some cattle that'd strayed. My gut feeling is he's innocent. He didn't know what was going on till we came upon them. He says he's just a hired hand and I, for one, believe him."

"Well Sheriff, the law is the law, and I swore and oath to uphold it. What would you have me do?"

"Isn't there some way we can charge him with a lesser offense? Something so we can let him go, after serving some time. There must be something you can do? The poor man is wasting away to skin and bones. He will hardly eat any food. All he does is pick at it. And he keeps saying to hang him and get it over with."

I liked Ben after I had gotten to know him better, and here I was now, practically begging for Ben's life and freedom. "Judge there must be something you can do."

The judge took notice of my concern and not wanting to lose a sheriff, said, "Son, I can see you're distraught and emotional about this matter." The judge leaned back in his high-backed chair and grasped his lapels with his thumbs, "Let me dwell some on it. I'll need to read up in my law books on the laws that have been enforced and acted upon in such matters as these. Give me a few days. I'll see what I can come up with, so neither of us will be accused of breaking any laws. Fair enough, Sheriff?"

I started for the door, turned and said, "Judge you'd better find something, because I don't want the hanging of an innocent man on my conscience."

I left the judge's office, stepped across the hall and entered the mayor's office. He stood at the window, hands clasped behind his back, looking out on his kingdom. He turned as I entered and said, "Good morning, Sheriff

Chad'tu," and glanced quickly back out the window, "It is a glorious morning, wouldn't you say?"

"Yeah, sure, it's glorious if you say so." I wasn't in the best mood after the short conversation I'd had with the judge.

"Mayor, I got an idea and I wanted to run it by you and get your opinion. What would you think if I had notices printed up and posted around town?"

"It depends. What would these notices have to say?"

"Since there is only one of me and I'm spread pretty thin here and there around town, I thought it might help to post a few town rules. Rules which would apply and be enforced by me, while in our town of Tombstone.

"And what did you have in mind for these here rules to say?"

"Well Mayor, I been a thinkin. First rule, if you fire a gun in town. You get a warning. Second rule, if you fire a gun after your warning, you spend one day and night or twenty-four hours in jail. Depends on the time when you are arrested."

"Third rule, the next time you fire a gun, we take the gun and keep it, and you go to jail. Then you'd have to buy yourself a new gun. And if you shoot someone you stay in jail till the judge says what to do with you."

I had been walking back and forth in front of the mayor's desk while I espoused my idea. "Well how does it sound to you?"

"Chad'tu … Sheriff, I like that idea. Wish I'd thought of it. Maybe it'll cut down on some of the shooting going on in town, just maybe. You got my blessings Chad'tu. Have at her son." the mayor said slapping me on the back.

I went directly to the print shop upon leaving the Town Hall. Hester the owner was working on tomorrow's paper setting type into the printing press. He looked up as the bell on the door tinkled, "Sheriff Chad'tu, what can I do for you?"

"I got something I want printed up. I need some paper so I can write out what I want to say."

Hester wiped his hands on an ink-stained rag and then handed me paper and pen and said, "Let's see what you got."

I wrote down what I'd discussed with the mayor word for word. "I want at the top in large bold print, 'Notice People of Tombstone.' and the rest put below. The sooner you can print it the better this town will be. Any questions?"

Hester read what I had written. "I don't have any questions sheriff," Then he smiled. "This surely will upset a lot of people." I started to leave as Hester said, "Oh! Sheriff one question, how many copies should I print?"

I stopped at the door, thinking for a moment as I counted up the saloons and brothels and a few other places that I might post the signs, and certainly some would get torn down.

"Why don't you print up say fifty to start with and we can see how that goes. Okay?"

"Sure, and Sheriff you can pick them up after ten o'clock tomorrow." He was still shaking his head and smiling as I closed the door behind me.

CHAPTER 35

I MADE MY nightly ride through town, everything was mostly quiet. I left the horse at the stable and walked to the hotel. In my room I stripped off my clothes, washed my face and went to bed, it had been a long day.

Refreshed after a good night's sleep I was up, washed and dressed, as the sun peeked over the horizon showing its first light. Not too many people were in the dining room as I entered, only a few early risers.

I ordered steak and eggs with fried potatoes and black coffee. It came served with fresh biscuits. The cook sure did know how to make biscuits. He made the best biscuits I'd ever tasted. There was nothing I liked better than fresh biscuits, smeared with jam.

Finishing my breakfast, I signed the bill and picking up a toothpick, I started working on the steak lodged between my teeth, I stepped out on the porch, it was still early and not many people were about. I savored the crisp fresh morning air and the lack of noise.

Standing on the hotel porch, I stretched, getting some of the stiffness out of my muscles. I pulled up a nearby chair and sat a while, watching as the town came alive. "Just another day in paradise," I thought.

As I sat there, my thoughts turned to Jaydeen, as they often did. What was she doing? Did she think of me as often as I thought of her? I wondered. Did she miss me? Not being able to see her was driving me crazy.

After awhile I figured I'd better get on with my job and stop daydreaming.

I walked down to the stables and on into the barn. Brannon was busy forking hay to the horses and a couple mules. He saw me coming, "Top 'o the morning to ya Sheriff," he said, spoken with a hint of an Irish brogue.

"Is my horse fed and ready to go?" I asked.

"Aye, to be sure, he'll be ready as soon as I can water him," he replied. He led the horse over to a wooden trough filled to the top with fresh water brought by the stable boy. After drinking, the horse tossed his head in the air, flinging a spray of water over anyone that stood near. "Ain't that just like a dang horse? You give 'em water and then to show their appreciation, they toss water all over you." He said laughing and giving the horse an affectionate rub.

I saddled up, stepped into the leather and headed down the street in the direction of the print shop. I didn't have a timepiece. Riding slowly along I returned a few greetings, I looked up at the sun and guessed it must be getting on towards ten o'clock.

I stepped down from the bay and looked up and down the street, taking in all that was happening. The boardwalk and street was quickly becoming filled with the comings and goings of its busy citizens. Nothing seemed out of the ordinary.

I tied the bay to the rail and entered the print shop. The bell tinkled and I was greeted by Hester.

"Howdy sheriff, you're a might early. I'm just now finishing up the last of them notices. Give me a couple more minutes and I'll be done. A copy of today's paper is on the counter if you'd like to catch up on the latest happenings."

Picking up the paper I walked over and taking a seat by the window where the light was better, I began to read as I waited for the printing to be finished. The headline caught my eye. In big, bold, black print, it read, ' JESSE JAMES SHOT AND KILLED.' Damn I thought, they finally got him and in his own home at that. Damn, shot in the back by his friend Bob Ford. Damn!

"Hester," I called out, "Is this paper telling the truth? Jesse James was shot and killed? How did this information come to you?"

"It came by a stage coach that arrived late last night. An hour or so after dark I think. Someone on the stage had the paper stating the whole story. Everyone on the stage swore it was all true. I decided to run the story as it was printed in that paper. I can hardly believe it myself."

The press stopped its creaking and rattling. Hester took the notices and setting them on the counter, said, "Be careful, some of that ink might not be all the way dry. Just sign this here bill and they're all yours."

As I was signing, I thought, the way of the west, the gunfighters, and bank robberies, was fast becoming the history of the past.

I headed for the Emporium. I needed a hammer and some nails to put up the notices. Sam was there as usual. I told him what I needed and why I needed it. He took one of the notices and quickly read it.

With a slight smile twisting his lips and frowning, he said, "You going to hang these all over town you say? Are you sure, you want to do this? This could bring you more grief and trouble than you bargained for. Are you sure you can handle the uproar this'll bring?"

"I'm not sure of anything right now, but all this shooting inside the town has got to stop. And me being the Sheriff, I'm going to stop it. One way or another, it's going to stop."

"Okay if you're that determined to get yourself killed."

He stepped behind the counter and handed me a hammer, and a small canvas bag filled with small nails. "Here you go, everything you need to get yourself killed, no charge. When you get through with the hammer you can return it to me."

"And if you're really determined to do this. I got a bulletin board over by the front door for folks to post things to sell and buy. Everyone that comes in usual looks at it. You might as well hang one of these on it." He said, as he put an arm around me with fatherly affection. "Just you watch yourself."

"Sam thanks for your concern. I'm pretty sure I can handle things, but it sure would be nice if I had a deputy or someone to back me. Brett's too far away, but if I get into real bad trouble, he'll be here quicker than a rattler can strike."

I posted the notice on Sam's board, shook his hand and left the store.

At the saloons, I posted a notice on the wall beside the swinging butterfly doors. By the time I was posting the notice at the third saloon, word had already gone ahead. Some of the saloon owners complained it would be bad for business. That I'd better watch my back, cause some of them hombres that come to town would have it in for me. I'd be disturbing their drinking and their fun of shooting up the places and raising hell.

A few days later, I had most of the six cells in jail filled almost to the maximum.

Every night I would arrest one or two that were drunk and had ignored my sign. I would lock them up. In the morning, I'd let the ones that had spent their time loose. Finally, it felt like I was getting something accomplished.

Tombstone had quieted somewhat but still had a ways to go before I'd be satisfied. A week had gone by with only a few minor disturbances.

I was bored, falling into a pattern of the same old routine every day. One day idly passing my time, I was setting on the porch in front of the jail. A saying of Brett's popped into my head. 'Never fall into a pattern of doing the same thing, the same way, every day, because someone knowing that can lay in wait for you.'

I thought about it and could see he was right. If anyone wanted me, it would be too easy. I would have to get out of the rut I had fallen into.

I was suddenly brought back to the present when a voice reached my ears. "Señor … Señor, Sheriff!"

I took my boots down off the railing and sat up. I saw Miguel running down the street, Straw hat waving in one hand and barefooted stirring up a cloud of dust that followed. He arrived in front of me out of breath, as usual.

"What is it Miguel? Is there trouble?" I stood and put a hand on his shoulder, "Calm down, catch your breath. What has happened that you must run so quickly to tell me?"

"Señor Sheriff," Miguel took a deep breath and blurted out. "John he say to run to sheriff … and tell sheriff … there is some new man in saloon of Lucky Lady. We never see him before. He be a stranger. Miguel took another breath and he look like maybe he want kill somebody. We don know for sure. He be askin' question … about the sheriff. John, he want you know."

Every time I start to get some peace and quiet and relax, something always happens.

"Miguel! Stop fidgeting. Tell me what does this man look like? Can you describe him for me? So I would know him on sight."

"Si, Si, Señor Sheriff. I tell you. He have a grey hat on head, dusty black boots, and black pants and … and a, how you say plad shirt?"

"You mean plaid shirt?"

"Si, he have a grey plad shirt. And he have on the gun."

"Was he wearing one or two guns? How did he wear his gun? Was it up high or down low?"

"Si Sheriff, I know." Miguel said holding up two fingers, "He have dos guns he wear down low like you. And they be tied around leg like you do."

Damn, just what I need in town another gunslinger. "How old did he look to be?"

"Maybe I think he look a little older than you. Maybe old as señor John … maybe? Not sure. And Señor Sheriff, he be a big tall handsome man. Señor John, he say, you should be careful."

"Miguel, has this hombre caused any trouble at the saloon?"

"No, he no cause any trouble. He have a drink and ask questions a lot. No trouble yet."

"Okay, Miguel. I guess I'd better take a look at this stranger before any trouble happens. You run on back and tell John I'll be along shortly. Okay?"

"Si, I go now, tell John, adios Sheriff." He ran off up the street leaving a trail of dust that hung in the air a moment before it settled.

I went inside the jail got my rifle and hat, then went out front, stepped into the saddle, and headed for the Lucky Lady Saloon. Maybe I might be riding into trouble, only one way to find out. Face it.

I tied the bay to the rail, stepped up on the porch, and swung in through the butterfly doors. I made a quick survey of the room. Everything seemed normal and peaceful. I walked to the end of the bar and John met me holding a glass of beer. He said in a low voice, "Howdy Sheriff. Did you get my message?"

"Yeah John, thanks for warning me." I took a sip of beer and with my elbows on the rail, I leaned forward. I looked for an unfamiliar face as I checked out the drinkers standing at the bar. My eyes travel from face to face, one by one, till I got three quarters of the way down the bar, and stopped on the grey plaid shirt. A face I didn't know was standing there drinking a whisky. It was a handsome face that had a deadly look about it.

Now I knew what Miguel had meant.

I looked slowly around the room for any other faces that I might not know and hadn't seen before. Grey shirt was the only one that was a new face. I didn't see anyone else that looked like they were new in town.

I'd already taken the leather thong off the hammer of my guns before coming through those swinging doors. I was ready for anything. Holding the beer in my left hand, I moved down the bar toward the handsome stranger. I edged into an open space to the left of the tall, lean, hard looking man. If need be I'd have my right hand unimpeded and ready to draw.

I stood there for a minute or two sipping on my beer, waiting to see if he would do anything. He didn't. He stood there seemingly unaware of me, sipping on his whiskey.

After awhile I struck up a conversation trying to find out who this man was and what business he might have in Tombstone. I started off with, "You're new in town aren't you? I don't believe I've seen you around and I know most everybody hereabouts. You just ride in today?"

He turned toward me and his eyes immediately flashed down, and back, so quickly that if I'd blinked, I'd have missed that quick look. That look, took in my tied-down double rig.

I could tell by the quick glance this man probably didn't miss much, if anything. If he was as fast with his guns as he was with his eyes, this man was someone to be wary of, for surely he would be very fast with his guns.

The stranger took a sip from the glass in his right hand, and said, "Yes, to your first question, and no you haven't seen me before, to your second question. And yes, I just now got into town to your third question. And this here is my second drink if you were going to ask. Do you object?" he said, in a mildly pleasant voice that held no animosity that I could discern.

He seemed polite enough, but so do a lot of cold-blooded gunslingers. I sipped on my beer taking my time and thinking about what to do next.

Making no moves, he stood there quietly sipping on his whisky. I was at a loss of what to do next. If Brett were here, he would know what to do. Brett always made friends with everyone if he could. He always gave everyone the benefit of his doubt. So I would try doing the same.

"Since you're new in town ... might I buy you a drink? I see your glass is almost empty." I offered.

"Why sure! You can buy me all the drinks you want. I'm not one to turn down a drink when it's offered, as long as the one offering is a friendly sort, which you seem to be."

I called John over and said, "John I want to buy this here feller a drink." John looked at me and raised his eyebrows with a look that said, 'you're crazy out of your head.'

"Yes sirre, John! Indeed! I said loudly, I want to buy this man a drink and welcome him to Tombstone. Give mister ... I turned and said, "I didn't catch your name. You might be?"

Smiling and in a deep pleasant voice he said, "You didn't catch the name because I didn't throw it." He laughed at his joke. "But the name is Jake, Jake Brandon and if you were going to ask where I'm from. I'm from down El Paso way, and if you got more questions, fire away."

I thought this guy has a real sense of humor. I heard of guys like this. Sometimes you didn't know if they were fooling with you or not.

He said, "Had a friend, I heard was up this way. Thought I'd stop by and say hello. Anything else you want to know, just you ask away, Friend!" He said the friend part a little sarcastically.

"I didn't mean to offend you Jake. I was just curious who you were, and where you might be from, that's all. I didn't mean nothing by it."

"No offense taken ... friend!" He sat his empty glass down and John was quick to fill it on my behalf. Jake raised his glass toward me in a gesture of thanks and taking a sip set the glass on the bar.

He said, "Friend, I have answered all your questions that you asked, and yet you still have not told me your name. If we're to be friends, I need to call you something besides 'Friend.' Or maybe Friend is your name?" He chuckled. "Don't you have another name that you go by?" he asked. With a twinkle of an eye and a smile on his face, he picked up his whisky. "And thanks for the drink," he said, taking a swallow.

Maybe he was leading me on, maybe he was out to get me. I didn't see how I could sidestep this one. I looked him in the eye. Brett always said if you were close enough to a man, always watch his eyes. His eyes would tell you when he was about to make a move.

I watched Jakes eyes for a reaction as I said, "You can call me Chad or Chad'tu or if you like by my official name ... Sheriff." I waited for the reaction that I was sure would come. I got a reaction alright, but it was one that took me by surprise, one that was completely unexpected, and that I was totally unprepared for.

"Well Chad'tu, it's a pleasure to finally meet you. I've been looking forward to meeting you ever since I heard about you. You look just exactly as described to me."

I must have had a puzzled expression on my face, along with some sign of apprehension showing. He could tell I was tense. He tossed down the rest of his whisky and smiled a brotherly smile, and said, "Don't worry; I'm not here to gun you down. I know all about you." He told me a few things about myself that only Brett and I knew. I couldn't believe this man knowing these things. Who was this man? How did he know all these things?

"You look just as Brett described you. Only you're a little bigger and a little brighter than he said you were." He clasped me on the shoulder, and laughed at my expression, an expression, which must have shown utter confusion at this point.

"Brett and I are old friends, we go way back to when men were real men and nobody fooled with us. Brett and I were the best of the best. Probably still are, the best gun hands that could be found anywhere in this country, and that's a fact. Although Brett did say if you'd been around at that time in our lives, there would have been three best guns. He says you're that good."

This man Jake was now treating me like a long lost brother when we had only just met. He was carrying on as if he'd known me all my life. Jake told me about him and Brett when they were younger and more than just a little wild. How they survived was a miracle he said, unless it was due to the fact that they were faster than any one with a gun.

The shadows were lengthening across the floor. It was sundown and soon it would be dark. It got dark quickly out here in the desert. "Jake it's getting late. Why don't we head over to the hotel and get something to eat. They got real good home cooked food. We could talk some more. I'd like to hear more about Brett. He won't tell me much about himself. What do ya say?"

"Sounds right good, I ain't had nothing since breakfast and my gut is telling me it's hungry."

We left the Lucky Lady, like two long lost friends that had just been reunited. Jake rode a big grey stallion. It was a handsome horse. I was beginning to understand a little about Jake, and I assumed the rest. Take for example the grey stallion, it matched his clothes, and altogether everything about him, was not to draw attention. At a distance, he and the horse could blend in with almost any type of country. To most eyes, he would be not easily seen or noticed, almost invisible to the naked eye. Untying our horses, we mounted up and rode to the hotel. On the way, I thought I'd had a pretty good horse in the bay that I rode, but after seeing Jake's I had second thoughts.

The hotel had a small area, with a bucket of water, a dipper and a basin, set to one side with towels as you entered the dining room. If a person wanted, they could wash their hands—if they were so disposed to do so. We hung our hats on the hat rack standing by the doorway. Then we availed ourselves, washed, and dried our hands. We sat at a table in the corner that was empty.

I had to laugh as we both sat with our backs to a wall and facing the door. That was the manner of a man used to using a gun. Always sit with your back to a wall was the rule, and most abided by it. The pretty waitress who was young and flirty didn't wait on us. I was disappointed. Instead we were waited on by a big jovial woman, must have weighed at least two hundred pounds, I'd guess. The wood floor creaked as she walked across it, but for all her size, she moved lightly on her feet like a ballerina.

We both ordered the T-bone steaks; it came with a healthy helping of brown beans along with a couple thick slices of homemade bread and butter. A cowpoke's delight.

After we had eaten our fill, Jake started to pay for his steak. I held up a hand, palm out and stopped him. "This supper is on me, and the town of Tombstone," I said. Jake watched as I signed the bill.

Jake looked a little puzzled. "You always just sign for what you want?"

"Yeah Jake, anything I want. I just sign my name and the town pays for it. A hell of a deal don't you think?"

"Better deal than I had down in El Paso." Jake replied.

"You were the sheriff down there?"

"Well sorta, I got paid for all the hombres I put in jail."

We took our hats from the rack and donning them, strode out onto the porch. I sat on the porch railing as Jake took out a small bag of tobacco. He rolled a smoke, stuck it between his lips and holding a struck match to the cigarette, he lighted it. It was a lovely evening in Tombstone.

While Jake smoked I said, "Tell me Jake, if you were just passing through, where you headed?"

A thought slowly started forming somewhere in my head, as I waited for his answer.

"Nowhere in particular, just riding and seeing more of the country till my money runs out. Then I s 'pose I'll have'ta get me a job." he said. Taking a seat on a nearby chair, he relaxed enjoying the smoke. Nothing was said for a while as he smoked.

I finally broke the silence, "Jake, I don't know how your money is holding out. You may have plenty or you might be almost broke. I'm not prying," I added quickly. "You say you're in no hurry to get anywhere ... and I been a-thinking. I was talked into this job, beings the former sheriff got himself shot and killed. I swung me a mighty fine deal in becoming sheriff of this here town. But to be honest, there are other things I'd rather be doing." Like seeing Jaydeen, I thought.

"And I was just thinking, since you're in no hurry. Might you see your way to help me out in bringing law and order to Tombstone? You could be my deputy, and when I was out of town, you'd have full reign over things. And too, I'm pretty sure that when I resign, the town would offer you the sheriff's job." Taking a deep breath, I waited. Knowing not what kind of response I would get, if any. Jake did not say a word. He just sat there smoking on his cigarette.

When he didn't answer I said, "Jake you could become Sheriff of Tomb-stone. It pays really well."

All I could see in the dusk was the glow of his cigarette. Still he did not answer. Maybe he just needed a little more convincing, I thought.

"Brett said, anytime I needed him he would come running to help me out. Think about it Jake. You could see Brett any time you wanted. No one could stand up to the three of us ... No one!

You could take some time off from your travels and replenish your money too. You said you got no place to go, you're just drifting through. And I would really like to hear more of your adventures with Brett."

Jake stood and dropping the cigarette on the porch, stepped on it with a twist of his boot, putting it out. "Damn kid! Don't you ever shut up? I'm trying to think. Yeah, all those things you say sound good, real good ... but I don't know ... I don't know if I want to be a lawman again. Let me think on it tonight, I'll let you know in the morning. Okay, kid?"

"Sure Jake, take all the time you want." I didn't want to make him anymore upset than I already had. "Where you staying the night Jake, you got a room anywhere?"

"Yeah, Chad," ... He stopped in mid sentence. "You know, the name Chad, doesn't fit the way you look and act. If you don't mine, I'll just call you Chad'tu." Putting an arm across my shoulder in a brotherly manner he said, "Seems to me Chad'tu would be a more appropriate name for a gunfighter sheriff such as you. And yes I got a room, right here in this hotel."

"That's right handy, I stay here too. Maybe we can have breakfast here in the morning and you can give me your answer then. That be okay with you?"

"Yeah, that's fine Chad'tu. It's too early for bed, what say we mosey over to a saloon and have a couple? Make us sleep better, and it don't hurt none to have the sheriff around in case some one wants to cause trouble." And off we went.

CHAPTER 36

PUSHING THROUGH THE swinging doors of the Lucky Lady, we were greeted by the smell of tobacco smoke that hung in the room like a grey cloud. It was noisy inside as usual, made by the many conversations, along with sounds of laughter, and scattered here and there cusswords. Everyone seemed to be having a good time. No sign of trouble.

John the bartender made his way toward us, stopping now and then talking to a customer. He finally got to us and asked, "What'll ya have, Sheriff?"

I said, "John I want you to meet Jake, a friend of Brett's and me."

"You're the fella that was doing all the asking about the sheriff. Pleased to meetcha, Jake. Now what can I get fer you fellas?" We both ordered beer. "Right lively crowd you got here tonight." I said, as John set two foaming beers on the bar.

"Yep, it shor is. Most of these hombres are from the cattle drive. They set up camp a little ways out from town. They're just passing through on the way to Tucson." he pointed down the bar. "You see that fella with the dirty big brim hat and grey beard. He's the boss trail driver. He says."

I turned to Jake and said "Want to take a ride out with me in the morning and check a few brands on that herd? See if they haven't picked up any strays with brands along the way that don't belong to them."

"Sounds like a right good idea you got there Chad'tu. If you hadn't said it, I'd have suggested as much to you. We'll have to get up early before they start moving them," he said finishing his beer. "We'd better turn in and get some shuteye. Most cattlemen start extra early in the day, before sunrise."

I gulped down the last of my beer, "I'm right behind you."

The next morning before sunup, we had our breakfast, saddled up, and were on our way out to look over the herd. The sky was just starting to lighten as we reached their campsite.

We found the man that John had pointed out to us at the bar, or rather he found us. He rode up, and asked. "What can I do fer you folks?"

"I'm the town sheriff and this is my deputy. We thought we might check a few brands on your cattle. That is, if you don't astonished look, as I'd said he was my deputy.

The boss trail driver said, "My name is Potter. You all are sure welcome to do all the checking you want. You go right ahead Sheriff. You and your deputy check all you want. But you won't find any brand other than the Rocking W." He went on, "And if you do, you're welcome to them."

Jake and I split up and steered our horses in and out among the milling herd looking for a brand that was not the Rocking W. I figured they must be close to two thousand head of cattle.

After a half-hour of checking, I waved Jake over using my hat to get his attention. We stopped our horses face to face. I asked Jake, "You see any brands that don't belong?"

"Nope, nary a one," was Jakes reply.

We rode over to the head man and I said, "Mister Potter, I thank you kindly for allowing us to look over your cattle. They look mighty fine and passed our inspection. And good luck on the rest of your drive."

We had hardly ridden a hundred yards when Jake jumped all over me. "What'd you say I was your deputy for? I didn't tell you if I would take that job. My answer was going to be this morning, and you know it."

"Don't get your feathers ruffled Jake. It was the easiest way to explain who you were. It's all I could think of at the time." We rode a ways without speaking. Finally, I said, "You did have all night to think it over. And ...?"

"Well," he paused, and then he burst out laughing as loud as he could. He slapped his leg. Tears were streaming down his cheeks. Finally, he got his laughter under control. Wiping the tears from his eyes he said, "I got you! You thought I was mad. I fooled you really good, didn't I?"

"Well ... I don't think it's all that funny. Yeah, you did have me fooled." I said, as I started to laugh at myself. "Yeah, you really got me a good one. Brett must have told you about the jokes we play on one another."

Jake pulled up his horse and we stopped. He said, "I did think a lot about all we spoke of last night and I did make a decision on it. And I decided," He paused looking for my reaction.

My reaction was quick to come. "For heaven's sake tell me what was your decision?"

He spaced his words and said, "I decided … I'll … be your deputy. How's does that suit you? Now are you satisfied?" If we hadn't been on horseback, I swear I would have hugged him. I was overjoyed that Jake was taking the job as my deputy.

Sitting there on our horses, I swore Jake in as my deputy before he could change his mind. I made Jake raise his right hand and I said, "Do you swear to uphold the laws of Tombstone and this territory of Arizona. Now it's official." I said. "You are now a genuine, bonafide deputy of Tombstone, except for the badge that goes with the job. I'll get one for you soon as we get back to town."

We rode into Tombstone and stopping at the town hall, I turned to Jake saying, "The mayor and the judge will want to meet my new deputy."

The judge didn't have much to say except it would probably mean more court work for him. He didn't appear to be happy to now have two law officers in town. On the other hand, the mayor was overjoyed till he heard how much it would cost the town. The mayor had asked, in an offhand manner, what I was going to pay Jake.

My new friend and now my new first deputy, pushed his hat back from his forehead and said, before I could get out a word, "He offered me sixty dollars a month, along with all the benefits." Jake looked at me with his pale blue eyes and winked.

The mayor's face turned red and he started sputtering, "That it was too damn much."

My mouth hung open. I'd offered Jake fifty dollars a month and no benefits. I could tell he was pulling the mayors leg. That Jake had a real funny sense of humor. I didn't know whether to laugh at the mayors' expression, or dispute the amount of money Jake had mentioned. I had no chance to do either.

Jake said, "Mayor I see your consternation and quandary over my out burst. And I do apologize for my sense of humor." He took off his hat and swinging it low, cavalier-like across the front of his body, bowed low before the mayor and said, "Please sir, do accept my sincere apology."

Jake smiled his best smile and then said, "Mayor, you don't mind if I call you Bill, do you? Mayor is so formal, don't you think?" The mayor turned an even deeper red and I thought he was going to have an apoplexy attack. We finally got him into his chair and I poured him a class of water from a white pitcher which sat on his desk. I took the newspaper from the desktop and started fanning the mayor. He took a drink of water and he started to calm somewhat.

Jake said, "Bill I didn't mean to upset you. So, tell you what I'm going to do for you and this fine town. I'll cut my pay from sixty down to ..." Jake paused dramatically. Walking back and forth in front of the mayor's desk for a moment, he stopped suddenly, turned and faced the mayor, and went on ... "Let's say down to fifty a month and benefits."

He was like a shark circling its prey. He paused again watching the mayor's reaction. "Oh! Yeah, I almost forgot the best part. And a dollar for every one I arrest that gets convicted, that fair enough for you Bill?"

By this time, Bill was the color of purple, and he couldn't have told you his name if you'd asked. He choked, fumed, and hawed. Then in a squeaky voice that hardly could be heard said, "Yes, Yes, that's fine son."

The mayor nervously reached out with a hand that shook and opening a drawer, reached in and fumbling around, pulled forth a shiny badge that had an indentation stamped on it reading Deputy Sheriff. He tossed it onto the desktop saying, "There you are Jake. Please try to keep the peace without too much shooting, if at all possible. And remember Jake you are now the second in command of the law in Tombstone."

That mayor surely was a windbag if ever I did see one. All he liked to do was use big words and talk a lot.

On our way out of the mayors office Jake pined on the badge and said, "Chad'tu there is something I should remind you of, for a time I was a bounty hunter. This is not the first badge I have ever worn. Not to brag, but as a matter of fact, I was the sheriff in several towns. Also I have been a U.S. marshal."

I looked at Jake with new respect. "No," I answered, "I did not know of those things. Brett has never spoke of you to me."

With a mischievous twinkle in his eye he said, "Between the two of us it shouldn't take long, till we have this town cleaned up. Don't you agree?"

"Yeah Jake, we'll have it cleaned up right soon." I had my doubts. "Those notices you posted around town was a hell of a good idea. Did you think that up by yourself, or did someone else?"

"Jake, give me a little credit. If those notices don't work, wait till I tell you my next idea. Most all the trouble is caused by guns. We make them turn in their guns at the jail when they come into town. Then when they leave, we give their guns back. No guns, no trouble, right?"

Jake shrugged his big broad shoulders, "Sounds good to me and it might work if we don't have to kill 'em to get 'em to give up their guns." he laughed.

For sure, that Jake has a strange sense of humor I thought.

"Jake lets make a round of the town and let everyone get a look at you, our new town deputy, and maybe get to know you a little."

We walked up one side of Main Street, then down the other side. Being friendly and smiling we walked along saying howdy and hello and sometimes shaking hands. We ended up in front of the Lucky Lady Saloon, by accident, luck, or just plain old fashion planning.

We strolled inside and waited for John to work his way to us. We greeted John, and ordered two beers. All that walking had made us thirsty.

Jake, rubbed his right hand and shook it, trying to get feeling back into it. "I ain't never in my life shaken so many hands before. That big fellow, the black smith, damn near crushed my hand. He has a grip like a vise and if I never have to shake another hand, it'll be too soon,"

"Jake," I said, "It's a darn good thing you're left-handed. We wouldn't want anything to happen to your shooting hand, now would we? You wouldn't be much good as a deputy if you couldn't shoot."

"Don't cha worry any about my shooting. I might only wear one gun on my left hip sometimes, but that don't mean I can't shoot with t'other hand. You remember the first time we met I was wearing two guns. Whenever I'm going into a situation, I always wear two guns."

"Chad'tu not to brag, cause I don't like braggarts. I'd bet ... I'm as fast ... or maybe even faster than you at drawing and firing and hitting what I aim to hit." Then as an afterthought he smiled and poked me good-naturedly in the ribs with an elbow, and said "You young whippersnapper."

"Well someday we maybe can have us a little contest. That should be fun. Jake we might even make it a three-way contest if we could tempt Brett to join us. That ought to make it even more fun, don't you think?"

Sipping on my beer, I thought about the contest I'd had with Sid and the appaloosa colt I'd won. "Jake all this talking about a contest reminded me. I won a bet from my friend Sid. He and his father have a cattle ranch, northwest of here. I'd say takes about a day or so to ride out there."

Jake looked at me. He could tell I was getting excited, by the way I rattled on. "It must have been a really large bet to get you all this excited, and you had forgotten it till now. So tell me Chad'tu what have you won, that has you so excited?"

I couldn't tell him about Jaydeen. He would probably just poke fun at me. "I said you won't believe this but I won the prettiest little appaloosa colt you ever did see. I need to ride out there and bring her back to Brett's and my place. I want to get started on her training and get her used to me"

"Now that you're the deputy, you can handle things in town, and I can take me a couple days or so off to get her. I can stop on the way and tell Brett all the good news about us. About you being a lawman again. Would that be okay, Jake?" Jake could see my mind was made up. It would do no good to tell me no.

CHAPTER 37

NEXT MORNING AFTER breakfast, I rode out on the way to get the appaloosa, and to see Jaydeen. Stopping at the gun store to see Brett I noticed he had hung a sign on a post out by the road. It read "GUNSMITH, New and Used Guns," and under that was printed; "We repair or modify to owner satisfaction."

Brett greeted me at the door with a bear hug and exclaimed, "Howdy partner, it's been awhile since I seen you. Tell me what's new with you?"

"Let me think." I rolled my eyes up toward the ceiling and shrugging my shoulders repeated his question back at him. "What's new with me, you ask. Well, for one thing, I got me a deputy. A right handy man I'd say except he's left-handed." I said laughing, trying to joke and make light of it.

Brett said. "Now who would be foolish enough to want to be a deputy, especially in a town like Tombstone?" Brett's expression was a mixture of dis-belief and that I might be joking with him.

"Some gunslinger rode into town, and before we had a showdown, to see whose gun was the fastest, and who would be the first to die. I thought to myself what would Brett do in a situation like that. Why, I'd bet Brett would charm and sweet-talk this gunslinger into becoming his deputy. So since, you taught me everything, that's what I did. I started talkin to the gunman and didn't stop till he said okay, he'd take the job."

I could tell Brett didn't believe a word of this tall tale that I told.

"Hell Brett, you know a lot of gunmen. You probably know this one. In fact, he did say something to the effect that the two of you had some sort of shootout down El Paso way. At least I think that's what he said."

I could see Brett was thinking hard. I really had him going this time. I'd finally got him a good one. I could not control myself any longer and finally burst out laughing at the expression on his face. I laughed and laughed till my sides hurt. Curbing my laughter I pointed my finger at him and said, "I got you real good that time. Admit it!"

Brett said, "Yeah you really got me good. Was this all a joke you pulled on me or do you really have a deputy?"

"I do have a deputy." I said, trying to draw it out as long as I could. "Would you like to know his name?"

"Getting information out of you is like pulling teeth from of a rooster's mouth. Spit it out and tell me this mysterious gunman's name."

"He goes by the name Jake, Jake Brandon. He told me the two of you use to ride together. He told me a lot of stories of all the shenanigans you two pulled. And I don't believe half of it."

"If Jake told you a story you'd better believe it's true. One thing about Jake, he always tells the truth. ... Well most of the time anyway."

"You okay Brett, being all along out here? I'm sorry not to have been able to get out for a visit. But now that I have Jake for a deputy, I can have more time to do some of the things that I want."

Brett answered, "I'm so busy repairing guns, don't have a chance to get lonesome, let alone bored. But it sure would be nice to see your ugly face once in a while." He laughed at my expression. "You know, I think of you as the younger brother I never had and I do miss not being able to see you now and then. So it surely would be nice if you could stop by more often."

"I miss our times together as much or more than you do." I answered. "Oh! By the way, thanks for sending Jake to see me. Without Jake, I'd still be stuck in town most of the time. Now I can come visit you on the way out to see Jaydeen and Sid."

"How did you ever talk Jake into being a deputy sheriff? That's what I'd like to know."

"This is the way it went down. You know John, the bartender at the Lucky Lady?"

Brett interrupted me saying, "Yes I know John. Isn't that where you got drunk one night?"

Ignoring Brett's interruption, I went on with my story. "Well John sent a message to me that some gunslinger was in town asking questions about the sheriff. I thought maybe some one had sent him to kill me. I didn't think I had made any enemies yet, but you never can tell."

"Anyway, I was watchful and ready for anything that might happen. I entered the bar and spotted the man right away. I walked down the bar, eased in beside him, and started a conversation trying to find out who he was and what he might be up to. Come to find out he knew who I was, but I still didn't know who he was. He kept talking and telling me things about me that I could hardly remember."

"Then he laughed at me. I was ready to hit him but I didn't … and then you know what he said? Brett told me all about you, and he laughed some more. I didn't know what to do, so I just stood there like a statue. He got me a real good one didn't he? It was your fault so that's why I had to get you back, didn't I?"

"Yeah little brother, you surely did get me a good one."

I stayed the night and caught Brett up on all that was going on in town.

We were late going to bed. It was like old times.

Being with Brett it just seemed like last week that I'd left to take some time off, and somehow got all caught up in this mess of being sheriff, all because of my visit with Sid. But reflecting back on it, it must have been more like three months. I didn't know. Who keeps track anyway. I felt more a man and so much more grown up than before.

I said adios to Brett, and was on my way, as the sun showing its bright face, rose above the arid desert plains. The thought of soon seeing my friends and especially the lovely Jaydeen gave me a warm glow. Sometime in the afternoon, I saw the low range of hills in the distance that the ranch nestled among. Urging the big bay into stepping out a little faster, my heart beat in anticipation.

Topping the rise, I pulled up the bay. I sat for a moment, looking down on the green lush meadows of the ranch. Smoke was rising from the chimney of the sprawling ranch house. Glancing at the sun, I'd say I was just about in time for supper. I sat there contemplating what they might be having for the evening meal.

A flash of light caught my eye from off a distant hill. It had come from the hill that rose behind and to the left of the house. I looked more closely at the spot from whence the flash had come. With the naked eye and at this distance, all I could see was a small dark spot. It could be a rider. Maybe Sid or his foreman Trace coming in for the evening.

I sat there awhile longer contemplating, I was curious about that dark spot. Then I remembered an old pair of long-range field binoculars in the saddlebags. Turning in the saddle I reached back undid the leather thong and flipped open the flap. Reaching inside, I rummaged around for the glasses, finally my fingers curled around the cold hard glasses. Pulling them out I dusted the glass lens with my kerchief. Satisfied with the cleaning job, I put the glasses to my eyes and adjusted the tuning knob in the center till the distant hill came into focus.

Moving the glasses back and forth across the hillside, I looked for what might have caused the flash that had caught my attention. I swung past a spot and then swung quickly back to look more closely.

Yes! There he was, a lone rider setting on a buckskin horse. He didn't appear to be moving. I tried to focus the glasses for a better image. That first flash of light, that had caught my attention, must have been a reflection of the sun from his glasses. The rider was doing the same thing I was; only he was looking toward the house with his glasses. What the hell is going on here? I wondered as I started on down the slope toward the ranch house.

Tying the bay to the hitching rail, I stepped away and gave out a loud shout, "Hello anybody at home?" There was no answer. Then suddenly the door was flung wide and framed in the doorway stood Jaydeen.

My heart skipped a beat. Standing there wiping her hands with a dishtowel was the love of my life, the woman I was determined to marry. The flowered apron tied around her did nothing to hide her womanly curves. Nor did the denim jeans and shirt she wore.

She was surprised when she saw me. "Chad, this is a pleasant surprise. It's been a while since your last visit. Quiet some time I must say. You're looking well. Come on in and catch me up on things."

Every time I saw Jaydeen, my tongue got all twisted up and I had a hard time talking. "Jay ... Jaydeen, I missed you." I stuttered, then quickly added, "And Sid and Trace too. Where are they? I can't wait to see them."

"They'll be along soon, its time for supper and they never miss supper. I missed you too you silly boy. I'd give you a hug but you can see my hands are covered with flour. I was about ready to put the pie I was making into the oven, and before you ask its apple. You do like apple pie don't you?"

"You made it special for me, didn't you? You must have known I was coming, cause apple is my favorite."

She motioned to one of the chairs beside the large table in the middle of the kitchen. "Sit down and make yourself to home."

"How did things turn out with …?" she hesitated, then said, "You know, the rustler you captured, and the one that was killed?" She gave a slight shudder.

I was about to reply to her question, when in came Sid, followed by Trace.

"Chad! I thought that was your horse out there." Sid said. "It's been awhile, how the heck are you?" He said giving me a big hug as I stood.

When he let go hugging me, Trace reached out his hand and we shook. "Good to see you again." he said. "We were just talking about you and wondering how you made out with the sheriff in Tombstone."

"That's what Jaydeen was just asking and wanting to know. I was just about to explain to her what all's been going on since I left here. Now that were all together, I only have to explain once, all the things that have happened since I last saw you."

With all of us sitting around the kitchen table, I started telling the events of the last few weeks. Supper was forgotten for the moment, as I revealed the events that had followed my departure.

After sitting in the saddle and riding all day, I didn't sit for long, my backside was feeling some aches. Standing, my coat fell open showing my vest with the silver star pinned to it. A gasp escaped from Sid, "What the hell …?" Followed by the question, "Is that a badge?"

They all stood and came close to look at the badge. I stretched out my hands trying to calm them. "Okay? I'll explain everything. Please sit down and let me tell you." They couldn't wait for me to explain. I started over again.

"The ride to Tombstone was uneventful," I said, "No surprises. The surprise was on reaching town to find the sheriff had been shot and was dead."

Trace didn't give a hoot if there was no sheriff. "Well did you hang that thieving cattle rustler?" He asked.

"Well no, we ain't hanged him yet. You see, him and me, we sort of … became friends. He say's he's just a plain old cowpoke and didn't know about the rustling scheme. And I believe him."

I told how I had put Ben in jail and with no sheriff to watch him. "Then I went to see the mayor and to complain. That's when he sweet-talked me into becoming the sheriff. That's why I ain't been out to see you all. I have been tied up in town trying to keep the peace."

"But we caught them red-handed." Trace said emphatically. "And further more, if you're caught in the act, you ought to hang. That there's the law in these here parts." They both said as one.

"Yeah, I know, but what if he's really innocent? I don't want to hang an innocent man."

"The Judge agrees with me. He's trying to find some law in his law books that says we can let him go free. Or maybe let him go with a lesser punishment, than to hang by his neck. If you got to know Ben like I have, you'd see he's a good man. He just threw in with the wrong bunch and got caught."

While we had been talking, Jaydeen had been busy. She had finished cooking supper while she'd listen to my problems. "Let's eat." she said, putting the food on the table. While we ate, we talked. I would look at Jaydeen out of the corner of my eye, and sometimes I'd catch her sneaking a peak in my direction. We took turns glancing at one another. Somehow, I just knew she had a feeling for me.

Forking a bite of beef into my mouth, I remembered the rider I'd seen on the way in. "Sid, you having any trouble here since we caught those rustlers?" I asked. "On my way in I saw a rider watching your house. He had field binoculars."

Sid replied, "You know, it's the damnedest thing, bout two weeks after we ran off the rustlers, we started seeing a lone rider now and then. When we'd ride toward him, he'd ride off. It's the damnedest thing. We don't know who they are, or what they might be after. Don't see 'em every day, only maybe once a week, sometimes twice. They seem to be waiting for something. Dang if I know what it could be."

Jaydeen took the steaming pie from the oven to cool. I could smell the cinnamon and apples. It sure did smell good. After the pie was cool enough, we each had a large piece with our coffee. It was heaven. I could see Jaydeen and me in a house such as this one, a house that I would build for her. And she would fix me meals, after a hard day's work.

Changing the subject I asked, "How's that young appaloosa filly doing? She should be about big enough to ride by now, wouldn't you say?"

Sid answered my question, "Yeah, she's big enough and old enough to ride, but we kind of were waiting for you to be the first to ride her, since she's your horse. Jay and Trace have been putting in some time with her. Mostly Jay's done all the work. Ain't that right sis?"

She blushed as she looked at me saying, "I wouldn't exactly call it work. It's more like me having fun with the filly. She is one smart horse if you ask me. When we get together and I tell her something, it appears she could read my thoughts, but most of the time she does what I want before I tell her. Then other times she gets a stubborn streak and just wants to run around me playful and teasing like ... "she glanced quickly at me" ... like girls some times do." Jaydeen quickly stood, saying shyly, she had to do the dishes.

I offered to help, as I picked up a couple plates and carried them over, setting them down beside the dishpan.

She declined my help and said, "No Chad, you go on out on the porch with the boys and have a smoke. I'll have these dishes cleaned up in no time and be out to join you all."

I guess she didn't know I didn't smoke. I never had picked up that habit, at least not yet. The three of us sat out on the porch watching the sun as it slowly slipped below the low-lying hills, casting a red orange glow above their tops and then was lost.

We sat and discussed many different things, including what those lone riders were up to. We could come to no conclusions about the riders, but we all sort of agreed that it might have something to do with the rustler incident.

CHAPTER 38

BEFORE SUN UP the next morning, we were having breakfast as the sun peaked out from a cloud-streaked sky and fell across the valley. It looked ike rain. This time of year, you could never tell which way the weather might go.

I was eager to see the appaloosa, but not so eager that I would pass up the chance to help Jaydeen clean up the breakfast clutter. She washed and I dried. We spoke little, but she smiled at me now and then.

When we had finished with the chore, she poked me in the arm and gig gled, "Come on, let's go see that filly of yours." Before I could poke her back, was out the door and running for the barn and corral. I chased after her but couldn't catch her. She was too fast. She was leaning on the corral railing, laughing when I caught up.

"Hey slowpoke, you finally made it. I thought maybe you'd show up sometime tomorrow," she said, looking over the railing. I followed her look and my eyes fell on the appaloosa that was walking over. Jay climbed up and sitting on the top rail spoke in a soft voice as the appey came to her out-stretched hand. The appey nuzzled her with a push of her soft nose in greeting.

The appey had grown since I'd last seen her, I'd guess three or more months ago. She sure was a beautiful horse and petted by an even more beau tiful woman. The horse was mine, and soon, I hoped the woman would be also. That's all there was to it, I'd expect.

"Well, what have you and Trace been teaching my horse?" I asked.

"We taught her to come when we whistle or when she sees us. We got her halter-broke. She leads and follows well. We got her over being skittish. She stands steady as we groom her. Isn't that enough?"

"Yeah I suppose so. I was only kidding. I think you have done wonderfully well with her."

I reached my hand out to the appey and she snorted and jerked her head back. Her dark eyes flashed open wide showing the whites as she sprang back and raced around the enclosed area. She finally settled down and came back towards us, cautious yet curious. She stretched out her head and approached us apprehensively her nostril's snorting and flared smelling.

Jay took my hand in hers, and we reached out toward the filly. Jay trying in her soft sweet voice to coax the appey not to be afraid of this stranger that sat alongside her. We climbed down from the railing to the ground inside the corral. Taking turns, we tried getting the appey to come to us. The appey would readily come to Jay, but with me, it was a different matter.

The appey would come close if my back was turned away from her. She'd walk cautiously one short step at a time, with ears pointed forward and smell me. When I turned very slowly to face her, she would give a snort, shake her head then take off running around the corral. We worked with the appey, trying to get her familiar and used to me, till late in the morning. It didn't appear to me I was making much headway. That filly had a mind of her own.

Jay said she was going in the house to fix something for us to eat, as it was getting along towards noontime. On her way she called out, "Keep trying, Chad. Don't give up. You'll get her used to you yet. Sometimes it takes a lot of patience to achieve a goal. But the main thing, Chad, is you just have to have a little faith."

Shortly after Jay left, I gave up and sitting on the ground leaned back against a corral post, I was thoroughly disgusted. I sat there chewing on a piece of straw, ignoring the whole scene and the appey. With my hat pushed forward, low over my closed eyelids, I sat thinking. What should I try next? What's the next step I should take?

A gentle nudge on my shoulder brought me back to the present. I just sat there not moving. Again there was a nudge against my shoulder this one was a little more forceful. I opened my eyes, still not moving. Peeking under the brim of my hat, I saw two hooves and a large velvety nose. I got a third nudge that almost knocked me over.

I raised my head and there stood the appey. I pushed back my hat and sat there looking at this horse of mine. She gave a kind of whistle through her nose. I reached out a hand. She smelled it, then gave me another nudge, to get up. I stood up and she didn't shy away. We stood face-to-face, friends at last. Maybe she wanted to show me who was the boss. Just like a woman, I thought.

As we stood there face to face, Jaydeen came out of the house and walked over to the corral, "I see you're finally winning her over. Didn't I tell you all you needed was a little patience and faith? Food's ready. You must be more than a little hungry; after all you've gone through this morning."

I didn't tell her I had all but given up of any kind of friendship with the horse. I reached out and gave the appey a rub on her neck. She in turn didn't shy away, but gave me a nibble on my ear. Jay laughed at the two of us. "I guess maybe I'll have some competition from her."

Walking back to the house, Jay asked, "You got a name picked out for her?"

"I hadn't given it much thought, but you're right. I should give her a name. Everyone names their horse don't they? Let's see ... I could name her Freckles, because of the spots on her rump."

"No, you can't. That's more of a boy's name." Jay pointed out.

"I know the perfect name." I said, "You told me to have patience and faith. I could name her either Patience or Faith. Since I didn't have any patience, I guess I'll name her Faith. What do you think? Do you like it?"

Thinking a moment, she said, "Yeah, I do! ... never heard of a horse called Faith."

After having a bite to eat we went back to see Faith. Of all the things, you'd lest expect, she came right up to me and nuzzled my ear. I had a feeling this might work out, that the two of us would develop a great relationship. Now if only I could get Jaydeen to nuzzle my ear.

The storm I thought we were in for had blown off and disappeared. Looking up at the clear blue sky gave me an idea. "Jay, look at this weather, a beautiful blue sky, not a cloud in it, and a nice warm breeze rustling the leaves in the trees. What would you say to us going on a picnic tomorrow, just the two of us? You need to get out of the house and have some fun."

Jay looked at my face that was almost pleading. Without so much as a blink, she smiled. "Why, Chad! That's a wonderfully great idea. We can go tomorrow after chores. I can make us sandwiches and we can go down by the stream. We can take along a blanket to sit on." She sounded happy. "Oh, Chad, I'm so excited,"

We sat by the stream watching the clear water, swirling and rippling over the pebbles that lay on the sandy bottom. A squirrel ran across the grass and disappeared up a tree. A blue jay scolded at us from the branch of a nearby tree, then flew off. Neither of us spoke, taking in the quiet and the beauty of it all.

After a few moments of silence, I cleared my throat and in the best voice, I could muster up. I looked at Jay's beautiful face and said, "Jaydeen I love you, will you marry me?" Then my throat tighten up, I couldn't swallow, and could get out no more words.

Jaydeen took my hands and held them in hers. She looked at my glassy, almost tearful eyes and after a long moment said, "Chad … Oh, Chad! … Yes! Yes! I love you too. I've loved you since the moment I first saw you. Why did it take you so long to ask?"

I choked out, "I was afraid you would say no. And that would have destroyed me."

We sat quietly then, neither speaking. We sat holding hands, happy. We watched the brook, as it bubbled and gurgled along its winding path. I thought … that stream … It would be like Jay and me, and our life together, bubbling along happily, as we wandered along the path of our life together.

The shadows were getting long and a chill was in the air as we rode back towards the house. Trace and Sid were at the house as we walked in all aglow. Sid took one look at our happy faces and immediately became suspicious, "Where you two been and what have you been up to?"

From the glow on our faces and our expressions, Sid wanted to know what had happened. From his look, I could tell he thought the worst, but hoped for the best. Sometimes he was overly protective of his sister and her virtue. Jay and me, we just looked at each other and grinned, we didn't reply. Trace had a concerned look on his face as Sid said, "Okay out with it, what happened? I know something's going on, so you two just spit it out right now," he demanded.

Jaydeen poked me in the ribs and whispered, "Tell them Chad."

Sid heard the whisper. "Yeah, go ahead Chad. Tell me! Tell me what?" he stood there arms folded, frowning expecting the worst. "Well? I'm waiting."

"Go on Chad, tell them." She said, grinning like a schoolgirl and pushed me forward.

"Well," I stuttered, "it's like this …" I paused, and then started again. "Well Jaydeen and me … we went on a picnic today. It being such a lovely day and all, we thought it would be nice."

"I hope you didn't … you know?" Sid said looking right at me. He took a deep breath before he went on, "Cause if you did you're gonna answer to me."

"Well it's like this, Jay and me are gonna get married. We decided today, while having our picnic. I asked her and she said yes. You're gonna be my new brother-in-law. And to answer your question, we didn't do what you're suggesting."

Sid sat down hard, as what I'd said sunk into his thick head. "If I'm going to lose my sister, I can't think of anyone I'd rather lose her to than my best friend," Sid said with a break in his voice. With a silly, happy grin on his face, he walked over and put his arms around our shoulders, giving us a brotherly hug. "I'm sorry for thinking … you know … Well when is this happy day going to take place? I don't want any more surprises from you two."

I shrugged my shoulders and said, "We just now decided to get married, and we haven't decided the when or where it will happen. For now, it probably won't be for a while, since there are several things that I have to take care of in Tombstone."

Then there's Brett and Jake, I'd have to break the news to them.

Sid said, "Well I'm glad you both are using your heads and decided not to rush into anything foolishly. I only have one sister after all, and I want her to be darn sure she picks the right man. Since you're a friend of mine, hopefully, you are the right man."

Jaydeen spoke up saying, "Sid, I know what I'm doing. Neither of us would do anything to hurt you, ever. I love Chad, were going to get married, so please be happy with our decision. It just happened so suddenly." She went on, "We we're having our picnic when we told each other our true feelings. We decided right then and there, that we were in love and we should get married."

"Well, it's plain to see you have feelings for one another," Sid said. Trace sat listening to the words flying like bullets, back and forth across the room. He sat quietly in his chair with his legs stretched out, his hat pushed back, smiling. His head swung back and forth, as he looked from one to the other. He was thoroughly enjoying himself, watching the ruckus the three of us were putting on.

Trace had had enough after a minute or two as the words flew, he said to all of us, "Would you all stop the bickering and just enjoy the moment of this great announcement." We looked at Trace and stopped our talking. We had forgotten about Trace till he spoke up. Then we all looked at each other and the four of us burst out laughing at the way we were acting.

After supper, having eaten our fill of fried chicken and mashed potatoes, along with biscuits and gravy, the four of us sat out on the porch. Relaxed and with a full belly, we talked of the riders that had been spotted around the ranch. Drinking coffee and smoking, Trace and Sid said they didn't know what to make of it. Neither did I.

We spoke about Jaydeen and me getting married, and when that might happen. My reply was, "It's probably going to take some time before that happens. There's a lot I have to do."

It was getting on, late into the evening. Sid and Trace saying they had to get up early tomorrow and brand cattle decided to turn in as it was getting late.

Jaydeen and I sat a spell longer. It was a beautiful clear evening, the stars sprinkled across the heavens, like a million fireflies. A nice warm breeze was blowing down from the hills. We sat holding each other, not speaking, content in our closeness to one another. Soon after the others, we too decided it was time to turn in.

CHAPTER 39

AFTER AN EARLY breakfast the next morning, I saddled up the bay, and put a halter on the appaloosa, and then I turned and kissed Jaydeen. Saying adios to Sid and Trace, I headed off down the trail toward Tombstone leading the appey that trailed behind me.

Thinking about Jaydeen, I rode along feeling happy and lucky she had said yes to my proposal. I finally settled down for the long ride back to town. I was looking forward to telling Brett about Jaydeen and me. I didn't know what his reaction would be. I would hope and guess maybe he would be happy for me.

My mind wandered here and there, thinking about all the things I had to take care of. I wondered how Jake was making out in Tombstone. And I thought about Ben, still in jail after all this time. I wondered if the judge had found an excuse to pardon him and let him out of jail. At least when I'd left he wasn't hung yet. I would soon find out when I got back to town in the next day or two. I had to do something about Ben's predicament, otherwise he was going to grow old sitting in jail.

Riding along thinking about all these things, a movement off to my right caught the corner of my eye. I turned my head to look in that direction, trying to see what might have caught my eye. I saw a rider, slightly behind and about half a mile off to the right. I wondered if it was one of the riders that had been spying on the ranch. If it was, why was he trailing me, if he was trailing me? I'd keep an eye on whoever it was riding in the distance there.

I continued on my way, keeping an eye out for anything that might unexpectedly happen. Sometime later I took notice the rider was still trailing me and still he was off to the side. I thought he might be on a different trail, maybe the one going straight towards Tombstone. The trail I was on would take me by Brett's gun shop.

Turning the bay, I rode in a southeasterly direction not in any big hurry, taking it easy and not pushing the bay. Hopefully I would arrive in time for supper. Brett would be pleasantly surprised. It would be another hour to Brett's gun shop. I looked for the rider off to my right, saw he had pulled ahead, and angled more off toward Tombstone, which eased my mind somewhat.

I rode into the yard and there was Brett, standing on the porch of the gun shop, holding a cup of coffee. I thought to myself, how the hell does he always know when someone's coming?

"Howdy partner. What's that you got trailing along there behind ya?" He didn't wait for my answer. "It looks to be a mighty pretty little filly, you got there. Is that the one you told me you won in a shooting match with your friend Sid?"

"Yeah, this is the one, ain't she a beauty?"

Brett sat his coffee cup on the porch railing, "Chad, holdup a minute and I'll open the corral gate for you."

I rode through the open gate and slid out of the saddle to the ground. I gave Brett a hug. "I'm glad to see you again partner." Brett closed the gate. I took the halter off and let the filly run loose. I turned to the bay, taking the saddle off and then the bridle, I carried them to the part of the shed, where we stored the riding tack and hung them on a special rail that crossed one end.

Brett asked in jest, "What new and exciting things do you have to tell me about this time?"

I said, "Oh … nothing much. Seems my friends out at the ranch might have a problem. They got unknown riders up in the hills watching them, with field glasses. They don't have no idea why their being watched. It might have to do with that incident with the rustlers, but that was months ago. They first noticed the riders maybe a month or more after we caught the rustlers. It could be connected with the rustlers, they don't know. Sid and Trace have ridden out to talk, but the riders ride away before they can get close. Thought maybe I was being trailed by one of them coming back into town. Then the rider turned off and headed towards Tombstone. So I must've been mistaken."

Brett, with me helping, rustled up supper. After supper, we went out on the porch and sat. Brett smoked, while we drank our coffee and talked some till dark. We finished the coffee and being late went in to bed.

Next morning after breakfast, I saddled up the bay. Brett said, "Chad if you or your friends need help, with those riders out at the ranch, just let me know and I'll be there to help with a lending hand—and my guns, if need be."

"Thanks Brett. For now, I don't think we need any help mainly because we don't know what they want, if anything. They haven't made any hostile moves towards anyone."

"Well, like I say, if you need help, just don't be shy and let me know."

As I rode off toward Tombstone, I yelled, "Brett, Take care of the filly for me, will you?"

"Yeah, I'll do that. I might even work with her if I got time. Maybe teach her some tricks before you get back." he yelled jokingly after me.

I waved goodbye and rode off. Two hours later, I rode into Tombstone. The street was busy with foot traffic and riders. I rode warily along down Main Street past the saloons and the hotel to the sheriff's office, keeping a sharp eye open for the rider who had trailed me. I tied up in front of the jail, stepped up on the porch and going inside looked around for Jake. Jake was not there, but Ben was. He was sitting on his cot in the jail cell. He stood as I came in and took hold of the cell bars, "Hello Chad, ain't seen you in a couple of days. Where you been?"

"I went out to the ranch where we had that run in with you and those rustling cowpokes. You remember?"

"Yeah, I remember." He uttered looking down. "That was one sad day of my life."

"I went out to pick up a horse … just now got back to town. Anything been happening while I was gone?"

"Naw, ain't nothing been going on here. At least they ain't hung me yet.

That's the good news.

Chad, he lamented, have you found a way to get me out a here yet?"

"No, not yet, but since you mentioned it, I think I'll go over and see the judge. Check with him to see if he's found a way we can get you out of here, legally or illegally. Ben, you stay here and sit tight, I'll find out what

I can. And Ben … don't go anywhere while I'm gone." I said, laughing. He didn't share my laugh. Ben didn't like my humor.

Standing on the porch of the jail, I looked up and down the street, with an eye for any riders acting strangely. Mounting up, I rode to the town hall to see the judge. The judge's door stood open. I walked into his office with one thing on my mind, determined I was going to resolve this Ben thing, one way or another. He looked up from the papers he was working on. "Sheriff Chad'tu! What brings you here so early in the day?"

"Good morning judge. How are you this fine morning?"

The judge removed his glasses and replied in a grumpy voice, "Not so good, my head hurts. I think I had too much to drink last night. I keep forgetting I'm not as young as I used to be"

"Judge, I hate to bother you this early, but it's about Ben. Have you had a chance to read through your law books? If you have, have you found a way to get Ben out of jail?"

"Yes, to the first question. And yes to the second question." He leaned back in his tall chair, and put his glasses on and rubbed his nose. "I think I have found a loophole."

He leaned forward elbows on his desk and placed his fingertips together said, "Back … Oh, maybe say five, six years ago a case like this one happened. There were two men thrown into jail and both clamed to be innocent. While awaiting their trial, it was found they were telling the truth. However, the judge in that case was too late. One of the men was hung before the judge could get them released. But the other one was set free."

"I think we can do the same with Ben," the judge went on. "Then we put him on probation for a while and see if he's going to become an upright citizen. What do you think Chad'tu?"

"You do that Judge. You draw up them papers for his release, deliver them to me at the jail today, and don't waste any time doing it. I sure as heck have been looking forward to this day. And today would be a good day for it."

"Okay Chad'tu, whatever you say. I'll get on it right away. There is nothing pressing on my agenda today anyway."

On the way out of the judge's office, I bumped into the mayor. Stopping and being civil, I said, "Morning Bill. I was just in talking to the judge. We're going to release that Ben fellow from jail. Everyone I spoke to about him likes him. Most all think probably he's innocent. What do you say? You got any argument against letting him out?"

"That's fine by me, Chad'tu. But if you're going to let him go free, the town would appreciate him paying us back for all those meals he consumed while he was incarcerated."

"Oh, one more thing mayor—the judge said something about probation. Whatever that might be? So do you think we can put that in, with the probation part? That he has to work until he pays back the cost of meals. We can have probation end when he's paid off the meals. How does that sound to you, Mayor? Would you and the town be satisfied then?"

"That would be fine, Chad'tu ... mighty fine." All the mayor seemed to think about was money.

"Well, let's shake on it, Mayor." We shook hands and I walked out, mounted the bay and rode about town looking for Jake. I finally found him, down at the stables. He was talking to Brannon.

Jake looked up, surprised, as I rode toward them, "Chad'tu, when did you get back to town?"

"About an hour ago and I been looking for you. Anything been going on while I was gone?"

"Nothing much, just a few drunks shooting off their guns and mouths, disturbing the peace," He laughed, "My peace."

I slid out of the saddle and pushed my hat up off my forehead. With my voice low so Brannon couldn't hear I said, "I think I was trailed back into town by a lone rider. Jake, you seen any strangers ride into town the last day or two?"

"Yeah, as a matter of fact—now that you mention it, I did see a rider. He was a stranger to me. No one I knew or seen before. He rode in yesterday evening just before dark, as I recall. I was just talking to Brannon about him. He was a stranger to Brannon too. He left his horse last night here at the corral. It's the mouse-gray horse over yonder," he said, pointing.

We walked over and checked the mouse-gray's rump for a brand. It carried one alright; a Rocking B-B brand. Neither of us new to what outfit it might belong. "He's probably down at one of the saloons getting drunk. Think we should see if we can find him, and maybe find out what he's up to?"

"Jake that sounds like dang good idea, the best you had in the last ten minutes."

We decided to start at the saloon furthest from the stable and work our way back. Jake and me mounted up and rode south to the edge of town, to the Four Aces Saloon. We tied the horses, went inside through the butterfly doors and bellied up at the end of the bar. It was just before noon. We looked up and down the bar as Gus the bartender approached. "Gus, we're looking for a man. You seen any strangers today?"

Gus studied hard, "Can't say as I have." He wrinkled his brow, thinking, "No, Sheriff, I don't recollect any strangers, just the normal crowd."

We thanked Gus, turned on our heels and went out, getting on our horses we rode down to the Lucky Lady Saloon. Inside, we had a quick look around and asked John if he'd seen any strangers in the last day or two.

"Yeah, strange you should ask. There was a fellow in here yesterday. Came in alone, about sundown I think. Had a few drinks and ask about our sheriff. He seemed kind of nervous-like. He asked a bunch of questions."

"What kind of questions?" Jake asked.

"He asked questions like, how long has he been sheriff and how'd he come to be sheriff, and what his name might be."

"I guess you told him all the things he wanted to hear." John shrugged his shoulders. "John, can you describe the fellow?"

"He looked to be maybe thirty-five years old, brownish gray hair, a weather-beaten face and he wore chaps and carried a gun. I didn't see what kind of horse he was riding. He was covered with dust. He looked like he'd ridden quiet some distance. Looked just like any regular cowpoke. Except, for a cowpoke he sure did ask a lot of questions and he looked around a lot. He wanted to know what the sheriff looked like."

"Well John, that was mighty nice of you to give this stranger all that information. If you see him again, please send for me. I want to talk to the man. Okay?"

"Chad'tu ... I didn't mean anything ... by given him that information." He looked at me apprehensively. "I hope you're not mad."

"That's okay John, forget about it. Only next time, just don't be talking around strangers when you don't know who they are."

Jake put his two cents worth in and echoed my sentiments. "Yeah, John, don't be so careless with your words. You never know who might be looking and gunning for us. And we don't like surprises, right Chad'tu?"

"Yeah Jake, you're right. We don't want any surprises."

We left, mounted up and rode to the next saloon looking for the stranger. We went north through town to the Last Chance Saloon. We dismounted, and stepped up onto the porch and walked through the doors into the bar. Shelley, the heavyset female bartender approached us.

"You fellows name your poison. What'll it be?"

"Shelley, you seen any strangers in here the last day or two?"

"As a matter of fact Sheriff, there was a stranger, a dusty, hard looking fellow. If you ask me, he looked like a cowpoke down and out on his luck. He left … oh maybe an hour ago."

"Did you see which way he went and what he might be riding?"

"Yeah I did, he left town heading in a northwest direction. I think he was riding a dark gray horse. I remember thinking there was something peculiar about him. Anyway he headed in a north west direction."

Jake and I rushed out of the bar, jumped on our horses, and rode fast out of town headed northwest. If we hurried, we might catch the rider. We rode hard, our eyes searching across the distant prairie. There wasn't a sign of anybody riding anywhere that we could see. After a half-hour of hard riding, we decided to give up and rode back to town. Dejected.

We talked as we rode slowly back into Tombstone. Jake said nothing worthwhile had happened while I'd been gone. He'd only had to jail six drunks for the night and then had let them go in the morning with a warning. Other than that, it had been quiet.

I told Jake we were going to let Ben out of jail, but the judge was going to put him on something called probation. I said, "Sounds to me as if he wants to see if Ben can behave himself. He also said Ben would have to pay back the town for all the meals that he had consumed while in jail."

Jake laughed, when I told him that. "Sounds to me like now they're charging you for being locked up, I guess that sounds like the damn politicians I know." he chuckled.

I looked up at the sun, which was directly overhead with not a cloud in the sky. It was hot and my stomach was telling me it was time for lunch. "Jake, you hungry?" I said as we rode along.

"Now you mention it Chad, I could go for a little something, I guess. What say we go over to the hotel? They got the best food in town. Sure beats that bar food." We drifted slowly down Main Street, stopped and tied the horses to the rail in front of the hotel. We crossed the porch, went past the front desk, into the hallway that led back to the dining room.

We strode into the dining room, hung our hats on the hat rack, washed up, found a table by a window, which looked out on First Street. We were in luck today. The young cute waitress by the name of Faye waited on us. "She sure is easy on the eyes," Jake said.

The special today was ham hocks and lima beans with homemade corn-bread. We ordered iced tea. The odor of cooking food that wafted from the kitchen made our mouths water in anticipation. From the smell of it, whoever was doing the cooking surely did know how to cook. We had apple pie for dessert, along with coffee. When we had finished, I remembered Brett had always said, leave a generous tip. You never know what it might bring you.

Faye smiled as we left, saying, "You boys have a good day now, you hear." We smiled back and said, "We sure will Faye." Grabbing our hats and a toothpick, we stepped out on the porch. We stood awhile picking our teeth looking up and down Main Street.

Everything seemed normal.

CHAPTER 40

W E MOUNTED OUR horses and rode to the jail. Opening the door and hanging my hat on a peg, I noticed a sheet of paper lying on my desk. Picking up the paper, I perused it. It was the release paper for Ben, signed by the judge and undersigned by the mayor. The paper also stated that I'd have to appoint Ben to some sort of work of my choosing to pay back the town for all the meals he had eaten while being locked up. I folded the paper, put it into the desk drawer, and locked it.

Taking the keys from a hook on the wall, I walked to the cell door in the back. Ben was standing there holding on to the bars of the cell. "Ben this is your lucky day you're a free man," I said unlocking the cell door.

With an unbelieving look and a crack in his voice, he said, "Chad'tu, I can't believe you're letting me out."

"Ben, I finally convinced the mayor and the judge of your innocence. They agreed to let you out. Only one thing ... there's a catch."

Ben looked worried, "What's the catch Chad'tu?"

"Well, it seems Ben that the officials want you to pay for all the meals that you ate while in jail. They told me to appoint you some kind of work, work that you will be paid for."

Ben said, "That don't rightly seem fair to me."

"Well at least you're out of jail and free, so I wouldn't complain too much if I was you."

"Well, I ain't exactly complaining. But it just somehow don't seem right to me."

I turned to Jake. "Jake what kind of job do you think we could have Ben do? They want him to work for the town, so he can make some money, and then to pay it back to the town he's getting paid by to do the work. Don't make much sense, does it Jake?" I said with a chuckle.

"Chad'tu you're right." Jake agreed. "Now let me see if I got this straight. The town's going to pay him for whatever job we have him do, so that he can pay the money back to the town for all those meals. That's real funny, but I suppose that's the way politicians think."

"Jake, what do you think we could have Ben do? You got any ideas?"

"Chad'tu, I been noticing the streets in our fair town got a lot of refuse on them. We could give Ben a bucket and have him pick up all the trash lying about on the streets. How does that strike you?"

"Jake, that's a darn good idea. And after he cleans up the streets what then?"

"Oh! We can surely figure out something." Jake grinned. I could tell Jake was enjoying all this.

So it was decided. Ben was now the man in charge of keeping the streets clean.

Ben stepped out onto the street a free man and headed straight for the hotel, first thing. He went to see the woman Kathryn McBain, who'd been bringing his meals, while in jail. They'd gotten acquainted and had feelings of a sort for each other. It had grown over the course of time she'd been bringing the meals.

It seemed ... I guess being in jail doesn't stop someone from falling in love with another, no matter whichever side of the bars they might be on.

Kathryn McBain was called Katie by everyone. She was a pleasant woman and well liked. She happened to be in the dining room when Ben walked in. She almost dropped the plate she was carrying when she saw him. She quickly delivered it to the man sitting at a table. Turning she hurried to Ben's side, taking his hand in hers in shocked surprise. "Oh! Ben, they finally let you out. I'm so glad."

"Katie, you ain't anymore glad than I am. I surely am glad to be free of that place. There is one thing I gotta tell you. There's a catch to my freedom. You know all those meals you brought to me."

"Yes darling, I remember and I was happy to bring them."

"Well they're going to make me pay for all them meals, but I ain't complaining, I'm out and rightly glad. Now we can see each other whenever we want. Anyway, I'm in no hurry to leave this town while you're here."

"Ben, do you have a place to stay?"

"No, I just this minute got out of jail. I decided to come straight here and give you the good news. The sheriff has given me the job of keeping the streets clean. Maybe I could get a parttime job here for after I clean up the streets. It sure would help me pay off my debt faster. Say, maybe I could get a room here in the hotel. What do you think, Katie?"

"Ben that would be wonderful, come to think of it I think we could use another dishwasher."

Katie was being called by a couple at one of the tables for service. "Just hold your horses," she called out to them, "I'll be right there." She turned back to Ben and said, "This very minute you go talk to the owner. His name is Mr. Barlow. He's the man at the front desk."

Ben approached the man standing behind the front desk and asked, "You Mr. Barlow?" The man looked up from his bookwork and said, "Yes, what can I do for you?"

"Mr. Barlow, I'm a friend of Katie's and she said you might need a dish-washer to wash dishes in the evening. If that is so I'd like to apply for the job." Barlow looked Ben up and down and said, "That Katie sure is a fine worker and if she vouches for you. Hmm ..." he paused. "Young man, tell you what I'll do. I'll try you out for a day or two, and if it works out, you're hired. How's that sound?"

Ben replied, "That sounds mighty good Mr. Barlow, I surely do appreciate the chance and I won't let you down, you can count on that. Oh, Mr. Barlow, there's one more thing. I need a place to sleep. A room I guess. Do you have one that I could rent?"

"Young man, what's your name?"

"My name is Ben Crackett and I've been locked up in that jail across the street over yonder, for a long time, for something I was not guilty of."

"Well, Ben Crackett, I'm not one that don't give a man a chance. So if you're a good dishwasher, I could give you a room out back above the kitchen and charge you half price for it."

"That sounds mighty fair, Mr. Barlow. I really do appreciate the chance. When do you want me to start?"

"You can start today, say five o'clock. The cook, Darnell is his name, will show you what your duties will be." He paused then said "Follow me, I'll show you the room." He reached up and taking a key from a hook on the wallboard, took him up the stairs toward the back and showed him a room that was dark and hot, being above the kitchen. He gave him the key to the room and then left.

Three days later, everything having gone well, Ben was washing dishes in the evening and cleaning streets in the daytime. Didn't leave much time for romancing Katie, but he found a moment here and there.

CHAPTER 41

ON A HOT muggy day about two months later, Ben was cleaning the streets when five riders rode into town. He glanced up, and stopped to wipe the sweat from his forehead.

The riders rode by without paying any attention to hiim. They only seemed interested in checking out the town. Two of them he recognize as being from the BB ranch, the ranch he'd worked for when he had been caught for rustling. He wondered what they were doing in Tombstone. This was a far piece from the ranch. These particular riders hadn't been in on the rustling of the cattle, but they did work at the ranch.

He thought about those riders for a while. Nothing good would come of it, he suspected. He hurried over to the sheriff's office, looking for Chad'tu. Chad'tu would want to know about the five riders being in town from a ranch that was so far away, and especially about the two cowpokes, he'd recognized.

Short of breath, he burst into the sheriff's office. Chad'tu and Jake were both there. They looked up as he spoke. "Sheriff, there's some thing you need to know and you too Jake. Five riders just rode into town from the Rocking AB ranch and this is a long way out of their territory. I ain't got no idea why they might be here or what business they might have. I got a bad feeling it might not be good. I just thought you two should know. I wanted to warn you, be careful on your rounds about town."

"Thanks Ben, we appreciate the warning and we'll be right careful with these five. At least till we find out what they are up to, won't we Jake?"

"Damn right Ben, we'll be real careful." Jake replied. Then Jake added, "Chad'tu ... you know I been thinking. Ben here has been an upright citizen for these last few months. What do ya think about us giving him his gun back? If were going to have trouble, it might be a good idea to have a little backup. What do you say?"

"Don't I have a voice in this?" Ben asked.

"Sorry, Ben, do you think you could back up Jake and me if it comes down to a shootout?"

"Well, I suppose Chad'tu, but ... I'm not much good when it comes to shooting. You both have been more than fair with me and I like you both. I surely would like to help you out anyway I can. If that requires shooting, I guess that's what I'll have to do."

Without another word, Jake walked over to a locked cabinet and unlocking it took out Ben's gun and gun belt and handed it to Ben.

Ben had a look of gratitude alone with a little fear, written across his face. "Thanks Jake, I felt a little naked walking around town without any protection hanging on my side and you too Chad'tu, thanks for believing in me. I'll do my best not to let you down."

"We'll let you know when and if we need you Ben. First though we have to find out what these cowpokes might have in mind."

Jake and I talked over what this might mean with these five riders being in town. It was unusual for riders to ride this far unless there was something on their minds. Like, maybe killing someone and that someone possibly could be either Jake or me, or both of us. It was something to think about.

Jake and I left the jail and rode to the edge of town. Stopping in front of the Last Chance Saloon, we tied our horses at the rail. Jake and I looked at each other while flipping the leather thongs from the hammers of our guns. I was somewhat scared. Jake smiled and told me to relax, it would be okay.

We walked carefully into the saloon with our guns holstered, but ready to be drawn if need be. Not knowing what might greet us was the hard part. Walking into the saloon, we stepped quietly to the side and stood at the end of the bar. No one had taken any notice.

Shelley the bartender came down and said, "I see you're back. What can I get you boys?"

"Two beers will do fine, Shelley." Shelley lumbered her way to the beer keg, and drew two beers. Returning she sat them in front of us, smiled, and said. "This one's on the house boys, no charge. Maybe I can get you to come in more often."

"Shelley," I spoke in a low voice, "You see those five cowpokes down there, the dusty looking ones? Do you know them?"

"No Sheriff, can't say as I do. They just drifted into the bar somewhere's about three hours ago. They sure been doing a lot a talkin', and they have been keepin' to themselves. I catch a word now and then, but nothin' that makes sense. I get the feeling though, seems to me like they're looking for someone. Matter of fact, from what parts I did hear, it sounded to me like maybe they were out to get the sheriff. Don't know for sure. It's just a feeling that struck me. Seems they don't know what the sheriff looks like or his deputy neither." she looked at Jake. "You two be right careful." She said walking off.

We drank our beer and watched the five cowpokes. They seem to be getting pretty liquored up, maybe for courage. We had another beer and watched a while longer. We couldn't decide what these hombres were up to. Maybe just having a good time, but it sure did seem like a long ways to ride just to have a good time.

Jake and I were even more cautious from that moment on. We looked hard at every shadow. We walked along the dark streets, Jake on one side and me on the other, making our rounds, checking doors and windows, and looking for any other strangers that might be in town. We walked the boardwalks around town, stopping here and there, looking into windows, and down the dark walk-through, that sometimes ran between buildings. It was getting late. We put a couple of rowdy drunks into jail, and decided to call it a night.

I met up with Jake the next morning, in the hotel dining room. After having breakfast, along with several cups of strong black coffee, we stood on the porch. Jake lit up a cigarette. Before starting our rounds, we talked and planned what we were going to do today.

Then there came an unexpected surprise. I could not believe what happened next, who would come running down the street, but little Miguel, barefooted as usual and out of breath. He ran up saying, "Señor Chad'tu," Gasping a gulp of air, "Señor Jake." Taking another breath said, "I have the bad news! John, he send me to tell you some hombres going to kill you both. John he say, be very careful. These be muy mean hombres. He don' know them he say."

"Thanks Miguel for the warning, and thank John also. We will be careful you tell him. Well Jake, I guess this is it. We'd better see if Ben wants to lend a hand, don't you think?"

"That'd be a damn good idea," Jake replied.

We found Ben with his bucket picking up trash along the streets. We told him the situation and asked if he'd join us, we'd be much obliged, that he was needed.

Ben pushed his hat back and looked at Jake, then me. He thought we might be joking until he saw the grim look on our faces. Without a word, he set his bucket down, pulled out his gun and checking it, said he was ready.

We stopped by the jail and I unlocked the gun rack, pulled out a couple of Winchester rifles and tossed one to Jake. "These might come in handy. Ben you want one?" I asked, as I grabbed a box of cartridges for the rifle.

"No, I think I'll have my hands full, with my trusty old Colt."

"Well I guess we'd best get a move on and see just how good these cow-pokes are. You two ready?"

"I might find a use for these," Jake said. Taking himself a box of shells for his rifle, we started for the door, Jake and me carrying loaded rifles and Ben carrying his empty bucket.

"Ben why are you still carrying that bucket, this is going to be a real gun-fight. Don't you realize were going to a showdown with these hombres ... with real guns? The bullets will be flying like hornets from a disturbed nest, once the shooting starts."

Ben looked thoughtful for a moment then said, "Well you all know how folks see me picking up stuff and keeping the streets clean. Well half the time people look straight at me, and don't even see me. Sort' a like I wasn't there, you know?"

"I figure to walk along behind you, picking up trash as I usually do. No one will take any notice and I can watch and keep your backs covered. If I know these fellows they wouldn't be afraid to shoot anyone in the back."

Jake looked at me and his face lit up in a grin. "Chad'tu, you know he's right. No one pays him any attention. I think it's a darn good idea. Chad'tu, you take one side of the street, I'll take the other, and Ben you bring up the rear." We agreed on the plan and started cautiously out into the street.

Jake crossed to the other side telling me to keep a sharp eye out and to watch for any movement from the second floor windows, balconies and don't forget the roofs. We parted and started walking along the boards. I watched the buildings on his side and he kept an eye on the ones on my side. We moved slowly along, carefully crossing open doorways and the walk-through between buildings, and looking through windows before passing them by.

The afternoon wind started picking up some. The signs that were hung, extending out from the face of some buildings squeaked as they swung on their hooks, whipped by the wind. A barn door slammed shut somewhere further down. Dust blew down the street followed by several tumbleweeds. A summer storm was coming. There was a feeling of static in the air. It was a good day for a gunfight, a good day for dying. I thought.

A horse and rider appeared suddenly from an alley walk-through. Without a conscious thought, my Colt appeared in my hand as suddenly as the rider appeared. But I did not fire, the rider was holding on to his hat with one hand as he steered his horse toward a saloon to take shelter. He was not a threat.

I was feeling jumpy. Then I felt that cold anger and hot feeling. Time seemed to slow for me. When I got this feeling, everything happened slowly. I looked back for Ben. He was twenty yards back, trudging down the street his bucket swinging in the wind.

Keeping a wary eye out I glanced across to where Jake was walking. Somewhat ahead and above Jake, a slight movement of a curtain caught my eye. Something had made that curtain move. Was it the wind that had moved the curtain or something else?

Keeping an eye on the window where the curtain had moved, I saw slowly being poked out at the edge of the window, a rifle barrel. At that same instant, I saw a flash from the barrel of the rifle followed by the sound of the shot. Wood splinters went flying from the doorjamb I was walking past.

I pulled up my rifle and shot from the hip, hitting the man in the window that had fired the shot. The rifle fell from his hands as he fell from the window and stumbled across the short balcony and fell onto the deck railing. The railing broke and he tumbled over it, hitting the dirt in the street, flat on his back. He lay there not moving.

Jake waved a hand at me in thanks. That's one down ... and four more to go. Carefully, I passed by the butterfly doors of a saloon. Ahead of me, I heard the breaking of glass. I guessed the sound came from around thirty feet further down the walk.

Jake held up a cautioning hand and I stopped. He quickly drew his gun and fired in the direction from where the sound of breaking glass had come. Damn he was fast; his movement was just a blur to my eyes.

Followed by the sound of more breaking glass, I heard something heavy fall. Then there was silence. The wind blowing was the only sound to be heard. Peering through the busted window I could see a body lying stretched out on the saloon floor amongst several broken glasses. He must have staggered back against the bar, knocking off several glasses as he fell. The odds were getting better; two down and three to go. Things were looking up.

We walked down another block, watching windows, doors and walk-through alleys. The wind was blowing dust as it pick up, making it hard to see or to hear. Nothing happened. Ben was still lagging along behind. Bringing up the rear, he still was watching our backs.

Stepping down from the boardwalk, I looked down an alleyway, and then quickly ran across to the next building. Across the street, Jake did the same.Walking slowly down the boardwalk, I stopped and looked into a saloon over the butterfly doors, then quickly crossed in front. I had taken no more than fifteen steps past those swinging doors when a shot sounded from behind me. I crouched and drew my Colt as I turned looking to where the shot had come.

A man stumbled out of the saloon through the butterfly doors and tumbled into the dirt at the bottom of the steps. He laid unmoving the wind blowing dirt over his still body. Ben stood in the middle of the street, a smoking gun in one hand and his bucket in the other. I yelled over the wind, "Thanks Ben." He waved his gun.

Three had gone down, only two were left.

With probably no more than a hundred yards to go, we approached the end of Main Street. We had reached the edge of town. Suddenly from an alleyway, a man jumped out with a rifle and started firing. I heard bullets zipping close by and the chipping of wood beside me. Before I could fire my gun, Jake shot him through the middle of his chests. Falling face down he clawed at the ground, he started to rise and Jake put another bullet into him. Then he laid still.

Four down. That left only one.

Suddenly, a man appeared at the end of the street. Standing in the middle of the street, his legs spread. He shouted, "Chad'tu, I'm gonna kill you. Call off your other men, and face me man to man, just you and me." He had the look of a gunslinger.

I stepped out into the middle of the street. Jake shook his head for me not to do this. I did not heed his warning. I did not care, this was a challenge. A challenge, I could not back down from and still call myself a man. It was time to see just how good Brett had taught me and just how good, had I become. It was time to find out.

Jake stood ready to back me as was Ben. I waved a hand for them to stay out of this. I knew most shooters were not very accurate, unless they were within thirty-five feet or closer to you, then you'd better be wary. And it didn't hurt none if you were faster and a better shot than the one that was shooting at you. I was not going to let this shooter get that close. I had practiced shooting at fifty yards and I was a dead shot at fifty yards. The dust blowing down the street didn't help any.

With my gun in its holster and ready to be drawn, I walked slowly toward the gunman. The stranger walked slowly toward me, his gun hung low at his side, holstered. His hand close to his gun and ready.

The dust was getting thicker and more tumbleweed's were being blown down the street. The wind had picked up a notch. When we got to the fifty-yard mark by my calculation, I told him that's close enough.

I called out, "Mister, it's your dance! Start the music whenever you're ready, and we'll dance ... go for it."

He wiped a sweaty hand on his dirty shirtsleeve. I watched his eyes as he stopped and stood there. It was hard to tell what this man was thinking. It took some time till he got his courage up. He started for his gun...

Before he could clear leather, I had drawn my gun and fired. He didn't fall for a second or two. I thought, hell I missed him. Then he fell to his knees and then crumbled sideways. He did not move.

I walked slowly up ready to fire again if need be. He was still breathing, but he was a dead man, he just didn't know it. His gun was still in the holster. He took a last breath and stopped moving.

Jake and Ben came running up as I stood there looking down at the dead man's body. Jake asked, "Chad'tu, you okay?"

"Yeah," I answered slowly. I was still holding the smoking gun by my side. "I'm okay, just a little shaken I guess."

"Do you know him?" Jake wanted to know.

"I never laid eyes on him. That was the first man I ever killed up close." I said, shoving my gun into the holster. "I'm okay, and you?"

"Well. I ain't been hit ... best I can tell, if that's what you're askin." Jake put his hand on my shoulder and said. "That was some good shooting you did back there."

I knew he was trying to distract me, from what I was feeling.

"Don't feel bad about killing a man. It was either him or you. It'll take you a time to get over the killing. But remember we're the law, and they brought the fight to us."

"We'd better get the undertaker and his wagon to get these bodies off the street before the people get hysterical." I said. "Anyway, I'm glad it's over."

"You did real well Chad'tu." Jake said, "And you too Ben, you did real good bringing up the rear like you did. Probable saved us from a bullet in the back."

"Yeah Jake he did, didn't he."

We stood talking, trying to unwind from the unpleasant incident. Hearing the sound of hoof beats the three of us looked up, still on edge and ready for anything.

A man appeared from out of the dust-blown street, riding a black horse. Stepping down out of the saddle, he tied his horse to a hitching rail. He wore a long black slicker, which he pulled back, exposing two low slung, tied down, black pistols on each hip. A real gun slick dressed all in black.

Not knowing what this gun slick might be up to, we slowly spread apart, putting some distance between our selves. Wondering what the man's intent was.

We were soon to find out.

He asked with a heavy accent, "Wheech of you hombres might be the sheriff? Thess sheriff they call Chad'tu. I hear he is very good with thee gun." The three of us hardly breathed, waiting for this gunman to make his move. I spoke up. "I'm Chad'tu ... Sheriff Chad'tu I am known by. And who might you be that wants to know?"

The three of us stood looking at the man, waiting for his answer. "Thee name is Shevara, Dom Shevara."

He waited for a reaction to his name. When none was forthcoming, he spoke again saying, "I am here and well-paid to kill you, Chad'tu." With that said, he reached for both guns. We all drew guns and everybody started shooting.

CHAPTER 42

FELT THE bullet as it ripped through my shirt and side. It hurt like hell and pushed me sideways. His next bullet whistled by my ear. Jumping to the side and rolling, I came up on one knee and fired, hitting him dead center between the eyes. He crumpled in disbelief and fell to the ground.

I looked for Jake and Ben, wondering if they'd been hit. Jake walked over to take a look. Jake pulled up my bloody shirt it seemed I was the only one hit. I asked, "Is it bad?"

"Naw, that's not bad," he said. "It's only a scratch, looks like the bullet went plumb through."

"Well, it feels like more than a scratch to me and hurts something fierce. Besides, you ain't the one that's been shot."

Jake laughed at me, saying he'd been shot more times than he could count. There he went again, trying to cheer me up.

I felt drained after all the excitement and weak in the knees. I put my arms over Jake and Ben's shoulders as they helped me stumble to the doc's house. The doc was standing on the porch, looking up the street, with one hand shielding his eyes from the blowing dust, when we came into view. He hollered out, asking what the hell was going on.

With the wind and dirt whipping around us, they dragged me onto the porch. The doc took one look at my bloodied shirt and said, "Hurry, get him inside." He held the door wide for us, and then the door was shut against the fury of the howling wind. "In here," he pointed, "Put him on that high table there." I felt like a baby as my two friends helped me up onto the table.

"Take off your shirt and let's have a look." The doc said. He pulled away the kerchief that Jake had used to stop the bleeding. "Hmm, nice bullet hole; looks like a wound a forty-four slug would make." He looked at the exit hole the bullet had made. "Hmm, this must be your lucky day. The bullet went clean through."

Jake said, with a questioning tone, "What do you mean Doc; he's shot, that ain't lucky?"

Ben said, "Yeah he's lucky he's not dead."

"Yeah Doc, why am I so damn lucky? Tell us."

"Well, if that there bullet had hit four more inches to the left or higher up, or even in the head, we'd be calling for Smithers the undertaker. That's why I meant, you were lucky."

The doc went to the cupboard, opened a door and took a brown bottle from a shelf that held many bottles. He turned, picked up a small cup and walked back. "Hold this," he said, handing the cup to me. He pulled a stopper from the bottle and poured a half cup of reddish-brown liquid into it, "Drink this."

With my nose over the cup, I smell it. It had a sweet smell to it. "What is this concoction and why do you want me to drink it?"

"It's laudanum. It'll help ease your pain—and the pain you're going to have when I start sewing up that hole going through you."

A half hour later, I was feeling no pain. The doc cleaned the wound thoroughly. "This is my sewing kit." he said. He opened the box and took out a large curved needle and some kind of thread. Threading the needle, he asked how I felt.

"I haven't felt this good since the first time I drank too much beer. Doc, what'cha going to do with that there needle, sew up a horse?" I said, then giggled and fell back on the table and drifted off to dreamland.

Doc looked at Jake and Ben. "Okay, the laudanum has numbed him down. If he starts to thrash around, I want you two to hold him down." They nodded in agreement, as the doc started sewing.

Ben grimaced and turning a little pale looked away, as the doc stuck his needle through my skin and started his sewing.

An hour or so later, I came out from the effects of the laudanum. The raw gaping bullet holes didn't hurt so much now as they had before. The newly stretched and stitched skin felt tight and itched a little. The doc said the operation was a success and was sure I would live. He told me to take it easy for a couple weeks and not lift anything heavy.

The next day the mayor sent for me. I had the stable hand saddle my horse. I mounted slowly, favoring my side. I settled into the saddle with a moan and headed for the mayor's office.

The mayor started to chew me out, wanting to know just what in the hell, was going on in his fair town. As I started to explain, the judge walked in and chimed in, "Yeah Chad'tu, tell us what the hell is going on?" They seemed to have no concern that I had been shot risking my life for the fair town of Tombstone. Their nonchalance perturbed me somewhat.

"Mister Mayor—Your Honor. This is what went down and the way it happened." I told my story of the incident, then added if they didn't like my conduct they could have my badge. My temper was heating up at being treated like I had done something wrong.

They both finally calmed down. The mayor sat looking at the judge, who was walking back and forth holding on to the lapels of his coat and mumbling to himself. They both agreed that I was still the sheriff and could keep the badge.

Starting to leave I stopped and said, "Oh, there's one other thing I want to say while we're all here together. I'm having signs made and posted on all the roads leading into town. The signs will read, 'Firearms are to be turned in to the Sheriff's Office at the jail on arrival. They will be returned to you when you leave. If you do not comply with this order you will have your guns confiscated and you will be run out of town without them.'" I stared hard at both the judge and mayor in defiance after I'd had my say. Their mouths hung open in amazement. I turned on my heel and strode out.

Two days later the signs were up and posted. I sure didn't want to go through another gunfight like the one that'd just happened. I might not be so lucky the next time.

There was a lot of complaining and grumbling from the cowpokes. There were complaints from others, whom you couldn't tell by looking what their occupation might be. After a few weeks, everyone settled into the routine and dropped their guns at the sheriff's office.

On a visit to the doc to have the bandages changed, he said the wound was healing nicely. "No one will ever know you were shot as long as you don't take off your shirt." He said with a grin. "But," he went on. "If I was you, I'd take a couple weeks off. You're still pretty weak from the looks of you."

Why shouldn't I take some time off? Jake could handle things; after all, he had been a sheriff once. I would talk to him about it.

Next morning, Jake and me were having breakfast, and I told him what the doc said about taking it easy for awhile. He agreed it wouldn't do any harm for me to take some time off.

With a mouth full of egg, Jake said, "You know I been doing some thinking. Ben was a big help out there. Shooting that there fellow who was about to shoot you in the back. I think you should take him off cleaning the streets and make him a deputy. What do you say?"

"Jake, how the hell do you come up with these ideas? I hadn't thought on it, but since you brought it up." I suddenly had the thought; this could work out fine for me. I would be free to visit Brett and mosey on out to see Jaydeen.

I guess I took too long to give my answer to Jake. "Well?" he asked again. "I think you got a right good thought there. And while I'm off recuperating you can train him on how to be a deputy and teach him some of them lawman's rules."

We started making the morning rounds. The town was unusually quiet this morning. Small groups of people stood around talking, probably about the big gunfight that had taken place. That was all people seemed to talk about lately. I hoped that the word of three guns against six would not be spread out of town. I knew deep down it would be talked about far and wide and probably for some months to come. Not much hope in squelching something like that. Yet a person could hope.

We spotted Ben, bent over picking up something. We rode up and greeted him with a good morning.

"Chad'tu how's your side?" He asked as he straightened up. "Does it hurt much?"

"Naw, it hurts some—but it's bearable." As we sat our horses and talked with Ben, I said to Jake, "You want to tell him or you want me to?"

Ben looked from me to Jake and spoke. "Tell me what?" He said a little nervous as he looked apprehensively at us. Ben couldn't tell by our poker faces, whether what we had to say was good or maybe bad.

I said, "Ben you're through cleaning the streets of Tombstone." Jake chimed in "Yeah, Ben you're through cleaning these streets."

He looked at us and said, "You're not putting me back in jail are you? I done everything you all told me to do and then some."

Both Jake and me lost our poker faces and burst out laughing at Ben's expression.

Ben didn't know what was going on. "Okay! What's so damn funny?"

"If you could just see the expression on your face," we said, between guffaws.

"Well it ain't funny to me, so tell me."

Jake spoke up. "The sheriff … that is … Chad'tu here is firing you from street picker—upper. And guess what?"

"What?" he asked and started to fidget as he looked at me.

"Well Ben, you done such a good job of cleaning the streets, I'm going to promote you to cleaning up the riffraff that drifts into this town." Ben stood there with a questioning look on his face. He still didn't get it. "Jake, explain what I just said to him."

Jake said, "Ben, Tombstone is an up-and-coming town and it's growing larger day by day. And each day the town attracts more undesirables, as you can tell …"

I cut into Jakes speech and said. "Jake! Enough of your orator skills just tell him."

Jake held up a hand and said, "Just you hold your horses there Chad'tu, I'm a gettin' to it, in due time. This is a momentous moment." Jake got down from his horse and stepped toward Ben holding out his hand. Ben didn't know what to do, so he stuck out a hand and Jake took it, pumped it up and down, and said, "Let me be the first to congratulate you on becoming the second deputy of this grand town of Tombstone." Ben was dumbstruck for a moment. Then what Jake had said started to sink in.

"Are you two sure about this? You must be joking with me. "He looked from one of us to the other. He could tell we were not joking by the serious look on our faces. "It surely is an honor you fellows want me to be a deputy. But … I'm not sure I can handle it."

"You did right well the day we had the shootout. So we talked it over and we both think you can handle the job. And besides that, you'll be getting a raise in pay."

As a raise in pay was mentioned he quickly said, "I accept." He must've been thinking about what Katie would say when he told her.

Later that day we gave Ben back his horse, along with a shiny five-pointed star. The judge swore him in, as an unhappy mayor looked on with a frown, probably thinking about the money this was going to cost the town. After getting things straightened out, Ben settled in and sort of comfortable with his new position, my thoughts turned to getting out of town and visiting Jaydeen.

CHAPTER 43

NEXT MORNING, I gathered a few belongings, packed my saddlebags and bedroll, told Jake where I was going and headed out. It felt like a great burden had been lifted from my shoulders. My wound was healing rapidly, only hurting when I twisted or tried to lift anything heavy. Other than that, I headed out of town in high spirits.

I took my time, and rode north, thinking about the past. It didn't help any. Two hours later, I rode into the yard of the gun shop. I was amazed that Brett was not standing on the porch to greet me. I wondered if something had happened to him. I pulled up my horse, dismounted and gave a holler, "Brett you in there?"

For a second or two there was no answer. Then from behind the house coming from the corral, I heard a yell. "I'm back here." Leading my horse around the house toward the corral, I saw Brett working with the appey. I thought she sure is a pretty little filly.

Brett walked over to the rail and leaned against it. "Well if this ain't a pleasant surprise," Pushing his hat back off his forehead he said, "What do I owe this visit to?"

"I thought it was time to take a few days and do some visiting."

Brett said, "A fellow stopped by here several days back, said something about trouble in town. Did you have trouble?" Brett looked me up and down, "You look okay. If there's anything you want to tell, I'd like to hear it."

Damn, it was only a few days after the incident and here Brett had already heard about the shootout. Word sure did travel fast. "Yeah, Brett it was nothing. Just something some cowpokes wanted settled. Jake, Ben and me settled it for them." I went on, "Seems now like it happened a long time ago. If I didn't have this scratch on my side, I would think it was all a dream. Anyway, the undertaker had a big boost in business."

Brett crawled through the corral fence with a concerned look on his face. He said, "Okay, how about showing me that little scratch." I pulled up my shirt and he looked at the bandages on the front and back of my side. He said, "Damn! I told you to be careful. Now you've gone and got yourself shot. You're damn lucky that's where the bullet hit, looks like it passed clean through. If it'd hit you anywhere else, you'd probably be dead now. You're damn lucky."

"Yeah, that's what the Doc said. A little bit to the left or a little bit higher... I'd be a dead turkey."

"You sure you're okay? You look a might pale." Concern tinged his voice. "How's Jake? He didn't get shot did he?"

"No he didn't get shot. He's smarter' n me. Maybe he was more careful, do you think?" Wanting to change the subject I asked, "How is the filly coming along? She seems to have grown some since I last saw her."

Brett said, "Don't try to change the subject, but yeah, she's a sweetheart. She's smart and she learns real fast." The filly walked slowly to the rail stuck her head over and gave Brett a push in the shoulder. He in turn, pushed her head away, but she just came right back and nudged him again.

"She seems to have taken a real liking to you." I said.

"Yeah, if I didn't already have a horse I might consider her as my main ride, but she don't belong to me. She belongs to you. It's about time you came out here to take care of your chores and some of the things you're supposed to be doing."

"Aw, Brett, what choice did I have? You know I've been busy keeping the peace and trying to enforce the law in Tombstone. And I ain't had much time for anything else."

"Yeah, I heard about all them signs you been putting up around town. Some of the people in town and a few out of town ain't so happy, I hear. Next thing you know, you'll be put 'n a sign up here on the front porch," he said, laughing. "You must be hungry after that long ride." He glanced up at the sun, which was directly overhead. "Put your horse in the corral and come on in. I'll rustle us some grub. It must be close to lunchtime. What do you say— you hungry?"

Brett held the gate open. I led my horse into the corral. Brett closed the gate and latched it. I took off the saddle and bridle and hung them on the rack in the lean-to. "Yeah, I guess I could eat something."

We walked into the house, going through the side door. Brett said, "It really is good to see you Chad."

"It's good to be back. I see you built a new shed and another corral—if you could call it that. And got yourself a cow. Now, just where did the cow come from?"

Well, Brett said, "This here farmer pulled his wagon up front one day. He had a rifle that was broken and he wanted me to fix it. He said he didn't have any money. First he wanted to trade me a bunch of vegetables, you know, corn, tomatoes, cucumbers, whatever. He said he was on his way to town and he didn't have any other firearm. He was afraid someone might rob him after he sold his produce, so he needed to get his rifle fixed to protect himself."

"He had a cow tied up behind his wagon. I said to him, mister you throw in that cow and I'll fix your rifle. I'll even throw in some bullets for it too, and son of a gun, you know he did. That's how I got a cow, and now I get fresh milk too."

"Brett, are you telling me you know how to milk a cow? It seems there's no end to the things you can do. Next thing you know you'll have a bunch of chickens and a rooster running around out there."

Brett smiled a silly lopsided grin, and said, "Already got that. Didn't you see the chickens out back of the lean-to?"

"Damn Brett, you're really gettin' domesticated on me. Next thing I know, you're goin' to become a farmer and give up being a gunsmith."

"Not on your life, I'll never give up being a gunsmith." he said, setting out some cornbread and beans that were cold. He poured milk into a glass from a pitcher. "Let's eat,"

"Brett, it sure is good to be back again. I really missed you. You're the only family I got."

"How long can you stay?" Brett asked.

"The doc said for me to take a couple weeks off and heal up."

"Is Jake the acting sheriff while you're taking time to heal up?" He asked. "Yeah, I made Jake temporary sheriff. He can handle it, since he was a sheriff before, and you know what else? Jake and me, we made Ben a deputy.

From a cattle rustler to a deputy, what do you think of that?"

Brett answered. "Yeah sounds like something I done back in my younger days. Although I don't think, I ever rustled any cattle. Might have killed one for some food, some time or t'other."

"Well all I can say is he kept Jake and me from getting shot in the back. He ain't too bad with a gun. He had a chance to shoot both me and Jake in the back if he'd wanted. Jake said he would work some with Ben on his draw, and handling of his gun."

"Jake knows his business when it comes to making his guns talk." Brett said between mouthfuls.

"Have you ridden the appey yet?" I asked Brett.

"Not yet, I was saving the honor for you, seeing's she's your horse. I got her halter broke and used to the saddle blanket on her back. She didn't balk at either one. She acted like it was something normal. She's one smart filly. Learns fast and is real easy going. She's gonna make you one fine ride."

I finished my plate of beans and stood. "Let's go see my fine ride." Going out to the corral, we slipped between the fence rails. The appey,

'Faith,' I had named her, gave a low whinny and pranced over and nudged Brett.

I said, "She acts more like your puppy than she does a horse."

I held out my hand. She stood a moment and looked sideways at my out-stretched hand. She swung her head close to my hand and smell. She tossed her head into the air, as if to say who are you.

I spoke quietly to her in a soft voice. "You remember me don't you Faith?" At the sound of my voice, her ears flicked forward. She lowered her head and took a step toward me. I stood not moving. She sniffed my hand again and then stepped up giving me a nudge that almost knocked me off my feet. Brett just stood there, as we made friends, until that last nudge when he started laughing at me.

Still laughing Brett said, "Now, whose puppy is she? You thought I'd spoiled her. Maybe I did just a little. But you can see she's just naturally friendly."

I put an arm around her neck, and with the other hand, I scratched between her ears while talking to her in a soft voice. Surprisingly, she seemed to understand my words.

Brett said. "I think you got her hypnotized. I bet she'd let you ride her right now. Want to try?"

"Aw, Brett I don't know. It might be too soon for me to try riding her, don't you think?"

Brett didn't answer; he just walked over to the lean-to, picked up a saddle blanket and saddle from the post where they were hung. On the way back, he snagged the bridle and said, "I heard a saying once, 'Faint heart never won fair lady.'"

Dropping the saddle, he handed me the blanket along with the bridle. Stepping back, he leaned against a rail and said, "Let her rip partner. Just remember, treat her like a lady. Be gentle with her … it's her first time." He chuckled at his remark.

I had no idea what he was talkin' about.

Faith pawed the ground. Then stood there waiting, like an impatient bride. Talking softly I placed the blanket on Faith's back. She only turned her head and looked back at me. I took the bridle, and with my hands, I warmed up the metal bit that would go in her mouth. I stepped slowly to her head. Still, she just stood there. I slipped the bit into her mouth between her teeth and then slipped the rest of the bridle up over her ears and fastened it behind her jaw … So far so good. I wondered what she might do when she felt the weight of the saddle.

I pulled gently on the reins and she turned and followed. We stopped beside the saddle. I reached down picked up the saddle from the ground and gently placed it on Faith's back. She quivered and stomped, then stood still. Reaching under her belly, I caught the cinch strap and timing Faiths breaths, I buckled it tight when she exhaled. It was then I realized I was covered with sweat. I was more nervous than Faith.

I looked over where Brett stood, his hat pushed back, with his face lit up in a broad smile. He was enjoying this. He moved his arms in an upward motion, telling me to go ahead and get on with it. I walked Faith around in a circle a few times, letting her get a feel for the weight of the saddle.

Brett called over, "You going to take all day? Can't you see she's ready for you?"

"What if she bucks me off?"

"You been bucked off before. Ain't nothing a man can't handle. You are a man aren't you?"

Brett's last remark was like a cocklebur stuck where I couldn't get to it. I stepped gently into the left stirrup and apprehensively swung my right leg over the saddle and slipped my boot into the stirrup. I became aware I'd been holding my breath in anticipation of being thrown off. Taking a deep breath, I sat waiting for that moment.

Brett took his hat off and swinging it around, shouted out, "Yahoo! See Chad, how easy that was."

As he spoke those words, Faith stamped a hoof and let out a snort as she arched her back ready to toss me. I pressed my legs tight against her sides, and made a clicking sound with my tongue and urged her forward.

She moved forward alright, she gave two quick bucks and then putting her head down she stopped suddenly. I grabbed the saddle horn to keep from being tossed over her head onto the ground. She stood for a moment with her head down not moving, just breathing hard. She pulled up her head and turned to look back at me. I swear, she smiled and that was it. She was docile as a lamb.

Brett laughed, "Now if that wasn't the damnedest thing I ever did see. That was the fastest I ever seen a horse broke." He went on, "Or maybe she was just showing you who was boss. You know like women do?"

I rode over to where Brett stood and stopped. Faith reached forward with her nose and gave Brett an affectionate nudge. I thought this was a good time to take Faith out for a stroll around the countryside and maybe a run, seeing as how I was already mounted and Faith seemed wanting to go. "Brett, you feel like going for a ride?" I asked.

"No. I got too many guns to fix, seeing as how I been short handed for awhile." He said chuckling at my chagrined expression. "But I think it's a good idea for Faith to get out and run some of that sassiness out of her. Wait and I'll open the gate for you."

Going through the gate, I let Faith have her head. She took off going hell bent out across the sandy dunes, weaving in and out through the sagebrush in a sudden burst of frivolous exuberance. Damn she was fast. I should have known with her long legs. She was quick and sure-footed; she didn't let up running for a good forty minutes it seemed. I thought I had me a better horse than most. We rode back in to the corral at a more leisurely pace than when we had left. The sun was dipping below the far mountain peaks casting a reddish, yellow glow into the sky.

After setting the saddle and blanket aside, I took some burlap and gave Faith a good rub down. I was feeding her some oats from a bucket when Brett came up.

"How did your ride go? You were gone so long I was about ready to come looking for you."

"Brett you won't believe what a horse I got myself here. She runs like the devil was after her."

"Fast is she?"

"Brett if she was any faster we'd now be over on the other side of those mountains yonder."

Brett laughed, "You wouldn't be joshing me would you?"

"Yeah, maybe just a might, but all kidding aside, she's the finest horse I have ever ridden, and that's a fact."

After spending a couple days with Brett, I told him I had an itch to see Jaydeen. I helped with the dishes after breakfast and then we went out to the corral. Faith walked straight over and ignoring Brett gave me a nudge with her nose, she was happy to see me.

Brett stood watching as I carefully saddled up Faith, not knowing what kind of reaction I might get from her. She snorted and quivered then stood motionless, waiting. "She sure has taken to you. It must have been the ride yesterday." Brett said "Looks like a love affair in full bloom."

As I rode out through the gate on the way to see Jaydeen, Brett said in an offhand manner, "You two behave yourselves you hear!" Then he let out a loud guffaw. I urged Faith to a gallop, my face flushed.

CHAPTER 44

A S THE SUN was setting over the mountains to the west, I rode in to the Brucker ranch. I didn't see anyone about, but there was a yellow light coming from the house, so I knew someone was there. I gave out a loud hello.

The door opened and there stood Jaydeen silhouetted in the open door-way, looking even prettier than I remembered. My heart gave a little flip-flop and started to beat faster.

Doing a quick hitch of reins around the hitching rail, I leaped over the steps onto the porch and grabbed Jaydeen in my arms. I held her close and whispered in her ear, "God I've missed you."

Jaydeen's body pressed tightly against mine, she reached up and put her arms around my neck. "Not as much as I missed you, I bet." Then she gave me a long hard kiss which I returned. I started getting warm, even though the evening was cool. Jaydeen Pulled back and took a deep breath. "Chad, come on in, the boys will be along shortly—somehow they never miss supper."

We sat at the kitchen table drinking coffee, while we waited for Sid and Trace. The kerosene lamp cast its dim glow and shadows flickered across the room. She looked at me. "Chad are you okay?"

"Sure Jay, I'm just fine—now that I'm with you."

"No! That's not what I meant. I … Oh! You get me so flustered sometimes I can't talk right."

She took my hands in hers and held them tightly, then started again. "Chad what I meant is, you haven't been shot have you?"

How did she know? I wondered. Then I put on my best manly face.

"What makes you think I was shot?" I looked at her questioningly.

"Oh, I didn't mean anything. Only a rider passed through here a few days back, told us about a big gunfight that had happened in Tombstone.

I was anxious and worried, you being the sheriff and all, that something might have happened to you. He said a lot of outlaws were dead, and by now were probably buried deep, resting in Boot Hill."

"Well as you can plainly see I'm alive and mostly well, except for a little scratch I got keeping the peace." I wondered if it had been the same rider that had told Brett.

Jaydeen would not shut up, 'till I had raised my shirt and showed her the stitched up wound that stopped bleeding a day or two after the shooting. The doc had said it was healing nicely and would leave only a slight scar.

Jaydeen took a long time to look closely at the wound. She finally straightened up and looked me in the eyes, and shook her head.

"What? What now?" I threw my arms into the air, exasperated.

"Damn doctor don't know how to sew. Look at those stitches, all crooked and everything. Hell I can sew better 'n that. ..." She added, "With my eyes shut."

"Damn, Jaydeen, you don't have to have a conniption fit, and get so excited."

"Oh Chad, I don't care about them stitches. I'm just so happy you're here and alive." She stood and poured us more coffee. "And what do you think would happen to our kids if you went and got yourself killed? Did you ever think about that?"

I almost choked on my swallow of hot coffee at her words. "Jaydeen, have you gone plumb crazy? You know damn well we don't have any kids, yet. We ain't even married."

"That's true. But if you go and get yourself killed, we won't have any kids at all, now will we?"

"Yeah, I see what you're getting at. But honey, that's my job—to protect the citizens of Tombstone."

"And that's another thing. After we're married, I don't want you being the sheriff. Okay? I don't want my husband and the father of my children to have a job where I never know if he's coming home in a box or not."

Then the door slammed shut, Sid took off his hat hung it on the rack by the door with Trace right behind him. Sid looked at me saying, "Chad it's good to see you. I hope we aren't interrupting anything?"

"It's okay Sid, you aren't interrupting. We were just having a friendly discussion about the kind of work I do."

"It didn't sound so friendly when we came onto the porch. As a matter of fact, we could hear the two of you going at it before we got to the hitching rail. Isn't that right, Trace?"

"Just leave me out of it; I'm not saying a thing." Trace said,

"Well," I hemmed and hawed, "You know how redheads are. They're said to have fiery tempers." I turned back to Jaydeen, and took her in my arms before she could show her temper at the last remark. I kissed her on the tip of her nose, and told her I was sorry.

"Well you should be," She lovingly hugged me around the waist to show she forgave me.

I let out a groan, and winced as she hugged me, putting pressure on my wound.

"Oh, Chad I forgot about your side."

We realized we both were saying we were sorry at the same time and started to laugh at one another.

"After we're married Jay, I'll see about getting into a different line of work. Okay?"

"Do you promise?"

"Yes, I promise."

"Okay," she said with a big smile, "Let's eat and talk about what you might be able to do."

Sid chimed in, "Yeah lets all talk about that. It should be a right lively discussion."

While we ate, we talked, throwing ideas out to one another. I could quit being sheriff. I could stay on with Brett and become a master gunsmith. My income would be enough for two people, but if Jay and me wanted a family, the pay wouldn't be enough.

"How about ranching? You could raise cattle along with a few horses," Sid tossed out.

"Yeah, I could be a rancher like you. Would you like that Jay?" I asked around a mouthful of beans. Before she could answer, I went on, "At least we would have enough to eat and in a few years, who knows? Maybe enough to feed more than two you think."

"Chad, that's a great idea. It would make me happy knowing you'd be home every night." Then Jaydeen went on, "But you don't know anything about cattle or ranching."

"Well I could learn, couldn't I?"

Sid said, "Hold on ... hold on! You all are getting carried away. Let's take this slow and easy and think it through." There was quiet for a moment, only the sound of forks and knives on china were heard.

I said, "Trace, you haven't said a word. Cat got your tongue. Or don't you have any ideas you want to throw in the pot?"

Trace, being the oldest, said in his mild way, "I learned a long time ago not to jump into things without thinking about it first. Seems to me, you're getting your cart before the horse, as the saying goes. Seems to me, you'd need to get yourself some knowledge and experience about the cattle business before you go leaping into something you ain't got no idea about."

He forked a piece of beef into his mouth, chewing thoughtfully, "Then too you'll need someplace to raise those cattle and horses ... you'd need a spread of your own. Did you think about that?"

"Yeah, all that's true," I admitted, "but you and Sid could teach me, couldn't you?"

Sid looked thoughtful. "I might give it some consideration, Chad" After supper, I helped Jay clear the table and while doing the dishes, we talked about what the future might bring. We were in love with one another, which was the main thing. Everything else would work itself out, somehow.

Jay slipped a light jacket on and we joined Sid and Trace out on the porch where they sat in the dark, talking. Jay and I sat on the long wood bench. Off in the distance, a coyote yapped at the full moon rising above the dark silhouetted hills. The night air had a chill to it. Fall was coming.

Jaydeen broke the silence with her soft voice. "The three of you haven't asked me what I think. While you all been discussing, I was thinking what would be best for all of us. This is the way I see it." She went on, putting her thoughts out there, like the tomboy she was.

"First thing, we get married. We need a place to live as man and wife. We have plenty of room here for Chad and me. Think about this, you'll have some one to help with the cattle and you can teach him the ins and outs. And you'll be keeping your cook and housekeeper awhile longer too."

I couldn't see her in the dark but I could tell by her last words, she was smiling. "Anyone object to my way of thinking?" She asked. "Let's hear it now." No one objected. So it was settled, just like that.

What a woman, I thought, and she was all mine or soon would be.

The next morning at breakfast, Jaydeen and the three of us discussed the plans she had in her head. She had decided that we should be married proper in Tombstone, by the local preacher. She would leave it up to Sid and Trace if they wanted to be there or not. She informed everyone she had shopping to do in town, which was one of the reasons she gave for getting married there.

No one disagreed with Jay on the issue. I was beginning to see who really ran this ranch and just who the boss was. She turned and gave me an ultimatum, telling me she had waited long enough and if I didn't want to marry her, she would find someone else who would.

CHAPTER 45

BEFORE THE NEXT week was over Jaydeen, was Mrs. Chad'tu. That woman sure did know how to whip men into doing what she wanted, and that's a fact. I'm not complaining, but sometimes I'm now known as Mister Jaydeen.

Brett and Jake, Sid and Trace, Ben and Kate, and the judge and mayor, had all been there for the wedding even though it wasn't held in the church. Jay didn't want a big wedding with all the hoopla that followed such an event.

Oh! I forgot, little Miguel was there too. He stood off to one side, bare of foot, holding his sombrero in his hands and smiling from ear to ear.

Miguel came up after the wedding and gave Jay a bunch of wild flowers, he'd picked for the occasion. Jay bent down and gave him a big kiss on the cheek, "Thank you Miguel, this is so sweet."

Miguel smiled, a little embarrassed, "Señora, pleeze take care of señor Chad'tu."

Everyone in hearing distance laughed.

Someone in the group insisted we go and have a few drinks to celebrate this great event. Jay didn't want to, but after much convincing, she agreed. She was only going to have one drink she said, if the rest of you want to get drunk ... for us just to go ahead and do it.

What a night. Everyone woke up the next morning with a throbbing, pounding head. Including Jay, who'd had more than just that one drink.

After breakfast, I told Jaydeen, Sid, and Trace to go on back to the ranch. I said I would be along in a day or two. I had some business in town to take care of. I rode over to the sheriff's office, tied up and went in. Jake and Ben were seated having a cup of coffee. Jake sat behind the desk with his boots up on it. Ben sat in a chair with his legs crossed, holding his cup with both hands. They both looked up as I entered. "A good morning to you," I said.

Jake replied, "How's your head this fine morning? Quiet a celebration we had last night, wouldn't you say?"

"It must have been a real wingding, because I don't remember a thing after that sixth drink. They must have been double pours is all I can say. How about you two, how do you feel?"

"Passable, passable, alls I can say. But I have felt better," Jake said, taking another swallow of coffee.

I looked at Ben. He looked like something the dogs had dragged home. "And you, Ben, how you feeling?"

"I feel like I been chewed up and throw'd up and spit out. I feel like hell, and I ain't ever going to have another drink."

Jake and me laughed at Ben and said almost together, "Yeah, till the next time."

I poured myself a cup of coffee and sat down in a vacant chair. I took my time and after a couple of swallows, I said, "I need to talk to you two. Now that I'm a married man, I'm going to resign as sheriff."

Jake's boots came down off the desk and hit the floor with a loud bang. Ben sat bolt upright in his chair spilling some coffee from his cup. They both had their mouths wide open with a shocked look on both their faces.

Jake was the first to speak and Ben was right there with his voice too. "You just can't quit like that."

"Jake, you been a law officer before. I think down El Paso way, you said, wasn't it? I want you to take over as sheriff, and Ben can still be your deputy. Okay with you, Ben? I hear you're becoming right handy with a gun." Taking a sip of coffee, I gave Jake a second to let it sink in.

"What do you say? Before you answer, think about this. We got this town under control and all sewed up. All you got to do is keep it that way. Oh, and before I forget, you'll probably get a big raise to boot. What do you say?" Jake didn't answer while he thought over the proposition. Finally, after some thought the first words out of his mouth was, "How much of a raise?" I knew talk about money would get Jake interested. "Oh, you could probably name the amount Jake. They would have to go along, seeing's you'd be the only law left. Ben he don't have enough experience yet." Jake said, "I got to think this over. Give me a day or two."

Ben just sat there with a dumbfounded look on his face. Finally, he shook his head and said, "What about me, do I get a raise too?"

"That's something you two will have to work out with the mayor. As I see it, he don't have much choice now does he?" I could see the dollar signs in their eyes, as the wheels turned in their heads, thinking about the proposition.

"Well, I think I'll head over to the mayor's office and tell him the bad news. If you all want to come along, you're sure welcome." They hemmed and hawed, but seeing my mind was made up, they grudgingly said they would go with me. They thought a force of three to face the mayor would be better than one at a time.

By the time, we got to the mayor's office it was eleven o'clock. I opened the door and the three of us traipsed in. The mayor sat behind his huge desk leaning forward, holding his head between his hands and moaning softly. He looked up, startled to see the three of us. "Gentlemen what can I do for you this … this god awful morning?"

As I laid out what I was intending to do and the plans that I had in mind. The mayor held his head and moaned louder. The more I said, the louder the moans became. By the time I'd finished telling my plans the mayor was almost in tears.

"Chad'tu," he started on me, "You can't do this to me. Please think about this great town of Tombstone. What will we do without you?"

"Well mayor, this is how I got it figured …" I sat on the corner of his desk. He didn't object this time.

"Yes, yes, go on," The mayor said impatiently.

"I've been thinking. Jake here was a marshal or sheriff down El Paso way, weren't you, Jake?" I pointed, "Ben over there has become right handy with his six-gun, ain't that right Ben?" Ben didn't say anything he just shook his head up and down along with a shrug of shoulders. "The only thing I can see that might be a problem is they both want more money, since they are moving up in importance." With every word that I spoke, the mayor moaned louder and louder, until he gave up and buried his head in his arms on the desk.

The mayor finally raised his head and spoke. "Chad'tu, you got me over a barrel. I have no choice but to go along with you fellows. Chad'tu, when do you plan on giving up being the sheriff?"

"How about right now," I said, as I unpinned the silver badge and handed it to him.

"Damn it, Chad'tu! Does it have to be this instant? I have to have time to get use to this here change."

"Make your decision quickly mayor, or the three of us will be out of here right quick."

The mayor stood up still holding my badge, walked around his desk and handed the badge to Jake. "Jake, I now officially appoint you the new sheriff of Tombstone." He turned to Ben, "Ben you are now promoted to be the new First Deputy."

He walked back and sat back down in his chair. He took out a cigar and lit it with a shaking hand. "Are you boys happy now?"

I looked at Jake—he smiled with a shrug of his shoulders. I looked at Ben—he rolled his eyes like he couldn't believe what had just happened. "It looks to me like everyone is happy with the deal except for you, Mayor. You don't look too happy."

The mayor started to say something, but I cut him off. "I know what you're going to say mayor—this is going to cost the town more money. Actually, it will save the town money. Think of it this way mayor; you will only have to pay two men now instead of three. So even though Jake and Ben will be getting more pay, you're saving money by not paying me."

With that said, I reached out took the mayor's hand and shook it saying, "It's been a pleasure doing what I could for Tombstone, Mister Mayor, Ah … Bill."

"Come on boys, we done all we can here." The three of us walked out of the mayor's office and into the bright sun and fresh air. Once outside I said, "Now wasn't that easy?"

"That sure was slick," said Jake. "I don't think I could have done it any better."

"Well thank you Jake. That's a compliment coming from you."

I had my doubts. Did I really not want to be the prestigious sheriff of Tombstone any more? I wondered.

Yeah, I did want to quit. I was tired of keeping the peace and getting shot at and not knowing when I might get the fatal bullet that would end it all. And then there was Jaydeen. It wouldn't be fair to her. I had, after all promised, I would be a cattle rancher.

The three of us were happy. Jake got to be sheriff; Ben got to be top number one deputy, as he put it. And now he could marry Katie, as he called her. And me, I was out of a job.

CHAPTER 46

WE HEADED BACK to the sheriff' office and I gathered up whatever belonged to me, throwing it into my saddlebags. I told the boys to keep a tight rein on things, keep an eye on their back trail, and try not to get killed. If ever they needed help, they knew where I could be found. We shook hands and slapped each other on the back. It was hard to leave these two, with all the things we had gone through together. It was like leaving family. I had a lump in my throat. In fact, besides Brett, they were the only family I had now. I said I would see them tomorrow morning before Jaydeen and me left for the ranch. We agreed to meet at the hotel for breakfast. While the three of us had been getting things straightened out with the mayor, Jaydeen had been buying a few things she needed out at the ranch. I had doubts about becoming a rancher. The corn had now been shucked as the saying went. However, I had my lovely bride Jaydeen, and I would soon find out if I was cut out for ranching.

I went looking for Jaydeen and found her at Sam's Emporium. She was buying some gingham fabric along with things to sew with. She said she wanted to make a new dress and me a new shirt. I frowned at the gingham, until she showed me the plaid cloth that was to be my shirt, and then I smiled.

We had supper at the hotel. Word of the wedding had spread. Everyone wished us well, especially Kathryn who thanked me for making Ben the number-one deputy. She hinted there would probably be another wedding soon, now that Ben was getting a raise in pay. Jaydeen and I were invited.

Jaydeen and I finished supper and I started to pay, when the owner of the hotel rushed up waving his hands and shaking his head saying, "No, No, No, you don't pay for your wedding supper, I pay."

"Well Ben that's right nice of you. I'm mighty obliged, thank you."
I turned and taking Jaydeen by the hand, I pulled her to my side. "Ben
I don't believe you've met my wife Jaydeen. Jaydeen, I'd like you to meet
the owner of this fine establishment, Ben Barlow…. Ben this is my wife
Jaydeen."

Ben took her hand and said, "Pleased to make your acquaintance, Mrs.
Chad'tu." Jaydeen blushed and did a slight curtsy.

We Strolled arm in arm about town, as we walked off the meal we'd
just eaten. We didn't talk much; I was feeling nervous about what would
happen when we went to my room for the night. I think Jay was a little
nervous too. Neither of us knew what to expect. We would just have to let
nature run its course.

The next morning we awoke still wrapped around one another. The
sun shone through the window bright and cheerful. It was going to be a
wonderful day, I thought, as I lay there looking at Jaydeen. I bent my head
down and gently kissed her soft sweet lips. Still half-asleep, she kept her
eyes shut; moaning softly as she passionately kissed me back. We didn't
get out of bed for another hour, it seemed like an eternity. When we did,
we were both flushed and fully awake. I felt that I had died and gone to
heaven.

Back in our room after breakfast, I told Jay I was ready for desert.
"Don't be silly Chad; we'll have plenty of time for that later," she said
laughingly. Then in a more modest tone, "We got all the rest of our lives
for that sort of thing."

We packed our few belongings and said our goodbyes to the people at
the hotel. The stable boy brought our horses, saddled and standing tied at
the hitching rail out front of the hotel. I tied my saddlebags on and started
to help Jaydeen with hers. It was a large roll; she was trying to tie behind
her saddle. Jaydeen declined my help as she finished tying the bundle tight,
I said, "Jay, I need to stop at the sheriff's office and tell the boys goodbye."

"Yes, I'd like to say goodbye to them too, they did seem so nice."

At the sheriff's office, Jake was sitting with his boots up on the desk.
He stood in deference to Jaydeen, and said, "Ben's out making his round
of the town."

I shook Jake's hand and said, "Jake, can't say it hasn't been fun knowing you. Tell Ben goodbye. And Jake, if you ever need help of any kind, just let me know and I'll be here for you."

"Thanks, Chad'tu, That's mighty good of you to offer, but Brett's already offered his help and he's a lot closer. I sure do appreciate it though." He jerked me to him, gave me a hug and slapped me on the back said, "It surely has been a pleasure working with you and if you ever get in a bind, just let me know and I'll come a running."

"Jake, have you seen Brett or the others? I thought we might all ride out of town together."

Jake let out a chuckle, "Yeah I saw the three of them this morning. They were on their way out of town, Said they had chores to do. Seeing you weren't up and around, they said something like, 'they'll probable spend a week in bed before they ever leave that hotel room.'"

At the remark, Jaydeen blushed and looked down.

"Sorry ma'am I didn't think." Jake said, with a shrug of his shoulders. Jay and me hit the leather and rode out of town. We finally were on our way, on our way to our new life. The life of an unknown future beckoned us with all the excitement and adventure that it might bring. We were in no hurry, so we rode along easy and talked of all the things we were going to do with our life together. There sure were a lot of things we talked about on that ride.

A couple hours later, we got to Brett's Gunsmith store. He was surprised to see us so soon. "I didn't expect to see you two for at least a week." he said grinning.

I looked at Jay and she was blushing again. Why do women have to do that? I wondered?

"Get down and set a spell." It seemed he hadn't noticed Jaydeen's blushing.

Jay rode a horse as a man would, astride its back. She probably rode better than I did so I didn't offer to help her down and neither did Brett.

Brett said, "If you all want to stay the night you're welcome, or were you planning on riding on?"

I looked at Jay for an answer; she shrugged and smiled but didn't say anything. I guess she was leaving it up to me, now that I was the man of the house. "Well it's a good two days ride out to the ranch. We might just as well spend the rest of the day here helping Brett. You two can visit some. We can spend the night and get an early start in the morning. What do you say Jay?"

"That's a wonderful idea. It will give me time and a chance to get to know Mister Brett, whom you speak so highly of." She said with a shy smile and a nod of her head.

Brett and Jay took to each other like a duck does to water. I felt a twinge of Jealousy as they got acquainted a little better than they had at the wedding. If I hadn't been married to Jay, and Brett wasn't my best friend, I would have taken offense to the way they were carrying on. I guess I was … jealous.

We didn't get as much work done, as we did visiting. Brett just wanted to sit and talk with Jaydeen. I think they were enamored with one another. Living this far out of town Brett hadn't had many women visitors. They finally got around and took notice of me setting there drinking my cold coffee.

It was getting late and we had to get an early start tomorrow. Jay and I went to the room that had formerly been mine and Brett went to his. My second night together with Jay was even better than the first. I just hoped we hadn't kept Brett awake.

The next morning over a breakfast of bacon, and fresh eggs from his chickens, along with strong black coffee, Brett grinning, asked how we had slept. Sheepishly we looked at each other and I said we had slept very well, thank you. Then being polite, asked how he had slept.

"Not too well. Too much noise, I think the horses were restless. I kept hearing snorting and a sort of whinny and a deep throated moan."

Jaydeen didn't say anything. So taking the bull by the horns, I said, "Sorry Brett but you know how it is." I looked at Jay for help.

"No I don't know how it is, why don't you tell me?"

"It's only our second day of marriage and … we're still sort of getting acquainted, you know?"

"Yeah I do know, even though I haven't had the pleasure of a wife, that I could call my own." He laughed at my bewildered expression and said, "Got-ya."

Jay chimed in and said, "What's he mean, Got-ya?"

I had to tell her about Brett and me playing jokes on one another. Saying something in a serious way so that the other believed it was for real. Once the other believed the line of bull that was being fed to him, the other would say, "Got-ya."

Jay understood what I had said, and in turn she said to Brett, "I'm so sorry that we kept you from sleeping. The snorting and whinnying came from Chad, the moaning and groaning came from me. You do know … Brett, how it is when a stallion and a mare in heat come together don't you?"

It was Brett's turn to look sheepish. He rolled his eyes the way he does sometimes and replied with a grimace, "Yeah I sort of remember how that goes." He looked down at the floor. He didn't know what to say.

There was a slight pause in the conversation for a moment or two. "Got-ya!" was the word that flew forth from Jaydeen's lips. Stunned,

Brett and I looked at each other in astonishment. It took a second or two to sink in then the three of us burst out laughing and tears came to our eyes.

Brett revived first, got control of himself, and said, "Remind me to never play that game with you Jaydeen, you're too damn good. You really did get me good." We all laughed again.

We all pitched in and cleaned the dishes then fed the horses and chickens and the cow.

We saddled our horses and each of us hugged Brett, and stepping into the leather we headed out, saying we would keep in touch. "Brett don't be a stranger," I yelled, "come on out and visit us at the ranch."

CHAPTER 47

WE RODE ALL day. Stopping before dark, we made camp as the sun set low on the horizon. After feeding the horses, we gathered a few dead mesquite branches and what ever else we could find that would burn and started a fire.

Out on the desert plains, after the sun goes down, it gets cold mighty quick. Working together, we cooked up some eggs that Brett had given us. Taking a little water from my canteen, I made the coffee. We sat eating our meager meal and talked about the future.

Rolling out our bedrolls and laying them side by side, we settled in. Holding each other for warmth, we fell asleep. Somewhere off in the distance a coyote yapped at the moon, as we drifted off to sleep and dream.

Next morning I stoked up the fire, added more branches, put on the left over coffee from last night and scrambled the three remaining eggs, since I'd broke the yoke of one, cracking it.

Kicking dirt on the fire, I smothered the flames. Throwing saddles on the horses, we mounted up and rode on toward the ranch. We should get there by dark if all went well.

Making our way through some boulders, the horses suddenly lifted their heads and blew out with a snort, ears flicking forward they started moving faster as they angled off around a large boulder. A small clump of mesquite and a yucca or two grew along side a very small pool of water. Leave it to the horses to find water. If there was any around, they would surely find it.

I looked up at the sun, almost directly overhead, and guessed it must be around midday. "Jay lets take a breather and rest the horses some." I stepped down and told Jay to hold my horse, while I tested the water, just to be sure it was not polluted with alkaline.

Kneeling down I dipped my cupped hand into the warm water and smelled it then stuck my tongue into it and tasted it. I took another handful and swallowed some. "The water is fine Jay, though it is a little warm, but it's wet and sweet." Standing I said, "Jay, give me your canteen." I grabbed mine from where it hung wrapped around the pommel, and reached for Jay's as she handed it to me. "I want to fill them before the horses muddy the water."

The horses were stomping around as I filled both canteens. They seemed impatient to get to the water and quench their thirst. I finished filling the last canteen and said, "Okay, the horses can drink."

Resting with our backs against its warm surface, we sat on the ground in the shade of the huge boulder, spared somewhat from the heat and the blazing sun. We sipped water from the canteens while the horses drank their fill.

"Sure is hot." Jay said wiping her forehead with a kerchief; she had dampened from the spring.

I didn't move but answered. "Yep you can rightly say that, but that's not what I'd say. I'd say its almighty damn hot."

Jay stood. "We've rested long enough; let's get on to the ranch and the beautiful green valley it rests in. I know it will be much cooler there." She said in a commanding tone.

"Yes your majesty! I'm at your command and service." I said with a great flourish of my hat and low bow. She let out a delighted squeal, somewhere between a squeak and a giggly laugh, which was so typical of her. I had to laugh too.

The rest of the day was uneventful, except for a dead steer that was some days old, that buzzards were still feeding on. We had scared them off as we rode up and now they were circling high in the sky waiting for us to leave so they could finish their feast.

It sure was hot; there was not a breath of air as we rode slowly along stirring up a small cloud of dust. Somewhat replenished from our brief rest. The horses moved at a faster pace, too.

We had covered a lot of territory when we finally caught our first glimpse of the low-lying hills that surrounded the ranch, telling us we were almost home. It wasn't my home. Yet, I would live there with Jaydeen, her brother and Trace, 'till I learned the cattle business.

Once that happened, Jay and me could find a place we could call our own. I smiled inwardly at the thought. I wondered what Jay was thinking. She was probably just happy to be getting back to the ranch that had been her home for so many years.

It was late as we rode in. I was tying the horses as Jay jumped down grabbed her purchases that she had bought in Tombstone and rushing into the house left me standing there alone. I finished tying the horses to the hitching rail, stepped onto the porch, and started into the house. Only to be almost knocked off my feet by Jay rushing out of the doorway. "They aren't here Chad!" Jay exclaimed frightened, "I wonder where they could be?"

The word 'be' had no sooner left her lips, when a flash of light coming off the distant hillside caught my eye. I looked, searching the hill. A reflection from something caught for an instance in the suns low setting rays. Upon looking closer, I saw there was movement on the side of the closest hill. Two horses were moving rapidly across the hillside headed in our direction.

I put my arm around Jay's slender waist pulling her close and said "Look yonder, I think that's them coming down from the hills now." The sun setting low over the hills, was shinning directly into our eyes, making it hard to see anything.

Jay looked up at me with her large green eyes. I pulled her close and kissed her passionately. By the time I was done with the kissing, Sid and Trace had ridden up.

"Hey you two, how's the newlyweds?" Sid said laughing, "Trace and me decided from all that kissing you two were doing you must still be in heat." Sid laughed again and this time, Trace laughed with him at his remark.

Trace stepped onto the porch and in his gravely voice said, "We ain't seen you for two days, you all getting along okay?" He pushed his hat back and stroking his moustache continued with his dissertation. "You two must be doing right fine from what I could see with all that hugging and kissing that was a goin' on."

I could tell Jaydeen was embarrassed by all their carryings on. She said, "I was going to fix us some supper but now I don't know if I will or not." Turning abruptly, she walked through the open door into the house. I thought she would slam the door but she didn't.

"Would you two take it easy? We just got in from a two-day ride across the desert plains. It was hot and dusty and with all the excitement of getting married and riding she's all wore out." Sid looked at Trace and Trace looked at Sid. They both had knowing smiles on their faces. "And might I just ask what you two are so smug and smiling about?"

"Well we wouldn't want to offend you, seeing' you got the fastest gun. We were just thinkin' it might not have been that long ride that tired her out." They looked knowingly at one another. They were about to split a rib. I could tell it was all they could do to contain their laughter.

"Okay you two get it out of your craw and spit it out. Just what's so damn funny?"

"Well we were just a thinkin' it probably wasn't all the riding she done, but all the riding that was done on her." They burst out with loud guffaws.

I had to admit their thinking might not be to far off. "Okay you two have had enough fun. Sober up and try not to upset our cook or were all going to regret it by going to bed hungry. Now let's go in and get some supper"

The next day after breakfast, the three of us saddled up. Today we were going out to check on the fences over in the north pasture and repair any that the cattle might have broken down.

Packing wire cutters, pliers, nails, and hammers into their saddlebags, Trace handed me two large rolls of heavy gauge wire, said, "Chad'tu you carry the wire." Trace turned toward his horse and stopped. "Oh! Damn near forgot the staples." he said grabbing a small canvas bag of staples which he handed to me. "Put it in the saddlebags along with the wire."

"Why do we have to mend fences?" I asked, as the three of us rode along the fence line looking for any breaks. "I thought all your cattle were free grazing and could go where they wanted."

"Since that cattle rustling episode, we decided to start fencing parts of the pasture to keep the cattle from straying off so far," Sid said.

We started up a slight incline after riding the fence line for a good hour or more. The fence ran up the side of the hill and then starting down, it suddenly took a turn and dropped off sharply. We followed the fence down the steep slope, our horses slipping and sliding on their haunches.

We found ourselves in a deep gully carved out by a recent rain. We found a sagging post and several strands of broken wire where several head of cattle had crossed recently, from the looks of the trampled ground.

"Trace, show Chad how to mend that broken fence while I go round up those strays." Sid yelled riding off at a fast pace. "Leave some of the wire off so I can drive them back through." he yelled back over his shoulder at us.

There wasn't a hint of a breeze. Being down in the gully resetting the post was hot sweaty work. This wasn't what I thought being a rancher was going to be like.

We were ready to restring the wire when Sid appeared. Whooping and a hollering and punctuated with a sharp whistle now and then, he drove six steers ahead of his horse. His horse whipping from side to side, kept the steers headed straight for the opening we had left in the fence.

The last steer bellowing made it through and we stapled the last few wires into place. "Now that wasn't so bad was it?" Trace said. He took off his hat with one hand and smiled, then wiped the sweat from his forehead with a sleeve.

"I didn't know ranching was going to be this hard" I replied.

Sid rode up and stepped down from the saddle. "What you two jawing about?"

Trace said, "Chad thinks this is hard work. Isn't that right Chad?"

"Yeah, that's what I said. I thought ranching was going to be easy, I thought all you had to do was get a bull and some cows and let em eat grass, have little ones and pretty soon you'd have enough to sell and make a profit." Sid laughed. "Chad … you think this was hard work, just you wait a couple weeks or a month or two, then you'll find out what ranching really is all about. Won't he, Trace?"

"Yep, I rightly would say he would." Trace went on, "Today so far has been a picnic. Mending fences is the easiest of all the chores we got to do."

"If you two are through talking lets get that last wire stapled on." Sid said, "We got a lot more fence to look at and it ain't even noon yet. It's still early so let's get on with it."

We found a few more places in the fence that needed fixing. They made me do the fixing while they stood around smoking and supervising. By the end of the day, my back hurt and my hands didn't feel any better, but I was an expert at fixing fences. At the days end we rode up past the house not stopping and going to the barn we unsaddled the horses and let them loose in the corral. Then we tossed hay out for them.

My lovely wife Jaydeen greeted us from the porch, as we walked around the side of the house. "You all get washed up, supper's almost ready. By the time you get all that dirt off it will be on the table and getting cold, so hurry up."

I walked up to Jaydeen and started to give her a hug and a kiss, she kind of hesitated, and said "You're all dirty."

I replied, "That's true, but what's a little dirt between lovers." Trace and Sid, shaking their heads, trying their best to ignore us, went on into the house to wash up.

Jaydeen stood apart from me and leaning over trying not to get dirty gave me a kiss on the lips. It was more like a peck than a kiss.

After the fellows and I had washed up, we sat at the kitchen table and had supper. All I can say is Jaydeen's almost as good of a cook as she is a lover. She'd made fried chicken, mashed potatoes, fried okra, and some white gravy along with hot black coffee. Oh, and I almost forgot the sweet rolls she'd made.

I was so thirsty from being out in the hot sun all day, that I had water to drink, instead of the strong coffee.

After supper, we all went out and sat on the porch, watching as the sun slipped behind the mountain peaks. The dusk of evening came rapidly upon our quiet little valley. Jaydeen wanted to know what I had done all day long. Trace and Sid laughed at her remark. They said I had learned how to fix fences today. "Ain't that right Chad?" Then they laughed again. Jaydeen wanted to know what was so damn funny about fixing fences.

Sid said, "If Chad thinks fixing fences is hard work. Wait till tomorrow, were rounding up several head of cattle that need branding, and were going to teach him how to use a branding iron. Then he can see what hard work is really all about, when we start the branding."

We smoked and had our coffee on the porch. We all turned in as we had to get an early start in the morning rounding up cattle that needed branding.

Jaydeen and I went to our room got undressed, turned out the lamp and crawled into bed. Jaydeen wanted to make love. I was so tired I must have fallen asleep while she was cuddling with me. I guess after awhile she gave up and went to sleep.

Still half-asleep, I awoke the next morning and reached for Jaydeen, she was not there. I heard the rattling of pans coming from the kitchen. She must be fixing breakfast. Getting out of bed I washed the sleep from my eyes and quickly got dressed

Walking softly, I snuck up behind Jaydeen, slipped my arms around her small waist, and kissed the back of her neck. She turned and put her arms around my neck and kissed me full on the lips. Then she pulled back and putting a frown on her face said, "A fine husband you are, in the middle of everything, you fall asleep."

"I'm sorry Jaydeen. I didn't mean to fall asleep. That's what happens when you're dead tired and I was dead tired. But I promise I'll make it up to you."

"I'll forgive you if you promise to make it up tonight. After all Chad, we are still newlyweds."

We stopped with our love talk when Sid and Trace walked into the kitchen and pouring themselves coffee, sat down at the table. I poured a cup for myself and joined them. Trace said, "Well Chad, today you're going to learn how to brand cattle. Are you ready?"

"I guess I'm as ready as I'll ever be." I said with a grimace. Taking a sip of hot coffee, "But I ain't really looking forward to it. I still ache all over from yesterday. I ain't used to this much work. I'm only used to riding and walking around and sometimes looking important."

CHAPTER 48

AFTER BREAKFAST, I kissed Jaydeen and went out to the barn with the boys. Getting our gear together, we saddled up the horses and rode out of the corral in search of the cattle we were going to brand.

Around nine o'clock we had rounded up about thirty-five head along with about fifteen strays, which were found down on the creek bottom.

We swung our horses back and forth, whistling, yelling, and swinging closed lariats at the laggards. Stirring up a cloud of dust, we pushed the cattle, into the holding corral.

Trace rigged up a chute of sorts that funneled in one steer at a time. With a rail slid across the chute in front to stop the steer, we would then slide another rail in behind, so the steer couldn't move. Earlier we had started a fire only a few steps from the chute. A branding iron shoved into the coals was glowing red-hot. Herding one steer at a time into the chute, we'd take that glowing red-hot yellow iron from the fire and press it onto the steer's rump. The smell of burnt hair and hide was something to get used to.

The steer would let out a loud bellow and sometimes they'd kick until we could slip the front rail from the chute to let them out. Then we'd do another one and then another one until they were all finished. By the time we had branded the last, we were dirty and sweaty. We called it a day and headed to the barn.

I hadn't realized that ranching was so much work. I wondered what else there was that I was going to learn before I was a real rancher. In the coming weeks, I found out that the chores were unending. You had to milk the cows, feed the chickens, slop the hogs, feed the horses, and sometimes had to fix a shoe they had thrown. Mend harnesses, repair wagons. Hell! I could go on for hours about things to be done.

That night in bed, I passionately kissed, caressed, and made Jaydeen very happy. I'd kept my promise to her.

We rode out the next day to one of the outlying pastures, and rounding up the cattle we found, moved them over to the next pasture. It was an easy day. Still, it did take us all day. Taking a break from the herding and driving of the cattle, I stopped Faith. Using my kerchief, I wiped the sweat from my forehead. I rolled and lit a cigarette. While taking a short rest, I gazed about the countryside.

It sure was a beautiful little ranch they had here. Someday, Jaydeen and I would have one as pretty or maybe even prettier.

I had no idea where or when or how I would find my dream ranch. As I sat smoking and daydreaming, I looked off into the distance at the range of mountains that lay dark and black on the horizon. Hard to tell how far away they might be. Sid rode up, stopped and rolled a smoke of his own. "Sid," I said pointing. "How far away you think them mountains are?"

"Oh, I don't know, maybe if I had to say, somewhere about forty miles. Maybe even further, it's hard to tell the distance of anything out here. The desert plain sometimes plays tricks on your eyes. Why, once I seen a lake out on that desert. I rode for it and just as I got close, it just up and disappeared"

"Have you ever ridden over and taken a look and seen what might be there?"

"No. When Pa found this place, he stopped looking and told us this was it. So no, I ain't ever been over there. Why do you ask, Chad'tu?"

"I was just daydreaming and wondering if maybe there might be grass and water over that way that maybe could support some cattle. If there was, maybe I could start a ranch on it. It was just a thought. I guess it is too far away."

"Yeah, it is a ways to get to them, I'd say."

No more was said about those tall black mountains in the weeks and months that followed. I guessed Sid had thought no more about it. Nevertheless, I couldn't stop thinking about them.

To me those mountains were like an itch you couldn't get to, to scratch. Ever time I rode out and looked at those mountains, I got that itch. Moreover, I wondered what those dark far away mountains might hold. I promised myself. One of these days, I'm going to ride over and check them out.

Ten months later, I still had not been to those black mountains. Yet they were always on my mind. The itch was still there, but now it was like you accidentally brushed up against a cactus, and got stuck by a thorn.

After a year, I purty much knew all there was to know about the cattle business. The cows had birthed their spring calves. Everything was going fine, except I was becoming more and more restless, wanting to see what might lie in those black mountains.

One morning after breakfast, I told Sid and Trace I'd been thinking about taking a few days off. All the work was caught up, the weather was warm, and they could get along without me for a few days as I had somewhere I had to go.

Jaydeen asked, "Where are we were going?"

Taking Jay's hands, I looked into her bright green eyes and said. "You're not going anywhere. Your going to stay here, where I'll know you'll be safe. I'm going to ride over and have a look at them black mountains that I been thinking about for the better part of a year now. I don't know what they might hold in the valleys that lay between their tops. There might be some danger for a woman. So I think it best you stay here."

Jaydeen tried to argue with me, but after awhile she could see it was no use. Deep down she knew I was right. It might not be a safe place for a woman. After all, there were still Indians roaming about the country. You could never tell if they were friendly or hostile 'till it was too late.

I'd packed my saddlebags with the things I thought I might need. Early the next morning after a hearty breakfast, I said my goodbyes to Sid and Trace. Turning to Jaydeen, I took my loving wife in my arms, held her tight, kissed her sweet lips, and whispered in her ear that I'd be back soon.

Stepping in the leather, I clicked my tongue at Faith and rode off to solve the curiosity in my mind about the mysteries those black mountains might hold … finally.

Faith loped along at a mile-eating pace with long easy strides. I slowed Faith to an easy walk now and then to catch her breath. She walked while I rolled and smoked a cigarette. When I finished the smoke, we were again riding at a fast pace.

Around noon I stopped and looking back, I could no longer see the ranch, only the tips of the hills that rose above it. I stepped down, poured some water from the canteen into my hat letting Faith have a drink. Shaking the water from the hat, I stuck it back on my head. Taking a drink from the canteen, I looked at the range of the hazy black mountains, which appeared to be not any closer than when I'd started. Sid was right they were farther than they appeared.

Back in the saddle, we moved on into the dry dusty desert plains, punctuated occasionally by a cactus or a clump of yuccas. Sometimes rock-hard black lava protruded from the sand. There was no wind and it had become increasingly hot, as the sun moved ever higher. We had slowed from the lope to a fast trot as the day wore on toward evening.

The sun set in the west dropping rapidly behind the ridge of the black mountains. We stopped and I tethered Faith, took the saddle off, and rubbed her down with the saddle blanket. Fed her some mesquite pods, she was content for the night.

I gathered dead mesquite and anything else that would burn clean and started a fire. Not knowing when or where we might be able to replenish the water supply, I didn't make coffee to conserve on what water I had. Eating the dried jerked beef and only taking a swallow to wash it down.

I unrolled my bedroll placing it close to the saddle. Taking the guns from around my waist and slipping the Winchester from its sheath, I placed them all, where they would be handy if needed. Taking off my boots, I crawled into the rolled out bed and lay looking up at the stars. My thoughts drifted to the mountains … the Black Mountains. I was obsessed. Then the mountains were pushed from my mind by my thoughts of Jaydeen and I fell asleep.

I awoke to the sound of thunder coming from the black mountain range. Even at this distance and in the gray light of the first dawn, I could see the dark clouds that lay over their peaks.

The air had that feel of static and a premonition that made one uneasy. Talking in a soothing voice, I calmed Faith. Throwing the saddle onto her back, I cinched it tight, and tied my bedroll behind it. We rode off in the cold grey morning without breakfast, before the first hot rays of the sun would strike us. We traveled onward toward those black mountains before the sun rose high in the pale blue sky to beat down on us with its searing heat.

By high noon, we had put several miles behind us. Faith was as eager to go, as was I. The mountains seemed to grow larger the longer we traveled toward them. The ground was still soft from an early desert shower that had awakened me with its thunder. Cutting down across a rocky ravine and riding up the other side onto the plain, I had not traveled a hundred yards, when I noticed fresh hoof prints made by several un-shod horses.

Pulling Faith up sharply, I quickly looked in the direction the tracks had gone. Damn, I thought, just my luck to run in to a bunch of Indians. I looked around the plains, but I didn't see any horses or Indians on horses.

I got down and looked more closely at the hoof prints. They were deeper than an un-ridden horse would make. They definitely carried riders on their backs. From the pattern and spacing of the tracks, there were five riders and they appeared not to be in any big hurry. The tracks led off in the same direction I was traveling, double damn my luck.

Not knowing if the riders would be friendly or hostile and not one to take chances I checked my Colts and pulled the Winchester from its scabbard.

Now I was as prepared as circumstances would allow, I rode warily on. It was not a good idea that I rode on the plains, out in the open. I needed to be hidden. Then I remembered the ravine that I had crossed. It seemed to run in the general direction that I wanted to travel. I would be better riding in the ravine than on these plains. Angling back, I rode down into the ravine.

The going was somewhat rougher and slower than out on the plains due to the many rocks and potholes that lay across its bottom. I rode ready with the Winchester's butt resting on my thigh.

I was out of sight and not easily seen. However, that worked two ways. I could not see anything that might be happening out on those plains. With that thought, I decided to take a quick look around and rode up out of the ravine.

I rode up over the edge and froze. My heart almost stopped. There facing me sat three young Indians on their painted ponies. About ten yards farther along sat two more.

For a heartbeat, we sat there staring at one another in shock. My rifle was pointed up towards the sky. I couldn't bring my rifle down to a firing position without being shot myself.

Only one Indian carried a rifle. I figured him to be their leader. The others carried bows. They must be thinking what to do, as was I. It seemed an eternity passed, but I'm sure it was no more than a few seconds.

I sat there dazed and unable to think clearly. Staring at the Indians my mind kicked in and started to function somewhat. If only I could talk with them. Maybe they would understand the Comanche tongue. I could try speaking with my Comanche tongue, and hope they might understand.

I slowly raised my left hand in a peaceful sign. The leader did not move but two of his friends shifted on their horses and started to pull arrows from their quivers. He barked an order and they stopped.

I remembered the language my Indian father had taught me and I spoke it now. "I come in peace and wish to do you no harm."

As I spoke, an amazed expression of disbelief, flashed across their faces. I could tell that they understood what I had said. They all looked sort of relieved I thought. They all suddenly started talking excitely to each other.

As they talked to one another, I took a closer look at them, now that I had gotten over my shock. They were a little younger than me. I didn't know who they were or where they were headed. Maybe I could find out before losing my scalp hair.

Using the Comanche tongue I said, "I come in peace, to see what the Black Mountains might hold in their valleys. I mean you no harm, my friends." I motioned with a slow movement of my hand toward the mountains. Their horses started to jump a little at my movement.

The Indian that held the rifle said, "How is it you speak with the Comanche tongue? You are not Comanche. You are dark of skin, but not dark enough to be a Comanche."

"I was found by a Comanche warrior who saved me from death and took me as his son. He had lost his wife and son in a massacre by the white devils. I spent many years with my Indian father. He taught me well." I sat proudly thinking of Shatika.

I spoke these words not as a white man, but as an Indian, "My Indian father's name was Shatika," I said proudly, setting up a little straighter.

"He called me Chad'tu." The Indians looked at one another, somewhat nervous, as I said the name Chad'tu.

The Indian that held the rifle said, "I have heard the name. Some call him the White Indian. It is said that he is good with all weapons, very, very good. Would you be that one?"

"Yes. I would be that one, my brother," I replied.

From his stern face, a ray of sunshine broke across his face and ended with a smile. He rode toward me and stopping by my side, he reached out his arm and clasped mine in a gesture of friendship and brotherhood. "Welcome, my brother."

He turned to his warriors and said, "This is our brother and no harm shall come to him from us or any others or you will answer to me." They all agreed with their leader. Soon everyone started to relax, the tension was lessened.

Red Dawn was his name and he was dark-skinned and handsome. He said they were out scouting the countryside for some one that had stolen several horses from their village. They had lost the trail and then they had spotted me. Then when I appeared out of the ravine without horses they were confused for the moment, and even more so when I spoke in their native tongue. Soon we all dismounted and even though it was the middle of the day, they built a hot fire and cooked a rattlesnake they'd killed earlier that day. I took out my pot and made some coffee.

We sat around like long lost brothers talking and eating. The rattlesnake tasted a little like chicken, only tougher. They didn't much like the bitterness of the coffee at first, then after a few swallows they change their minds. We seemed to be one big happy family. Still, I kept an eye on them.

The only thing I can say is it was a damn good thing I could speak Co-manche, even though I spoke it somewhat haltingly from lack of use.

I asked about the Black Mountains and if there, was water and grass enough for some cattle. Red Dawn spoke for them. He said their village lay over the Black Mountains at the far northwestern end. He had grown up there and he'd explored and hunted those mountains since he was a small child.

Pointing toward the mountains and indicating a notch that was between the two tallest peaks. He said, "A valley such as you seek lies between the two mountains." He said it held much wild life as he had hunted there many times. The valley was lush with grass, with a stream running through it that held fish.

The way he described it, it was just what I was looking to find. I told him about Sid's ranch that was a few miles over the horizon. I explained that I was married and was looking for a place to start a cattle ranch.

He smiled when I mentioned I had a wife. He said he had not one but many admirers but so far, he was not ready to choose a wife. After awhile he smiled again and said, "I am having too much fun being a single unmarried brave to get married." he paused, "But there is one that is special. Maybe one day she will be the one. If that happens, Chad'tu, you must come to the wedding ceremony."

I told him if he sent word, I would come. I would come un-afraid I told him. We each stood and embraced the other and he said, "Some day we will meet again my brother. Go in peace."

"Good hunting," I said and headed off toward the mountains. "I hope you catch those horse thieves." The Indians mounted their horses and quickly disappeared into the desert plains, only a cloud of dust marking their departure.

As Red Dawn and his braves departed, I felt relieved. I had not known I was so tense. All in all, it had worked out well. I pointed Faith west and rode on toward the Black Mountains and the notch in them that Red Dawn had pointed out.

CHAPTER 49

SOMETIME IN THE afternoon of the fourth day, the ground changed from flat plains to a gradually rising one. The rocky sloping ground rose ever more steeply, toward the mountains that reached up almost touching the grey clouds that hung in a grey sky.

Faith worked her way around the stunted twisted trees, which grew about the hillside, punctuated occasionally by low growing brush. Here and there small patches of scrubby tuffs of grass fought for space to grow.

The hillside became increasingly rockier as it sloped more sharply upward. I searched for a trail made by animals which would lead me to the safest route up this treacherous mountainside. Soon I found what looked to be a path that angled off diagonally across the contour of the hillside, perhaps made by deer, antelope, or maybe even dangerous javelina boars.

Following the trail and keeping a sharp eye out. I slowly rode Faith up the mountainside. I paused at times to look around and give Faith a chance to rest from the steady climb upward. Rolling a smoke, I looked back down the way we had come. It was a breathtaking sight. I could see for miles. I looked for Sid's ranch. All I could see in that direction was some low-lying hills that were a long ways off.

I finished my smoke and rode on. The higher I rode, the greener, thicker and taller the trees grew. The grass was taller, but not much. The sun was high when we stopped on a small shelf jutting out of the hillside. I tied Faith to a tree branch and gave her water from my hat. I took out some jerked beef to chew on. While Faith nibbled at the grass, I walked out a ways and took a good long look around. I decided it wasn't too bad, but not exactly, what Red Dawn had described.

I decided this must not be the right place. Being on the mountain, I could not see the notch he'd pointed out. I trusted my senses that it must lay more to my left, so I stepped into the saddle and rode on, still following along that faint trail I'd started on. Soon I was hearing the twitter of birds from the trees. A good sign, which meant there was water somewhere close by. A bush suddenly shook and a rabbit bounded away.

Wildlife was becoming more abundant, which was another good sign. I looked up at the sky to get an idea of the time. I watched a hawk circling high looking for his supper, I suspected. It was getting along toward evening. I had a couple hours left before dark by my reckoning. There was still time to find the valley.

Riding Faith through thick brush that was shoulder high, we came out the other side of the ridge onto a small plateau.

I stopped and gazed down at the most beautiful, lush green valley I'd ever seen. It was so pretty, it took my breath away. I wanted to shout and jump with joy. I had found my ranch.

I got down off Faith and picked my hat up from the ground where I had flung it in my excitement. I dusted it off and stuck it back onto my sweaty head, knelt down, and gave thanks to the one above that watched over all things.

My mind was churning as fast as a windmill turns in a high wind. So many thoughts crowded into my head all at once. I told myself to calm down, take deep breaths, relax, have a smoke—be calm.

I picked up loose rocks and stones, and built a fire pit. I gathered up dead branches of every size, along with some brush and piled a goodly supply nearby that would last through the night. It might get downright cold this high up. I didn't know how cold it might get, but I didn't want to freeze to death. It was better to be prepared. I thought of Jaydeen, how excited and happy she would be to see this valley.

Before the sunlight faded completely I started the fire. I explored the plateau looking for a cave or an overhanging outcrop, where I might be better protected from the weather. I found nothing but the shear granite stone as it rose up the mountain. The plateau butted up against its ragged surface that rose straight up as far as my eye could see in the failing light.

Walking alongside this massive stone façade, looking for an opening, I slipped suddenly without warning. I fell, trying to catch myself and landed on my rump in soggy wet earth. What the hell, I thought, pulling up a handful of dripping brown mud. I hadn't found a cave but something much more important, I had found a seep. A seep meant water.

I decided right then and there, this was where I'd build the ranch house. I would build it close, but not to close to the seep, so getting water would not be a problem for Jay. Building the house, lumber would not be a problem either with all the trees that grew close by

It was too dark to see more so I went back to Faith and the fire. Faith was chomping contentedly at the grass. I stroked her neck and said, "Welcome to your new home." At the sound of my voice, she swung her head around giving me an affectionate nuzzle. I took a halter from the saddlebags and staked Faith with a long tether, so she'd have more freedom to move around.

I placed the saddlebags and saddle close by the fire. I pulled up clumps of dry grass and gave Faith a good rubdown. While I groomed her, I told her what a great horse she was. She tossed her head up and down a few times as if she understood my every word. Who knows, maybe she did.

The night was rapidly getting colder. I got out the coffee pot, poured in water from the canteen, put some grounds in and placed it on a stone at the fires edge. I couldn't wait to have me a cup, it would warm me. I loved the taste of hot coffee. Now what did I have to eat to go with my coffee?

I still had some salted pork left. No, save that for breakfast tomorrow, I thought. I rummaged in the saddlebags and found some jerked beef. Ma had always said, 'Beggars can't be choosey.'

Now where in the world did that thought come from? I hadn't thought about Ma for years. Now all of a sudden her words pop into my head … strange.

I thought about my Ma. From what little I could remember, she was a hard-working woman. She would have loved this place. Then I put Ma out of my mind and bit off a piece of the hard jerked beef. The coffee was ready. I poured a cup, sat down on the saddle and stretched out my legs, relaxed.

For a moment, I watched the fire as the red, yellow and blue flames shot up. Then the flames would die down, only to blaze up repeating the movement in a different pattern. They did a dance of flickering different colors. Yellows entwined and mingled with the red, and occasionally a blue flame would flare up.

Yes, I thought this is the life for me, out in the open and nobody to answer to. I looked up at the star filled heavens. The stars twinkling and shinning bright, my thoughts went to Jaydeen. Well I guess I did have one that I had to answer to, Jaydeen.

❖

Red Dawn and his four warriors rode off in a northerly direction, headed toward the far distant mountains. They hoped to cut the trail of the horse thieves. They wandered back and forth for an hour or so across the desert without success, trying to pick up the trail they had lost earlier. They had yet to come upon the hoof prints of the stolen horses and those who had stolen them. They had ridden for a couple hours and still had not come upon any tracks made by the stolen horses.

Red Dawn drew up his pony, stuck his arm high over his head, and with closed fist, let out a screech such as an eagle might make. It was a call for his braves to come close. Upon hearing the screech, the braves' heads went from looking at the ground toward their leader. Seeing his fist held high, they rode rapidly to him.

Once the last brave approached, he spoke. "We are not covering enough territory fast enough the way we are searching. I have a new plan. We will spread far apart from each other to a distance that we can still see each other. Then we start in a northern direction and zigzag as we ride forward. We can cover far more ground faster."

Red Dawn envisioned his plan as a large net cast across the desert to snare his prey. The plan worked. They came across tracks, left by eighteen to twenty unshod horses, being driven by some that were shod. The tracks appeared to Red Dawn to be maybe two or three hours old. The sun sat low at the edge of sky. There was no time to waste, before darkness fell and the hoof prints left by the horses would be lost in the blackness. They grouped together and with a yell, started in hot pursuit to catch the thieves before dark set in.

There was a low rumble of thunder some distance behind them. Red Dawn looked back at the low-lying black clouds moving slowly across the desert in their direction. They would have to hurry if they wanted to catch the horse thieves before the storm caught them.

As the evening drew close, the wind picked up some. It brought with it the fresh smell of dampened earth. Several Russian thistles tumbled and bounced along with the dust, past the Indians, being driven by the wind like a bunch of herded cattle. The cowpokes called them tumbleweeds.

As the tumbleweeds rolled by, Red Dawn looking up and back saw the dark clouds were almost upon them. Whipped by the stinging dust and air-borne weeds, they rode on looking for shelter from the storm. Before the clouds and the rainstorm reached them, they had found shelter in the side of a low hill that had several large rocky outcrops. By the time the storm caught up to them, they had settled in for the night, building a small fire for warmth. From a small pouch that each carried they took food of parched corn, dried deer meat and ate in the cold wind-blown rain.

Red Dawn and his braves were up before sunrise, the storm having passed by them in the night. The slight rainfall along with the wind had wiped out any tracks that had been made. Red Dawn was upset; the desert was now wiped clean. Discouraged, they headed for home, which lay on the north-west end of the black mountain range. It would take eight days for them to get there.

CHAPTER 50

THE NEXT MORNING, I had some of the salted pork along with my coffee. My food was sparse. If I stayed long, I would have to kill something to eat.

This was a fine morning after the fury of the storm last night. The air was fresh and clean and by the time I finished breakfast, the sun was peeking over the horizon. It was a cold morning, but not that cold, considering how high up I was in these mountains.

Feeling like a kid, I started exploring the plateau. Reaching down, I scooped a handful of dirt in my hand, the ground crumbled and smelled like rich soil. It would grow Jaydeen a good garden. The ground, as much as I could see backed up to the hillside which was purty much all granite.

I walked several hundred yards along the granite façade and approached the edge where it started a gentle slope downward. Standing on the edge, I saw a most wondrous sight. A waterfall, from somewhere high above the plateau where I stood, cascaded out from the mountainside and fell several hundred feet, hitting on a granite outcropping with a rushing roar, and then tumbled several hundred feet more into a small lake that had been carved out of the earth and stone that lay far below. The angle of the sun on the spray made multi-colored rainbows. It was the most beautiful thing I'd ever seen. I stood for several minutes mesmerized and transfixed by its sheer beauty.

Enough, I thought. I have to find an easier way up to the plateau if I'm ever going to build a house here. The air was crisp, fresh and clean as I walked back to camp. Taking my hatchet from a saddlebag, I made my mark on a tree. Walking further, I made another mark on a tree. All in all, I marked ten trees with the same mark, making my claim to this part of the mountain.

Saddling Faith, I broke camp. I had no idea how to find an easier way down or an easier way back up. I spoke to Faith, "Okay girl this is going to be your new home so you'd better find an easier way to get up here." I clicked my tongue and gave her a gentle nudge with my boot heels. She started off slowly not knowing what I wanted of her. I gave her free rein and didn't guide her. Although I did say, "let's go home."

I sat in the saddle waiting, watching her moves. She wandered around and then started slowly down the steep, shale-covered hillside toward the lush green valley that lay some distance below. I'd found from experience, animals most always, seemed to find the easiest and safest way down a hill. I marked Faith's downward progress making it a part of my memory. She did find the easiest way down, and that was the trail I would use from now on.

The trees became fewer as the valley begin to flatten, giving way to tall lush green grass that grew up to Faith's belly. Riding through it was like a boat moving upon waves as the wind rippled across it. It had a wonderful fresh smell, not quit like fresh cut hay. I can't quiet describe the smell. When I smell fresh turned earth, it smell's to me, like the brown color it is. This grass had the smell of a green color to me. It smelled wonderful.

Riding across the meadow I turned in the saddle and craning my head, looked back and up at the magnificent cascade of water falling down the rocky side from hundreds of feet above and ending in the lake, before overflowing and wondering off, finding its way through the lowest parts of the meadow and snaking off across the field of green.

Taking several large rocks that lay about on the ground, I stacked them three on the bottom and one on top as a marker. I did the same in several different spots farther along as I rode. Just in case, anyone wanted to dispute my claim to this ground. It was shortly past noon by my calculations and placing the fourth stone atop the last marker, I mounted up and headed for home. I looked forward to telling Jaydeen the good news.

Red Dawn had been right though, about the valley. The directions he had given me were dead on. It wasn't his fault if I couldn't follow them. What's more, if I had followed them, I would not have found the plateau where I would build our house.

I just hoped I wouldn't run afoul of any Indians on the way back to the ranch. They might not be as easily persuaded as Red Dawn, that I was friendly. The ride back was uneventful except once I saw a cloud of dust off in the distance, raised by twenty or more Indians as much as I could tell from this distance. They did not see me, as I rode with just my head showing over the edge of a ravine I had run across earlier that day. The ravine was running in the direction I wanted to travel, so I'd taken it.

On the way back to the ranch, I scouted some of the territory over which I rode, to become more familiar with it. I came across a seep that supported a couple trees out in the middle of nowhere. It was a good thing to remember, in case I ever needed water. It seemed to be about halfway back to the ranch.

On the eve of the fifth day, I rode into the yard of the ranch. There was smoke coming from the chimney and the sweet smell of the cooking food coming from the house. It smelled almighty good, after the food I had been eating. It seemed like; I was always just in time for supper, or any other cooked meal.

When I walked in and Jaydeen saw me she stopped. She set a steaming pot back onto the stove, rushed into my arms, hugged me tightly, and smothered me with kisses, and said, "Thank god your safely back."

She finally stopped kissing me. "Oh Chad, I missed you so. I'm so glad you're finally home." She held me at arm's length, looking at the silly grin on my face. "Is that grin on your face for me … or maybe it's for some of my fine home cooking?" she joked. "Chad I don't know how you do it, but you always seem to arrive just in time to eat."

Sid and Trace had been sitting at the kitchen table watching Jaydeen's passionate welcome. "It surely is good to have you back." Sid said, standing. "After nine days, we were starting to worry, wondering if you were coming back, or maybe some Indians gotcha. Jay was starting to worry some, isn't that right Sis?"

Jaydeen said, "Truer words were never spoken. However, Sid exaggerates, as I was only a little worried. The fact is I have missed you terribly." Giving me a coy look, she brushed her long red hair back from her face where it had fallen and said, "Now set yourself down, you're just in time for supper." Without stopping his jawing, Sid gave me a hug and slapping me on the back the dust flew. Stepping back from the dust he quickly said, "You and your clothes could sure stand some washing, I'd say."

I stuck my hat on the wall peg and pulling out a chair, I sat down at the table. Taking the coffee pot from a trivet that sat in the middle of the table, I poured myself a cup. It sure did feel good to be back, and it was good that they had missed me.

They started asking me all kinds of questions. What had happened and what I had found. I started off telling them of the Indians I'd come upon, and how my Comanche language got me out of a real bind and a worst situation.

How in my speaking with their leader Red Dawn, he had told me of a lush valley which lay somewhere up in the Black Mountains and had pointed me towards it. Finding the valley after some miscalculations on my part, I quickly decided it was exactly the kind of place I had pictured. I wanted a place with plenty of water and an abundance of tall grass and solitude and this place seemed to have it all.

"Jaydeen, you will love it," I said. "It's the perfect place for us to build our ranch. And Jay the best part, we'd only be a four or five days ride at the most from this ranch. Maybe we could visit one another sometimes."

I told of the wildlife in the area. Along with the grass and the water, it would make for good hunting. I told of the beautiful waterfall which fell hundreds of feet. I told them the view from where I would build the house on the plateau, you could see for fifty miles and maybe more. I was so excited in my telling, they all three got caught up in it.

Placing a plate on the table for me, "We'd better eat before the food gets cold. We can talk while we eat." Jaydeen said. She placed a large platter of steaming golden brown fried chicken, a bowl of mashed potatoes with a hunk of butter melting in its center, along with gravy and fresh made buns.

We ate, talked, and discussed plans for the new ranch and house that I would build for Jaydeen. "I really missed you Jay and I surely did miss your cooking, too." I said, taking another bite of crunchy chicken. By the time we'd finished eating, we had pretty much done all the planning.

Now it was deciding how to go about it. I needed a wagon and a couple of mules, to haul the supplies and material I'd need in building the house. It would take money. Since I'd been sheriff, I'd not spent much, except for a new shirt or pants and some socks and underwear. Therefore, I calculated I had enough. If I didn't, I could always get a loan.

I sat at the kitchen table and wrote down all the things I thought I'd need. Sid and Trace suggested some things, as did Jaydeen. I wrote all those things down too. The lantern had burned low by the time we'd finished the list. It was late. Tired as we were, we were still excited as we turned in and hit the sack.

Next morning the sun was shinning over the hills when we awoke. We all had slept late.

After a hasty breakfast, Trace and Sid headed out to do chores. I talked with Jay. She was still very excited about the prospect of our own place and could hardly wait to see the valley. She said it sounded so beautiful she could hardly wait to see it.

She wanted to go to town with me for supplies, but I talked her out of it, saying she should stay here and start packing what she wanted to take to her new home. I told her I would get the supplies I needed in Tombstone, and from there I would go to Black Mountain to build our house. When I returned for her, we would be leaving.

I went to the corral and catching Faith, saddled her. After kissing Jay, I stepped into the leather and taking the reins headed for Tombstone, a happy man.

I rode up to the gunsmith shop at noon of the third day. Brett was in the corral, working with a handsome jet-black stallion. The stallion was completely black except for a white blaze that ran between his eyes like a jagged slash of lightning. The horse rearing and snorting didn't want to cooperate with Brett's commands. Brett was working hard trying to break and train the stallion to his commands.

Unnoticed as I rode quietly up, I said, "Hello Brett, What 'cha doing with that stallion?"

"Hi Chad, What's it look like I'm doing? I'm breaking him to my ways."

"Well for a minute there, it looked like you were trying to teach him to dance, the way he danced around with you hanging on." I said laughing. He stopped and taking the halter off, let the stallion run loose in the corral. He walked over and crawled through the railing of the corral, and using his hat, dusted himself off. "Chad, what a pleasant surprise, what brings you to town? I was about to have lunch, you want something to eat? Get down and sit a spell. Tell me what all's been going on with you? Catch me up on things."

I stepped down out of the saddle, Brett gave me a hug. "Well." I started, "I found a place to start me a ranch."

"Where might that be?"

"You know those Black Mountains way over yonder? The ones you can barely see from here."

"Yeah, I know of them."

"I found a place up a verdant valley in those mountains, and that's where I'm gonna build a ranch for Jaydeen and me and our children, if we have any. I'm on my way now to Tombstone for supplies to build me a house. I reckon I'll need me a wagon to carry all the things I got to buy, and I guess a couple mules to pull it. And if I have any money left over I might be able to get a hired hand to help me out."

Brett was happy for me. He told me to hurry up, build that house, and fill it up with some kids so he could be an uncle to them. I didn't visit long, as I wanted to get that house built, and start on those kids Brett talked about. Not to say I wouldn't like to have a son or two and maybe a red haired, freckle nosed little girl that would look like her mother.

CHAPTER 51

RIDING INTO TOMBSTONE, I went directly to the Emporium. Tying Faith to the hitching rail, I walked in and asked Sam Elliot about getting supplies. "Hello Sam. What you doing back there?" Sam was bent over doing some rearranging behind a counter. He stood up with a surprised look on his face.

"Chad'tu, it's been a long time since I laid eyes on you. It's good to see you again. What can I attribute this visit to, business or pleasure?"

"Both. It sure is a pleasure to see that you're in such good health." I said laughing, as I looked at his shirt that was stretched tight across a large stomach.

"Cut that out. It's not my fault I haven't missed any meals." He smiled good-naturedly at me and said, "I know you didn't come in just to comment on my waistline. What else can I do for you?"

"I'm going to build me a house up in the Black Mountains, the ones you can barely see north-west of here. I got me a list of things I'll need. And if you think of anything I didn't put down, just add it in." I said handing my list to Sam's outstretched hand.

"My, this is a purty long list," he said looking it over quickly. Then he added, "I believe I have most of the items you require. Except you got written down here you need a wagon and mules to pull it. I ain't got those. I suggest you go down to the stables. Maybe Brannon can fix you up."

"And Sam, I sure could use somebody to give me a hand and help me with the hauling and the building of my house. I can't pay much, but if you know of anybody, it sure would be appreciated."

Sam rubbed his chin and thought a moment then said. "Say, there was a young fella through here just a couple days ago, looking for work. I don't know where he went, but I told him to put his name on the 'Sell or Need' board out front. You might check it. Someone might have posted a wagon and a team of mules for sale, on it."

"Thanks Sam." I started to leave.

Sam called out, "How you going to pay for all this?"

"Don't worry Sam, I got money I saved when I was the sheriff and I might say it's a right tidy amount. And if I run a little short … Brett would probable stake me, don't ya think?"

Sam smiled, nodded his head. "Yeah you're right, he probably would at that and if he wouldn't, I'd probably extend you some credit since I believe in you. You could always pay me after you get your cattle ranch going."

I stepped out on the porch, taking a look at the board that was nailed up beside the front door. It held notices stacked on top of more notices. It was surely a mess. Some had dates. Most had nothing to tell how long they'd been there.

After some looking and a lot of digging, I found a note that said 'looking for work.' It had a date only two days old. It must be the fellow Sam had mentioned. It was signed 'Ned Blaylock.' It said he could be found at the hotel or the stables.

I tried the hotel first, it being the closest. Ben the owner was on the front porch with a broom, stirring up a cloud of dust. "Hi Ben, how are you?" I said stepping up on the boardwalk.

Ben stopped his sweeping and looked up. "Hello Sheriff. Dang, I plumb forgot, you ain't the sheriff anymore. What brings you into town, Chad?"

"I'm looking for a fellow goes by the name of Ned Blaylock. He has a note on the Emporium, 'Sale or Need' board. Says he can be reached at your hotel. You heard of him?"

"What's he done?" Ben asked, suspiciously.

"Nothing I know of. A note posted at the Emporium, said he was looking for work, and I'm looking for someone to hire. Do you know him?"

"Yeah, he walked in here couple days back. Seemed like a fairly decent young lad. Said he was down on his luck and was looking for work."

"So … do you happen to know where I might find him?"

"Well, I felt sorry for him, so I got him hoeing weeds out back of the hotel." I must have given Ben a puzzled look because he immediately said,

"In case of a fire, you know. Sure don't want to lose my hotel by it burning down."

"So he already has a job with you. I guess I'll have to look elsewhere's."

"No, No, I only gave him the job temporarily to cover his room and board. He's all yours if you want him." Ben quickly replied. "Seems like a nice pleasant enough fellow and he's a hard worker."

I went through the walkway beside the hotel and around back. There was a young sandy-haired fellow with no shirt, chopping weeds like there was no tomorrow. His chest glistened with sweat mixed with the dust he was stirring up. Seeing me, he paused in his chopping. Leaning on the hoe handle, he fixed his eyes on me. I walked over, steering clear of the cloud of dust and dirt.

He was a husky young man, maybe eighteen or nineteen. He looked to be maybe a couple years younger than me. He wore ragged blue denim pants, with suspenders that ran up over his bare chest to hold them up. He looked more a farmer than a cowpoke.

"Is your name Ned?" I asked.

"Yeah that's my name. What might I do for you mister?" He replied in a pleasant sounding voice.

"My name is Chad'tu. I hear you're looking for work, that right?"

He straightened to his full height just shy of six feet, took a kerchief from a hip pocket and wiped the sweat and dirt from his eyes. He looked at me and said, "That's a fact, Mister Chad'tu, I surely am."

"What can you do," I asked, "besides chop weeds?"

"Anything you've a mind for me to do, I reckon." he said, as he swung the hoe at a weed.

"You know anything on how to go about building a house out of trees? You know … logs."

"Well, when I was a kid, back in Arkansas, I helped some in the building of the town church."

"I'm gonna build me a fine ranch house up in those Black Mountains about fifty miles or so from here. How long it will take to build, I don't know. If you'd like to help, you're hired. I'll feed you and pay you four-bits a day. What do you say?"

"Well mister, I don't know you. How do I know you'll pay?"

"Until just recently, I was sheriff of this here town. Ask anyone in Tomb-stone, they'll vouch for me, but don't take all day to decide, because I got a lot of things I have to get done. I can't waste time. I want to get this house built before winter comes with its snow and rain."

"Okay, I'll take your word that you were sheriff. You look to be an honest man ..." It was more a question than a statement he threw at me.

When he saw I wasn't going to respond, he spoke up, "Okay, I'll come to work for you, but there's one thing mister you ought to know. I don't have a horse, or any other means of transportation. So how will I be able to go with you?"

I was happy he'd said he would work for me. "Don't worry; you'll have either a horse or mules you drive from the seat of a wagon." He started swinging the hoe again at the weeds.

"Ned, set that hoe aside and come on. You work for me now. Go see Barlow and collect what pay you got coming."

Ned came out of the doorway followed by Ben, who said, "Take care of the lad, Chad'tu, he's a good worker."

First, we headed over to the stables to see about getting a wagon and some mules to pull it. Brannon was there and no, he didn't have any mules or a wagon for them mules, he didn't have, to pull. Wondering what to do, I stood there and pondered my situation. Brannon spoke up. "I here tell there's a farmer out south of town that's been having a hard time. He might consider selling you a wagon and a couple mules. Might be worth your time to ride out and see."

"How far out might this farmer be?" I asked.

"Oh, an hour or so of easy riding, I'd say."

I needed a horse for Ned. Today I was riding Faith and the big bay that I had been riding, was out at the ranch. I wanted to keep the bay horse for me as an alternate ride. I guessed I'd have to buy another for Ned. "Brannon you got any horses you'd sell cheap? Ned here needs a ride."

"Yeah, I got one or two I might sell. Don't know about cheap, though." We walked out back of the barn and took a look at the horses.

There was a buckskin horse that looked like it might do. I haggled a little with Brannon about the price. After a few minutes, we agreed on a price. For another six dollars, he threw in an old used saddle and blanket along with a bridle.

We saddled the buckskin and together we rode off to find the farm Brannon had spoke of. He had given me good directions. What he'd said was an easy one or two hour ride, only took an hour and half.

As we rode up to the old weather-beaten farmhouse, three mangy dogs ran from around the corner barking furiously, their tails wagging, belying their intent to attack.

The barking of the dogs had aroused an old bearded man in worn bib overalls. He stepped out onto the porch, the screen door slamming shut behind. He wore a beat-up straw hat. Walking out on the rickety porch, he yelled at the dogs to stop their damn barking.

"Howdy," I said, "Brannon, the stable owner in town, sent us. Said you might have an old wagon you weren't using that you might sell and possibly a couple mules to pull it."

"Well young fella, that's a fact. You done come to the right place, at the right time. I'm moving out of this hell-forsaken country and headin' for Cal-a-for-nee, and I ain't taking much with me. So yeah, I got a wagon and several mules."

"Out back," he said stepping down from the porch. "The wagon's out back by the barn."

He led the way and we followed, with three dogs sniffing at our heels. The wagon wasn't much to look at, but I was desperate. "How much you want for the wagon and two of them mules in the corral over yonder?"

After some dickering, we agreed on a price. He wanted me to pay for the harness also. I balked and told him I wasn't paying a cent more than the agreed upon price, and he should just let me have the harness. He could see I wasn't budging, so he gave in.

We picked out two mules that looked healthy. The old man showed Ned and me how to hitch them up to the wagon. Ned seemed to know about such things but it was new to me.

I paid the farmer as Ned tied his horse to the rear of the wagon and climbed up on the wooden seat. I rode beside the wagon watching Ned maneuver out onto the dirt road and we headed on back to town.

On the edge of town, I called out to Ned to drive the wagon over to the Emporium. Ned pulled the wagon up to the loading dock and stopped the wagon alongside. He tied the reins around the tall brake handle and stepped across onto the porch.

Sam hearing the wagon walked out and said "Well, I see you found yourself a wagon and some mules."

"Yeah, we did Sam. Brandon down at the stables didn't have a wagon, but he told me about this farmer a few miles out from town that might have one. Had to dicker some to get the right price, finally we agreed on a price." Ned just stood there. "Sam I think you already met Ned, he's going to help me in building my house."

Sam reached out a hand and said, "Pleased to meetcha."

"Sam, when do you think you might get the wagon loaded with all the supplies?"

"Well let me see." He did some figuring in the air, his finger stuck out in front of his face. "That is quiet a lot of supplies you did order. It's going to take some time to gather them up, but I reckon I could probably have it all for you and loaded, say sometime tomorrow. How's that sound, Chad'tu?"

"If it's the best you can do, I guess I'll have to settle for it." If I had to wait, that's what I'd just have to do, although I really was anxious to get started on the house. The wait meant I'd have to stable the mules for the night.

Sam took another look at my list, "Well, from the looks of all these supplies you got written down. It appears its going to be a right dandy, house I'd say."

CHAPTER 52

TOMORROW CAME SLOWLY. The wagon being loaded high and tied down with a tarp over the top and two full water barrels, strapped one on each side. Anxious to get started, we headed out on our way to the Black Mountains. Being familiar with the surrounding countryside of Tombstone, I headed off from town at an angle. Taking the shortest distance as the crow flies, we would bypass the town of No-Name.

It was rough going. We got stuck in a ditch only once. After a couple hours of sweating and hard work, we managed to get the wagon out and rolling again. Four and a half days later, we approached the bottom slope of the Black Mountain range. Everything seemed much as I'd left it. Looking around for the trail and finally finding it, I signaled for Ned to follow me up.

Driving the wagon up the mountainside, Ned followed me steering the wagon around and over the rock-strewed trail that cut back and forth across the mountainside. We angled up the mountainside for the shelf that lay high above the valley floor, where we would build the cabin.

It wasn't easy, with only two mules pulling the heavily loaded wagon. Finally, after one whole day we managed by pushing, pulling, and with the horses helping the mules, we got the wagon up onto the shelf. Dirty and sweating, Ned and me were plumb wore out. It had been rough going. We cleaned up and celebrated some that evening. It wasn't as much a celebration as it was a relief that it was over. We had arrived.

We tended to the animals. Then too worn-out to cook, we ate jerked beef washed down with coffee. We finished the last of the coffee, laid out our bed-rolls, banked the fire, and crawled into our beds. We must have been dead tired. We didn't awaken 'till we heard the twittering of birds. The sun was well up the side of the mountain.

We took the morning of the first day relaxing and recouping our strength. I sat talking about the house. Ned sat there listening as I talked. "Come-on I'll show you where I want to build." I stood and picking up a nearby stick, used it to scratch an outline in the dirt of the shape the house would be. "What do you think, Ned?"

Ned smiled and said, "It seems a might big, but if that's what you want, it's going to take some time to build."

"Yeah," I thought for a moment and said, "We'd better unload the wagon and fix up something to keep our four-legged friends from straying." I looked at the four animals that were still securely staked on long tethers from last evening. They were content, chomping on the tall grass.

We'd driven the wagon close to the shear granite mountainside, stacked the supplies up against that cold hard stone, and covered it with the tarp. We picked up two axes and a ten-foot long crosscut saw that had a handle sticking up at each end. The kind lumberjacks use.

I looked to where the tall pine trees had grown up close to the shelf. They were far enough away from where I would build the house. I figured it would be a good place for the barn. I could use the shear granite mountainside as one side making it part of the barn.

After we had sawed through six trees, we were starting to get the hang of it. Taking a break, I rolled a smoke and lit it. Looking at the felled trees thinking, what a mess we had created.

Axes in hand, we started chopping off the branches, turning the trees into long logs which we would saw to the length we needed. Using some of the branches for post, we built a three-sided corral using the granite mountainside as one side. For the time being, we used the wagon as a gate to close, the eight-foot opening. With the wagon unloaded, it could easily be rolled across the opening to close it. The sun heading westward dipped below the mountain tops casting a giant blue-grey shadow across the valley. It wouldn't be long before dark.

Next morning we started on the house. Taking shovels, we started digging a trench about a foot down and a foot across following the rectangle outline I had drawn in the dirt. It wasn't long till we had our shirts off, the sweat beading and dripping from our exertions.

My idea was to fill the trench with some of the loose stone, which lay about on the flat shelf. To give the first logs we would set on them a good base. We sawed tree trunks to the length we wanted and soon we had the first course of the house completed. We left space for two doors.

The next day we notched logs and fitted them at the corners alternating the pattern with each following layer of logs. By that evening, we had fitted and stacked the logs knee high. Some we had had to cut notches and fit in wood pins. The house was slowly taking shape.

We had devised a tall tripod with a long pole tied across its top to use as a lever to lift the logs up to where we could maneuver them into position. After three weeks we had front walls seven feet high and rear walls eight or nine feet. My idea was, when we put on the roof, it would slope down toward the front and run out over the top of the porch I had envisioned.

It was back breaking work. In the main living area facing out where the porch would be and overlooking the valley and desert below, we left openings for two windows.

With the walls up, we concentrated next on building a fireplace for warmth and the cooking of food. We had no idea what we were doing. It was mostly trial and error. We used mostly the square looking stones that we could find, along with a few flat-sided ones.

In my wandering about looking for flat-sided stones, I had found a spot of earth which some called adobe. It was hard as hell but with a pick, we got out a plentiful supply, which when mixed with water turned into a clay-like mixture. We used the adobe to fill in the cracks left between the stones.

The fireplace opening was about five feet wide and about four feet in height. We used a long stone to span over the opening. It was difficult to get that stone up and into place. The chimney reached up a foot or two above the back wall. I couldn't believe how fast the house was coming along. Ned knew a lot about building, and what he didn't know, we figured out between the two of us, using plain old horse sense.

We finished poking adobe into the spaces left between some of the stones using our hands and a short stick. When we had finished we stood back and admired our work. "Now that's a fireplace." I said, wiping my forehead and smearing a streak of adobe across it.

Ned looked at me and laughed, "You look like an Indian on the war path with that adobe smeared across your face." His remark made me think. At heart was I still an Indian, or was I one of the paleface breed? That question flashed through my head and then was gone.

We felled smaller trees for the roof. I didn't have any ideal how to do the roof to keep out the rain and snow, which I was sure there would be an abundance of, come winter. We decided to lay the smaller stripped trees as close together as possible, and then we laid smaller poles crossways over them and tied everything together with rope. When we had finished we went inside to see how it looked. It looked fine except for one thing, it would never keep the rain or snow out.

Ned said, "I seen houses with dirt and grass growing on the roof. Maybe we could do that."

"We could use adobe … No that would be too heavy. What we need is some sawed lumber boards. We could overlap them and then it would be purty water tight, don't you think."

Ned asked, "Where we gonna get sawed lumber-milled boards out here?"

"Hey! I just remembered I got some sawed lumber in the bottom of the wagon. I laid it in first cause it was flat and wouldn't take up much space. Let's go see if there's enough to cover the roof. I was gonna use it to make furniture and such. But a good weather tight roof is more important don't ya think?"

It didn't look like there would be enough to cover the roof and porch, but maybe there might be enough to cover the house. We could always figure out something for the porch.

We hauled the lumber over and I crawled up the log ladder onto the roof. Ned stayed below and passed the boards up to me. When he'd finished passing the last board up I called down, "Ned, get two of those hammers I bought and bring a bag of those long nails too."

We started just past the edge of the front wall nailing the boards down to the poles we had laid the day before. Overlapping the boards, we slowly nailed our way up. I didn't know if there would be enough to cover the roof, but I had my hopes. Almost to the top, I could see we were going to run short. Damn! If only I hadn't added that extra storeroom. I would have had enough to finish the roof.

We were both down on our knees hammering away when Ned suddenly stop his hammering and leaning towards me whispered in a cracked voice,

"Chad'tu we got company." he motioned with his head toward the tree line. He looked scared.

Without standing, I slowly looked in the direction he'd indicated with his nod. There at the edge of the clearing sitting quietly on their ponies, almost hidden in the shadows of the trees, watching us were three Indians.

Hells fire, here we were up on the roof and our belt guns were hanging down below on a fence post. The rifles were leaned up against the house on the porch. No way were we going to get to either one, without an arrow sticking from our chest. Damn.

I was thinking fast on how to get out of our predicament and thinking it was stupid of me to be so complacent to be without a gun. Squinting, I took a long hard look at them three Indians. I didn't see any war paint. They looked to be a hunting party that had just stumbled upon us. They still hadn't moved.

Ned nervously said, "I don't want to die. I'm too young to die Chad'tu. What are we going to do?"

I took a closer look at the ponies. One of them was a paint, I'd seen somewhere. It suddenly came to me that Red Dawn rode a pinto with markings of that color. I told Ned not to make any sudden moves, just act like they're not there. I stood and raised my right arm up with my palm open and said in the Comanche tongue, "Red Dawn is that you?"

The Indian let out a whoop, and started his horse in our direction.

Ned was shaking in his boots as the Indians came closer.

Sure enough, it was Red Dawn. Boy, I was never so glad in my life to see an Indian, especially one that was a friend. I turned to Ned, "Its okay I know these Indians, and they're friends." Using the ladder, I climbed down off the roof. Ned hurrying stayed close behind and followed as I walked over to greet Red Dawn.

Red Dawn slid off his horse and walked toward me, holding his rifle high overhead with one hand, he yelled out a greeting.

I walked forward and grasping Red Dawn by the forearm gave him a pat on his back and said, "How are you my brother."

"I am fine my brother. I see you have found the valley of which I spoke. What is this thing you are building? Is it your tepee? I see that you cannot fold it up and move it to a different location. Chad'tu, you are stuck here forever."

"Yes, this is where I will live till the end of my days with my woman." Red Dawn said nothing more for a moment. "Red Dawn, as my friend you are always welcome to my home and my fire."

"I am glad to have my friend here with me on my mountain." Red Dawn said. "There are enemies here sometimes."

I wondered what he'd meant by enemies. I let it pass and said, "What brings you here to my plateau? I see you only have two of your braves with you."

"No Chad'tu my friend, there are five of us. We have been hunting and we have good luck. We killed a deer which two of my braves are gutting at this very time. Soon after they finish, they will bring the deer and follow us to this place." All the while Red Dawn had been speaking; he had walked curiously around Ned, looking. After making several circles around him he asked, "Who is this man that is so nervous?"

I didn't know what to say so I replied, "He is a cousin that has come to help me build the great Tepee.

"It is good that he is of your blood. You can tell him to stop his trembling. Tell him he is lucky. I will do no harm to him."

Fear written across his face, Ned looked on, not understanding a word as Red Dawn and I spoke together using the Comanche tongue. Ned finally asked in a choked voice, "What'd he say?"

I put a grim look on my face and told Ned, "He said he would not scalp you today because you are so afraid. He say's he will wait till you are not afraid." I turned to Red Dawn and told him in Comanche what I'd said. Red Dawn broke out in laughter and I did the same.

Ned just stood looking at us, not understanding. I finally explained the joke was at his expense.

"I don't think it's so damn funny." he said, giving me an ugly look. Then Ned's expression changed as the missing two Indians rode in from the trees. One had a small deer in front of him slung across his horse.

"We shall have a feast of celebration for our meeting again." Red Dawn said. The two who had brought in the deer dumped it on the ground and started to skin it. The sun was going down and they wasted no time. The other two braves started a fire to cook the meat.

Red Dawn said, "Show me inside your tepee Chad'tu. I wish to see what you have done. I took Red Dawn inside the still unfinished house.

He looked around nodding and grunted a few times. Then he said, "My tepee I like better." and that was it.

He looked at the cleared ground around the house and grunted his approval. "You have planned well Chad'tu, from where the tepee sits you can protect it easily."

"I hope to live in peace here and hope it never comes to having to protect it."

As we walked around, I showed him where I would build the barn. He looked at the makeshift corral and said if I were going to keep many animals, I would need a better corral. I laughed and said, "That's for sure."

The smell of roasting venison reached my nose making my mouth water in anticipation. It had been a lone time since I'd had roasted deer meat. We dragged over a couple of logs close to the fire to sit on while we ate and to keep warm. The chill of evening was setting in but the seven of us were content, as we sat eating the hot venison.

These were the same braves with Red Dawn I'd met on that fateful day. They remembered the coffee I had made, and asked if I had more of the black liquid. I told them yes, I had more coffee and that I would make some. So along with the deer meat we had coffee to wash it down with.

Red Dawn and his braves camped outside in the woods while Ned and me slept inside the unfinished house. Just before I dropped off to sleep, Ned said "Do you think they will kill us as we sleep?"

"No, Ned. They won't kill us. We are friends. Now stop your worrying and try to get some sleep. We got a lot of work to still do on this place."

When we awoke the next morning, the Indians were gone. We hadn't heard a sound. Red Dawn had left some of the deer meat hanging from a pole of the roof that jutted out over the porch. He always seemed to share with me whatever he had.

We still lacked a foot or two of having enough sawed boards to finish the roof. I was short of lumber, on account of that damn extra storeroom, I'd wanted. I would need to buy more lumber to finish the job. Hell, come to think about it. I didn't even have lumber enough for the two doors or the windows. I could see I'd not planned as well as I had thought. I thought about the dirt floor in the house. What was I going to do about that? Shale came to mind.

In my exploration of the surrounding area, I had discovered a slide of shale that had slid and crumbled down from a different kind of rock off the mountainside. There were a lot of flat different shape pieces of a fairly hard material of clay and stone that had been compressed together. I could use that for a floor. I didn't know if it would hold up, but being composed partly of stone, I thought it worth a try.

On the other hand, I could lay some timbers across the dirt from one wall to the other and then cover them with saw-milled planks. Still, I had no such sawed wood at my disposal. Shale it would have to be, at least for now.

Sweating and dirty but with the wagon loaded with shale we drove it to the house.

Leaving the wagonload of shale by the front door, we unhitched the mules and returned them to the corral. With no wagon to use as a gate we had cut some long, small in diameter logs to reach across the opening, effectively keeping the horses and mules contained.

As we were unloading the wagonload of shale beside the front door, a thought occurred to me. Why not send Ned to Tombstone for more lumber and supplies. Deep in thought, I stood there thinking. Ned asked, "Chad'tu, you got that look on your face. What now?"

"Just thinkin it sure would save a lot of time if you went to Tombstone and got us more sawed lumber and a few more supplies." I could see Ned did not like the idea.

"Hell I bet you could make it there and back in a week's time." After some discussion while unloading the wagon, I convinced Ned to go. The next morning Ned left for Tombstone.

CHAPTER 53

AFTER THE FIRST day of working alone on the shale floor of the house, I realized. Without Ned's constant chatter, I was lonely, Around noon, two days later, as I laid shale, a shadow fell across the doorway. My hand reached for my gun, then stopped. I saw Red Dawn standing there. "Red Dawn what brings you back?"

Red Dawn looked around and said, "Where is young paleface that trembles?"

"I sent him to get more supplies from the white village. He didn't want to go. Is there trouble with the other Indians that pass this way?"

"There is no trouble I know." he said.

"That is good, for he is young and somewhat afraid." We walked out of the house and stood in the yard looking down at the valley. "I don't see anyone with you. Where are your braves?"

"I sent them over the mountain, with meat we killed, to our village." Red Dawn looked at me with concern, "Chad'tu, my brother, you look tired."

"I am a might tired, but the sooner I finish the house, the sooner my wife can join me. That's why I work so hard."

"Chad'tu, you need rest." His face brightened, "Take some time we go hunting together on the beautiful land of this mountain. I will show you where the plentiful game abounds."

After a somewhat lengthy discussion, Red Dawn convinced me to hunt with him. He said we would hunt the 'Indian way,' no guns, only bow, arrows, and knives. I think he wanted to see if I was as good as he'd heard. There was always that question in other minds … if I was really as good as they'd heard … and as good as I said.

After the run-in with the rustlers, I always carried my moccasins and bow along with arrows just in case I needed to be an Indian again. To me, this was one of those times. It seemed to me that there was always someone wanting to challenge me.

Tossing in enough of the fresh cut grass that I had stacked near the corral, I saw to it that the horses and mules had enough to eat for the two or three days that I might be gone. I didn't have to worry none about water, since I'd built one corner of the corral across a trickle of water that seeped out of the rocks and into a rough-cut trough.

I shucked my clothes and slipped on my Indian clothes, wrapped my guns and ammo in my bedroll, and with Red Dawns help, hid them under a pile of rocks. As we finished placing the last rock, Red Dawn looked upon me, "My brother, with those clothes you are changed. You truly are a white Indian."

I smiled at his words, "Lead me to the hunt. We will have meat for the evening meal," Then I laughed as anticipation lit up his face.

Red Dawn told me of a pass across the mountaintops, through a lush valley that lay between two peaks high up. It led towards his village at the northwestern range of the Black Mountains. He'd been hunting when he'd accidently discovered the valley and the short cut from one side of the mountains to the other, he explained. Instead of going around the mountain and taking four days to his village, he used the pass cutting two days off. Soon we would be hunting in the valley of which he spoke.

I took one last look at the ranch house as we started off on foot. With an easy, loping pace, we covered a lot of ground as we traveled across the mountainside in an upward direction. Only slowing to a walk, after an hour to rest and catch our breath. Red Dawn looked at me with approval, "It is true what I have heard. You truly are the great white Indian. Only an Indian could run as well and keep up with Red Dawn."

I grinned, "Red Dawn, my Indian father Shatika, taught me to run all day at a faster pace than what we have been doing—of course it was not all up hill. I must admit, I am somewhat out of condition, not having run for awhile."

We walked on a ways, not talking, then I broke the silence, "Red Dawn, it sure does feel good to be out here with you. I cannot believe the freedom, being unhindered by guns and boots."

"White man wear too many clothes. I think Indian clothes better," was all he said as he took off running with me fast upon his heels.

We didn't stop our ascent till he found the trail he'd been looking for. We had been moving rapidly for some time and traveled several miles in our upward journey. Red Dawn took my shoulder, pointed me to an outcrop of granite, "Come, I will show you the way to my secret valley." I looked to where he pointed. I couldn't see a way past the granite outcropping, and said so.

"Follow me, I show." He led me to the outcrop. As we approached, I could see there was a narrow crevice where it had pulled away from the mountainside. It was just wide enough for a man. At the time, I wondered if you might not get a horse through too.

We walked into the gap and stepped carefully, not to trip over the loose rock. We followed the dark crevice along for a time. Finally, we reached an opening and stepped out onto a granite ledge into the blinding bright sunshine.

We stood for a moment while our eyes adjusted. Soon, I looked out over a small valley, lush with tall green grass bending as the wind whipped across it. Tall pine trees surrounded the meadow. Where the rocky mountain pushed in among the tall trees grew a few stunted scrub oak, their gnarled roots exposed over the rocky surface searching for substance.

It was a pretty little valley and quiet. There was only the sound of the wind blowing through the pines, 'till the screech of a hawk high up reached my ears. I looked up at the sound and saw a large hawk gliding back and forth, as it hunted, looking for prey.

Red Dawn looked at me and smiled. "It is beautiful. Do you not agree?"

"Yes, it surely is," I answered. "It's so pretty, it sort of takes your breath away."

Holding a hand across his brow, he looked at the sun. "It will be dark in an hour or two. If we are not to go hungry, we should hunt for food." Red Dawn reached up and pulled an arrow from his quiver, and I did the same. "You hunt that way." he said, pointing toward a stand of tall pine trees off to my left. He left me standing alone as he moved off to his right at a fast pace. It seemed a race, to see who would make the first kill. I grinned at the challenge, and raced off for the pines.

When I reached the tree line, I turned and looked for Red Dawn. He was nowhere in sight. He sure could run fast. If I could make my kill before Red Dawn made his, it surely would raise his esteem of me.

Cautiously, I entered the woods. My senses became heightened and attuned to the surroundings, reverting back to the teachings of Shatika and all he had taught me. I crept slowly through the shadows cast by the tall pines, looking for any tracks made by an animal, stopping to listen for any sounds an animal might make in its moving. After several yards, I spotted deer droppings on the ground. I squatted down and picked some up to see how hard it was. It was still soft but cold. Not a day old, I thought.

I looked around and soon found hoof marks that led off through the trees. From the tracks, it appeared there were three deer. I checked the wind direction. Luck was with me, the wind blew across from my right side. With the direction the wind was blowing, the deer would be unable to catch my scent.

I heard the trickle of water before I came to a small stream bubbling along over rocks that lay beneath its surface. The ground was muddy where the deer had stopped to drink. I looked up the stream, not a deer in sight. I looked down the stream, still not a deer to be seen.

Crossing the small stream, I bent and looked at the tracks that paralleled the meadow and headed up toward the tree line. The deer were keeping to the shadows of the trees, making them difficult to see. Following the tracks for a short distance, I stopped where the tracks had turned off into the woods. Standing very still only my eyes moved while I searched for the deer.

A branch cracked up the hill. Out of the corner of my eye through the trees, I caught movement. I moved my head slowly in that direction. Two does were lying down and a buck standing guard.

I nocked an arrow and crept silently forward. I was within twenty yards and yet they were not alerted. Slowly, I raised the bow and pulled the bowstring with the nocked arrow back to my cheek.

I was ready to let the arrow fly, when suddenly the buck stiffened and looked back over his shoulder in the opposite direction of where I stood. Something had startled him. My arrow drawn, I steadied myself and waited for a clean shot.

The buck turned and with his back to me stood staring at something. I had no kill shot. He jerked his head up and shook it. The two does alerted by the bucks' movement jumped up ready to spring away.

Not having a shot at the buck, I quickly changed my target from the buck to a doe. Letting my arrow fly, it struck the doe just behind the forelegs, burying itself deep into its chest. It fell to the ground, kicked a couple times, and then lay still. The buck and other doe had bounded into the woods.

I let out a loud whoop and called out to Red Dawn of my kill. I was answered immediately by a similar call from where the buck had been looking. Coming from that direction was Red Dawn, on the run. I stood looking down at the doe when he arrived by my side. Silently, we both stood there staring at two arrows, not an inch apart, protruding from the doe's chest. I looked up from the arrows and said, "I shot first, it's my kill."

Red Dawn disagreed and claiming the kill said, "No Chad'tu it is my arrow that entered first." It was not a contest, but if it had been it would be called a tie.

I'd been taught by Shatika to carry several rawhide strips wrapped around my waist when I hunted. Taking the strips from my waist, we used them to hang the deer from a nearby tree branch. We skinned and gutted the doe. We went to the stream I'd crossed and washed the blood from our bodies.

We cut a sapling, went back to where the doe hung, dropped it to the ground and tied the front legs together, then the rear ones. We slipped the pole between the tied legs, carried the doe, to the stream, and hung it from a tree branch.

Making camp, we started a fire in a pit. We cut off part of the haunch and hung it over the fire to roast. After eating our fill of venison, we lay on our stomachs and drank from the cold water of the stream, since there was no coffee.

From a small pouch I carried, I took some tobacco. As I smoked, we talked about our childhoods and growing up. I sat with my back against a tree. Red Dawn had chosen to recline on a pile of pine needles. The more we talked the more easily the Comanche language came to my lips.

With dark approaching, we banked the fire, made a bed of pine needles and turned in. I laid there relaxing, with the sound of the gurgling brook in the background. There in the dark, I thought about Red Dawn and the pleasure I'd had hunting with him. An owl hooted, and far away, a wolf howled at the half moon that hung high among the stars. We were becoming more than brothers as he put it, we were becoming fast friends.

The next morning we ate cold leftover meat and again drank from the stream. Red Dawn wanted to show me the pass on the other side of the valley that led to his village. We proceeded at a comfortable pace toward a notch in the mountain peaks that lay at the far end of the valley. Two hours later, we stood on an outcrop of granite that jutted out into open space. Standing on the edge, he pointed northward and said his village was too far to see, but was at the foot of the mountains he pointed out.

He wanted me to go with him and meet his people. He'd told them of the white Indian he had met. They were curious and wanted to see this great white Indian he spoke so highly of. "Red Dawn, I would like to meet your family and friends, but there is not enough time. I must get back and finish my house. I am sorry to disappoint you. I will come another time."

"Yes, my brother— after your teepee is finished and you have time. You will then come." he said these words with a long sigh.

"I promise," I said, hugging him.

We headed back to camp and as we approached, it became a foot race to see who would get there first. Again, it was a tie. We raced into camp and collapsed falling into the creek. Exhausted from the long run, we washed the dirt and sweat from our bodies. Revived somewhat by the cold mountain water and in a playful mood, we started splashing water at each other and laughing. It was a great water fight.

We freshened up the pine needles that were our beds and cooked more venison for supper. With our bellies full and being tired after a strenuous day, we collapsed onto the needles and quickly fell asleep.

Next morning after breakfast, we cut down the deer and pushed the pole between its still tied legs, and headed toward the hidden crevice that led down the mountainside toward the ranch house. Approaching the ranch house, we took care not making any noise. We looked around and nothing seemed to have been disturbed that I could see.

I took off my Indian clothes, put on my denim pants and a shirt, and then retrieved my guns. I hung them where they would be handy if needed. Then I looked to the animals, and threw some fresh hay into the corral. Red Dawn stayed the rest of the day, saying he would leave the next morning.

The sky had begun to lighten as Red Dawn gathered up his horse from the corral. He cut off a hunk of the deer, and left the rest for me.

Feeling lonely after he left, I busied myself laying the rest of the slate on the floor of the house. It looked right nice when I was done. Ned was still not back, but he should soon be arriving with the load of supplies. I could not just sit idle and wait for him.

I started off sawing down a few trees with the long-saw for the building of the barn. It was difficult and time consuming, but it did keep me busy. Using an ax, I chopped off the jutting branches from the trees I had felled. Hitching up the mules, I dragged them one at a time to where I had laid out the outline of the barn.

Taking a break, I rested from my endeavors, caught a cupful of water from the seep and sat down on a log. I wiped the sweat from my forehead with an arm and took a long drink from the cup. I rolled a smoke and as I sat smoking, I counted up the days Ned had been gone. He should be getting here soon unless he'd run into trouble.

I stood and looked out across the valley into the desert plains searching for any sign of him. There was nothing as far as I could see. Then I remembered the field glasses I carried in my saddlebags.

Retrieving the glasses, I looked out over the plains again. This time I could see much further. I swung the glasses back and forth across the plains methodically, moving from the foot of the mountains and then searching further out.

After five or six passes, I saw a small dark dot that did not blend with the brown of the desert. I watched that dot with the glasses for some time. It appeared to be moving in my direction, but it was too far out to ascertain if it was Ned and the wagon. Another hour or two and I would know if it were Ned—or something else.

Hell, I thought, I'm to the stage where I can't do much building by myself. I'd been working hard and had neglected Faith. On the spur of the moment, I figured to saddle up Faith, ride down and meet whoever it was. Faith pranced around a bit before she settled down. She was happy to be going,

I followed the switchback trail down from the plateau, to the bottom where it ran into the meadow. Riding through the waist high grass to the deserts edge, I was just in time to meet the dusty wagon. Perched high on its wooden seat, sat a sweating Ned.

"Hi Ned, you look a might tired. How did it go—any problems?" Before answering, he pulled the wagon to a halt, took off his hat and wiping the sweat from his brow, "It was a danged long hard trip, being alone and all. I sure am glad to get back here with my hair still attached to my head and not hanging from some Indians belt."

"Since you made it back with the supplies, I take it you didn't run into any trouble."

"Well, to tell the truth, I was a might scared once. I was halfway across the plains when I saw some Indians, must have been about twenty of 'em. They were riding far out on the horizon. I was lucky; they never took notice of me."

"Well, we best get this wagon up to the plateau before dark." The wagon was not as loaded as it had been the first time we'd gone up this hillside. The mules pulled it easily over the switch back trail to the ranch house where we unloaded it.

After building a fire in the fireplace, we washed up and cut a hunk of meat from the deer, hung it from the hook that was made for that purpose, and swung it in over the fire to roast. While the venison was roasting, and smelling mighty good, Ned and I set about the chore of cooking up a kettle of beans and a pot of coffee. When the meat had cooked enough, I swung it out from the flames. I carefully took it from the hook, and laid it on a board. Whipping out my knife, I sliced off several pieces.

Having no table yet, Ned and I sat on the floor eating. Ned stuffed his mouth full and swallowed the food so fast you'd think he hadn't eaten for three days. I had to laugh at the way he was going at it. We slept in the house, on our bedrolls that night, and ever night after that.

Next morning, bright and early after breakfast, we started work on the barn. With Ned and me working together, the barn progressed rapidly. Within the next few days, the walls rose to a height higher than the house.

We rose early one morning before daybreak and headed out of the house to wash up, only to find a deer hanging at the edge of the porch. It was gutted but not skinned.

Ned looked at me with a startled look and exclaimed, "What the hell! Where do you suppose this deer come from?" He looked with fear towards the edge of the woods. "Who would hang a fresh killed deer on our door step? And why?"

"Calm down. Let me think." I was as startled as Ned but I would not show it. "It must be Red Dawn's doing … a gift of food, for friends."

With the coming of light, I looked at the ground around and in front of the porch. Sure enough, I found faint tracks made by moccasins in the dirt. I called Ned over and pointed out the tracks. "See, an Indian was here and by the tracks there was only one. It could only be Red Dawn."

He looked at me and said, "I didn't hear anything, did you?"

I had to admit, I hadn't heard a thing. "Indians are very good at not being seen or heard, whether it is dark or daylight. They are like ghosts. If they don't want to be seen they probably won't be."

Every few days after the incident, with the deer, we would find a couple of wild turkeys or other game, hung from our porch. We never heard or saw a thing. It was a daunting feeling and somewhat frightening for Ned.

We never went long without fresh meat. It had to be Red Dawn. My feelings for him were growing deeper with each passing day.

CHAPTER 54

'D CHANGED MY mind about building the barn as a lean-to, up against the granite cliff. Instead, I would build the walls straight up, which would make them stronger. Then I could build the roof on a slope over to the sheer facing of the granite mountain where a ledge running across its face would support the weight.

In a month, we had it mostly completed—except for doors and some other odds and ends. I must say, Ned was a right handy carpenter. Together with his expertise, we fashioned a table along with a couple chairs which were sturdy, but not near as good or as pretty as store-bought ones. We didn't have to eat sitting on the floor anymore, thank god.

There was not much left to do to the buildings except for doors and windows. One day standing, back I surveyed our work. I got the bright ideal to run one side of the corral up to the barn where there was an opening for a side door. It took hardly half a day to accomplish building it to the barn's side.

I was becoming more and more anxious to go and get Jaydeen. It seemed I hadn't seen her in a long time. My heart ached for her. I wanted to feel her warm body pressed against mine. I wanted to taste her soft sweet lips and feel her arms around me, god how I missed her.

She wasn't so much on my mind as long as we kept busy, but in my spare time, she was all I thought about. I wanted to get her and bring her to our new home. I hoped she would like it, and be proud of it and me for building it. Ned could tell I was getting impatient and wanting to go get her.

One morning Ned said, "Chad'tu, you been driving me crazy, the way you been moping and acting lately. I can tell you want to go get Jaydeen. So go, will you? I'll feed the animals and watch over the place while you're gone." So I saddled up Faith and started off, then I stopped suddenly thinking Jaydeen had things she would want to bring along with her. That being the case, I'd better take the dang wagon and that would take me longer.

Ned stood watching from the front of the barn as I turned Faith around and rode back. "You forget something?" he asked.

"Yeah, I forgot she has things she'll want to bring. So I'm gonna have to take the wagon."

Together we hitched up the mules to the wagon. Taking Faith's bridle off, I replaced it with a more comfortable halter, and tied her with a long lead to the tailgate. I removed her saddle and slung it into the empty wagon.

Stepping on a rung of the wagon wheel, I reached up grabbed the long brake handle and swung aboard and sat on the hard wooden seat. I gathered the reins in hand and yelled out a loud "Haw." The mules started off down the trail of switchbacks that would lead us off the hill onto the desert plains.

I was happy. Soon I would be holding Jaydeen in my arms.

It took several long dreary days, a 'driving that danged wagon across the desert plains. It was a tedious, time-consuming and uneventful journey. As far as the eye could see, nothing but cactuses and a scattered few creosote bushes. Sometimes I'd see the track made by a sidewinder snake, looping across the sandy dirt. On a very rare occasion, a coyote would pop up, springing forth from the shade of a bush and take off running.

The sky was a dull blue-grey without a cloud in it. It was unduly hot as the sun beat down mercilessly with a vengeance. The perspiration had soaked through my shirt which stuck to my back like a second skin. The dust hung in the air, kicked up by the wagon and mules, and sticking to my sweat covered body, soon turned my skin from brown to gray, emphasized by the lines of sweat that rolled down my face.

It was getting on toward evening of my fourth day of travel as I drove the rig into the yard of the Brucker ranch. No one was around that I could see. I jumped down from the wagon and rushed to the front door. Without knocking, I swung it open and yelled for Jaydeen. There was no answer. The house was empty. I wondered where everyone could be. I knew Sid and Trace were probably out doing something on the ranch that needed their attention. Where was Jaydeen, probably out riding around the hills on her horse?

Well, there was nothing for me to do except wait. I went out to the wagon and drove it around by the barn, unhitched the mules and turned them into the corral. I untied Faith from the wagon and turned her into the corral also.

Going back to the house, I was set on having a cup of coffee while I waited. The coffee pot was cold when I picked it up. Shaking it, I could tell there was no coffee left in the pot. Getting water and grounds, I made some. When the coffee was ready, I poured myself a cup and sat at the table waiting. Pouring myself a third cup, I went out on the porch, sat on the bench, and waited.

Deep in thought, I looked out toward the meadow in front of the ranch house which held a few head of cattle. I sat thinking to myself. The place I'd picked for Jaydeen and me was prettier than this place, and this place is mighty pretty.

I rolled a smoke and sat waiting for someone to show up as the sun glided towards the hilltops. Sticking my legs out in front of me, I crossed my legs one booted ankle over the other, leaned back against the house and closed my eyes.

I was awakened by the sound of hoof beats thundering into the yard. Opening my eyes, I could see it was Jaydeen. Seeing me sitting on the porch, she jumped hurriedly from the horse and raced to me. She threw her arms around me and gave me a kiss that I would not forget for some time.

"God, Chad'tu how I've missed you, we get married and then you run off. I have not seen you for months."

"Well, I have been busy building you a castle on Black Mountain. I have finished building it, and now I have come to take my princess and bride to that castle high on the mountainside."

"Aw, Chad'tu, why are you talking so funny? You know I'm not a princess."

"Well, my sweet darling Jay—to me, you are a princess."

"That's so sweet of you Chad'tu. No one has ever called me a princess."

"Where's your brother Sid and Trace?"

"Oh they're out moving cattle from one section to another. They should be in shortly." She stopped talking long enough to give me another kiss, then said, "They never miss supper, they'll be along soon. Speaking of suppertime, I'd best get in the kitchen and start cooking. You must be hungry after your long journey."

"Yeah, I'm so hungry I could eat a … what-cha gonna cook?"

"Well, we butchered a hog last week. I was thinking about having ham hocks and lima beans, along with biscuits, and coffee, and maybe frying up some okra from the garden. How does that sound, honey?" She asked, giving me another hug and kiss.

We broke off hugging and kissing when we heard hoof beats. Holding hands, we walked out of the kitchen onto the front porch. Jaydeen shaded her eyes against the setting sun and yelled out to Sid and Trace. "Look who's here, my long-lost husband, Chad'tu."

Dismounting, they walked over with grins on their faces. "Well it's about time you showed up. We were beginning to wonder if the Indians gotcha. How the heck are you?"

"I was just telling your sister about the castle I built for her up in the mountains. I told her I'd built it for a princess."

Jaydeen butted in saying, "I told him I was not a princess but he did not believe me."

"Well, my darling Jay, to me you are a princess. Don't you two agree she's a princess?"

"You could say she is a Princess." Trace said looking at Sid. "But Sid would probably not agree with you, he'd probably say she's more like a thorn in the side," he said laughing.

"Well, I have come to take my princess to her castle, as soon as she gets all her things together."

Jay said, "You boys can talk and joke all you want, I'm gonna fix supper." Jay with a toss of red hair turned on her heel and walked back into the house. Laughter followed after her.

I told Sid and Trace about the house and the barn that had a corral. I said I wanted to get back as soon as I could. Seein' I didn't want to leave Ned alone for too long. I had brought the wagon to carry anything Jaydeen might want to take. "Anytime you all take a notion come for a visit."

Stepping down from the porch, I picked up a stick. "I'll draw you a map. See this is where your ranch is and this is the Black Mountain range." I said, drawing in the dirt. "And this here peak is the highest one, so if you head for it and a keep a little to the left of it, you'll run right into our ranch. I'd say it's about a three-day ride, four at the most. When you decide to come, be sure and keep an eye out for hostile Indians. Some are friendly and others don't take kindly to the white man moving in and taking his land and shooting their food." Finally, I stopped talking and took a drag off my smoke.

Sid stood there taking in all I'd said. Trace, being older, said, "You shore do talk a lot for wanting to be a rancher. Maybe instead of becoming a rancher you should become a politician. Did you ever think about that?"

"Aw, come on, Trace. I just got excited telling you two about my ranch."

"Where you going to get the cattle to stock this here ranch?" Trace wanted to know.

"Well I figure to start small and breed a few cows with a strong bull and soon I'll have enough to sell like you do."

They laughed, "At the rate you're talkin', it'll take you twenty years to build a herd." Trace reckoned.

I scratched my head, they were right; it would take a long time. "Okay, what should I do? You two seem to have all the answers."

There was a long silence following my question. Then Sid said, "You do know that half the cattle here on the ranch belong to Jay. You could start with those."

Jaydeen had been listening and suddenly turned from the stove and said. "What about dad, doesn't he have any say?"

Sid stood; walking to his sister, he put an arm around her and said, "I don't think dad is coming back. I don't know what's happened to him, but by my reckoning, he's been gone over two years. I think if he were coming back, he'd be here by now. Don't you think?"

Jaydeen with glassy-eyes said, "Yeah you're right Sid … I don't think dad's coming back. But I don't know if we should take half the cattle."

"Sis, we can talk some more on it after supper." Sid said, seeing Jaydeen was upset.

After supper, I helped Jaydeen with the dishes. It was like old times, her washing and me drying. I kept kissing the back of her neck and she kept hitting at me with a soapy hand. We acted like two little kids. We finally finished up the dishes and taking our coffee went out and joined Sid and Trace on the porch. We continued the conversation that had started before supper.

I rolled a smoke and lit it, "Ain't any use talkin about the cattle and how we might divide the herd fairly. I need to get Jaydeen to her new home and settled in for now. Then we can come back and get the cattle that we agree on." We all agreed to forget it for the time being. We sat drinking our coffee and smoking, enjoying the cool of the evening and each other's company.

The next morning Jaydeen picked out what she wanted to take and we loaded it onto the wagon. When we were finished, the wagonload was piled high.

We said our good-byes and with a slap of the rein's and a haw, the mules started pulling the wagon out through the front gate. Jay sat beside me on a blanket she had covered the hard wooden seat with. I'd tied Faith along with Jay's horse to the tailgate and they followed along behind.

When we passed through the gate, both of us turned and waved to Sid and Trace. I turned the team and we headed the wagon west toward the hazy Black Mountains that lay far out on the distant horizon.

CHAPTER 55

WE HAD MADE it safely across the desert plains, without any unexpected events, nor did we see any Indians. On the eve of the fourth day, we arrived at the valley which lay below the ranch house and at the foot of the Black Mountains.

Looking high up the mountainside toward where the house sat on the plateau, I could faintly make out a thin tendril of smoke rising slowly up the face of the rocky mountain. Ned must be cooking.

We followed the switchback trail back and forth across the face of the mountain making our way slowly upward to the plateau where the ranch house sat.

The higher we traveled, the larger Jaydeen's eyes became. She looked back down the trail toward the desert plains, mouth open in awe, eyes taking in the tall green grass of the valley that moved from the evening breeze in ripples like waves on an ocean. She said she could not believe the beauty of the valley.

Upon our reaching the plateau, my darling wife took one look at the ranch house and poked me in the ribs. "What a pretty house. In a way, it does look like a castle. We must be at least a thousand feet higher than the desert plains." She went on, "And sitting here on the mountain's edge like it is … the beauty of it all takes my breath away. It's just more than I had ever dreamed it would be."

The wagon had hardly come to a stop when she jumped off and ran toward the house wondering how the inside would look. Would it look as good on the inside, as it did on the outside? In her haste, she almost knocked Ned down as he came out the door. I greeted Ned, then got down off the wagon and followed after Jay.

She was like a kid with her hand in a candy jar. She was so excited she could hardly contain herself. She turned and put her arms around me, pulled me tight and gave me a big kiss. "Chad'tu, you are so wonderful to build this all for me."

I took her by the hand. "Come; let me show you the barn." I led her around behind the house and showed her the barn, with the attached corral.

Trying to contain her excitement, she finally said, "It is more than I ever expected. You've done a wonderful job, building our new home. You're right. Chad it is a castle high in the sky."

Ned had a pot of beans cooking on the hook in the fireplace. "Ned, what are you having with your beans?" I looked and saw nothing else.

"I ain't got around to that part yet," he laughed. "You did bring more supplies, didn't you?"

"Sure," I replied. "You don't think I'd take that long journey without bringing back supplies, do you?" We brought a slab of bacon along with meat from a pig that Sid and Trace had butchered. Cutting off a hefty slice of bacon, we cooked it along with the beans. After four days out on the plains, it tasted mighty good.

I poured another cup of coffee and the three of us stepped out on the front porch.

Jay and I sat on the porch swing Ned had built, rocking back and forth. Ned sat in a chair facing us. As the evening wore on, with the coming of darkness, the stars lit up the night sky with their little lights shining brightly. It was a beautiful, clear evening and I was happy and content to be with the one I loved.

The next morning after breakfast, I said to Jay, "Let's go for a walk. There're still some things I want to show you. I saved the best for last."

Walking with Jaydeen in the direction of the far edge of the plateau, I had her close her eyes for the last surprise and I led her with eyes shut the last few steps. I took her by the shoulders and turned her so she faced toward the waterfall that cascaded down from high up off the rocky mountainside.

"Okay Jay, open your eyes."

It took Jaydeen a moment to realize what she was seeing. "Ooh ..." She said breathlessly, looking at the falling water as it cascaded down, roaring over the face of rocks, before plunging deep into the pool that lay far below. "It's the most wondrously, beautiful sight I think I have ever seen.

Its shear beauty takes my breath away. The way the morning sun reflects back from striking the falling water and … Oh look! There's a colorful rainbow hanging in the mist."

We stood there quietly, listening to the distant sound of falling water. I stood behind her with my arms wrapped around her waist, holding her tightly against my chest, I nuzzled her soft neck. Neither of us said a word, lost in the moment.

She turned, kissed me and said. "I am so happy. I never want to leave this place. It's so beautiful, peaceful and quiet … and most of all, I'm so glad you're my husband."

—∘∘▪◉▪∘∘—

The summers were great, but the winters were something else. It got downright cold in the winter and sometimes it would snow. The first year on our ranch was hard, but we managed.

That first year, we made several trips across the plains. On one such trip, Sid, Jaydeen and me agreed to our taking only fifty head of cattle and one bull. It took us a little over four days to drive the herd to our valley. Once there, the cattle smelled water and made a beeline to the creek. After their thirst was satisfied, they proceeded to make themselves at home, wandering about, grazing on the tall grass.

That first year was something to remember, most of it all good. One day Ned and me were out in the barn with pitchforks, stacking the hay we'd cut. We were working up a good sweat, when suddenly from the house came a terrified scream. Jaydeen was in trouble. Not knowing what the trouble might be, we took one look at each other, dropped the pitchforks and raced for the house. We were ready to protect and defend her.

I ran as fast as my long legs would take me, skidded around the corner of the house, and almost fell. I took a deep breath, and then burst through the door and my eyes found Jaydeen. Jay's pale face looked at me, speechless, and she pointed to an open window where an Indian was peering in.

I started for the Indian, then stopped, as Ned came crashing in about that time. He stopped as I held up a hand toward him. "I'll take care of this," I said, and started for the Indian. Again, I stopped—then I burst out laughing.

The face of the Indian sticking through the open window belonged to Red Dawn. He had not been around for several months. Jaydeen held a hand to her mouth in fear, as I walked toward the window.

I stopped in front of Red Dawn, reached over and gave him a half hug, and spoke with my Indian tongue, "I have not seen you for a long time my brother. I was wondering if something bad had befallen you."

With one hand on the windowsill, Red Dawn leaped through the open window, as Jaydeen gasped. He threw his arms around me, "Yes, my brother I have been busy. But now I find time to visit with my white brother." He looked in Jaydeen's direction. "Your squaw?"

Jaydeen look apprehensively at the two of us, not understanding the Co-manche language.

Getting over some of her fear, she stood with her arms folded across her chest. "Will someone tell me what is going on? And you Chad ..." she said pointed a finger at me. "What's so damn funny? I'm about to be scalped by an Indian, and you laugh."

I would say she was as agitated and mad, as only a red-haired vixen could be.

"Jaydeen, calm down, this is the Indian I told you about. Come meet my friend and Indian brother. He means you no harm. He only comes to visit me. He has been here many times bringing food, while Ned and me struggled to build this house." After some convincing, Jaydeen came and stood by my side. "Red Dawn, this is my wife."

Red Dawn walked cautiously over. With some trepidation, he reached up and felt Jaydeen's red hair. Jaydeen stood like a statue, showing only a slight shiver as Red Dawn gave her hair a stroke, letting it run between his fingers. He grunted and said. "I have never seen hair the color of fire. It is nice."

After an hour and not yet having her hair lifted from her scalp, Jaydeen started to feel slightly more comfortable.

We skinned and gutted three rabbits and a squirrel Red Dawn had killed. Jaydeen cooked them for supper along with biscuits and white gravy. The meal was good, according to Red Dawn. He kept asking for more hot coffee.

He slept outside that night to Jaydeen's relief. The next morning, he was gone. On the porch beside the door, he'd left a handful of wild flowers. Jay, a smile on her face bent and picked them up, moved by his thoughtfulness.

After breakfast the first thing she said, "Chad, I want you to teach me to speak that Comanche language."

"Sure, if that's what you want. Its okay with me, but it won't be easy." For the rest of the year, when I wasn't doing chores, I'd help her with the Comanche language. She learned fast. I'd say she had a natural talent for picking up a different language.

The next time Red Dawn unexpectedly showed up, she greeted him unafraid. Haltingly, she spoke to him in his own tongue. I watched for his reaction.

Red Dawn was taken aback and astonished by her crude words. He stood and studied her for a moment, then with a large grin, he spread his arms wide and stepped forward. Before Jaydeen could escape, he wrapped his strong arms around her and let out a whoop, "You have done well to learn the Co-manche language. I am now proud to call you my sister."

Jaydeen was flustered. Quickly, she recovered her composure and gave a tight smile, "As do I accept you my dark skinned brother."

Red Dawn made so many visits after meeting Jaydeen, that I had the feeling he only came to see her. I confronted him one day with my thoughts. He laughed at me, saying I talked like a man that was crazy in the head. He said his feelings over time had really grown toward 'Jaeen' as he called her. He admitted he loved her … but only as a sister.

"It is good Chad'tu she is your squaw. Or I maybe would take her away and make her my squaw." He laughed at the expression that flitted across my face and then disappeared just as quickly when he said, "I love her almost as much as I love you my brother. I would die protecting you both from any harm that would befall you."

I grinned, "That is good. I'd much rather have you as a friend than an enemy."

Upon one of Red Dawn's visits, he said he had told his father and the people of his village of me and of the woman with the hair of fire. The people of the village did not believe there was a woman with hair of fire.

Over a period of months, he had begged for us to go with him and meet his father, mother and his people. Things were caught up at the ranch, so we finally gave in. We left Ned in charge and went with Red Dawn to visit his people.

CHAPTER 56

U P THE STEEP mountain trail and through the hidden crevice we rode, passing across the lush secret valley to the far side, we followed Red Dawn. He led us down a wandering trail with an occasional bush growing haphazardly out between the rocks, a trail made faintly visible by the passing of various animals.

Sometimes we rode fast. Other times on foot, we would lead our horses cautiously, as we worked our way slowly along a shear cliff edge, hundreds of feet above the rocky bottom. One misstep and our journey would be ended. There were rockslides where huge boulders had fallen and tumbled across the trail, now lay buried deep into the earth from the force of their downward plunge.

Working our way around these obstacles, we steadily made our way down the mountainside toward the northwest tip of the mountain range. Topping a ridge, we came suddenly upon Red Dawn's village that sat in a sheltered valley between two ridges that ran down to meet the desert floor. The trip was quicker than I'd expected, taking only two days.

Red Dawn cupped his hands around his mouth and let out the ear-piercing screech of an eagle. The people that heard turned at the sound, recognized Red Dawn and waved. Then seeing two palefaces, they scattered like grains of wheat blown across the prairie, grabbing children they quickly disappeared into their teepees. Only the braves stood their ground, ready with arrows fitted to their bows.

Getting closer, he called out saying we were friends, the ones he'd told them about. "They come in peace and no harm should be done to them—or you will answer to me, Red Dawn."

When we walked into the village, the warriors put their arrows and bows aside and crept close, not knowing what to expect. We were soon surrounded by the half-naked Comanches. They paid little attention to me, and came closer only to look at the woman with hair of fire.

I glanced at Jaydeen, who seemed to be holding up. She stood stiff, with a brave, fearless expression on her face. She had never in her whole life thought she would be surrounded by Indians without being scalped.

Red Dawn spoke to Jaydeen, "Jaeen speak to my people with Comanche tongue."

Jaydeen looked at me for guidance. I shrugged my shoulders, "It's your show ... have at it."

She hemmed and hawed, stuttered out a few words that sounded nothing like what I, along with Red Dawn's help, had taught her.

Red Dawn looked at me; I shrugged my shoulders. He said to Jaydeen, "Do not be nervous, my little sister. They are only curious. They have never seen a white woman, especially one with hair of fire. You try speaking again." Jaydeen was becoming less afraid. She cleared her throat and tried again, "My friends, I greet you with warmth and love in my heart." The braves stepped back, surprised by the words she spoke. Though the words were not fluent and perfectly spoken, they understood. They stood talking excitedly among themselves and laughed, the tension among us had been broken. Soon, the women and children came from the teepees to see this white woman with hair of fire, who could speak in their tongue.

A tall handsome man with long white hair and dark sun bronzed-skin exited his teepee. He stood stoically for a moment, taking in the chatter of the excited Indians. Then he moved forward toward the crowd. The crowd parted, making way for this tall, noble, white haired man, as he made his way with long strong steps. Stopping in front of Red Dawn, he bent and said something.

Red Dawn turned to me and Jaydeen, smiling he said, "This is my father, Chief White Cloud, chief of all that you see before you ... Father, this is Chad'tu, my white brother that I have spoken of many times, and his wife, Jaeen."

White Cloud said, "My son has spoken often of the 'White Indian' he takes as a brother." He turned to Jaydeen, and took her hand, "My son did not lie; you are beautiful as a red sunrise or the rising of a full moon on a dark night. You bring light into the dark."

We met Red Dawn's mother, Quiet Dove, who suddenly appeared from the Chiefs teepee. She was a small woman with a quiet beauty about her. Even though she was older, she had retained much of her beauty. Still, she was not as beautiful as my Jaydeen.

We stayed two days, leaving on the morning of the third. Everyone had wanted to touch Jaydeen's long red hair. The tribe had welcomed us without reservations.

On the occasion of our leaving, Jaydeen asked for my knife. She took it from me, and proceeded to cut off a small handful of her long red hair. She handed the locks to Chief White Cloud with a smile, "Thank you for your kindness."

Red Dawn escorted us back over the mountain along with three braves who wanted to see the teepee I'd built. Upon seeing it, they said if I ever needed to move it, it would be very hard to fold up and carry away. We all laughed at the remark.

The Indians stayed that evening, eating our food out on the open front porch. The Indians preferred to sleep outside which was fine by me. The next morning they were gone, not having made a sound in their leaving.

———•••⦿•••———

Before riding on, my last thoughts were those of sweet remembrances of days long past. When Jaydeen and me were newly married and starting our life together. What great times and fun we had together.

Over and over again, I had thought about my entire past life as I pursued those that had taken my darling Jaydeen. I sorely wanted her back alive, but if that were not the case, there would be those that would pay, and they would pay dearly for my beloved Jaydeen, you could be sure.

CHAPTER 57

SLADE HAD HURRIEDLY ridden off across the desert in a cloud of dust, headed for California with only a canteen of water and no weapons. Soon he was lost from sight as he crossed over and disappeared behind a sandy ridge. I meant what I'd said to Slade; if ever I saw his face again, he was dead.

With no further thought of Slade, my thoughts turned to exactly how was I to get Jaydeen back alive, without loosing my own life. I prayed for guidance as I turned my horse and headed again for the Whitlock Mountains.

Except for this cattle-rustling rancher Bernard Blackburn, who was called B-B, anyone who held a grudge against me had either left the country or were dead. To my knowledge, I had not met Blackburn. I couldn't figure out for the life of me, if I'd never met him, how could I have become his enemy? I rode on, but my thoughts kept coming back to the incident with the cattle rustlers. My instinct said it had something to do with those rustlers—but for the life of me, I couldn't figure it out.

My thoughts went back to Jaydeen and the three wonderful years we'd had on our ranch on Black Mountain. That first year had been hard, even though it had also been good. The cattle had calved, the herd had increased in size, and best of all, it was the year I found the abandoned wolf pup, that I'd raised and named Track.

I took my eyes from the far distant trail of dust left by Slade's horse and looked for Track. I cast a glance at my back trail and to each side but I didn't see him. Then, I turned forward in the saddle and looked ahead in the direction I intended to take. I saw Track sitting on the trail a hundred yards ahead, waiting. Damn smart wolf, I thought.

Drawing even with the wolf I reined up. Stepping down from Faith, I called Track to me, knelt down and hugged him. I told him to stay close and not wander off. We were on our way to get Jaydeen, and since I rode alone, his help would surely be needed.

At the mention of Jaydeen's name, Track's ears flicked forward and he wagged his tail, and looked down the trail in the direction of the Whitlock Mountains. I swear that wolf understood every thing I'd said.

On the afternoon of the third day, the mountains still lay a day's ride ahead on the horizon. I had no plan. Still I rode on, hoping something would come to mind. Could I just ride in and take her without being shot? That was a question I'd find out tomorrow or the day after. It was a desolate country. In my northward journey, I'd seen no one.

I rode along, trying to devise a solution to my problem. None seemed to be forthcoming. Soon it became dark as I rode on toward the Whitlock Mountains. I made camp that evening in a ravine. I did not know how far away I was from Jaydeen and the cowardly hombres, who had taken her. I was not about to take any chances on being seen.

Gathering up dried branches, I built a small Indian fire that could not be seen from the ravine. I made coffee, chewed on a hunk of hard jerky, and searched my mind for a solution to my problem. None was forthcoming. I put out the fire and needing rest, crawled into my bedroll that lay close-up against the far bank.

Gray and dreary, the dawn came,—which did not help my mood much. I rebuilt the fire, put on the coffee, and chewed on another piece of jerky. After having coffee, I saddled Faith, checked my guns, mounted up and rode on—heading toward who knew what. I still hadn't come up with a way to get in and out with Jaydeen and me alive. I could only hope and leave the rest to God.

Out of habit, I watched my back trail from time to time. The sun poked through the overcast sky sometime around noon. Looking back in the direction of my trail, far back on the horizon, a faint cloud of dust seemed headed my direction.

Thinking it might be unfriendly Indians, I rode on with a wary eye on that cloud of dust and the surrounding terrain. Whoever they were, the cloud of dust was rapidly getting closer. I became increasingly worried. Indians or cattle rustling gunslingers, it seemed they would be catching up to me within an hour or two.

I started looking for somewhere I could hide and defend myself. The cloud of dust grew steadily closer. I could now make out two separate clouds of dust. That meant there were only two riders.

I didn't know what to make of it. Earlier as I'd ridden up out of the gully, I'd noticed some low hills a distance off to my left. I veered off and headed in their direction urging Faith into a gallop. I hoped there would be some sort of protection for me and Faith, if it came down to a gunfight.

Reaching the hills, I was lucky in finding a rockslide with huge boulders dislodged by a recent rain. I hid Faith behind a large bolder and took the Winchester from the saddle scabbard; I found a place higher up in the rocks and waited for the two riders. I was not taking any chances.

The trailing cloud of dust stopped and hung in the air a moment, then was slowly blown away by the morning breeze. From my vantage point high up, I could see they had found what was left of my campfire and camp. It was not long till they came on again, riding hard.

As they approached the rockslide where I was hiding, they slowed their horses and looked about warily. I could see they had their rifles out and ready. I still had no idea who they were. Their faces were shaded by the brim of their hats and at this distance; they were not close enough to make out who they might be. One rode a big shinny black stallion; the other hombre rode a large grey horse.

I watched and waited, as they rode closer and closer. Looking about they were being very careful. One was looking down and following my trail while the other kept watch over the hills. When they had ridden close enough for a rifle shot, I called out, "That's close enough." They stopped their horses and looked up, I asked, "You all looking for something inparticular?"

One of them, the man on the jet-black horse, yelled back, "Yeah, we are." He looked up at the rocks trying to spot me. When he couldn't locate me, he said, "You might say were looking for a friend of ours, goes by the name of Chad'tu."

When he said the name Chad'tu, it was then I recognize that voice. I stood up and yelled back, "Brett, is that you?"

"Yeah, I thought I recognized Faith's hoof prints. She always did throw out her right hoof. I'd say you were a might jumpy ... put that rifle away before you hurt someone."

Slowly I lowered my rifle, and asked, "Who might that be with you on the grey?"

"Hell Chad'tu you done lost your eyesight? It's me, Jake."

"I would say you two are a ways from home. What brings you out this way, and in such a big hurry, anyway?" I said, climbing down from the rocks.

Brett said, "Well, there was this fellow come by the gun store t'other day, and in our conversation he said, some cowboy had got himself shot up by a fellow called Slade. It seems this Slade fellow had bushwhacked the cowboy as he rode into town."

"He told me the fellow had a wolf dog with him. Biggest damn wolf he ever did see. That man and his wolf corralled the bushwhacker in the saloon. He said that wolf was a growlin' and gnashing his teeth like he wanted to rip the fellow apart. He said that Slade fellow turned white as a sheet, and stood frozen like a statue. Then he said this here cowboy walked right up to this Slade feller and took his gun from him. Said it was like taking candy from a baby. He walked him out of the saloon like a lamb."

"The man that told me all this said that's the last he'd known of it, except..." the man paused in his telling me his news. I could see he was thinking if he had overlooked anything. The man seemed to suddenly remember, and finished with his telling. "When he took that mans gun, I heard something said between the two of them, about the taking of a woman called Jaydeen." After telling of the incident the man had told him, Brett said, "Now, there is only one Jaydeen I know of in these parts. It could only be your wife, so I got a hold of Jake and we rode out here to lend a hand. You can sure use a hand, can't you?"

Jake had been silent as Brett told his story, now he spoke up. "I bet you could use all the extra hands you could muster up, especially ones that are fast with a gun, right?"

"Damn it, you're right on that account, I have never been so glad to see anyone. You are the answer to my problem. Between the three of us, we got six guns and three rifles, should be enough to take on a small army. Yeah, I surely could use the added help of you two. But I'm curious, how in the hell did you know where to find me?"

Brett answered, "The fellow that told me mentioned something about some mountains to the north, and there ain't no mountains north except those that are straight ahead."

"Having no time to spare after the fellow told his story. I saddled up, and sent word to Jake by another cowpoke that happened to be passing by on his way to Tombstone. He was to tell the sheriff I needed his help and what direction I was traveling. It took me a day or so to cut Faiths trail and by then Jake had caught up."

"Well however you two got here, I surely am glad to see the two fastest guns in the territory."

Side by side, the three of us rode on toward those mountains that we would soon be reaching. "Have you got a plan?" Brett wanted to know.

"No, I have no plan. I was just going to ride in and take my chances. Hell, I don't even know if Jaydeen is still alive. And if she is alive … I don't know what they might have done to her … you know?"

Brett said, "Well, we need to have some sort of plan don't you think? Jake."

Jake replied, "Let's stop, and let the horses rest. We have been pushing them hard. While the horses rest, we can talk and make out some sort of plan. Even if it's wrong, any plan is better than no plan a' tall."

We built a small fire for the making of coffee, then the three of us hunkered down drinking our coffee. We talked, putting out ideas. I'd told them the whole story as far as I knew it. We still could not come to a unanimous decision on a plan, so we decided to let the chips fall as they might.

That night we made camp in a gully behind a low hill. We didn't build a fire in case there were eyes about. We ate cold, tough jerky, and washed it down with water from our canteens. Keeping our guns handy, we turned in early.

Next morning we saddled up and headed for the unknown confrontation that was sure to come. It was not long before we sighted the ranch. The sky was lightening to a nasty grey; the sun was still below the horizon.

Brett was riding out a ways on my right side, checking the hills for any movement. It was still early. Jake rode far out towards the very edge of the hills to the left of me. With our Winchesters cocked and ready, we rode on, trying not to make a sound.

The sun peeked over the low hill, casting a long shadow across the hill-side and the valley floor. There was a glint of brightness, followed by a bright flash, coming from the hillside off to the left. A bullet ricocheted off a nearby boulder.

Jake had not been seen by the shooter. Quickly he returned the rifle fire, firing several shots in rapid succession into the trees from where the muzzle flash had come. He was rewarded with cuss words, painful and loud, followed by silence. We no longer had the element of surprise. Alert and wary, we rode on toward a sprawling ranch house set at the bottom of a wooded hill.

Two fast riding gunmen rode toward us with rifles blasting. The three of us fired back hitting the two riders and knocking them back out of their saddles; they fell hitting the ground and lay not moving.

Three more gunmen cut down on us with rifles, from somewhere high up among the trees and rocks.

We needed to get to a defensive shelter. We kicked our horses into a full out dead run. The only shelter in sight was the ranch house. The three of us took off for the ranch house like the devil himself was nipping at our heels. With bullets, kicking up dirt around us we rode our horses up on the porch jumped down and quickly started returning their fire.

Suddenly, the door was flung open and two hombres stepped out with their six-shooters ready to fire. Jake hardly batted an eye, with lightning speed, he drew his Colt with his left hand and casually shot them both, then holstered his gun, turned back with his rifle and continued firing toward the guns up on the hills. With the three of us concentrating our gunfire at the flashes from their rifles. The fight was soon over.

Cautiously, I made my way toward the open door. A quick glance into the room was rewarded with a shot that splintered the door jam just above my head. Crouching low, I lunged, hitting the floor hard, I rolled some distance, saw the shooter and fired. My bullet hit him in the chest slamming him backward over a cowhide couch. Behind me, Brett and Jake swiftly entered the room. Seeing no one about, we carefully made our way through the house with our guns drawn.

The sound of echoing gunshots faded from my ears. Still I could not hear a sound. It was to damn quiet after all the gunshots that had been fired. I couldn't hear any noise of feet shuffling about. My concerned for Jaydeen grew in the deadly silence. My heart beat faster as I looked around the empty room for her. Then I yell out her name as loud as I could. "Jay! Where are you? Are you here?"

No answer was forth coming.

A worried frown on my face, I looked at Brett and Jake. Looks of concern were apparent on their faces also. I started for the door on the far side of the room. Cautiously I opened the door; it led only to an empty room. There was another door on a sidewall. Maybe she would be in this next room. I hurried toward the door. Brett said, "Take it easy Chad; after all, you don't want to go and get shot."

My senses slowly came back and my head cleared on hearing his words. I carefully opened the door a crack. No shots were fired, so I took a quick peek, there sat Jayden. She was gagged with a bandana and tied to a ladder back chair and guarded by two ugly hombres. I flung open the door and shouted, "Let her go or you're dead men." Caught by surprise they jumped behind Jaydeen using her as a shield. I was so afraid for Jaydeen my hands trembled. I desperately hoped she wouldn't be hurt or worse killed.

I'd been nervous and anxious through this whole rescue thing. I was afraid of hitting Jay from where I stood but Brett and Jake had clear shots as the two gunmen focused their attention on me.

Confused by our sudden appearance a look of surprise crossed the gunmen's faces. They reached for their still holstered guns but were not quick enough as Brett and Jake's guns spoke, spewing, out their message of death.

A look of startled disbelief was written on their faces as they crumpled to the floor. They were dead before they hit the floor. It was a good thing Brett and Jake were dead shots. Maybe that's where dead shots got its meaning. If they shot at you, you were dead.

Brett and Jake went in search of other gunman as I rushed to Jaydeen. Quickly I untied her. The rope fell to the floor as she stood, shaking. I grabbed her with my strong arms to keep her from falling. Joy and gladness filled my heart. Jay looked at me with those deep green eyes, and I bent and kissed her softly, on her sweet lips. "You're safe now." I said, holding her tight in my arms. She let out a sigh of relief. Neither of us spoke we just hugged in a silent loving embrace. A great burden had been lifted from my shoulders, Jaydeen, my love, my wife, my life, was safe.

Jaydeen looked into my eyes and smiled. "Chad, you are my valiant and brave prince. I knew you would come.

Brett and Jake had returned dragging along an old man they'd found hiding in a closet. When asked his name, he drew himself up and he proudly said, "My name is Bernard Blackburn, and you're on my property. Please get the hell off it."

"Well Mister Bernard, we're gonna take you to Tombstone to see the judge for abduction of a woman, holding her against her will, and for cattle rustling. They'll probably hang you." I said. "There's one question though that puzzles me. To my knowledge, we've never met. So why are you trying your damndest to kill me?"

The old man would have collapsed, had not Brett and Jake been holding him up. In a shaky voice he answered, "You ... you killed the only reason I had for living ... you killed my son."

"Hell mister, I don't even know your son."

His voice trembled and he said, "His name was Brice and he was just sixteen, when you gunned him down. I loved him dearly; I ... I wanted you to pay ... the same as he did."

The name rang a bell, and I remembered the want-to-be gunslinger, cattle rustler kid. I said, "If I hadn't killed him someone else would've." I felt sorry for the old man; there was no need for us to tie him, he was through. Jay, with her arm around my waist had listened quietly, while I had done my talkin'.

Brett and Jake rounded up the rest of the gunfighters, that hadn't already fled. Altogether, we had B.B. and three of his cattle-rustling gunmen.

In a moment of silence, Jaydeen asked if I'd been hurt. I put my arms around her, and told her again how much I loved her, and no, I was not hurt. Then I asked, "My princess, are you ready to go home, to your castle?"

"Yes." Jay answered in a tired, weary voice, and leaned weakly against me, "Yes Chad'tu, I surely am ready to go home ... to my castle up on Black Mountain." Putting her arms around me, she gave me a weak kiss.

Brett and Jake looked at us, grinned and slowly shook their heads, "For god's sake Chad'tu, don't dilly-dally, take the lady home." Jake said, "We'll take these varmints in to the sheriff ... Oh dang, I plum forgot with all the excitement. I am the Sheriff." he laughed at his joke.

Brett was smiling, "Go on, and get the hell out of here Chad'tu, you done caused enough trouble for one day." Then they both laughed at my dumbfounded look.

We found Jaydeen's horse and saddled it and we all rode together some distance then parted ways. Brett and Jake headed for Tombstone with their prisoners. Jaydeen and me, we headed for home. It would take a few days. Now that we were together, it didn't matter much when we got there.

I turned to the beautiful red-haired woman who rode beside me and said, "Jay, it's gonna take several days to get home. Even as the crow flies, we can't make the ranch in one day. We're gonna be spending a couple of days out here in the open."

As the sun sat low on the plains, we stopped to make camp; we tethered the horses where there were a few wisps of grass growing. We stripped off the saddles and made camp before nightfall. Making a fire, we had hot coffee and jerked beef.

I took my bedroll from the saddle and spreading it on the ground said, "I'm sorry this is the best bed I can give you."

Jay revived somewhat, said with a mischievous smirk, "It looks like a wonderful bed, if you'll share it with me?"

I answered, "I will share with you only if you don't make me sleep on the ground."

Jay caught my meaning and laughed. Slowly she took off her clothes and slipped under the blanket, "Well?"

I stood mesmerized watching my wife disrobe. As the last word left her lips, I was already, half undressed, and a second later, snuggled close to my wife's warm body.

We lay on our backs and gazed up at the thousands of stars. I reached for Jay's hand and held it for a moment, before I turned and kissed her with a passionate long deprived kiss, which lasted for minutes. Jay responded, and moaned softly, as my hands caressed her. Then suddenly temperatures rising, there was a burning desire of moans and groans and then a long silence … broken only by a sigh. Then there was silence.

Entwined and happy to be with one another again, we gazed up at the stars in the heavens. We laid there quietly not speaking, just holding one another. Suddenly a shooting star flamed across the heavens.

Howling at the bright full moon, the large grey wolf watched from a resting place high a' top a boulder close by...

Other book of:
Kelsie R. Gates

THE
TREASURE
OF THE
CRYSTAL CAVE

~A Fairy Tale Fantasy~

CHAPTER 1

The Arrival ~ A Key

THROUGH THE FURY of the dark night and howling wind she fell. Lightning filled the sky with bright flashes of its anger. Like a banshee, the wind whipped about her, grabbing with its cold wet fingers, at her hair and flapping gown. It ripped at her as she tumbled toward Mother Earth.

She franticly caught her breath. For a moment, she searched her mind for the correct words, which would slow her fall. Gasping for breath, she screamed out the words. Instantly, no longer than a heartbeat, two beautiful white glistening wings, sprouted from her back.

With a strong flap of wings, her descent slowed. She landed softly on the damp grass of a meadow surrounded by huge tall trees. She pulled her long black hair back from her face. Her dark eyes flashing, she surveyed her surroundings. Miiliinda looked like an angel, dressed as she was, in a shimmering silver and white silk gown, its edges trimmed in gold. Although beautiful, she could well take care of herself, for she had been trained by a mage in the arts of mystical magic

That was easy she thought. Having only recently acquired her magical powers, which sometimes worked, and other times didn't, due to the wrong words spoken, she was sure. At the open end of the meadow were granite boulders of every size and shape strewn across the ground, as if a giant hand had tossed them there.

In all of her sixteen years, never had she seen such a forest as this. Living in Chinnder, she had never seen trees that were as tall as the ones that surrounded the meadow. She stared up at them in the murky gloom of darkness, barely able to see their tops. They must be at least three hundred feet tall and as big around as the Quark where she had been born. Between the giant trees were many smaller trees, their branches reaching up and out. Reaching for what? They looked like small children reaching up to be held by loving arms. She guessed they must be the offspring of the giant trees.

Looking about the strange forest, she laughed nervously into the dark night. "Ha! Ha! Ha! My name is Miiliinda and I have magical powers, so do not dare fool with me." She finished with a forced smile, wondering where she could possible be.

She gathered up several soft damp twigs along with tuffs of grass. With a few spoken words of magic, the dampness disappeared. Then another ancient word was spoken. The twigs and grass became alive and interwove, forming a bed of sorts, a place upon which she could rest.

Tired, she stretched and lay down on the bed made of thick grass. Pulling her long black hair close around her for warmth, she laid her head upon the grass-covered twigs and closing her black almond shaped eyes fell fast asleep.

She slept lightly. Even though asleep, her subconscious mind reached out searching the edges of the forbidding forest. Sometime later, she awoke with a start. Something had gently touched her mind. Sensing a presence at the edge of the woods, she pretended to still sleep, her eyes closed. Not reacting and focusing all her senses, her mind probed instantly toward the place from which it emanated.

Without moving, she opened one eye slowly, peered at the dark quiet forest. Nothing moved. No wind rustled through the branches, no night birds sang, just deathly quiet. Still, something had awakened her. Taking a second, she wondered what to do? *Mother always said, face your fears.*

Faster than the blink of an eye, she sprang to her feet, spun quickly three times. Looking about she stopped, pointed a finger into the foreboding darkness and yelled, "I know you are there." Unable to penetrate the darkness she paused, catching her breath, she glanced apprehensively to the left and right. "Who are you?" she said in the bravest voice she could muster.

Unaware she was clenching her gown, she waited for a response. Again, only silence answered her question. Losing some of her fear, she took a small step forward and stopped. Raising a small fist, she yelled at the forest once again. "I'm not afraid of you, I'm not afraid of anything on this earth. I am Miiliinda, and… and I have many powers, so step forth, before I get really angry." Still, nothing moved.

From the corner of an eye, she caught a flash of movement, just inside the forest edge. Quickly she turned and glimpsed something white, moving at great speed among the trees, really just a blur of white it moved so fast. Then it was gone. *Did I see something, or was it my mind playing tricks.*

If something is out there, I will create an invisible shield, to protect me, And, with a few magic words, she did. This magic shield will protect me against everything. With that thought, she pulled her gown tightly around her for warmth and lying back on the makeshift bed feeling safe from all things, she fell fast asleep.

The next morning she stood, stretched her arms out, and yawned. Cautiously she looked across the dew-covered grass toward the still dark forest. Not a movement or a sound, did she see, or hear, just silence. Strange, there was no sign of life, no birds, no deer, no scurrying of little mice among the leaves.

Why was she here, and just where, was here? This place looked nothing like where she had been born. Confused, she looked around wondering.

Dawn started to break, dark and dreary, it looked like rain. Suddenly chilled and shivering she thought, *I'm not dressed for this.* With her magical powers, she created a black leather jumper laced up the front and trimmed with white fur, thick white leggings and knee-high black boots. In case it did rain, a black ankle length cape with a hood and pockets, which should keep her dry.

Making sure she was alone, she peered about, then removed and discarded her gown, tossing it carelessly onto the ground. She then proceeded to dress in her newly created clothes. Walking to a small grey boulder, she sat upon it, and with some effort pulled on the boots. "There, that should keep the cold from me." she said.

Looking up, the grey clouds were transforming into white fluffy ones, which were being blown rapidly toward the horizon. The sky was starting to clear. One stone stood out, it sat in the midst of the many varying shaped and size of grey boulders. Strangely, out of place, it was black and tall. It pointed ominously toward the sky like a bony finger.

Curiosity getting the better of her, she stood, looked around making sure it was safe, and took a couple of steps toward the black rock. It seemed so out of place. Why would a tall thin obelisk be here among all these grey boulders?

With this question in mind, she walked forward to investigate. As she drew closer, she saw something shiny partially buried in the dirt at its base. She bent down and scraped some of the dirt away. Something was there. Grasping an edge, she tugged and pulled at the metal object until it came free from the earth.

Standing she brushed more dirt from the object, and then turned to tap it against the obelisk to remove the rest of the dirt. As she looked at the aged and weather-beaten black stone obelisk, she noticed old letters hewed into the stones rough surface. The object in her hand was forgotten for the moment. She reached out in wonder with her fingers to brush the crusted dirt from the letters to better read them and touched the cold stone.

The instant her fingers touched the black stone she received a severe jolt of energy that lasted only a millisecond, but which sent her to her knees. Stunned and dizzy, she paused a moment and took several deep breaths. Her eyes blurry, she tried to focus, shaking her head to clear it. Not touching the stone, she wondered what had happened.

She stood looking down at the carved letters on the stone. The dirt and weathered abuse the stone had endured for who knows how long, made it difficult to read. She tried anyway. Unaware her lips were moving, she read aloud.

One will come...
To save country and kingdom
Blown in on a dark night's wind
Down to earth like an angel
On wings of white gossamer
Having the sweet innocence of a child
Fearing nothing... and no one

Standing there, still in a daze, she wondered what it meant.
Recovering from the jolt she'd received, she brushed a wisp of hair from her face, bent and picked up the object she'd dropped. Holding it up, she looked closely at it. What an odd shaped thing it was. What could it be?

Then slowly it dawned on her, what she held in her hand was a wonderfully old, large silver and gold key, attached to a short, silver chain. She had never seen a key shaped as this one, or of such beauty. Surely, whoever owned it would not have thrown away such a key of this value. Someone must have lost it. She wondered what it fit and how it had ended up here.

Who could have lost this beautiful key?

Well, she might look for whoever lost it and return it to its rightful owner. Where should she start? How could she find them, that was the big question.

As she held the key, it slowly started to change shape. Morphing into an entirely different shape, the key was still beautiful, but different. Startled and amazed, but not afraid, she wondered how this could be. Was the key alive? She did not sense an entity, or was it some form of magic. Maybe it was cursed, or enchanted, or maybe it was under some sort of spell.

Holding the beautiful key in her hand, she turned away from the black obelisk a puzzled expression on her face. Startled, she dropped the key, almost fainting.

www.ingramcontent.com/pod-product-compliance
Lightning Source LLC
Chambersburg PA
CBHW051635180726
48284CB00006B/1737

Introduction

Maribel Morales

Mary Hunter Austin (1868–1934) was a self-declared feminist, and many modern critics agree that she was in fact an active feminist.[1] She was an essayist, a poet, a novelist, a short-story writer, a lecturer, and a naturalist, publishing thirty-five books and more than 250 articles, stories, poems, and other short pieces. Her extensive literary production is matched by her wide range of interests in issues of her time concerning race, class, and gender, and she made significant contributions to feminism, modernism, regionalism, and Native American studies. In fact, she was a pioneer in the modern roles of feminist, environmentalist, and advocate for Indian and Hispanic minorities. She wrote about these issues with a "sharp moral vision" that continues to stimulate readers a century later (Walton ix).

During her lifetime she was a well-known and accomplished figure in American letters. Shelley Armitage explains that Austin's "tremendous accomplishments were acclaimed by critics in her lifetime and upon her death in 1934" (16). In fact, important literary figures of the time, such as Joseph Conrad, William Butler Yeats, and George Bernard Shaw, praised her work. Henry Seidel Canby, who was Austin's literary executor, wrote a memorial in which he described Austin as "one of the great American women of letters of our time" (11), who "had won her right to a prominent place in American

---

[1] Austin's feminism has been regarded as the foundation of her work by scholars such as T.M. Pearce, and even her nature writings contain elements of feminism. Marjorie Pryse in the introduction to *Stories from the Country of Lost Borders* (1987) situates Austin within the group of regional women writers and active feminists of her day. Although there is a general consensus on Austin's feminist views, Janis Stout has analyzed Austin's novels with an emphasis on the conflicts and inconsistencies of her advocacy of feminist ideas ("Mary Austin's Feminism" 77–101). Stout argues that there are traces of ambivalence or even counter-feminism in some of her novels (*Through the Window* 40).

literature" (11). Carey McWilliams wrote in the *Los Angeles Times* in September 1934, "Mary Austin became, in many respects, the most remarkable woman her generation ever produced in America" (qtd in Mallios 125).

Nevertheless, a few years after her death in 1934 she was virtually forgotten. Despite her impressive productivity and her acclaimed literary reputation, Austin is less familiar today than some of her contemporaries such as Charlotte Perkins Gilman and Willa Cather. One reason for this decline is suggested in the extensive profile of her career and style. Melody Graulich, for example, explains that Austin was once largely neglected because "she wrote in indefinable genres about borderless subjects" and that "ironically, the range and variety of her work led critics to dismiss her as an eccentric dilettante" (*Exploring Lost Borders* xii). In addition, Austin's nature writing places her in a tradition of American nature writers such as Henry David Thoreau, Ralph Waldo Emerson, and John Muir, but for years Austin was, as Linda Karell explains, "pejoratively labeled a minor female regionalist writer" and excluded from the canon of American literature (21). Other scholars believe that Austin's feminist ideas are the cause of the "long critical neglect of her work" (Stout "Mary Austin's Feminism" 78). Nancy Porter, for instance, claims that "assertion of a feminist perspective on most subjects" contributed to the decline "of her reputation even in her own time" (307). Yet another reason for Austin's neglected literary career could be that her "often abrasive and egocentric" personality and the controversies surrounding her life have overshadowed her literary career (Blackbird and Nelson 1).

The critical renaissance of Austin's works is attributed mainly to the effort of contemporary feminists and environmental movements. Recent reprints of Austin's nature works and her feminist novel *A Woman of Genius* (1912) have gained her new readers and attention. *Santa Lucia* (1908) is another of Austin's feminist novels that deserves attention because of its detailed descriptions of the situation of women and their deep emotions and frustrations, and its criticism of marriage and the conventional values that deny women the freedom they desired. As Esther Lanigan suggests, the theme of "a woman's place in the modern world of the 1910s and 1920s" is present in the content of Austin's early novels and this makes them "worth reading in their entirety today" (*A Mary Austin Reader* 14).